The LIGHT *in an* IMPENETRABLE NIGHT

Paige Trevisani

ISBN 978-1-0980-5317-8 (paperback)
ISBN 978-1-0980-5318-5 (digital)

Christian Faith Publishing, Inc.
832 Park Avenue
Meadville, PA 16335
www.christianfaithpublishing.com

Printed in the United States of America

CHAPTER 1

OPTI Day

The dizzying crowd baffled me. I meandered behind my family as we gathered on one side of our town's Main Street, trying to make sense of the crowd's eagerness. Barriers blocked off the street while police officers patrolled the sidewalk so no one would cross over. I gripped my red balloon as tight as I could, determined to keep it from escaping into the sky. I just received it from what my father called a street vendor, and I had to ask him whether it would make me float away. My father reassured me I would stay on the ground; however, if I let go of my balloon, it would disappear forever into the open endless sky above. Faith, my oldest sister, whispered that I would see the balloon again in heaven even if I let go, and my worry subsided.

"How long would I have to wait to see it?" I asked.

She smiled. "A very long time. Good thing the earth has plenty of balloons. Don't worry though, God would take care of it until you arrived."

"Hey, Abby. I want that balloon. I saw the red one first!"

"No, Scar." I huffed at my other older sister, Scarlett. "It's mine. *I* saw it first!"

"Mom!"

"No fighting, girls." My mom cut in as my younger sister, Renée, began to fuss in her stroller. Mom shot a nervous glance at Dad and she looked back at us with a stern expression. "Get along or you'll both get a time-out when we get home."

Scarlett narrowed her eyes at me but left me alone.

The parade started. Jets shot through the open air like comets. Fire engines, emergency vehicles, and police cars rolled along the parade route, followed by a convertible with a chauffeur in the front driving the town mayor. The mayor wore his all-white military uniform with medals and a silver plate attached to the left side of his chest with a name I recognized—OPTI—engraved into it. He waved to the crowd as they roared with excitement. I didn't know much about the mayor, though I imagined if so many people liked him, I would like him too. Behind the mayor, a neat formation of what looked like soldiers the age of teenagers marched in their matching white uniforms. People threw cans and bottles at one of the boys, the youngest of them who appeared about fourteen years old. I couldn't imagine why. Then came the float that motivated the assembly and the music changed to our national anthem. I learned it in school but never sang it.

As one, people around us began to sing:

> It's OPTI Day.
> Make no mistake,
> It's OPTI, we praise always.

The float came into view. A giant screen perched upon it with a luminous colorful brain in the center. It pulsed as the float moved it along, as though it danced.

> When our world may seem
> a frenzy.
> OPTI lends a hand to the needy,
> Oh, in you we live truly free.

> Don't shed a tear.
> If our minds align,
> With OPTI's might
> We can see delight nears.

Behind it, OPTI's Youth marched, their chins raised high; a group comprised of young boys, the youngest about ten years old, and behind them, a similar group of young girls wore floor-length flowing purple skirts, their title: OPTI's Lilacs.

> It's OPTI Day
> Make no mistake
> It's OPTI, we praise always.

All at once, people surrounding the float began to bow—grandparents, mothers, fathers, teens, children—all poured out their devotion to OPTI in this way. I watched my father gaze in speculation at the screen and the others who bowed before he bent over at last. My mother crouched beside him.

> With endless treasures and trophies
> Rain down joy upon our heads
> Lead us to achieve our wildest dreams
> OPTI, please reign supreme...

Faith remained one of the only people—aside from Scarlett, Renée, and me—who didn't bow. She stood steady and motionless, without a trace of hesitation. The boy who had objects thrown at him also stood.

"Follow our example, girls," my mother said. "Faith, you too."

Scarlett and I exchanged worried glances. Despite our mother's demand, Faith didn't move. I looked at her for guidance and she shook her head as if to tell me not to bow either.

> Prolong our days,
> the crowd continued to sing.
> In your mighty way,
> Keep us in good health
> When we have a spell...

"Girls," my father said, his voice rising. In fear, Scarlett and I glanced at each other again; something deep inside me told me to listen to Faith. I couldn't explain the feeling. In any case, I held my position behind the barriers that encased the parade route. Faith and the boy were visible to everyone, and despite the stares they received from the people bowing, neither of them made even the slightest movement toward the ground.

> With OPTI
> We incorporate,
> Under one identity
> None should dare stray.
>
> OPTI is the one and only.
> Ruler of all our hearts and minds,
> No one is above you
> Dear OPTI, our love for you is true.

The song provoked sadness in me at this moment. I frowned as I heard the lyrics saying no one ruled above OPTI. It hurt my heart. Faith told me that God created us all and held the most power in the universe. OPTI couldn't rule above God. I ignored my father, despite the fear in my throat from his anger, and held out my hand to Faith. She took it and then Scarlett's. Renée cried in her stroller, and without releasing my balloon, I placed my other hand on it so she could join too. The police officers patrolling us also bowed to OPTI, and therefore, they hadn't detected the people who stood.

The entire OPTI float froze in the middle of the parade route and I realized the screen on the float had two sides. OPTI could see in front and behind.

"Bow." I heard OPTI's voice boom for one of the first times in my life. I knew OPTI by just the image. When OPTI spoke, the ground seemed to shake and I looked to my mom for comfort. She wouldn't return my glance; her head bent toward the sidewalk beneath her. The brain pulsed as it waited for Faith and the boy to obey.

Faith held her ground and kept her gaze turned away from the screen while OPTI stared right at her. Instead her eyes rested on the boy and his on her, strangers yet united somehow through their defiance.

"Take care of the boy," OPTI said. "Make him bow."

An officer rose from the ground and strode into the middle of the road to stand before the boy. The officer stared at him through the white helmet that concealed his face, as though giving him a chance to bow. The boy stood, unflinching.

Then the officer raised his hand and struck him across the face so hard he stumbled, fell onto the hard pavement below him, and seemed to fall unconscious.

"You're next if you don't bow," my mother whispered to Faith as the police officer peered at her from afar.

Faith trembled as she stared at the unconscious body of the nameless boy and appeared as though she wanted to cry. She clenched her teeth, her jaw tightening as she awaited the looming punishment.

"Bow," OPTI said again, even louder so it seemed to echo.

Even so, Faith would not move, as resolute as a statue.

"Never," she answered.

The officer approached her, and once again, he struck and I watched my sister fall to the ground like the boy had.

"No!" I cried simultaneously with Scarlett while Renée shrieked in her stroller. Out of fear and worry for my sister, I lost my grip on my balloon's string. It slipped from my grasp and drifted into the air. I couldn't catch it in time. I could only watch in dismay as the red balloon floated away, high into the sky and into the unknown, lost forever—or at least, until I reached heaven.

"Continue," OPTI ordered.

I listened as the music struck up again and the floats moved along, still holding my sister's trembling hand.

> It's OPTI Day
> Make no mistake
> It's OPTI, we praise always
> It's OPTI, we praise always…

CHAPTER 2

Shifting Shadows

Nine months later

My mom never wanted me to come from a broken home. Even in her strife, she did her best to keep our family together, intact. She told me to always care about my siblings because they were all I had in this world. As a child, getting along with all my siblings didn't come easily. My eldest sister, Faith, and I always played together the most. Though as she grew older, her schoolwork made her too busy. Whenever she couldn't play, I would sit in her doorway, crying until my mother came to escort me away. I adored my baby sister, Renée, and sometimes, Mom didn't even have to ask me to watch her when she cooked dinner in our kitchen. However, my other older sister, Scarlett, and I hated each other. We always fought over everything. Mom said we fought all the time because the two of us were close in age.

"How can I get along with Scarlett when she never listens to what I have to say?" I asked my mom as I helped her in the garden one afternoon.

My mom sighed as she covered one of the seeds with soil. "I know you two don't get along right now," she said. "One day, you will realize how lucky you are to have her, all of your sisters."

My eyebrows scrunched up on my forehead. "I don't think we'll ever get along," I said.

She paused to relinquish more seeds into the muddy earth. "I guess we'll have to wait and see then."

A few weeks later, I sat at my desk in my math class when a voice came out of the loudspeaker. "This is an emergency alert. All schools in our district are having a lockdown…" The deep voice repeated the words over and over.

"What's a 'lockdown?'" I asked my friend, Claire, who sat beside me. Before she could answer, the teacher told us all to quiet down and to hide.

"Why are we hiding?" I asked another girl named Teresa. She shrugged.

Other students were asking the same questions and the room filled with their buzzing endless chatter. The teacher had us count with her to ten to gather our attention. When our class reached ten, a definite silence hung over the room aside from the teacher's guiding voice as she urged us to gather at the back of the classroom. My classmates and I had to sit down, making sure to stay very quiet and still. The teacher turned the lights off, darkening the classroom aside from the soft glow of light slipping inside from behind the curtains. It reminded me of the times when I would wake up in the middle of the night to all the shifting shadows on the walls of my bedroom, moving about like mysterious night-time creatures. My mom would reassure me that monsters didn't exist and the shadows were curtains whenever the window was left open in the summers. None of those shadows could hurt me. However, on this day, uncertainty claimed my mind.

It seemed like hours that we sat on the story-time carpet and I found it hard to remain seated. I had so many questions. I hadn't figured out what a lockdown meant. Fear swelled in my throat. I didn't know who we hid from and Scarlett told me once that I was not good at hiding. She found me every time. Sometimes when Faith played with us, she would always find me first, making Scarlett the winner. It made me so mad and I would burst into tears. In spite of losing, Faith would promise to buy me a chocolate bar the next time she passed the candy store, on her way home from school, and she always lived up to her promise. If I won at hiding this time, maybe she would buy me *two* chocolate bars.

After some time, my fear subsided when no one came for us and it made me happy to know I won at this game. Instead of fear, all the waiting bored me to tears and I wished I could go home. My eyes drooped enough to take a nap. I rubbed them.

Then another announcement played, "The lockdown has ended. All students are free to go home."

I cheered, along with the rest of the class, in excitement for our extra-long weekend. Right before summer too!

My joy came to an abrupt halt when the teacher spoke.

"You're free to go," she said. "Stay safe on your way home."

Her face struck me with hazel-brown eyes gaping with fear; she appeared as though she had just entered a cemetery at night. When I said goodbye to her before I left, I examined her eyes once more and the hazel opals portrayed a pronounced sadness beyond words. I never forgot it.

She opened the door for us in glum silence. I couldn't imagine why her expression emanated distraught. It left an ache in my heart, and my stomach churned. I knew then that something horrific had happened; I didn't know what.

Scarlett and I shared a seat on the bus this time. Her face was strained with worry.

"Do you know what happened?" I asked her.

"No," she said. "We'll have to ask Mom when we get home."

When my sister and I arrived at our bus stop at the bottom of our long driveway, we couldn't find our mom waiting for us as usual. It had rained all day and traces of the wet weather revealed itself in the patches of mud and puddles around the driveway.

"Where is she?" I asked Scarlett as I scanned the drive, expecting to see Mom walking down it. I turned back to Scarlett to find she had already begun heading up and I hurried to catch up to her. Her long dark-cherry-oak hair rested behind her ears, her face pale. A sharp line stood out on her forehead.

"Do you think something happened to her?"

I watched her face as she gazed ahead of us, her eyes searching the top of the hill.

"Why isn't she here? Do you think she's home?"

"I don't know!" Scarlett burst with a sharp glare. "Stop asking me questions."

We made it to the front door and Scarlett rang the doorbell. I peered through the windows beside the door. I couldn't see Mom walking toward us to answer the door. It scared me and I stuck close to Scarlett as we went over to the garage. I realized Faith's car wasn't in the driveway either. I had assumed Faith would have the day off too.

"Where's Faith?" I asked Scarlett. She refused to speak once more and plugged the code into the garage. Mom had her write it down in her notebook in case of an emergency. When we entered the house, the sound of my mother's firm voice informed us that she was in the kitchen. Scarlett hurried down the hallway and I followed her. We found our mom pacing back and forth on the phone. Renée sat in her high chair with a plate of food that she picked at. She waved to us and smiled. My mother's voice shifted to one choked with fear and it seized my attention.

"I need to know," she spoke. Scarlett and I watched her in worry. "The police wouldn't let me in to see. I couldn't find her outside the school with the other students when I got there…could you please check to see…the names?"

Silence filled the room and my mom turned around to see Scarlett and me waiting for an explanation. Neither of us could ask any questions while she talked on the phone. She entered the family room and began to pace.

"It's Faith, Faith Richardson."

Another pause.

"No, you must have made a mistake."

We waited with bated breath.

"No! No!" Her voice sounded as shrill as an alarm. Renée started to cry and her face reddened.

"It's okay, it's okay." I crossed the room to Renée who kept crying. I would have picked her up. Unfortunately she was too heavy for me to carry. Instead I laid a hand on her shoulder.

"Mommy, Mommy!"

I rubbed her back to soothe her.

"No! No!" Mom shouted again.

Renée's wails rose in a crescendo as I watched Scarlett hurry over to the family room. The hair on the back of my neck stood up. I trailed with caution behind her. My mom continued to cry "no" in the same voice which grew softer as she stopped in her tracks. Even though Renée's screams had quieted down by now, the full volume of them echoed in my ears. My mom fell to her knees and clutched her chest as she lay her entire body against the carpeted floor.

"Mom, are you okay?" Scarlett asked and knelt down beside her. I went to the other side of my mom and imitated Scarlett. I reached out a tentative hand to place it on my mom's back. In solemn silence, I observed her as she wept.

"It's okay, Mom," I said. "Scarlett will call an ambulance. Just get up."

She didn't move and continued to cry. Renée's wails had softened into a soft whimper. Scarlett and I exchanged glances, unsure of what to do. Then Scarlett laid herself down beside her and I did the same, both of us placed our hands around her back. What else could we do?

Together we held onto our broken mother for what seemed like forever.

My mom recovered from her sobs and put Renée down for her usual nap. Afterward she sat Scarlett and me down at the dinner table. We stared at our mother in anticipation. I couldn't sit still.

"What happened?" I asked. "Are you hurt?"

"No...well, yes, and no," she said, her forehead lined with worry.

"Did something happen to Faith?" Scarlett asked. "Is she okay?"

"No. She's gone."

"Is she lost?" I asked. I remembered when we lost our cat, Pearl. To me, only cats could go missing, not sisters.

Mom gazed at Scarlett and me for a moment as if deciding how to answer. "Yes, she's lost."

"Should all of us look for her?" Scarlett asked in concern. "She can't have disappeared forever."

"She did. She left forever," Mom insisted, her face grave. "She's resting now."

Scarlett shook her head in fury.

"No, Mom, she can't be," she protested. "Faith promised...we planned to...she planned to take me to the doll store this weekend to buy her a new outfit."

"Is she in heaven?" I asked.

"Shh." Mom glanced at the screen behind us where OPTI's form often materialized. OPTI lived there as involved in our family as we were, ever-present as he watched over us all. "Heaven doesn't exist."

"But, Mom—"

"Enough," she said. "Don't anger OPTI. He is the one we should praise."

I held my tongue even though it made me angry. I didn't understand why it would make OPTI mad. Where else could Faith exist if not in heaven? After a moment of silence, Mom spoke again.

"It's her time to go. I know it's difficult to understand. When you are older, you will." She spoke as if to convince herself.

"Did her battery run out?" I asked. I thought of how sometimes my OPTI-Pad died from playing too long. "Maybe we can give her some."

"People don't have batteries, *idiot*," Scarlett hissed.

"I'm not an idiot," I retorted and crossed my arms. "*You're* an idiot."

"Enough, girls," Mom said. "We need to treat each other kindly. You only have each other now. Just the three of you."

Scarlett and I stopped glaring at each other for the moment.

"I want Faith back," Scarlett said in a soft voice. Mom pulled the two of us into a hug.

"I do too," Mom agreed, her eyes moistening. Her tears surprised me. I didn't see her cry often. It troubled me and my eyes welled up.

"How did Faith die?" Scarlett asked.

My mom waited a long time before she answered. "She was at school and…she…someone, a very bad person chose to make her body stop working."

"The monsters got her?" I asked. In alarm, I looked around the room as I checked for any shadows.

"No," my mom said. "Monsters don't exist. Shadows can't hurt us."

My mom's words comforted me for the moment. I tried to imagine what happened and none of it made sense. Would it happen to me or my other siblings? Should I feel afraid?

And like that, a nameless monster had stormed into my once seemingly peaceful world and shattered it into a million irreparable pieces.

For the rest of the weekend, Mom forbade us from watching television besides movies. A girl named Ashley became our babysitter for both days. Dad sat at his desk in his office with the door shut. I had tried on previous occasions to see my dad while he worked in the study. It always made him angry though.

"It's rude to interrupt someone as busy as me," he would say. I would hang my head and leave the room in confusion and hurt.

The babysitter seemed nice, except when she made cookies with us, some of them burnt and the rest hurt my teeth. Renée had to get hers broken into tiny pieces so she essentially ate crumbs. Faith always knew how to make them soft and doughy. She could bake well and I recalled the scrumptious taste of the chocolate mousse she once made us. Ashley's failed attempts made Scarlett, Renée, and me more upset.

After, we gathered in the family room to play with our toys. Scarlett excused herself to use the bathroom. I focused on playing with my toy castle and the knights, princesses, princes, and dragons. Renée played along with me and we came up with fun stories together. Sometime later, Ashley got up from the sofa to check the bathroom.

"Scarlett?" she said in the midst of her knocking. "Scar? Are you in here?"

Silence.

Renée and I got to our feet and hurried over to Ashley as she opened the door.

"She's not in here," Ashley said. "Where do you think she went?"

"I don't know," I said with a lump in my throat. "I hope her body didn't stop working too."

"She'll be fine," Ashley assured me, though she bit her nails. "Let's look for her."

The babysitter, Renée, and I rushed around the house in search of my lost sister. We checked every bedroom, closet, and even under our beds. Although the babysitter said Scarlett would be fine, I didn't believe her at this point.

"What if we never find her?" I said in panic. My entire body quaked.

"I even looked under her bed," Renée said, raising her hands in question.

A memory resurfaced from more than two years ago when my mom carried Renée in her belly.

Mom would take us for walks around the neighborhood and Scarlett and Faith rode their bikes. Mom strolled with me since I hadn't learned how to ride a bike and I wouldn't get one until my next birthday. Whenever Scarlett and Faith reached the end of a street and began to turn the corner, I would always call for them to stop out of fear that they would disappear.

"Scarlett," I called as I stepped outside to search. "Scarlett, come back!"

A small whimpering sound drew me to the edge of the forest in our backyard and to a nearby tree. I hustled over to the tree to find Scarlett crouched behind it, hugging her knees and crying. Her bike lay on its side on the forest floor, forgotten. Happiness filled me when I found her, to know she hadn't disappeared forever like Faith.

"Why are you hiding?" I asked.

"Go away, Abby," she said between sniffles.

I knelt down beside my sister and placed a wary hand on her back. She didn't nudge me away this time and I rubbed her back. In this moment I understood what my mother had meant. I knew I should care about Scarlett no matter how much we fought.

"I couldn't find Faith," she said, glancing up at me in dismay. "I checked the meadow. Remember our secret hideout? She wasn't there..." Tears streaked her cheeks as she wept, and I wrapped my small arms around her in comfort.

Sometimes I forgot Faith's body stopped working. I would open the door to her room to ask her to play tag with me. However, when I didn't find her at her desk completing homework, writing in her journal, or lounging on her bed to watch a show on her own television, then I would remember all over again—Faith wasn't around to make me laugh anymore or tickle me until I couldn't breathe. Instead I sat in the doorway and wailed. She'd vanished as if she hadn't even existed.

"Abby, don't go in Faith's room," my mother would say to me. "Faith isn't there anymore."

Eventually I listened to my mother and stayed away. I still imagined that Faith lived in heaven with God which soothed me. For the moment, I kept it a secret.

CHAPTER 3

Flowers Die

Faith's sudden death remained difficult to discuss with either of my parents. I learned to hide my grief in silence, unheard and buried deep down in my heart. Keeping quiet presented difficulties because I cried more than the rest of my family. One time, before Faith died, my dad found me crying after Scarlett called me stupid. He bent down so his face almost leveled with mine and wiped away one of my tears with his thumb. After a slight moment, my dad spoke clear and succinct. "Never let anyone see you cry. You'll only give them more reasons to tease you."

At that, he rose to his full height and retreated back into his office, closing the large wooden door behind him.

Shortly after Faith's death, I found my father on the front porch. He gazed out at the forest that provided security for our home from prying eyes. When I came out, he peered down at me for a moment and then gave me a hug. "You'd like a new bike, wouldn't you?" he asked.

I nodded in excitement. "Oh, yes, please, Dad," I said.

"Well, I'll get you one now," he said. "I'll make sure it has flowers. You like those, don't you?"

I nodded. "Yes, flowers are pretty."

"Did you know there's a type of job called a botanist?"

I clung to my father's words with intrigue.

"They study plants." He went on. "Plants are remarkable. The most lethal weapons and, at the same time, the best antidotes. If submerged in darkness, some plants will stretch their stems out as far as possible just to access sunlight, just to survive…Unfortunately just like us, flowers die."

Although my father explained what a botanist did, my mind filled with so many questions that my brain whirled. What did *submerged* mean? What kind of plants can survive darkness? Then another far more pressing question came to my mind.

"Why do people—and flowers—die?" I asked him.

"It's the wicked way of the world," he replied in a calm smooth tone. "Everyone must die, one way or another. Not even the strongest people can conquer death. However, strength and endurance can help you last a lot longer."

"Can people who die ever come back?" I asked. "Maybe God will give Faith back if he sees how sad we are without her."

My father chuckled. "Foolish girl. There's no God in this world," he said, "just life and death. Don't think such thoughts about God. OPTI is the closest thing humans have to God. If you worship OPTI and are strong, you can live a good life."

I stared at my dad with wide eyes. Why would he say God didn't exist? "But, Dad, God created us," I said. "Faith told me so once. Why wouldn't he be real?"

"God didn't create you," he said, "OPTI did through me. OPTI is the god of this world. Faith lied to you. She's gone and you'll never see her again."

Tears formed in my eyes. "Why would you say that, Daddy? It's not true! God made me. Faith isn't a liar, she's not!"

"It is true," my father replied, a gleam in his eyes. "Don't worry though, someday with OPTI's help, humans will discover how to triumph over death."

He patted me on the head before slipping into his car to drive away. Scarlett came out as he left and mustered a wave. She waited with me for him to return with the bike. I knew I should feel excited yet Dad's words lingered in my mind. It felt as if he'd scolded me for more than spilling grape juice on the carpet. Why would he say such horrible things about God? I couldn't wrap my head around it. A few hours went by and I waited with diligence, my mind consumed with his last words. Scarlett gave up after some time to go eat dinner and brought mine out for me. In the end, the evening light shifted to night and there was still no sign of him. Tears pooled in my eyes.

"Why won't he come back?" I asked Scarlett.

For once, Scarlett didn't tease me for crying. Instead she put a hand on my back the way Mom sometimes did as I had after Faith died. I leaned my head on Scarlett's shoulder as I cried. She didn't even push me away. We sat together, wondering how our once-peaceful world had gone so wrong.

We didn't know what to tell Renée. As the days passed, my hope that my father would return lingered and I would sit out on the porch in the evenings, after school, even as the evenings turned to twilight with mosquitos out, waiting for him to come home. I never saw his car slip into view. Scarlett joined me on some evenings. In the end, our mother had to come out to tell us to come inside and that he wouldn't return. It didn't make sense to me and I racked my brain for an explanation. Where did my father go? Where did he go to after work? Why didn't he want to sleep at home? Would he come back when my birthday arrived? I asked my mother all these questions on repeat.

"I don't know," she would answer every time until she grew angry with me. Also Scarlett would glower at me when I asked these questions so I stopped asking my mother for some time. I wanted to tell Renée that our father would return soon. However, my mother said not to mention it at all to Renée.

"He made his decision." I listened to my mother tell a coworker the following Saturday evening while Scarlett and I played with our toys in the living room. I stared in dismay at my dollhouse and tried to make sense of a story for these dolls without a father and an older sister. "It's final. He's not coming back. He didn't even leave a note."

Renée slept upstairs so she didn't know that our father disappeared for good. Later when my mother's friend left, without many words, my mother directed Scarlett and me to our rooms for bed. When I reached my room, I encountered a problem. I didn't know how to put my pajamas on without my mom's help because my pajama top had buttons. So I exited my bedroom to wander down the hall to my mom's bedroom behind two double doors. I tiptoed inside the dark room and found my mother already in bed and asleep. I crept around the large bed to the side where she slept. I touched her arm.

"Mom, I can't put my pj's on," I said.

She didn't answer. She remained in the same position with her eyes closed.

"Wake up," I said and tugged on her arm.

She groaned and shifted onto her side, away from me. "You can do it yourself. You're old enough now."

"But, Mom," I whined. "I don't know how."

"Ask your sister to help you then."

I stood at the side of the bed, staring at my mother's back and growing nervous about being in darkness. Before whenever I feared the dark, my parents would tell me that they would protect me from any monsters. On this night, I couldn't feel certain. I had one parent left.

"Please, Mom."

She released a heavy sigh and sat up in bed, irritable. I stepped back so my mother could get out of bed and she beckoned me to follow her to my room. My mother helped me get my pajamas on.

"Do you think Dad will come back for my birthday?" I asked when we finished.

"No," my mother said.

"He promised to get me a bike," I said. "Maybe that's where he is—at the bike shop."

"He's not at a bike shop, Abigail," she said, her voice becoming sterner. "He is gone. Forever."

I stared at my mother. She had dark circles under her eyes, which were resolute and without a trace of hope. At her words and her expression, I burst into tears and uncontrollable shaking.

"He's not gone," I said through my sobs. "Where is he?"

"I don't know," my mother said. "Get to sleep."

At that, my mother left my room while I continued to cry. However, before Faith's body stopped working, she told me if I ever felt sad, I could pray. She said all you have to do is to put your hands together and talk to God. She informed me if I prayed, God would answer my prayers. So that night, I climbed into my bed and folded my hands together.

I pray Faith and my father will come home. I pray I can have a family again…And I pray the shadows won't get me too.

I waited and searched around my dark room and out the window to settle my gaze on a bed of twinkling stars. I expected I would hear the doorbell in the next moment, and in my excitement, I hurried over to my window to peer down at the driveway. When I gazed down at it, nothing had changed. My father's car didn't slip up the driveway and no one came to the front door.

That night when I fell asleep, despite the shadows, I had a dream about my sister Faith. I could see her face and she laughed at something. It made me disappointed when I awoke and her face disappeared—it made me afraid I would forget what she looked like.

My birthday came the week after my father left home and I would turn seven, only three years until I turned ten. However, my mom cancelled the plans for my birthday party at the local botanical garden. We planned to spend the day exploring the eccentric shapes of the bushes as well as the enchanting flower arrangements. The first time, just my immediate family came, and this year, I wanted to invite my friends. When my mother told me we had to cancel it, I cried all day. She explained we didn't have the money to host people at the garden. Instead we had a small birthday party at home with the family I had left. I recall gathering around the kitchen table in front of my dull vanilla cake.

When I made my wish, I asked for my father to return and for Faith to wake up. As I did, the hope that had blossomed in my heart and endured—lit all this time—wilted with the suddenness of the candles when my breath extinguished them, the wisps of smoke vanishing into nothingness.

CHAPTER 4

The Edwins

Eight years later

The dismal dawn at the Edwins' house left me nauseous about the approaching summer day, June 1—my fifteenth birthday. Pale light shone through the windows and stung my eyes. I could still hear my mother's screams from last January as she broke down in the kitchen one gloomy afternoon. We were yet to know why, only that we had to leave home and OPTI entered us into the foster care system as a temporary arrangement until she recovered.

The Edwins treated us with unimaginable cruelty. My limbs ached all over, bruises covered my arms though my wounds reached far deeper than my skin—indescribable pain in every fiber of my being. Scarlett rolled over on the small bed we shared, nudging my shoulder as she struggled to find room. Renée, now ten years old, slept curled in a blanket on the hard wooden window seat. Last night had been her turn to sleep there. I offered to switch with her but Renée insisted with more emphasis after the ordeal I went through two nights before.

My thoughts preoccupied my mind to the point where I couldn't sleep anymore and slid off the bed to the floor. I kept my eyes on Scarlett for a moment as she rolled over to replace my previous spot. Even in this moment, with my sisters near, I lacked comfort; and I curled in on my stomach, hoping to quell the hunger pangs. I knew what it could cost; I knew the time would come again to try to steal from the fridge, my only way to sustain us yet risk detection. Our sole relief from the Edwins occurred when they sent us to school—and by sent, I mean forced to walk there. Even when it rained. For months, Scarlett and I tried a few times to ask the Edwins if our mother recovered. They refused to tell us and threatened to hurt us if we kept asking.

The door to our room flew open and in walked Mrs. Edwin. In her hands, she carried three black dresses.

"Get up, you filthy girls." She spat. "We have visitors today. You'd better clean yourselves up. I have some dresses for you to wear while they are here." Mrs. Edwin tossed the black lacy dresses into my hands and I handed one to Scarlett and another to Renée.

We all did what Mrs. Edwin told us.

"Who do you think the visitors are?" Scarlett asked as she brushed through her wet hair. This morning we had access to a shower for the first time in a while. Mr. and Mrs. Edwin often complained we wasted water.

"I don't know," I said as I examined myself in the mirror which I hadn't done in at least a week. My cheek displayed a fresh bruise. "Whoever they are, they might help us."

When the guests arrived Scarlett, Renée, and I went downstairs to sit beside one another on the living room couch. The polished leathery sofa seemed as though it had just arrived from the furniture store. I took in the rest of the room and noticed the washed floors; a smooth polished wooden floor replaced the original thick layer of dust. The box of pizza that used to sit on the coffee table disappeared, and instead, a fancy cheese platter substituted it. Scarlett, Renée, and I fidgeted in our matching black lacy dresses that itched with black nylons entrapping our scrawny legs. Mrs. Edwin had taken to dousing our faces and any exposed skin in a white powder before they permitted us to enter the room, concealing any blemishes that might have signaled our troubles. While we sat on the sofa, I gripped Scarlett's and Renée's hands as though using all our strength to will our chances of freedom. Mr. and Mrs. Edwin sat on either side of us. A stout man in a sleek business suit lounged on the opposite couch with cuff links on his wrist emblazoned with OPTI, and beside him, a woman perched wearing a beige dress. She pursed her lips and clicked her pen on repeat.

"Hello, girls," the woman said. "This is Mr. Bourdin, and my name is Martha. What are your names?"

"I'm Scarlett, and this is my sister, Abigail, oh, and that's Renée," Scarlett replied with narrowed eyes as if she sized both Mr. Bourdin and Martha up.

"Now I'd like to check up on how everything is going here," Martha said, pausing in her pen-clicking to pull out a clipboard from her bag.

"You're due for a visit from our company. Since a month ago," Mr. Bourdin said, scratching his thin beard. "I'm afraid we've gotten behind schedule."

"Oh, not to worry," Mr. Edwin said, "There are no concerns here."

"That's great to know," Mr. Bourdin said, putting one arm behind the couch above Martha's head as though he gazed at a television. "That will make our jobs a lot easier."

"Well…" Martha interjected with a pointed look at Mr. Bourdin who pulled out his phone, "we did learn about some calls made. Something about an adolescent girl with a dog collar around her neck in the backyard and noise disturbance…Mr. Bourdin?"

He raised an eye from his phone. "Yes, yes," he said, "I believe that's why I'm here as well."

A smile swept across Mrs. Edwin's face. Mrs. Edwin had pleasant features: soft shoulder-length dark hair and a convincing cheerful smile. "Oh, it seems you've made a mistake. Why on earth would we do such a thing? And to a young girl?" She placed a thin hand on Renée's head. I eyed the spidery hand with long crimson polished fingernails on my younger sister's head, wishing I could swat it off.

"We're bringing it up because the neighbors complained," Martha explained. "Something about hearing barking and growling. We want to make sure this home you've provided for these young girls is safe."

"Martha, didn't you hear her response?" Mr. Bourdin said his eyes glued to his phone. "She said we made a mistake."

"It's true," Mr. Edwin insisted, turning his beady eyes on me as if in warning. I huddled closer to my sisters. "The neighbors must have thought they saw a young girl when it was actually our dog." He patted the head of his fearsome-looking German shepherd who growled at Scarlett, Renée, and me whenever we walked by him.

After the dreadful boring conversation about the Edwins' concern for fostered youth, we all gathered in the hallway to bid Mr. Bourdin and Martha goodbye.

"Mr. Bourdin, I need to speak with you in private," Scarlett's voice came out in one breath, knowing we had just a few minutes. "Please, it's urgent."

"I don't have much time," he said, showing us the time on his phone. "I have to get back to the office."

"Please," I begged. "It won't take long, we swear."

Mr. Bourdin's eyes flickered from me to Scarlett and then to Renée. At last, he sighed. "All right, all right," he said, "I suppose I can spare at least one minute of my time."

"Could we go outside?" I asked. "It's private."

"Follow me," Mr. Bourdin said, striding for the front door. We trailed close behind until we stood outside on the front porch. "Now what could be so urgent?"

"The Edwins are evil," Scarlett blurted.

"They keep us locked up in our room or the basement if we do something wrong," I added. "They made me sleep outside once… and have done…such…horrible things to us." I shuddered, unable to contemplate voicing them all aloud.

"The rice that they make us kneel on hurts." Renée pressed.

"They lied when they said they would never hurt a child," I said. "I'm the one they put the dog collar around."

"They keep the fridge locked," Renée added.

"We're always so hungry. They don't give us enough to eat."

"We're not safe here," Scarlett finished.

While we spoke, Mr. Bourdin eyed us, perplexed.

"Hmm," he said. "I hear what you're saying."

"So you'll help us?" I asked. "Are you going to take us away from here?"

"I'm afraid not," he said, seeming calm despite the urgency of our situation. "Those are very grand accusations."

At his words, my hope dissipated.

"But they're horrible to us," Scarlett said, her eyebrows furrowing. "And it's your job to place us in a safe home."

"Listen," he said, peering down at us as if we were too young to understand, "I know change can come with difficulties. The Edwins are your caretakers now until your mother is better and they get to set the rules in their house, including administering punishment as they see fit."

"Their punishments are cruel," I said. "We never did anything to deserve any of those punishments." Though often, it felt like we had.

"That rice feels more like torture to me," Scarlett muttered.

"I'm not sure how rice is a torturing device," Mr. Bourdin said, looking dumbfounded. "Let me put it in simple terms for you. See, you might think I have all of the time in the world to worry about you girls. You must also realize this is a business. OPTI's business."

"It's not a *business*," I retorted. "It's a matter of life or death."

"People in business aren't concerned with accusations with no proof," he replied. "Only solid facts matter and earning profit and salaries for my employees directly from OPTI and generous donations. Haven't you heard of the story of the boy who cried wolf? But you three should rejoice to know that you are the golden geese."

"You can't treat us like we're piggy banks," Scarlett growled, stepping forward, and I had to grab hold of my sister's arm to keep her from retaliating. That wouldn't end well. "And we most certainly aren't crying wolf."

"Besides it is also OPTI's decision for you to reside here," Mr. Bourdin said. "You should thank OPTI for providing you with shelter, with food, and the freedom to go to school."

"So you're not going to do anything?" I cried in exasperation. With a last bout of hope, I pulled up my sleeve and extended my purple-blotted arm. "Not even with these bruises running down my arms?"

Mr. Bourdin appeared unmoved by my display and, with a mere shake of his head, said, "Why do you have to cause so much trouble?

I'd rather resolve this in a much more peaceful way. I'd suggest you talk one-on-one with Mr. and Mrs. Edwin about any issues. Other than that, nothing more should happen. Perhaps it will do you good to learn some discipline. As a boy, my father would…oh, never mind that. Now enough complaining."

Renée started to cry, and Scarlett glowered at Mr. Bourdin. I then glanced at Scarlett for her reaction. She nodded in agreement, a signal, a message that the time arrived to put our plan into action. Our survival depended on it.

"Now I'll leave for a vacation to Vermont in a week." Mr. Bourdin droned on. I turned my attention back to Mr. Bourdin, though my mind rested on Scarlett's defining look that seemed to seal our fate for the rest of our lives. "You've got to get there before the bed-and-breakfasts get too crowded. So I most likely won't see you. I wonder if my assistant could get a picture of the three of you before I go. It would benefit some other adolescents and children if you helped market this foster care system so that they can have a place to go."

Scarlett opened her mouth as if to protest but she didn't get a chance as Martha emerged from the house, followed by the Edwins who threw nasty looks at us. Mr. Bourdin and Martha failed to notice. Not that it would have mattered.

"Martha," Mr. Bourdin said to his assistant. "Why don't you take their picture now?"

Martha nodded and gestured for Scarlett, Renée, and me to move closer together. I placed a hand on both my sisters' arms. I didn't care to muster even the smallest smile.

"You three are not very photogenic." Martha noted as she examined us. "You should smile more often. It makes your face look prettier too."

"Why don't you get one of the Edwins?" Scarlett asked then, nonchalant.

Renée and I gazed at our sister in curiosity.

Martha found this a wonderful idea, and soon, the Edwins posed at their front door as their pictures were taken. As the camera flashed, Scarlett told Renée to stay put and came close to me so she could whisper.

"The next moment we have, you got it?"

"I think I may have something that might help," I said and my hand reached into my pocket to feel the soft petals of a flower between my fingers. Even as my fingers interlaced with them, a sinking feeling of dread permeated my heart. They became our only choice, our only hope. Like the roll of the die, the odds of our plan's success lay in the balance.

Renée looked at us in question.

"You'll find out soon enough," Scarlett informed her as we distanced ourselves. My mind buzzed in thought like a live wire, my breath settled into gasps riddled with apprehension.

CHAPTER 5

Awakened

The Edwins got away with their lies about leaving me outside with a dog collar around my neck mostly because of Mr. Bourdin's refusal to help us. The Edwins caught me trying to "steal" food from the fridge for Renée for the third time in a row. Mrs. Edwin slapped my cheek, and then Mr. Edwin forced me outside to spend the entire night in the cold pitch-black. Mr. Edwin put the dog collar around my neck two nights before Mr. Bourdin came to visit and I almost wondered if I'd survive until the next day. An OPTI screen perched on the back porch under an awning, its brain watching me and surveying my night of terror out in the cold.

I began the night staring in defeat at the sunset as Mr. Edwin placed the collar around my neck and taped over the buckle so I couldn't remove it. He left me standing in the middle of the muddy backyard, surrounded on all sides by a tall fence with slits between each board. Toward the back of the yard sat a medium-sized gardening shed and a garden blooming with flowers, bushes, and trees.

I watched the sun as it sunk below the horizon and thus began my countdown until the dawn broke after an endless night. The surge of clicking crickets overwhelmed the surrounding forest, and mosquitos feasted on my bare skin. I shivered as I attempted to swat the mosquitos.

Darkness fell all around me, lulling the creatures of the day to sleep and the light of the moon called to the beasts and critters of the night. I lay down on the grassy ground to sleep and tried to avoid the mud. I wrapped my arms around my body to keep warm. My plans expired when a light drizzle softened the ground, deepening the muddy patches until I had to choose between standing all night and getting dirty. I chose to get dirty. Like I did every night at the Edwins' I put my hands together and prayed I would survive the night and go home. Praying turned into a routine I'd kept throughout the past few years, though I often doubted. I still believed, however, I persisted in uncertainty about whether my prayers were heard or answered.

My stomach growled. My plan to steal from the fridge involved satisfying my own hunger as well, and now, I would spend another night with my stomach aching for food. So would Renée, I suppose. Although I felt guilty for my failure, I couldn't do anything about it. The Edwins barely fed us. Scarlett and I resorted to smuggling food for Renée. Otherwise Scarlett sometimes gave me some of her food and I would share some with Renée, so in that sense, Renée's appetite remained satisfied. However, that meant Scarlett and I would go hungry.

Unfortunately tonight, I didn't have Scarlett to give me any food and I didn't have either of my siblings for comfort. My siblings became the part of living at the Edwins' that I didn't hate. They made survival possible for me.

I tried to lull myself to sleep on the muddy ground when I saw some glowing fireflies, like fairies, heading for the garden. Curious, I got up and followed them to where I found bushes growing raspberries. I began to eat the berries, hoping the Edwins wouldn't find out. I noticed some hemlock growing and moved away from the poisonous plant. Then my eyes settled on something else—a plant I recognized from spending hours gardening with my mother; the clustered white elderberries surrounding crisp white petals spread open as if in greeting. My thoughts turned to the plan Scarlett and I had formed—finding a moment, any window of time, to run away from the Edwins and go home. We figured our mother must have recuperated by now and the Edwins held us hostage from returning home. Having foster youth made OPTI spoil them with all sorts of gifts, and as soon as we left, they would have to wait for a different group of children to get any more rewards. We couldn't wait around for any moment; we needed to create time. So I plucked some of the valerian petals and stuffed them in my pocket. Afterwards I found a tree close to the bushes and settled underneath it for shelter from the rain. My clothes were soaked by now. Fortunately the tree prevented some of the raindrops from falling on me, allowing me to escape the drizzle.

A sudden cry in the night echoed from the forest; a cacophony of barking accompanied it. I shuddered at the noise and surveyed the fence, trying to peer through the slits. I couldn't see anything. The barking came again followed by a sharp howl and a chill ran down my spine. I noticed something else: the fence had one of its gates left open at the side. Then I knew I was in immediate danger. Against the fierce howls and echoing squealing barks that grew in volume, I sprinted across the yard toward the shed.

The pull of the chain halted me, hindered by a small pole in the ground. I stood feet away from the door of the shed but not close enough to get inside. If I tried, the collar would choke me. My hands seized the collar, searching for the buckle. I pulled at the tape wrapped around it. I would need scissors to cut it off. I tried to pull the collar up over my head. Mr. Edwin had fastened it too tight around my neck so I couldn't pull it off. I needed to get inside that shed however I could.

The barks came nearer, thundering in my ears as the coyotes came closer. I ran back the opposite direction and grabbed ahold of the pole. Amid the snarls from right outside the fence, I pulled on the metal pole, trying to free it from the ground. It shifted; aside from that, it remained in the ground. I could see the dark shapes of the coyotes as they circled the fence, searching for a way inside. With all my strength, I pulled again and the rod released from the ground, uprooting the earth around it. I couldn't believe it worked. I didn't waste any more time and ran across the yard into the shed and closed the door behind me. Darkness swallowed me yet the unknown became a haven. The coyotes continued to yap. One of them must have entered the yard because the growls intensified as it scratched at the door. My heart raced. I found myself now trapped. I trembled and prayed I would live.

"Don't worry, I'll save you, my child." I heard like a whisper; the voice left me speechless and, at the same time, comforted me, the kind of comfort I'd yearned for ever since arriving at the Edwins'. "You'll survive."

A light came on inside the shed, and now, I could see the tools and pots lining the shelves and a tarp in one corner. As I surveyed the room, the snarling and scratching noises subsided in minutes. They were gone.

I stayed in the shed for the rest of the night, under the tarp that provided me with some warmth. I spent the night crouched on the floor, wide awake and sobbing. God heard my prayers; he even whispered I would survive. All this time, I thought I'd lost my connection to God in the blur of the years after my father left. On this night, my faith reignited with blooming strength.

The Edwins would have punished me for finding me in the shed but they received complaints from the neighbors and didn't want them to know what they were doing to me. The next morning, they sent me back to school with my siblings. I prayed to God it would never happen again. That night, God's presence evidenced itself in a way I never thought possible. I'd never forget it.

CHAPTER 6

Night Fright

Tonight was my night; the night when Mr. Edwin would send my sisters to our room and keep me to himself in the basement. It made Mr. Bourdin's unhelpfulness all the more upsetting. We were defeated, doomed, left to be violated, waiting in desperation for our mother to get better so we could go home. Before the time came, we waited in the basement with the door to the first floor locked. We sat on the dingy mattress with a hand-towel-sized blanket and our two jackets to keep the three of us warm. Dinnertime arrived, according to my watch. Scarlett and I were to prepare it as we did most nights when my turn came.

"What do you have that can help us?" Scarlett asked.

My stomach churned. "I have these." I unfolded my hand to reveal a small pile of white petals sitting in my palm.

"What are they?" she asked.

"They're valerian petals," I explained. "I picked them from their garden. They make you fall asleep if you eat them."

"That could give us our chance," Scarlett said. "If he falls asleep, we can make our escape."

I glanced from Scarlett to the petals.

"Come on. If you hide them well enough, he'll never know."

"I'm worried it's not a good idea. It doesn't feel right."

She put a hand on my shoulder. "It's the only choice we have. You nearly died the other night, and what he does to us reflects a certain kind of death. It's survival."

I stared at her.

The door to the basement opened and light blasted into the room. A small tremor ran down my spine.

"Blond girl and dark-brown-haired girl." Mr. Edwin's voice carried down the stairs. "Come out of that basement and prepare me my dinner."

I stepped away from Scarlett and led the way up the stairs, leaving Renée behind. My legs shook. I walked past Mr. Edwin who wore a buttoned-down shirt and a pair of work pants, and as he locked the basement door, I walked down the hall into the kitchen.

"What shall we make?" I asked.

"Spaghetti," he said, his eyes firm and a glint of amusement apparent in them.

Mr. Edwin left the kitchen for the living room where the glowing brain of OPTI rested on a screen. My eyes wandered around the kitchen and noticed three steaming mugs that were different shades of green, with what looked like tea, sitting on the kitchen counter near the sink.

"Do you think they're for us?" I asked Scarlett.

She looked at me. "Put the flower petals in there. *Now*," she whispered.

I met her gaze and my thoughts turned to what awaited me tonight. Anything except *that*. This sedative became our chance for freedom, to finally return home. I pulled the petals out of my pocket and tore them into the tiniest bits and put them in each of the hot mugs.

"They'll all sink by the time we're done," Scarlett said.

I nodded and opened the cupboard beneath the stove to find a large pot. I filled it with water and lifted it onto the stove. Scarlett took a frying pan and began to make the meat sauce. I hoped it would turn out better than last time when the pasta was crunchy. I poured in the noodles and stirred them around, waiting for them to cook.

"Is it ready yet, girls?" The brutish voice called from the living room as I drained the pasta. The television buzzed and I could hear the muffled sounds of the news. "It'd better be. I'm starving and I don't like waiting."

"Almost," I said. My eyes flitted away from the noodles to study the mugs. The white petals of the flower had disappeared to the bottom of the mugs by now. My gaze shifted back to the noodles as I checked the pasta strainer to make sure the noodles were soft, feeling my heart thumping. Could inducing Mr. Edwin to sleep work? What if he found out? Footsteps from behind us foretold Mr. Edwin's entrance, each step thudding in my ears as his feet met the linoleum. He sank onto the wooden chair at the table, making it creak and wobble.

"It better not feel too hard or rubbery," he warned me as I used tongs to place pasta onto an empty plate and Scarlett spread the meat sauce onto it. I took several long breaths to quell my pounding heart, so loud it surprised me he couldn't hear. "If it is, you'll regret it."

Scarlett gripped the wooden spoon like a constrictor as she mixed the sauce around the pasta. Steam floated up from the meat sauce, and I exercised caution as I carried the hot plate over to the table, placing it before Mr. Edwin. He flashed both of us a smirk with his fresh polished white teeth.

"You're not a very smart girl, are you?" he said, looking at me as if he were sizing up prey. "You've forgotten the Parmesan cheese."

"I didn't know you wanted it," I replied.

"Well, you'd better listen next time," he said. "Unless you want your sisters to get hurt."

I bit my tongue to stop myself from retaliating. Scarlett remained quiet too. I turned and fumbled in the fridge for the Parmesan cheese, wanting to avoid any imminent backlash. At first, I thought I had lost my sight—my vision blurred in my haste.

"How hard is it to find one bag of cheese?" Mr. Edwin said, pounding his fist once on the wooden table like a judge's gavel.

My mind went blank and Scarlett had to come over to find it. It had rested right on one of the side shelves where I'd searched. I wondered how I'd missed it. I took the cheese from Scarlett and sprinkled a light layer onto the pasta.

"More," his gruff voice commanded, and I added the Parmesan cheese with even more precision. "Add it quicker next time."

Before he picked up his silverware, Mr. Edwin reached a rough hand out to lay it on my cheek and his thumb rubbed my chin. I repressed a shudder under his hand but didn't dare express my distraught. I didn't want to give him a reason to hit me.

"You're lucky that you're a pleasing sight," he said, "or I would have no reason to keep you around. You'd live on the street on your own in a day, if it weren't for me."

He lowered his hand and twisted in his seat to pick up his fork, the silver glinting at me like the blade of a knife as he dug into the spaghetti.

"Don't just watch me eat," Mr. Edwin growled while he chewed, exposing the unbearable contents of his mouth. "Turn away so I don't have to eat while looking at you both."

I backed up toward the counter, fear seizing me with the thought that he might rage over his meal. I released an aching plea, a prayer in my mind for it to stop, for the terror to end. Scarlett and I turned to the pan and large pot, consuming ourselves with tidying up. I noticed Scarlett's neck craned, her eyes peering over her shoulder as the man slurped up his spaghetti, his lips smacking together with wet noises. I cringed as I eased the heavy pot into the sink. I turned the water on and realized I'd made a mistake. The water in the pot sizzled. I jumped and turned the faucet off.

"I don't care if it burns," Mr. Edwin said. "Clean it."

I turned the water back on with shaky hands and grabbed the sponge. I squeezed dishwasher soap onto a sponge, squished it together, and then started to scrub the pot. I jerked my hand back as my skin brushed against the metal of the pot, grimacing in pain. When I finished, Scarlett had to wash the pan and she refused to let me do it for her. She hissed a few times in pain while she scrubbed the pan extra hard.

I glanced over my shoulder at Mr. Edwin and saw that he had finished his plate of pasta. He noticed my look and gave me a wide grin.

"When you're finished cleaning," he said, "I have a special treat to give you both."

He got up out of his chair and walked over to the counter where the three green mugs were perched, steam rising from them. He picked up two of the mugs and handed them to us and then placed the last dark-green one on the kitchen table. Scarlett put the clean pan down on the counter and we both turned to take them.

"Drink it up," he said, "it's just tea."

Scarlett and I exchanged glances and then looked down at our tea. I believe we both realized in our guts that Mr. Edwin had contaminated the tea. This random act of kindness couldn't come without repercussions. My night had come, I knew. Perhaps he'd had the same idea we had and drinking this would put us to sleep, perhaps, so I couldn't struggle. I couldn't decide which situation was worse—to live through it awake or asleep. I also didn't know why Scarlett received one too.

"No, thank you," Scarlett said and she stepped forward to place her mug onto the table. She eyed me as though begging me to put mine down. I followed suit and put my soft-green mug back down.

For once, our refusal of his orders didn't make Mr. Edwin mad. He grabbed the third green mug and went to sit back down at the kitchen table. His eyes were bright with amusement.

"You think I've put something in those mugs?" Mr. Edwin said and laughed. "Well, who do you think the third tea is for?" He picked up the third green mug and held it up for us to see. Then he poured the tea into his mouth and swallowed a large gulp. As he drank, his grin transformed into a grimace.

"S-something…" I heard Mr. Edwin begin and then break off in a gasp. "This doesn't taste—" He wheezed again. Scarlett and I gasped and glanced at each other in uncertainty. His hand clasped his neck as he struggled for breath.

Something had gone very wrong. "Scarlett," I cried, whirling to look at her with wide eyes. "What's going on?" I knew Mr. Edwin took his last breaths. At the same time, I couldn't comprehend it.

"I-I…" She swallowed. "I think he's been poisoned."

I watched in distraught as the mug of tea slipped from Mr. Edwin's stubby hand, falling with a clang against the tiled floor, shattered into chunks, and released the liquid contents onto the floor. I could see the bits of what looked like white petals. Except there were more bits of petals than I remembered putting in there.

"Are you sure you used valerian?" Scarlett asked me.

"Positive," I answered, calm despite the terror that consumed me on the inside.

Mr. Edwin's now-swollen hands closed tighter around his neck as he began to take sharp breaths as if he had emerged from a body of water.

"What should we do?" I asked. Scarlett fixed her gaze on Mr. Edwin.

"I don't know, I don't know, I don't know," she answered and crossed the room over to the phone. "Call an ambulance?"

"What if the police come?" I asked. "They'll think we did it. We'll go to jail."

"We can't just…just leave," Scarlett said. "We'll receive even more punishments."

"But if they come, they're going to place us in another foster home or, worse, juvenile detention," I said in distress. "Even if we go to another foster home, what if it's worse than here?"

"How could our situation become any worse?" Scarlett cried in exasperation and picked up the phone. She called an ambulance and gave the address, hanging up after without mentioning her name.

I wanted to scream. I squeezed my eyes shut, trying to imagine living at home with Mom, safe and secure. My ears were unable to escape his desperate gasps. I could only stand there, paralyzed and helpless. After another loud clunk and a slosh of liquid, an ominous silence covered the room. Even when silence arrived, I found no escape—as if I could hear his huffing breath materialize in my ear.

I opened my eyes and looked again.

The other two mugs were tipped over; hot tea pooled out onto the wooden surface of the table and streamed over the edge in steaming splatters. Mr. Edwin's large form slumped over in his chair. My hands shook; my stomach flipped, feeling queasy. I couldn't comprehend it. We had just watched a man die. Could I have done it?

"What do we do, Scarlett?" I asked, glancing at her strained expression with alarmed eyes. "He's dead now."

"Look," she said then and examined the contents of the third mug. "There are more pieces of petals in that mug. We didn't do it, Abigail. He put something in there. Why else would he give tea to us out of the blue?"

My eyes studied the small pile of petals, and I agreed with Scarlett.

"The petals could have come from a hemlock," I said, recalling the bed I saw in the garden during my night of terror, the recognizable purple stalks—a harbinger of death. Our mother warned us about going near the plant all the time, particularly when Faith, Scarlett, and I visited our secret hideout, a small clearing in the woods. She taught us to look at the stem before touching any white-flowered plant. "It looks similar to valerian. I didn't have any sort of negative reaction to touching the petals so they couldn't have been hemlock."

"Well, no matter," she said. "We need to leave. We need to go home. Mom can help us. I think…she'll explain our situation to the police."

My weary heart now wrung with guilt. What could we do? I could only stand here for the moment, my mind frozen. I watched the puddle of tea on the tabletop; some of the hot substance dripped over the edge of the table and each drop echoed in my ears when it met the linoleum.

Ding! Dong! Ding! Dong!

The strike of the grandfather clock reverberated from the living room, announcing the end of the hour and seemingly springing to life as its chime sent a jolt through my heart and mind like one of those dreams when you miss a step.

Dong!

The cue for our escape plan had come. I inched toward Mr. Edwin, a tentative hand reaching out for his smartphone that lay on the table, unlocked. I avoided looking straight at his pale face to suppress my guilt-ridden heart. I opened the maps icon, typed in our destination, and snapped several pictures of the town map. Scarlett began digging through his coat pockets until she found his ring of keys.

Dong!

Scarlett passed me the keys and I unlocked the pantry while Scarlett hurried to the front door. She gave one of Mr. Edwin's empty briefcases to me and I exchanged the keys for it. I stuffed the bag to the brim with as many nonperishable foods as possible as well as some bread and water bottles.

Dong! Dong!

Scarlett already had the basement door unlocked and yanked it open. I stumbled down the stairs in the pitch-black, hoping I wouldn't fall; my heartbeat hastened and I dripped with a profuse cold sweat like I had the stomach flu.

"Renée!" I called. "Renée!"

"Abigail? Is that you?" Renée asked.

"Yes, it's me. And Scarlett. Come on!" I cried. "We have to leave. *Now.*"

My vision had adjusted to the dark room and I could see Renée rising from the mattress. She still wore the same lacy black dress from two days before, and I watched her reach for the two jackets we had. As Renée's face came into focus, I could see a fresh bruise on her cheek. Another pang of guilt mingled with the next chime.

Dong!

"What happened?" I heard Renée ask, her voice choked in fear.

"There's no time to explain," I cried. "We have to go!"

I turned around and ran back up the stairs to Scarlett. I could hear Renée following behind with rapid footfalls.

CHAPTER 7

An Endless Road

In the dead of night, we trekked our way along a winding road. Scarlett guided Renée and me along with the map on Mr. Edwin's OPTI-Phone. We seemed to travel a forever road, making me doubt we would make it out alive, especially after the coyote attack. In my arms, I carried Mr. Edwin's briefcase with all of our nonperishable food and bread. Icy tendrils of air attempted to trickle inside the embrace of my jacket, making me shiver, and I hugged my torso to keep warm. Above me, a gleaming fresh waning moon shone against the dark yet clear star-sprinkled sky. A forest enclosed the road on both sides, increasing the penetrating darkness and the forest's dissonance; screeching crickets and the trickle of a nearby stream followed us along with the occasional hiss of leaves. I sent a half-hearted prayer for help to the sky.

A sharp hoot met my ears like an alarm clock, keeping my attention focused on the crisis at hand. I heard a sharp intake of breath from in front of me. Scarlett came to a sudden halt and I knocked into her, fumbling with the briefcase.

"What was that?" Scarlett gripped my arm as she stared into the forest.

"Cut it out, Scar," I huffed at her for what felt like the hundredth time. "Stop freaking me out, please. We're never going to get anywhere if you keep jumping every two seconds."

"Did you hear that sound though?" Scarlett said, seeming to have ignored my complaint. She preoccupied herself with peering into the woods alongside us. I followed my sister's gaze, studying the thick forest whose trees and bushes spilled out onto the sides of the road. The leaves of the bushes brushed against my nylon-covered legs and sent chills down my spine. Weeds grew along the forest's edge, choking the life from the various plants. At the sight, I tasted dread in the back of my throat as images from the day threatened to break into my mind.

A soft howl pierced through the night this time and Scarlett clutched at my jacket, dragging my reluctant mind back to the task at hand. In alarm, Renée whimpered and grabbed on too. Fear flooded my veins, twisting and turning with adrenaline, more fervent after my night spent outside. I remembered what I'd heard from God—that I would survive—and I grasped the idea as a crutch. I clung to that comfort as though it was a single pool of light guiding me through the winding roads on this night. Another cry came from the forest.

"I heard another howl," Scarlett said, her voice choked with fear. "Didn't you hear it?"

"Don't worry," I assured her and Renée. "The howl sounded more like a hoot, probably an owl or something. Let's try to focus—"

"I heard a howl. What if there's a coyote?" Scarlett looked at me with wide eyes like she would jump out of her skin if it ended up being true.

"A coyote?" Renée cried. "Please, no coyotes!"

"There's no coyote." I interjected, almost as a reflex before Scarlett and Renée could start panicking.

Scarlett nodded and both she and Renée let go of my jacket. Scarlett released the air she held, attempting to relax. "Yeah. There's no coyote," she murmured to herself.

"I hope there's no coyote," Renée said.

"Oh no, I've lost my place on the map now," Scarlett said as she studied it and tried to rediscover our position.

"You have to try remaining calm," I said, "or we'll never make it."

Just as I spoke, bright lights emerged from the dark road, speeding toward us.

"Hurry," I urged my sisters as I started off the side of the road. "We need to hide. In case she's after us."

Scarlett, Renée, and I scrambled inside the edge of the woods, hiding behind one of the thicker trees. Scarlett clung to a tree, looking back and forth from the car to the forest as if she couldn't decide which situation seemed worse. Renée found a bush and crouched behind it, shaking. I held onto the bark too and it gave me a sense of safety for the moment. When the car disappeared around the next bend, I could breathe a sigh of relief. "Let's keep going." I stepped out from behind the trees and Scarlett and Renée followed. I paused to brush off some leaves sticking to Renée's lacy black dress.

"Can I have some more bread?" Renée asked. "I'm so hungry."

"Yes, fine." I pulled the briefcase off my shoulder and unzipped it so I could rummage for the loaf of bread and one of the bottles of water. We still had several cans of soup and corn that I had managed to grab before we left. "No more after this though." I handed the bread to Renée. Before she could begin to take it, Scarlett snatched the bag of bread from Renée.

"Hey," I said, "let Renée have some."

"I get it first," Scarlett demanded and took out some bread. "You were fed a lot at the Edwins'."

Renée fumed. "Give it back!" She reached out for the bag.

"Give it to Renée," I told her.

"Fine, here," Scarlett said, tossing the bag to Renée who had to put her hands out to catch it.

"Don't throw the bag like that again," I yelled at Scarlett. "I don't know how long we're going to travel and we need to preserve as much food as we can."

"Jeez, relax," Scarlett said.

"You're telling me to relax after you nearly lost us a meal?" I said with my voice choked in irritation and panic at the same time.

"And I can't feel afraid of a coyote?" Scarlett retorted. "Maybe I'm the one who should take charge of how we should travel. After all, I am the oldest."

"If you want to take charge, then keep guiding us." I spat back. "I don't trust you with the responsibility of the food."

"Well, I'm tired of starving while Renée's stomach is perfectly satisfied," Scarlett countered. "How is that fair?"

"Please stop arguing," Renée urged. "We need to focus on where we're going."

Scarlett looked as if she wanted to hurl an insult at me. She swallowed and cast her eyes upon Mr. Edwin's phone.

"Well, it's going to take us around another twenty minutes," Scarlett said. She held the phone in front of my eyes which displayed the map. The tick indicating the train station was positioned a mile away.

Renée groaned. "I'm so tired."

"We can't stop," I said. "We have to make it aboard the train tonight. We can try to sneak aboard."

"Out of this awful town, finally," Scarlett said.

"Where are we going once we get there?" Renée asked.

"Home," I answered. "We're going home."

"Do you think we'll see Mom there?" Scarlett asked in a quieter voice.

"I don't know."

As we continued walking down the dark road, I reached into my pocket and pulled out a plastic ziplock bag containing a small clear capsule. The capsule contained a piece of thyme that looked like a star. It belonged to a thyme bush in my mother's flower garden at home. I remembered each type of flower and plant residing in my mother's garden: daisies, cornflowers, tulips, daffodils, valerian, and her favorite, thymes. Thymes were distinct in that they were evergreen. Yet the leaf in the capsule, deprived of its stem, no longer emanated a vibrant green but faded to a bland vulgar brown. Its texture, dried and delicate. I imagined now that garden became barren, the flowers wilted and limp. My dream of a full and thriving garden this summer had been disrupted.

"Do you think she's returned by now?" I glanced up from the capsule. "Mrs. Edwin?"

"I don't want to think about it," Renée replied. She shivered in her black lacy dress, and I paused to give her my jacket to keep her warm.

Scarlett rolled her eyes and grimaced. "That witch, you mean? Yeah. Why?"

"If she has, then she'll probably have found him by now," I said in a hushed voice. "Her husband…I'm sure she called the police."

"There's no proof we did it," Scarlett said.

"Right. Except they know we were there when Mr. Edwin died. We need Mom to explain it to the police. They'll believe her."

"What if OPTI saw you?" Renée asked. "He can find us wherever we go."

"Maybe OPTI will let us go home if he knows what we went through at the Edwins'…" I trailed off, hoping my siblings would agree. I remembered the OPTI screen in the backyard during my night of terror. It didn't help me escape at all.

"Why did he put poison in the tea?" I asked, after a moment of silence. The dread in my throat returned. "Did he try to kill us?"

"Probably," Scarlett said. "I don't know why though. What would he have gained?"

"I don't know," I said. "He already had our money for child support, what more could he have wanted?"

"If only he hadn't drunk the tea," Scarlett said, "then he wouldn't have died."

My eyes moistened with tears, and I played with the skirt of my dress. "If only I hadn't collected what I thought was valerian."

"What's valerian?" Renée asked. "Why did you give it to him?"

"They're a type of flower," I replied. "A strong sedative. Mom let us grow them in our garden in case one of us had trouble sleeping. I helped her grow them. That's why I remember."

"I remember them now," Scarlett said. "They would have helped us escape without detection and without Mr. Edwin having to die."

"We shouldn't have given them to him in the first place," I said. "I don't know why we did." I folded my arms, wishing I could escape the gloom of my guilt.

"We had to escape," Scarlett said. "You nearly died that night you spent in their backyard. The petals were our way out."

"I'm scared," Renée said.

"It had to stop somehow," Scarlett went on. "If only he hadn't tried to poison us, we could have left in peace…"

I lowered my head to face the ground again; my heart ached and it wouldn't go away. "Do you think we should have stayed?" I asked. "Is this a mistake? What will happen if Mrs. Edwin finds us?"

"I don't want to go back there," Scarlett said, her face grim once more. A hint of a bruise lingered on her neck. "I think I'd rather live out here in the dark alongside this forest than back in that basement."

We all shuddered.

"We won't," I answered despite my uncertainty. "We'll get to the train soon. We're close to the station. Then we will go home. I hope the police aren't looking for us." As brave as I wanted to be, my hands fidgeted with my capsule.

"Why do you still carry that plant sample around?" Scarlett asked. "It's dead."

"It's important to me," I replied. "They remind me of home. When Mom got sick long before her breakdown, she told me to make sure to take care of her garden."

"I miss her," Renée said.

My eyes softened as I put an arm around both my sisters' shoulders.

Just then, more lights—flashes of red and blue—came toward us.

"Get behind the trees," Scarlett urged us, her fearful expression transforming into one of determination.

We clung to the trees behind the roadside bushes. My eyes gaped as I fixated on the road.

A police car sped past us and slowed to come to a stop along the side of the road, a few feet past where we hid. Its lights blinded my vision, giving me spots and making me dazed.

"Stay down," I whispered.

Scarlett jumped and ducked behind a bush, trying to make herself as hidden as possible. She looked like she wanted to say something but she remained silent.

Through the window of the police car, I could make out the misshapen silhouette of a police officer. An eerie stillness filled the atmosphere of the dark forest as we waited, hoping we concealed ourselves enough that they wouldn't come looking for us. Then the door of the police car opened on the passenger side. I recognized Mrs. Edwin's dimmed skinny figure standing outside the car near the edge of the forest. The driver, an officer wearing a familiar white uniform, got out as well and walked around the car. The pair came closer and stopped to stand alongside the right side of the car and I held my breath, praying that they wouldn't see us.

Mrs. Edwin spoke in a low voice to the other larger muscular figure, and I could see the glint of silver form the name OPTI written over his heart. They were walking closer to the forest, speaking in murmurs. Then Mrs. Edwin turned her head toward the forest, searching its depths; and finally, the policeman shined a flashlight in the forest, and as hidden as we were, we could not escape detection with the light shining in our direction. Mrs. Edwin pointed at us with a long sharp fingernail. I shuddered; I could still remember the times it would scratch at my skin.

"There they are." Mrs. Edwin's voice sliced the air. "They're in the forest. And look that brat has my husband's briefcase and the other has his OPTI-Phone."

It took me some time for my initial shock to wear off. I turned to my frightened siblings. "*Run!* We have to run!" I nudged Scarlett and Renée forward so we could begin to run for our lives through the forest. Mrs. Edwin seized my wrist and dug her nails into my skin as she pulled me back.

"Stop, let go!" I cried as Mrs. Edwin's fingers dug even more into my skin. "Scarlett, Renée, run!"

Scarlett and Renée only shifted their feet, looking at me in disbelief. "Not without you," Scarlett said for my ears. "Mom told us to stick together, remember?"

"Neither of you are going anywhere," Mrs. Edwin said. "Especially not after what you three did to my husband." Mrs. Edwin choked on her words and burst into mournful sobs.

"I can't allow any child or teenager to run away," the officer said.

"We didn't do it," Scarlett cried. "Mr. Edwin did it. He drank the tea with the poison in it and that's how he died. He intended to poison us."

"How dare you accuse my husband of trying to poison you," Mrs. Edwin said, glaring at Scarlett. "You three poisoned him!"

She looked at the officer for the verdict.

"If you're not guilty," the officer said, "then why did you run from the scene?"

I ignored his question with my outburst. "Just let Scarlett and Renée go," I pleaded when I sensed our explanation would prove futile. "Officer, please let my sisters go. They didn't do anything. Only me."

Scarlett and Renée opened their mouths and I knew they were about to say they did it too. I couldn't let them do that.

"I swear I'm to blame," I shouted over their words. "I knew that flower was poisonous. Please don't arrest my sisters. They had nothing to do with it."

"But—" Scarlett and Renée said together. I gave them a firm look to silence them.

"We were also responsible," Scarlett said, much to my displeasure.

I looked from the officer to Mrs. Edwin. Mrs. Edwin had recovered from her sobs and her eyes flashed.

"They should all receive a punishment for what they did," Mrs. Edwin said, wiping her eyes with the backs of her hands. "They should all go straight to jail."

"Actually," the officer said and looked down at his OPTI-Phone and then grabbed at my other wrist. His straight face looked dutiful and certain. "I received notification from OPTI. He says Abigail put those poisonous petals in the tea. You are under arrest." He took the briefcase from my hands, handed it to Mrs. Edwin, and then withdrew a pair of handcuffs. I turned around with a defeated sigh, putting my hands behind my back. My face fell as I acknowledged my defeat and fear settled in my gut about going to jail.

I could hear sirens in the distance, and Mrs. Edwin looked triumphant. "More officers are on their way to collect you all and deal with you as they please. They know all about what you did." Then she leaned down to whisper in my ear, "And you can assure yourself you'll get everything you deserve. I'll make sure you never see your dear sisters again."

I stared at Mrs. Edwin in horror as the sirens blasted in my ears. The additional flashing red and blue lights made me feel dizzy as a couple of police cars pulled up on either side of the road. In spite of my dizziness, I turned to Scarlett and Renée.

"This is your last chance," I said to them. "You have to run!"

Scarlett and Renée remained where they were, not budging an inch.

The officer let go of me to reach out and grab both Scarlett's and Renée's wrists.

"Don't think about running again," Mrs. Edwin snarled at them. "You won't get far with the police on your tail."

"We weren't going to run," Scarlett said and then looked at me. Her gaze turned back to the officer. "OPTI is wrong. Our sister didn't poison the tea."

"I don't make the decision on who's guilty, OPTI does," the officer said. "He saw it and he knows."

Four police officers, all donning the same crisp white uniform, got out of their cars and a couple walked over to Mrs. Edwin and the male officer who found us. Mrs. Edwin waved at them as they approached.

"Over here," the male officer said. "We've found them."

"Abigail is the one that murdered my h-husband," Mrs. Edwin added. At that, Mrs. Edwin let out another wail, tears flowing from her eyes, and I knew that her tears were somewhat genuine. It made my gut tighten with guilt. I knew I didn't do it; however, for some reason, I felt like I had. Another officer came over to rub Mrs. Edwin's back. "I was so generous to take them into my home," she continued, "and this is how they've repaid me."

The officers listened to Mrs. Edwin's wails for a moment. Then I felt a hand on my arm and turned to see one of the officers, a female, had come up behind me without me noticing.

"Don't take her away from us," Renée said. "Please don't." Her pleas were met with the male officer's stern expression.

"You have the right to remain silent," the female officer recited as she began pulling me across the road and toward one of the vehicles.

"*No!* Abigail!" Scarlett shouted through her tears.

"Please, she's innocent!" Renée cried.

The male officer who had first found us pulled Scarlett and Renée toward his car. They were both placed inside while I watched in despair.

While on the brink of tears, the female officer shoved me into the back seat of her vehicle. The sharp bright glare of the lights, along with the wetness in my eyes, made my vision blur again. As I looked out the tinted window of the car, I could see Mrs. Edwin wearing an unmistakable malicious grin. The female officer got in the front seat, and her presence drew my eyes to the dashboard where a screen had been placed with the gleaming multicolored brain of OPTI. The sight of it gave me goosebumps. Here OPTI appeared again, always present, observing each moment like an outside spectator; yet now, OPTI became the judge of my future.

OPTI didn't scare me when I lived at home as a child. OPTI seemed not to notice me then. Now I had been accused of murder and I feared OPTI's wrath against me more than anything else. Now I would receive the punishment of a criminal.

CHAPTER 8

Convicted

The drive seemed to last forever. We stopped once at a gas station so I could use the bathroom while under strict supervision. I spent the drive with my thoughts on my sisters. What would happen to them? Were they going to live with Mrs. Edwin again? Or maybe, perhaps—in the best case—they would be taken home to live with Mom again? I prayed with all my might that they would make it home, even if I couldn't be there with them. It would make me feel better to know they were safe. I longed to join them. Here I faced a punishment for what OPTI claimed I did. I wondered though, if I had put those valerian petals in the tea, could the petals have been hemlock instead? We never should have used them for our plan. I suppose we should have stayed and waited to go home. But if we had, we never would have made it alive. The image of Mr. Edwin slumped over in his chair, his beady eyes open, empty and gleaming white, still haunted me. Why did I even collect the petals? Why couldn't we have waited for an opportunity to escape instead of creating one? I couldn't stand the tidal wave of guilt that engulfed me and made me feel as though I deserved this punishment. Maybe I did belong in prison. I sighed as I settled into my bleak unknown future. I could only wait for it to happen as though it were an unpleasant anticipated entrance into a haunted house. I resolved to stare out the window at the landscape of open fields. All I could gather was that we remained in the same country. At least this road didn't make me feel claustrophobic like the road my siblings and I had tried to escape on, but this road didn't lead home, leaving me torn.

I continued to gaze out the window, allowing my mind to shift back to thoughts about my siblings. It could be months, maybe even years, until I see them again; and I had no idea where the other officer took them. How would I find them? What if Mrs. Edwin did something terrible to them and I couldn't save them? I wish I could see their faces one more time and express how much I love them and always will. I knew I would spend every day of my new life sending prayers above that they were safe and I would one day see them again. Tears filled my eyes during the car ride and I let them fall. Crying made my hands ball into fists; it didn't change our situation. We were still separated.

After a lengthy, heated cry, my eyes drooped. Every time I closed my eyes, a flood of frightening memories involving Mr. Edwin sipping the poisoned tea terrorized my mind. The memories made me cry harder, and soon, my cries turned into aching sobs over everything that had happened.

Sleep overpowered my fears, and without noticing, I drifted off to a dreamless sleep. When my eyes opened, they gazed at the rising sun that transformed the sky into a fearsome orange. An expansive dull-gray concrete building lay before me, surrounded by barbed-wire fences.

The female police officer slid out of the car and then pulled me out. Many other police cars sat in the parking lot, looking shiny and sleek like sports cars. A large screen bearing OPTI's unforgettable form loomed over the front entrance. The officer raised her badge to the screen, and with a ping, the gate swung open. The officer pressed a hand against my back as she guided me inside. I reminisced on my last moments of living in the outside world, free from prison. I seemed to have lost the little freedom I had in the first place. Since Mom became ill, I had been carried from one place of confinement to another, and I wondered if I would ever be free of it.

As the officer led me to the front entrance of the building, I looked around and could see the barren grounds within the fence that surrounded the concrete prison. I hoped I could spend time outside. I liked to spend time outdoors but no garden, no flowers, and no relief existed in the dreary landscape.

The female officer raised her badge once more to the OPTI above the door of the building. With another ping, the double doors swung open and the officer ushered me into a lobby with officers sitting in a small room behind a glass window at desks. A full-body security scanner was built in beside the office. The female officer insisted I sit on a bench in the lobby while she gave the other officers my information.

After a moment, the officer with a large build exited the small room and spoke to me. "Stand against that wall." He pointed to a portion of the lobby's wall painted white with black lines. I hurried over before the officers could push me there. The same muscular officer handed me a sign with the date and my name. He had a camera in his other hand and took my mug shot. The light from the camera made me feel dizzy, and when I saw the photo of my pale face and tired eyes, I saw myself as a real criminal, my hands dirty with the crime of murder. I had to remind myself that I didn't do it. There may have been hemlock in the same mug as the valerian and Mr. Edwin poisoned himself while trying to poison Scarlett and me. For the second time in my life, I came close to death and Mr. Edwin ended up dying in front of me. I wanted to tear out those memories and our entire stay at the Edwins'. I wanted to go home where I could feel safe; I feared more misery awaited me here and I couldn't escape. I gazed out of the small windows at the top of the lobby walls; my breath quickened like I suffocated. I just wanted to be free.

After my mug shot, the muscular officer took my fingerprints.

"Step in the scanner," the female officer told me once my fingerprints were collected.

I followed her order, stepping inside and raising my hands while the machine scanned me. They discovered the capsule with the dead thyme and took it away, the last trace I had of home. The female officer then guided me to what looked like a room at a doctor's office. The officer directed me to sit on a big chair with wide armrests and lay out my arm for a blood test. A doctor entered the room to take my blood. After that the doctor recorded my height and weight. Then I was given a white jumpsuit with a black lapel with OPTI embroidered in silver to replace my lacy black dress. At last, the officer escorted me down several long hallways lined with doors leading to rooms I could only conjure in my imagination. I entered a small room with a small bed, a toilet, and a barred window. The door shut and the lock clicked. I had no idea when I would be out next or even if I would be fed. In any case, I expected I would feel bored here.

In the next moment, I realized the barred window was a screen that may or may not be an imitation of the day outside. I resolved to climb into the hard bed and close my eyes.

After what seemed like two seconds of sleeping on what felt like cardboard, a loud honk like a trumpet woke me. I noticed the window displaying the weather outside showcased a schedule from waking up until bedtime. Most activities were labeled simply as "class" while others had more specific names like "swim trials." Swim trials? In prison?

My door unlocked and creaked open. I watched several prisoners in matching white jumpsuits march past my cell. I took that as my cue to follow them. Most of the prisoners appeared about my age and their eyes were set as they strode. A few of them who noticed me shot me venomous glares that made me nervous. I did my best not to display any evidence of fear. I followed the stream of prisoners down another hall and along more halls until we reached a door with a window looking out onto a large swimming pool and across from it were two doors labeled "Male" and "Female." I entered the female door into a changing room with a bathroom in the back. There were lockers with names written on them. I found mine near the back of the change room where the showers were. Inside the locker I found a one-piece white swimsuit, a headcap, and goggles. I put them on, my mind occupied with questions.

I rushed to get dressed to keep up with the other prisoners. When I closed my locker, I found I didn't have a lock. This meant I had to risk my jumpsuit being stolen and I tried not to draw attention to myself and become a target. I left the changing room and walked with bare feet across the hall and into the poolroom. The room was vast and a dome arched high above our heads made out of glass so that it displayed a cloudy sky. The domed windows were the highlight of the room. As I expected, giant screens of OPTI hung over both walls at the ends of the pool. A police officer in a bulky white uniform stood near the backdoors. Other prisoners stood across the far side of the swimming pool, standing behind the diving boards, and each lane had its own line. The people in the front were the scariest-looking. Both the men and women had toned brawny bodies and most of their eyes were hard and cold. I noticed their swimsuits all had a star over their hearts. Seeing them made me more nervous for this swim trial. My past experience with swimming was joining a swim team at six years old for a couple years. Other than that, I had little experience with exercise. My favorite activities at home involved reading books about science, conducting observational experiments of nature, gardening, and performing in the school plays. I couldn't do any of those activities here.

I swallowed my fear and found a place at the back of the line at the front of the pool. I noticed that even the prisoners in the back of the line were in decent shape and I knew this would not turn out well for me.

An instructor stood to the far left of us and said, "As many of you know, OPTI expects for me to teach you the art of swimming. I will do as OPTI has commanded and nothing less. I expect hard work from all of you. If you do not work hard and you do not participate, you will suffer hefty consequences."

"It's all true," a prisoner whispered to me, her face etched with worry. "Terrible things happen here to those who refuse to obey OPTI." She spoke with a tremble in her voice that reinforced the threat in my mind.

"Those in the star group can step onto the diving boards," the instructor announced.

I watched as the prisoners in the star group marched forward to climb onto the diving boards in a track start, each with one foot forward.

"Ready?" the instructor shouted. "On your marks. Get set. Go!"

Each member of the star group lurched forward in smooth succinct dives, propelling through the water with seamless grace. I watched with bated breath to find out who would place first. One of the members of the star group in the far-right lane broke to the surface and another in the center trailed behind him or her. I couldn't tell who was who with the matching white caps. The star group battled head-to-head, and at first, it seemed like they would tie. Then out of nowhere, one of the star members surged forward, seizing the lead and creating distance between him and the other swimmers. It didn't take long before that prisoner made it to the other side and turned to go the opposite direction. They were all spaced out now after the kick turns. I grew more anxious as I watched them and wondered if I would have to do the same. I'd never gotten to that level of swimming. How could I know how to do it here?

After another lap, the person in the lead touched the wall first. He got out of the pool and now I could identify his tight facial features. He stood tall with a strong build that surpassed the others, making them look lean. He took off his swim cap to reveal a head of dark-blond hair, messy and long like a surfer. His nose was wide, his cheekbones high, and a smile of triumph brandished across his face.

"And the winner is Luke!" cried the instructor, and Luke touched the star that branded his swimsuit. At his touch, the star glowed and flickered like flames of a fire.

"Now it's time for our beginners to go," the instructor said as the star group got out and dried off with towels. I inched forward. No one else stepped forward with me, and the instructor surveyed the group of prisoners. His eyes fell on me. "It looks like it's only one of you then. You—what's your name?"

His gray hair was slicked back on his head, and he gazed at me with fierce eyes.

"I-I'm Abigail," I replied.

"It's your turn to prove whether you're strong enough to survive here. You were brought here because you're a criminal. Now you need to make up for it if you ever want OPTI to forgive you. If you can't, well, you'll be removed by OPTI. Just as OPTI made you, he can kill you. Are you up to the task?"

"Yes," I replied, my voice quivering. Kill? Did he mean I would be killed if I couldn't pass this swim trial? Dread plagued me, making me nauseous.

"Do I have to instruct you on everything?" he said, his voice rising. "Get on the diving board."

I hurried to get on the diving board, trying to ignore the pressing stares of the other prisoners. I did my best to imitate the stance the star group had assumed. My belly filled with butterflies with the idea of having to dive in and swim those same lengths.

"Ready. Set. Go!" the instructor announced.

I moved a few moments after "go" and dove into the water, doing a belly flop instead. When I regained control, my arms floundered around me, my legs kicking, my whole body trying to propel me forward. I had a miserable form; changing it would be impossible without any training. I put all the force I had in my body into swimming; I swam for my life, the adrenaline shooting through my veins. When I wore out, I willed myself with all my brainpower to keep going, to struggle through each exhausting stroke, to try and catch my breath despite my panic. The entire situation made it seem like I experienced a nightmare where someone chased me—and I was losing.

I almost reached the other end of the pool, preparing to do a kick turn. I spun around and water filled my nostrils, making me cough and come up for air. I endured the sting in my nose while I swallowed as much air as I could. I carried on swimming for the final lap and slugged back to the starting wall, void of breath and energy. When I recovered, I scanned my surroundings. I should have expected it beforehand, though I had focused, with all my strength, on the goal of completing the race to the best of my ability that I didn't pay attention to the roaring laughter filling the poolroom from the gaping mouths of the other students. A few of them from the star group were doubled over as they guffawed at my performance. The instructor glared at me in fury but even that didn't scare me as much as OPTI's menacing pulsing shape now visible on a screen against the wall.

CHAPTER 9

Goner

"She's a goner," a boy from the star group cried. "OPTI definitely won't be pleased."

"The worst performance I've ever seen," a girl squealed with a snicker.

"Oh, come on," another said in between chuckles. "It's only her first time. She'll improve eventually."

"Eventually?" Another boy from the star group chortled. "There's only so much time. I can't believe OPTI put her in this particular prison in the first place. She's going to need plenty of training all day for months to get to where we are."

"Enough," said the instructor. "All of you, go back to your bedrooms and get refreshed for breakfast. You stay put, girl. We'll need to report the results to OPTI and then we'll see what you're going to do."

I climbed out of the pool as the students began to file out of the room to the change rooms. I remained standing, dripping wet and cold on the pool deck as I waited for more instructions. A police officer wearing the typical white uniform and a helmet that concealed his face approached.

"Come with me," said the officer and he handed me a spare towel.

"You should treasure this moment while you can," the instructor said as I followed the officer. "OPTI may decide to dispose of you and you certainly won't like what happens next."

I shivered and didn't want to imagine what could happen to me. I followed the officer out the backdoors and down a long dim corridor.

"Don't worry about what the coach said," the officer spoke in a low tone. "You didn't do as poorly as they said. You'll survive."

"Thank you," I said, still trying to stay oriented to my surroundings while feeling so terrified that I felt faint. His words assured me. I had no idea who was underneath the helmet; however, they emitted a perplexing soothing energy that I'd never experienced from anyone before.

We turned at the nearest door on the left and I faced a room full of television screens. When I arrived, they turned on and showcased OPTI's radiant multicolored brain. I prayed I would survive whatever came next.

"Looks like Abigail here didn't pass her swim trials," OPTI declared as its brain pulsed up and down.

"I hope you won't give any punishments," the officer said. "After all, it is only her first day."

"Poor behavior won't go unnoticed from me, fool," OPTI spoke. "I know the punishment needed for her to excel."

At that moment, a green light appeared, coming from a machine in the shape of a black box with a hole cut into it in front of the main OPTI screen. I realized the contraption was a 3D printer. It printed out what appeared to be a silver metal bracelet with OPTI engraved on it.

"Put it on, Abigail. Put it around your wrist," OPTI spoke in a firm voice that made me hurry forward, tripping over myself to reach the printer. I picked it up and fumbled with the bracelet as I struggled to put it on. "Now, Abigail, let me show you what happens if you perform as poorly as you did today."

The glowing brain pulsed even harder, and then at once, an electric surge rippled through my body. I yelped in pain from the sting.

"I'm sorry," I cried as the pain became more intense. "Please don't hurt me. I'll do better next time, I swear."

"I believe you," OPTI replied. "But you must be punished in this way until you truly learn. You're a murderer and murderers deserve to be punished." The bracelet jolted me again, bringing me to my knees as my teeth gritted in pain. "Both of you may go. Know that if you dare take it off, you'll be met with an even worse fate than those shocks."

I didn't doubt that there would be more severe consequences. OPTI shocked me again and I cried out as the pain increased. "Please stop," I begged. "I'll do better next time."

"You'd better," OPTI responded. "Take her to the change rooms, Byte. Then, Abigail, join the rest of the prisoners in the cafeteria."

Byte, the officer, nodded and then grabbed my arm to lead me toward the door. It took a bit for me to keep up with Byte, and in the meantime, the bracelet sent a shock through me again.

"Speed up!" OPTI boomed after me, making even Byte tremble as he gripped my arm.

I stumbled as Byte pulled me forward, and then, another shock reverberated through me, making me trip again.

"Come on," Byte said. "OPTI will track everything you do now. You can only do your best to listen. You don't want to know his worse punishments."

Byte escorted me back down the corridor and down the stairs, through the poolroom, and then we parted at the change rooms. I went to open my locker and, of course, my white jumpsuit disappeared. Panic consumed me and my eyes welled with tears when several more shocks surged through my body, making me double over in pain, the tears falling faster. I resolved to leave with my swimsuit still on and occasional shocks stung me, making me grimace with each step. My time at this prison had turned into a nightmare in such a short time. As predicted, when I finally found the cafeteria obnoxious laughter and jeers bellowed throughout the large room, seeming to bounce off the concrete walls. After the cafeteria workers presented me with moldy bread and a sliver of butter, I searched for a table. The tables were all crowded, and when I went to sit at the nearest one, a girl with bright-orange hair threw a menacing glare in my direction. At last, I found a spot at a table but the group shuffled over so I sat on the end by myself, in my wet swimsuit. I ate my meal, wishing I was invisible and trying to avoid eating any mold.

I sighed and started to feel very homesick. I would give anything to be free of this prison and to be home with my mom, Scarlett, and Renée. I had nothing to remind me of either of them. At home, I had been comfortable. Even with my father gone and Faith passed, things weren't too bad at home. I wondered if Mother still stayed in the hospital. I gazed out the windows at the muddy weedy grounds, trying to substitute the bleakness with an image of a flower garden in full bloom. Perhaps if I kept conjuring better images in my mind, I could survive the dull atmosphere.

Tears welled in my eyes. Another jolt passed through me.

"No crying." The coarse voice of OPTI came booming at me through the glowing brain on the two-sided television screen that hung over our heads, encouraging more laughter and jeers in my direction.

I willed myself to stop. OPTI's warning only provoked my despair and a tear escaped anyways. It trailed down my cheek before it plopped on my lap. I wanted to give up. I felt like I may never be out of this enduring life of punishment and failure. I couldn't decide which place's conditions were worse, the Edwins' or this prison. I couldn't cope in either place and every breath ached. I grew tired of just trying to survive. Hope only gave me more despair. I prayed a scream for help and cringed from the memories that rushed in of me putting those petals in Mr. Edwin's tea. Even so, I wondered if I should let OPTI have his way with me. I wasn't cut out for the amount of work involved here. Perhaps death would be a release from all this pain. But as my tears turned into sobs and the bracelet shocked me several more times, I dug into what remained of my strength. God told me I would survive and I hoped it carried over to my time in prison. I couldn't give up. I remembered what my father had once told me about the curious nature of plants. I knew I needed to become like a plant shrouded in darkness and emerge to survive.

CHAPTER 10

Spiraling

After breakfast, I left still hungry. I returned to my cell and sighed in relief to find a white jumpsuit had been placed on top of my bed. I hurried to change into it. When I finished, I looked around the hall from my room's doorway to figure out where we would be sent to next. Then I heard a beep from my window and realized the screen had a schedule on it again. I saw the word *chemistry*, followed by *history*, and then *lunch*. It surprised me that this prison gave us the opportunity for education since I had no idea when I would be out to even use it. I tried not to waste time and went on a search for the correct classroom.

When I arrived, late and stressed, I sat in the back row, hoping to blend in with the other students. We were in the middle of a unit on chemical bonding incorporated with ionic bonds and covalent bonds. The class had no real teacher; the police officer who OPTI called Byte stood at the door. He didn't speak a word to us. Instead of a teacher, there was a screen displaying a slideshow while a robotic voice gave us a lecture. Prisoners in the star group were given note-pads on tablets for note-taking. Those not in the star group received used notebooks and pencils. I received a chewed-up greasy pencil with one sheet of blank paper to take notes on. I didn't need to take many notes on this though. I already knew much about chemistry and biology. They were my favorite subjects in school, and I became an avid reader on subjects of anatomy, biochemical mechanisms, and botany. The atmosphere seemed to transform into a world of interacting tangible and intangible elements, working together for life to function.

When my father left, he didn't take any of the books on the shelves in his study. So one day, when I had nothing to watch on the television and without my mother's supervision, I entered the polished oak door to examine the neat bookshelves and pulled out one on organisms and the elements. The material absorbed my attention and I ended up reading an entire collection on living things. Weeks later, I had memorized the properties of several elements as well as the process of ATP production in the body during exercise. I also memorized the properties of most of the plants grown in my mother's garden. Despite OPTI's attempt to hinder my progress, I endured the class without having to take as many notes. It lifted my spirits, and for the first time at this prison, I felt confident.

In the middle of the lecture, OPTI's image replaced the slideshow.

"We have a new prisoner," OPTI said, each word slicing the air with the precision of a knife. "Why don't you introduce yourself? Your name, why you're here, and your birthday."

I stood. "Hello," I said with a quivering voice, addressing a classroom of people who turned around to stare at me like they thought I was bizarre. "I'm Abigail. My birthday is on June 1, making me fifteen years old."

"And why are you here?" OPTI demanded.

I swallowed. "I murdered a man."

The class erupted in gasps and whispers. My initial success in the class became replaced with utter failure and I wished I could hide away from it.

"Now, Abigail, can you tell me and the class what an ionic bond is?" OPTI said.

At first, I hesitated, uncertain of OPTI's intentions. Trying to remain calm, I answered, "An ionic bond is a type of chemical bond that occurs between atoms when they have opposing charges. It's possible for it to form between an anion and cation as one is positively charged while the other is a negative charge. They don't take on a solid shape and usually occur between a nonmetallic and metallic atom."

"Very good, Abigail," OPTI said with a hint of sarcasm. "This has been your best performance all day."

The prisoners roared with laughter, slamming the desks and falling back in their chairs. I couldn't help the fury that boiled in me. I was determined to try harder at everything. My efforts felt foolish.

"Say thank you, Abigail," OPTI said.

"Thank you," I said, thinking about the shocks, though I couldn't figure out why I thanked OPTI.

"One more question—is glass a liquid or a solid?"

"It's a paradox," I answered, remembering the book I'd read about the states of matter. "Glass is in a state between a liquid and a solid called an amorphous solid."

I waited a moment before anyone spoke.

"Sit down, Abigail," OPTI said.

I did as OPTI said as the other prisoners whispered about me. Class ended and I followed the other students to a classroom for history. We studied a book called *OPTI's Glory* about OPTI's many accomplishments. Since I just arrived here, I hadn't read the text, of course, and received a zero when OPTI quizzed us on it. OPTI announced my score to the class in the midst of a brutal shock and I received more bouts of snickers and jeers from the rest of the prisoners. I breathed a sigh of relief when a bell rang to announce the end of class.

My stomach already grumbled for lunch even before the bell rang. When I arrived at the cafeteria, the expired tomato sandwich made me lose my appetite. I forced myself to eat it anyways, sitting at the same table as I had at breakfast. I remained alone. No one spoke to me. Then without warning, I felt something slap me in the back of my head. I twisted to find two slices of bread and a single tomato strewn on the floor as a group of boys from the star group threw their heads back in roars of laughter. I sat there, staring in glum silence while I tried to hold down my nauseating sandwich, wishing I had some company to make me feel better.

As I prepared to leave to get some time to rest before whatever frustrating class came next, one of the boys from the star group's table stood up and held a plate of rotisserie chicken in his hand. He was the strongest one, the one who had won during the swim trials—I remembered his name, Luke. He started walking past all of the tables and I thought he was about to leave out of the doors, but he surprised me by passing the exit and coming over to my table.

"What do you want?" I asked and jumped as if I expected another shock to run through me.

"Here," Luke said, placing the plate of fresh untouched chicken before me. "You can have my lunch."

I stared at him. He didn't seem surprised for he grinned back at me. His eyes were ice blue and glinted in the false light that came in through the window. "Why?" I asked.

"No reason," he said. "You seemed hungry…more hungry…I couldn't stand to watch as you ate that gruesome tomato sandwich."

"I didn't ask for you to do this," I said, pushing it away from me. "You can have it back."

This made him chuckle. "I wanted to do something generous," he said. The rest of the star group watched and laughed along with him.

"Well, don't be," I said. "I don't need your sympathies."

"Oh, you may say that now. Wait until a few days and you'll be begging for my help," he said. "The only way you stay here is by keeping up with the rest. It's more of a survival-of-the-fittest kind of prison as I'm sure you already know. Better to focus more on evolution than chemistry here or you're wasting your time."

"I've figured that out," I replied.

"I'm glad," he said, "and good luck."

After that, he left, leaving the plate of chicken behind. It smelled delicious and I devoured every last piece, right down to the bone. I tried to avoid making eye contact with Luke so as not to give him the satisfaction.

The afternoon comprised of a couple more classes in geometry and computer science. I found out OPTI had us separated between boys and girls in both subjects. I felt confused in geometry with only a power point and I didn't have much experience with computer science. I struggled to keep up, trying to ignore the shocks when I answered the practice problems. When I looked around the room, most of the girls, even those in the star group, were gazing in confusion at the power point because it taught advanced material and moved too fast for us to take any notes.

When dinner arrived, I had to stuff my queasy stomach with an overcooked meat loaf and watery gravy. I imagined I would get food poisoning at some point. I noticed that the star group ate fresh bowls of soup and Luke took a huge bite into a cheeseburger. He caught my eye and winked. I averted my gaze, wishing he hadn't noticed.

"It's a movie night." I overheard a girl with brown hair in a ponytail say to her friend at the table beside mine.

"That's my favorite type of night," she replied, "thanks to OPTI." Her green eyes glistened, dazed, as if she lived in a far-off world, and she giggled as if someone had tickled her. "OPTI is beginning to like me." I noticed she wore a bracelet similar to mine. I wondered if at some point, that would be me, and the thought made it even harder to keep my dinner down.

"What kind of movie is it?" My voice came out when no one else spoke. The girl with brown hair threw her nose up at my question as if she was trying to decide whether she would give me the silent treatment or sneer at me.

She chose to sneer.

"It's usually a horror-movie theme. OPTI rewards us for our hard work by letting us relax with a movie. Though in your case, you may not enjoy it. It might be too scary for you."

"I won't be scared," I said in defiance, though I couldn't feel certain.

"You need to improve and obey OPTI," she said. "Otherwise you're a goner."

Her friend and the other girls at the table laughed.

I narrowed my eyes, ready to protest, but I had something on my mind. "Do you know what happens to those who don't win OPTI's favor?" I asked; as I said it, I began to fret over what would come then.

"No," said the girl with the faraway expression. "We're not to know the specific details of OPTI's plan for when people fail."

"It's bad though," the brown-haired girl said. "We've lost a few who came in like you, and then one day, they disappear."

"The last one couldn't get his form right in the kickboxing class, remember, Karen?" her friend said. "He reached exhaustion halfway through the class and had a breakdown from the amount of shocks it gave him. I saw him in his bedroom crying, and within the next few hours he vanished."

"OPTI knows what he's doing though," Karen said. "Crying is weak."

Before any of us could say any more, a bell rang.

"Movie time," cried the dazed girl. "If you're good, you'll be provided with popcorn and soda."

On the police officer's instructions, we filed one by one out of the cafeteria in order of our placement in OPTI's eyes. That meant that I waited at the back of the line and Luke stood in the front. I waited, growing anxious as I neared the auditorium. The line came to a halt at a pair of double doors. Luke opened it and then propped it open for us all to file into the expansive auditorium. It had several rows of plastic chairs. In the middle were seats with cushions for the star group. I found an empty plastic chair near the front since I entered last which meant I had to crane my neck back to see the screen. A large screen stretched down in front of the stage and a projector hung overhead. On the screen appeared OPTI's usual form and everyone applauded. I gave some half-hearted hand-touching and then gasped from the sting of the shocks. The movie began and the red glow on the screen confirmed it as a horror movie as Karen mentioned. I watched as a werewolf came onscreen and ventured into a village to feast on its inhabitants. I couldn't figure out why OPTI required us to watch horror movies.

I cringed as the werewolf munched on the villagers, sinking its teeth into their flesh and tearing their limbs apart. I tried to cover my eyes at the most gruesome scenes. Each time I did, the bracelet shocked me back into focus on the scene before me. No one else appeared to be frightened in the same way as me. Most of the star group cheered when the werewolf overpowered one of the villagers and bit him to turn him into a werewolf through an excruciating transition. When it ended at last, with the pack of werewolves eating the remaining villagers, I breathed an enormous sigh of relief. We filed out of the auditorium and back to our cells. As soon as I arrived, exhaustion hit me from the long day of swim trials, classes, and that horror movie. I couldn't believe this was just my first day.

I entered my cell and found myself beginning to enjoy the peace and quiet that my bedroom provided. The fake window exhibited a starry sky that OPTI's appearance interrupted.

"Your peace and quiet is a service of mine as well," OPTI's digital voice whispered. "It must be earned."

I grimaced as the screen displayed a horrifying image of the werewolf from the movie. I jumped from the shock that rippled through me, seemingly for no reason. My sense of peace had limitations here and I dreaded having to endure more of this prison tomorrow. I laid down on the hard mattress of the bed, pulling the worn and dirty blanket over me to escape the stale cold of the room. I waited for OPTI's glowing brain to disappear before I dozed off.

CHAPTER 11

Fight or Flight

I woke up the next day to a shock that moved through my body and jolted me awake. I checked the clock on the screen that doubled as my window. I ran late—for kickboxing? Why on earth were we doing kickboxing in prison? I barely had time to think about it because the shocks were more intense now than ever.

"I'm sorry, I'm sorry," I cried, hoping OPTI would hear me. I started getting dressed in my jumpsuit and the shocks subsided.

"You're late. Hurry!" Boomed OPTI's voice, loud and clear, through the screen at my window. I could be certain other prisoners heard it.

I nodded and hurried to the locker room, putting on a pair of shorts and a plain white T-shirt. A mangy-looking sports bra was provided. It fit too loose which would make my efforts today more difficult. There were decent gloves at least. I prepared myself to try and do better today than I had during swim trials. My stomach grumbled. I knew I would have to wait to be fed until after this brutal workout so I did my best to ignore it. Amid shocks, I hastened out of the almost-bare locker room and found the door to the gym. On the court of the gym, a black mat spread out beneath the boxing bags. When I arrived, the instructor surveyed the room with their OPTI-Phone. An OPTI screen hung on one of the walls of the gym. OPTI watched us all, radiating a blur of colors. A policeman stood near the doors as added supervision, most likely Byte.

"You're late," the female instructor said to me. "I expect more effort from you for the daily assessment."

I groaned, received a shock, and then hurried over to settle on the bleachers. I sat down next to the two girls I'd spoken to in the cafeteria. As soon as I sat down, they stood and moved away from me.

"Everyone grab some gloves and a punching bag."

I did as she commanded, looking forward to redeeming myself with this exercise. We started with right hooks and left hooks. Then we moved on to roundhousing and incorporated it with some planks and crunches. Once again, I had trouble keeping up with the rest of the prisoners. The star group did their moves in perfect synchronization and their bags didn't slide—they jumped across the floor.

I fought for my life. My punches were floppy and I couldn't get the right form. My bag shifted an inch. Plenty of shocks hit my body throughout the lesson. I pressed on, throwing some left jabs, right hooks, roundhouses, kicks, and then doing them all in the same pattern. Sweat dripped down my face as the lesson progressed. It intensified the longer we practiced until sweat came in torrents as if I sat in a sauna. My arms and legs were on fire and began to tremble. I carried on in spite of the shocks I received every time I hesitated or used the wrong arm or leg. I punched and kicked as hard as my body allowed until I panted and had to stop to place my hands on my legs in exhaustion and terror. Another shock ran through me and I kept going.

Finally the bell went off again, announcing the end of today's lesson and the beginning of breakfast. By that point, I felt faint from hunger. I would have eaten my own glove if it was edible. We filed out of the room in a hungry, sweaty throng down the corridors and into the cafeteria for breakfast. The prisoners separated from me as usual so I sat alone, once again, at the end of one of the tables. This time, I had a bowl of bland and watery oatmeal for breakfast. The bland taste made me gag. I yearned for something more filling and tasty. I began to wonder what all of these activities were for and had an impulse to ask those girls again. They refused to make eye contact with me.

After a long day of the same classes, I spent my evening poring over the mountain of homework I had been assigned in each of them. It almost took me all night to get it done, and most of the assignments required me to read the textbook as though I hadn't been in class at all. I got a few hours of sleep.

The next morning came sooner than I wanted it to and we had swim trials again. I staggered out of my cell, fighting my drooping eyes and nearly walking into the door to the locker rooms. When I arrived at the poolroom, the prisoners were lined up as usual. This time, the assessment had greater severity. The instructor demanded us to swim four laps of breaststroke in perfect form and at a good time for our level. Just taking in the pool's length exhausted me.

The instructor called the star group forward. I watched Luke as he dove into the water, gliding with ease in a torpedo position before breaking the surface and emerging in front. He swam head-to-head with a few other star group members. The one on his left kicked as hard as he could and even passed Luke once. Luke overtook him in the end. He grasped the wall and surfaced with a wide grin on his face while the other boy scowled. I wondered what Luke did that put him in such good shape. What did he do to survive and gain OPTI's favor? Had he always been in that sculpted shape?

After the star group swam for their test, the rest of the students had their turn until, at last, I was left to compete against the less-skilled prisoners. I lined up and copied the other prisoners' stances on the diving board. I took a deep sharp breath. The instructor announced for us to go and I dove headfirst into the water. I didn't do a belly flop this time and it gave me a boost against the other prisoners. The cool water seemed to turn my brain on but my need for sleep made my movements sluggish. My arms and legs were heavier. I willed my arms and legs to pump faster and I ended up gaining some distance. When I reached the end of the pool, I completed the kick turn better this time and remembered to exhale through my nose as I did, despite being a tad sloppy. I hoped I would do well enough to pass today. I arrived at the second lap now and held my ground in front of one prisoner. Yet my happiness over my improved performance got the best of me, especially when I reached the middle of the third lap and my arms and legs burned with exhaustion; my energy had drained, and before long, the prisoner behind me passed me and it took immense effort to take on the fourth lap. I pushed my arms and legs even harder as I tried to regain my momentum. My body pressed forward, though my effort proved futile. The prisoner I had originally swam in front of finished when I'd traveled halfway across the pool. I heard a chorus of boos as I made it to the finish and grabbed onto the wall, gasping for breath. I looked up at the instructor who reflected my dismayed countenance. I knew I would face trouble again. At that moment, more shocks reverberated throughout my body, making me grit my teeth in pain.

"Out you go," the instructor commanded us and I obeyed reluctantly. I didn't want to think about what punishment came next. I feared I would disappear like the other prisoners Karen and her friend mentioned. "You're all done for today—all except for Abigail and Luke. Both of you need to follow Byte."

I prayed with all my might that I would come out alive. I wondered why Luke came too, and this thought distracted me for the moment as I dried myself off with a small towel that had already been used and was the only one I could use.

"Take them, Byte," the instructor demanded when Byte hesitated. "If you don't, I will."

"Follow me," Byte said through his helmet. "Both of you."

I followed Byte out of the poolroom. Luke walked by my side on the way there, though I knew his strides were much longer than mine. I knew we were heading back to that room with all the OPTI screens. I tensed up as if more shocks vibrated through me, however, none came. I found I dreaded the silence from OPTI more than the past shocks. We reached the end of the last corridor that led to the room with all of the television screens broadcasting OPTI's image at all angles and turns.

"First, Luke, you step forward," OPTI commanded as soon as we entered, and Luke did so with a bow. "I want to congratulate you on your performance today and so far."

"The honor is truly yours," Luke replied. "You have provided me with the equipment and strength needed to succeed."

I rolled my eyes at his gushing speech. Another shock silenced me. Luke noticed and glanced at me with a curt look that said my behavior wouldn't serve me.

"Thank you, Luke," OPTI replied. "You stand as a standard for what the other prisoners should be, especially Abigail whose performance has been laughable. You may step back now and know that there will be a ceremony from which to honor you with a badge for all your hard work. Only those in the star group will be allowed to go and you all will be served a buffet."

Luke bowed and then stepped back.

"Abigail, step forward," OPTI said, his voice becoming aggressive. On some of the screens appeared scenes of the various classes I had been in. I watched myself struggling to perform well in all of them except for chemistry, though OPTI didn't acknowledge it. My heart thumped in anticipation of the looming punishment.

"You have performed poorly too many times," OPTI went on. "It may be time for your time spent here to come to an end."

"No, please," I begged. "I can do better. I swear." Though I doubted I could.

"Don't kill her." Byte backed me up. "She's right. With time, she can improve."

"Enough. Your words mean nothing to me, Byte. Step into the next room, Abigail."

A light turned on and I realized a shower with glass walls surrounding it was built into the wall.

I had no idea what would happen if I stepped inside. I predicted it might lead to my death or some form of torture.

"Step into the room, Abigail," OPTI said.

My head spun and I grew faint, my ears ringing and my vision blurring.

"Abigail...Abigail...Abigail." I felt someone carry me—Luke. He placed me in the shower room.

When I returned to consciousness, I looked up to see a showerhead above me, water gushing down on me in torrents. Water surrounded me as if I was on a coastal shelf. I rose to my feet and found what seemed like a million OPTI's staring at me from the various screens.

"Goodbye, Abigail."

"No." I gasped. I looked at Luke who stood, looking at me as if he regretted putting me in here. Byte carried out a heated argument with OPTI and Luke. The water continued to pour. I could only hear OPTI over the rushing water.

"That's enough," I cried. "Please don't fill it up any more. I'll be better."

"It hasn't looked like it," OPTI replied. "You fail to keep up and your performance has been embarrassing. If you want to live and be free from punishment, I expect the best here, and if you can't do the best, then you die. After all, you're a mere human. If you want the right to live, fight for it."

"No, no, no, no." I gasped again and the water rose to my torso. I pounded the glass with as much force as I could muster but it wouldn't break and my knuckles hurt. It seemed ever since that night with the coyotes, I kept approaching death again and again. I tried to hold on to those words. *Don't worry, I'll save you, my child. You'll survive.* I clasped my hands in prayer, my sole hope in all this madness.

"Please, God. Please help me."

"What did you say?" OPTI roared and I knew I had done myself in further. "God can't help you, Abigail. I'm the voice of God."

"Please," I begged to God and held my hands together so tight that my nails were digging into my skin. My mind screamed a prayer that I would live once again. "Please help me. I'll do anything."

The water kept flowing, without ceasing, in buckets, reaching my chest. It leveled with my neck and I cried out again in panic, "I'll do anything! *Please!*"

The water pooled over my mouth then my nose. I struggled to keep my head above the water, and in moments, darkness took over.

CHAPTER 12

Revival

I awoke in a place I'd never seen before. The sky above me mirrored the rich blue of the sea. The ground was layered with sand like a desert. Peace blanketed and revived my soul. Above me stood a man with his arms outstretched, wearing robes as blue as the sky above. Water poured down on me from his hands. I knew without seeing his face that the man was Jesus, and he gazed down at me with a beautiful smile. My breath caught, and my heart filled with an indescribable happiness. I started to cry, a blur of joy and sorrow, and my eyes opened again to a dull room surrounded with screens, all deadly black.

I lay on the floor of the shower, coughing up water from my lungs, my head lifting up as I did. When I recovered, I looked around in shock that I was alive.

"Get up." OPTI's voice met my ears as the screens flickered on. "Now."

A shock tore through me before I could even blink. Suddenly a hand reached out and I could see that Luke remained here. Byte stared at me in concern, his helmet off, his brown eyes complementing his dark skin. Luke grabbed my hand and started to pull me up. I let him help me to my feet in the midst of the shocks. They subsided as soon as I stood. Water dripped from my body and I shivered from the cold. Luke offered me his towel that he had brought from swim trials and I wrapped myself in it to dry off.

"What's going on?" I asked, my eyes flitting around the room again. "I'm not dead?"

"No," OPTI's booming voice replied. "You've been spared."

"Why?" I asked.

"Tell her," OPTI commanded.

Luke spoke. "Byte suggested that I volunteer to train you." I glanced over at Byte, my mouth agape. He nodded, his expression heartfelt and his eyes emanating sadness beyond words. "OPTI has agreed to let me help you get better. If you don't get better, you will die. For now, you'll live."

"Thanks, Byte. Luke," I said, my body shaky.

"You may go now," OPTI said, "You're on probation, though I expect to see you improve."

Luke tugged my arm to lead me out of the room. I followed and his hand fell away.

"Thanks again," I said to him. "Though I'm starting to wonder whether death would have been a more peaceful solution."

"You might think so now," Luke replied. "Most people fear death. Even you or you wouldn't be standing here. No one knows about the afterlife, not even OPTI, probably."

"I think I know," I said so Luke couldn't hear. Like a flame igniting, my faith in God restored itself ever since that night I'd spent in the Edwins' backyard, and Byte saving my life was like a miracle and an answer to my prayers.

We left the poolroom to reach the locker rooms.

"How about we start tomorrow at 6:30 a.m.?" Luke suggested.

I nodded. I needed to improve so I could stay alive. The peace I felt in my dream made it easier to breathe.

I didn't have any nightmares tonight when I went to bed. I enjoyed bliss with a dreamless sleep and despite the darkness hanging over me since I arrived here, my heart radiated with joy from my encounter with Jesus. When my alarm sounded at 6:15 a.m., I found my mind alert with questions and thoughts whirring about the dream. The water that flooded from Jesus's hands seemed to have missed me because I thirsted for more, to feel refreshed and whole. Instead I felt grimy and incompetent. I brushed away those feelings as I willed myself to roll out of bed and prepare for my practice with Luke.

I went to the locker rooms to change for practice at exactly 6:30 a.m., my mind still on my dream-like mystical experience with Jesus and feeling like a weight had been lifted from my shoulders. I knew I had been baptized, cleansed of all my past sins, and the release I felt exhilarated me. Under OPTI's rule, my parents would always tell me that we should rejoice in the freedom he granted us. But OPTI's rule only cast me in darkness and despair. Freedom felt foreign to me, marvelous like the sparkling of a stained glass cross cast in the rays of a golden sun. Jesus's appearance reassured me that somehow I would survive and find freedom. I realized I didn't have to do anything to earn a miracle. Jesus didn't ask for anything in return. With that in mind, I prayed in desperation for a greater miracle that would free me from OPTI's control. I knew Jesus walked with me, by my side with every breath I took. No matter how much it ached.

Luke waited as I hastened to change into my swimsuit in the locker room and exited, determined to practice. Luke put his hands on his waist and observed me as I approached.

"You're quite slow," Luke said. "We were supposed to start by now."

"Sorry," I replied. "I'm not ready for this practice."

Luke removed his hands from his waist to extend them toward me. "May I?" he asked.

"Sure," I said.

He placed his two hands on my cheeks, cupping them, gentle yet firm. I'd never connected like this with a boy and my stomach flipped. Heat rushed to my cheeks and I wished I could turn my head away.

"Close your eyes," he said.

I hesitated.

"Just do it." He spoke again.

"Fine," I grumbled as I shut my eyes.

"Take a deep breath."

I did so, inhaling and then exhaling as directed.

"Good," Luke said, his voice quieting into a lull. "Now imagine yourself swimming. How do you feel?"

"Panicked," I replied. "I have to make it to the other side so I don't get shocked or die."

"Pretend there are no shocks and no other consequences," Luke said. "How do you feel?"

"Anxious," I said. "I want to do well."

"Try and relax," Luke said. "Imagine yourself completing the laps with strength and endurance. If you swim with a strong mindset, you'll most likely perform better."

I did as he told me and imagined myself swimming with ease across the pool; it seemed too good to be true. However, I wanted to survive, to prove to OPTI and all the other prisoners that I was good enough. So I held onto that image of me gliding across the pool and urged myself to focus on that goal.

"Take another deep breath, the deepest you can."

I breathed in through my nose for a moment, feeling my lungs expand and then contracting as I exhaled out my mouth. I reimagined myself racing across the pool, my arms churning through the water and my legs propelling me forward. I visualized finishing each lap with a perfect kick turn to push myself even farther along. I pictured finishing at a good time and hearing cheers from the other prisoners rather than laughter.

"Now open your eyes," Luke said, and as I did, he removed his hands from my cheeks. "How do you feel?"

"Relaxed," I replied, "and more confident."

"I thought so," he said. "You needed it."

"Thanks," I said, "though I don't know what this has to do with anything."

"It's related because performing well in swim trials is all about your mindset," he said. "If you're doubtful, you're not going to swim as well."

"That makes sense," I said. "Now am I actually going to swim?"

Luke chuckled. "Yes, of course. Get on the diving board."

I climbed to the top of the diving board and bent over. Goose bumps covered my arms as I anticipated the cool water against my bare skin.

"Your task is one hundred meters in one minute and thirty seconds. Ready and...go!"

I dove, slipping into the icy blue water and emerging for air. My lungs ached from nearly drowning and my senses were alert as if it was happening again. I struggled against the rapid beat of my heart as I flung my whole body forward in freestyle. I pushed out all the thoughts of being in that shower, no matter how much they fought to invade my mind. After two laps, it seemed like I'd completed all four laps, and once again, I fought for my life. Exhaustion overpowered me. I completed the final lap, fighting against the soreness in my arms and legs, thrusting all my energy into it. My hands reached out to grasp the edge of the pool and my whole body collapsed into rest.

"How did I do?" I asked when I gathered my breath.

Luke wore a wide grin. "Two minutes and thirty-two seconds."

I sighed in exasperation and he chuckled.

"You'll get better in time," he said. "You're not conditioned enough. If you want to live, I suggest you try harder. Now again. Four laps."

"More?" I groaned.

"Yes, more if you want to gain some muscle and speed."

I nodded and repositioned myself on the diving board.

"Ready and...go!"

I plunged back into the water and held my body in a torpedo for as long as I could and then resurfaced for another round. My exhaustion made me sluggish but I kept swimming in the hopes of growing more muscles. I spent the next half hour completing four laps over and over again in about two minutes and thirty seconds each time. I didn't improve my time by the end of it and held onto hope that my body would get into shape. By the time I finished, I barely had enough energy to climb out of the pool.

"Ready for kickboxing?" Luke said with a grin.

"What do you mean?" I asked. "Our meeting is over."

"Kickboxing is at 7:30 a.m. and OPTI expects a good performance."

I groaned. "I have no energy," I said, and at the mention of OPTI, my heart sped up and my throat tightened.

"That doesn't matter here," Luke said. "There isn't much time for rest. Good luck."

Luke started toward the door to the poolroom while I panicked over my bleak future.

*****

Every morning, at 6:30 a.m., Luke and I continued our training sessions, focusing mainly on swim trials. My hard work proved successful. I began to grow some muscle and endurance, shortening my swimming time by five seconds. As much as I improved, I also grew in exhaustion and my performances during the actual classes lagged. More shocks came at me every time and it felt like my efforts were hopeless. I found myself on the verge of death that seemed to hang over my head like a reaper's scythe. My only release from exercise and classes occurred on Sunday. I spent the day in my cell, trying to catch up on sleep while I had a pounding headache. I longed for another dream of Jesus and prayed for a miracle to improve in my athletic and academic abilities so I wouldn't die.

When Monday came, I met Luke in the gym to train for kickboxing class. Luke waited there, and when I approached, he gave me a high five.

"Get your gloves on quick and let's start," he said.

I put them on and positioned myself in front of a punching bag. I followed Luke's instruction, sending a right and left jab on cue. Luke had me practice this one movement multiple times until my arms hurt. He wouldn't let me put them down though.

"Please," I said, gasping. "It burns."

"It's supposed to if you want to get stronger," Luke replied. "Just like swimming."

"Only for a moment," I begged.

"All right, fine," he said, and I dropped my arms, feeling the burn settle in and then subside with rest.

"Now up again," Luke said. "And this time, with no rest until you've finished."

Sweat poured down my heated, red face as I threw punch after punch at the bag before me.

"You're improving." Luke noted. "Though not by OPTI's standards."

I finished the exercise and rested my head against the bag.

"Get ready for another set," Luke said and began pounding the bag, shifting it farther forward than I could have.

"Show off much?" I said in response to Luke's smug look.

"Only occasionally," he said. "Get in position."

I got back into my form behind the bag and, on Luke's command, aimed several hooks at the bag, wishing it moved as much for me as it had for Luke.

"Harder, harder," he shouted at me. "I know you have it in you."

"Garrhh!" I groaned as I flung my fists harder and harder at the bag. It trembled but failed to move. My slim arms couldn't overpower the bag as I would have liked to. Sweat dripped from my armpits and my forehead dampened. I panted, my arms were on fire and a voice in my head shouted at me to quit now, to let go and resign to failure. Another voice reminded me of how it had felt when OPTI almost drowned me, and I kept going, fighting through not just to get better results but also for my own survival.

"How much do you want it?" Luke said when I started to lower my arms. "Push harder if you want to change your body to OPTI's standard."

"It burns!" I shrieked midpunch.

"Let it burn," he said. "Feel the burn, and eventually, it'll feel good."

I carried on throwing out the hardest punches I could muster.

"Last ten seconds, make it count," Luke hollered, heaving a few punches on his own bag.

"Ten! Nine! Eight! Seven!" My knuckles burned and I wanted to collapse onto the floor.

A bout of energy hit me and gave me a charge. "Six! Five! Four! Three! Two! *One!*"

I fell onto my knees before the bag, gasping long and fast. My heart hammered like a drill. I removed the gloves from my aching hands and stretched them out, each individual finger felt like they could have grown muscles themselves from this workout.

"You did it," Luke said, putting a hand on my shoulder. "You can celebrate today."

OPTI's image hung overhead on the same screen built in to one of the walls. I noticed it pulsed.

"Good work, Abigail," OPTI said, and I sighed in relief that I didn't receive more shocks. "That just might be enough to please me."

I returned to the locker room. My higher spirits were short-lived while I changed for swim trials. Once again, my energy depleted itself, and when I arrived in the poolroom, the instructor announced for us to complete a one-hundred-meter race in butterfly. Fatigue plagued me; I didn't even get to finish the race despite reaching the beginning of my fourth lap. I almost preferred to feel the shocks than the ominous silence that befell me when I failed. A deep strain resonated from my chest, making me want to expend more energy to perform even better so the pain would subside.

For months, Luke continued to coach me in both swim trials and kickboxing; and over time, I began to shave off time of my swimming and the punching bag began to move farther backward with each hit. I could feel my body changing; muscles grew in my arms and legs and it felt good. OPTI served me better food, and I didn't feel the shocks as often. The dream I had had stuck with me and left me with questions. I couldn't imagine why Jesus would appear to me, of all people, when I was a prisoner. It made me question if I truly murdered Mr. Edwin. I hesitated in praying about it, to even let my mind occupy itself with thoughts about my past. Did I really use the wrong type of flower? Did Mr. Edwin put the hemlock in the tea? I knew enough about hemlock to know that even a touch could cause a skin reaction and my hands had no trace of a rash.

Luke started to gain my interest in more than just as my coach. I was motivated to perform better to impress him, to set my eyes on his charming grin when I cut my swimming time to two minutes. With each success came more excuses to get closer to him, to slap my small hand against his larger one in a high five or to receive a gentle encouraging pat on the back, to exchange heated glances upon greeting. I couldn't tell if my feelings were shared. My crush on him grew as each week passed until I couldn't stop thinking about him.

By the end of summer, I swam the one hundred meters in one minute and forty-eight seconds. When I reached the wall, I fell backward into the pool out of joy and exhaustion.

"You did it!" Luke cried and held his hand out to help me out of the pool. I got to my feet and he pulled me into a hug so my face rested on his neck. I couldn't help but give him a gentle kiss on the neck. A shock, more painful than the others, hit me and knocked me to the ground in agony. When I looked up, Luke's joyful countenance had morphed into one of anger.

"Get out of here," he growled.

"I'm sorry," I apologized. "I just—"

"I don't want to hear it," he said and it felt like he'd slapped me.

Dripping wet and without a towel, I hurried away from Luke and out of the poolroom. Tears welled in my eyes and I cringed as more shocks hit me. Not even the shocks could compare to my wounded heart.

The next morning, I arrived at the gym for kickboxing practice with Luke and it disappointed me to see that he wasn't there. OPTI didn't speak to me at all, and when I entered the room, the OPTI screen turned black. I waited for about ten minutes for Luke to turn up. He hadn't come yet. I resolved to train on my own today, and each pound of the punching bag became an echo of my frustration and pain. It became apparent to me that I had to survive on my own now. Perhaps the threat of death crept nearer.

When I arrived at swim trials the same morning, the star group surrounded Luke. He pointed at me, and all at once, the group feasted their eyes on me with sharp glares. I couldn't deny the way it tore at my heart. I hid my face from them by gazing down at the floor so none of them would see the tears that dropped from my eyes.

More weeks passed and I still had no trainer. I vented all my energy and pain into each punch of the boxing bag and each lap of the pool. My body had transformed over the past few months; my abdomen tightened, my butt toned, my arms and legs boasted with muscle. I prayed each night for an end to my pain from OPTI's cruelty and Luke's rejection. I trusted that I would somehow survive this too. And I did—this time, without Luke to help me.

Despite my improvement, I lacked some crucial aspects of my life—freedom and family. I wanted to know what freedom tasted like. I groaned for it day and night. The dream I had of Jesus seemed like a promise of freedom. Through my faith, I could trust in finding freedom from any storm.

By fall's arrival, I passed a couple of star group swimmers in a one-hundred-meter race. However, no one said a word to me after and not even OPTI uttered a word of praise as if nothing had happened at all.

"OPTI wants to see you, Abigail," the instructor said. "Alone."

A thought rose that this was the day OPTI would finish his job and kill me. I groaned, feeling frustrated that my efforts were overlooked. I took a towel from one of the bins, wrapped it around me, and exited the poolroom with my head down. I and slumped through the corridors in dismay until I found the door to OPTI's room. I stood before OPTI's colorful form and waited with an ache in my chest to hear what he would say.

"Abigail." OPTI spoke, sharp like a military commander. "You've been here for several months, facing a punishment that could last for the rest of your life for what you did."

"I understand," I replied, wondering where this conversation could be headed.

"Committing a crime means you lose rights and privileges you would have had if you hadn't done it," OPTI said.

"I know."

"Which is why it might surprise you that I'm going to release you."

"Release me?" I asked. It did surprise me.

"You can go back home. Your siblings are there with your mother," OPTI said. "Your life no longer belongs to you. Your life and what you do with it is up to me. In three years, you'll complete a training program different from this to serve as one of the members of my police force or military, whichever one you qualify for."

"Police force?" I said. "I can't be a police officer or in the military. I'm not nearly that qualified. I've never wanted to be either of those."

A shock took me to my knees before OPTI's brain.

"It does not matter anymore what you want, you foolish girl," he said. "But I see potential in you and your life calling should be to serve me, your leader in everything. This is going to be your life, and if you don't want this life, well, death is your only other option."

CHAPTER 13

Return

I gazed up at my home as the cab swung around the curves of the steep driveway. The bushes lined the driveway's path like a colorful forestry escort, guiding me into another, more personal and enclosed world. After much time spent away, locked in a concrete detention center with barely any windows, the splatter of autumn color on the forest's trees transfixed my gaze as if I'd never laid my eyes on them before. I longed to lose myself in the forest's trails, discovering and observing brooks and rabbit holes, ponds and meadows; one meadow in particular held familiarity as Faith's choice of meeting ground when she taught my siblings and me about the Bible. I shifted my eyes from the forest to stare at the home that stood before me; dove-like white paint on the sidling with dark window shutters. The circumstances weren't ideal; I no longer had control over my future. For the moment though, I felt at peace at the one place I most wanted to be. The cab stopped at the top of the driveway and I got out with nothing in my hands. My mother had prepaid the cab so I didn't have to worry. My back dampened from sweat and I lifted my mane of hair off of my back. I looked up at the house that I had grown up in and something felt different. I had lost my freedom, Faith was gone forever, Father still hadn't returned, and the beds of flowers were dying in the cool autumn weather.

A chill ran through my entire body, deep under the surface of my bones.

"I made it," I whispered to myself. "I'm here." I breathed out. "Home."

I remembered my time at the Edwins' and my struggle to make it home—one way or another—with my siblings and me intact. Fortunately they had made it home without me. I couldn't help wish that I hadn't missed so much time with them. I thought I'd never see them or my home again. I walked up the front steps to the front porch, memories drifting into my mind of a younger version of myself—of my sisters. When I glanced over to the side of the house, I almost thought I saw a young Scarlett doing cartwheels on the grass, an echo of childish giggles bubbled in my ears.

I rang the doorbell—the chime reverberating in my eardrum, echoing the distant sounds of my childhood. No answer came. No sound, except for a light breeze brushing its cool air against my skin. I moved over to the window, trying to peer in through the curtains and only seeing the top of a white sofa. I remembered the times when I would come home to the house locked with my mother out running errands and had to look for the key in the flowerpot. I searched for it now, digging through the dirt until, at last, my fingers brushed against the metal edge of a key. I turned the key in the doorknob, having to jerk it a few times, and then, at last, the door swung open. I stood in the doorway as if I expected someone—my mother in particular—to make an appearance.

No one appeared. Just silence.

I stepped into the foyer, looking up at the chandelier that hung from the high ceiling and the dark wooden staircase that led up to the bedrooms. I breathed in the familiar scent of home—memories filled my mind of greeting my father at the door, baking chocolate chip cookies with my mother and sisters, and snuggling with Faith on the living room couch to watch the gardening channel.

I walked toward the archway leading into the kitchen. Then stopped short at the sight of the white linoleum. My vision blurred and shifted. The earsplitting sound of china shattering reverberated through my ears, causing another deep chill to run through my bones as I heard a childish scream. I swung my head from right to left, trying to find the source. Nothing was found. It seemed like a memory of some sort. My mind blocked it, and then suddenly, it flew from my mind as swift as a bird from a tree.

A door creaked as it swung open and I could hear a low hum that drew closer to me until I came face-to-face with Scarlett, chatting on her OPTI-Phone, her dark hair in rivulets down her back, glossy and smooth as if she'd come from the hair salon. Her nails were sharp and pristine and natural makeup enhanced her features, accenting her olive-green eyes. Without waiting for her to finish her call, I wrapped my arms around her.

She uttered a goodbye into her phone and lifted it away from her ear as she hung up. "Abigail? You're home?"

Her arms wrapped around me in a tight hug and then we stepped apart.

"Yeah…" I mustered. "Didn't OPTI tell you?"

"He told Mother you would be coming home," she said. "He didn't say when. Good thing I'm home. I've missed you."

"I missed you too." I echoed her statement.

"I'm so sorry you had to go to prison," Scarlett said, her voice choked. "It should have been me."

"You didn't do anything, Scarlett," I said.

"Neither did you," she replied.

Then I stepped back from the hug. "Where's Renée? And Mother?"

"They'll be here soon," she said. "Mother is picking up Renée from school. Call time is at 5:00 p.m. and I have a lot to get done for the party."

"Call time for what?" I asked. "What party?"

Scarlett looked surprised for a second and then smiled. "I'm performing tonight in the school play, *Tartuffe*. I play Mariane. You should come! And there's a cast party here tonight. You can meet my friends and get a head start at school. You'll be popular in no time."

"I'd love to," I said. I felt a dull pain in my chest and my forehead scrunched. I wouldn't know anyone at the party. I feared I would make a wrong impression.

A knock on the door called my attention and I hurried to answer the door. My mother stood there with Renée by her side.

Renée launched herself into my arms and I spun her around, her feet leaving the ground. I planted a kiss on her forehead. My mother watched us, and I turned to give her a hug.

"I'm so glad you're better," I said and tears dripped from my eyes.

"Me too, Abigail, darling," she said. "OPTI even granted me a promotion at the firm."

"Congratulations!" I said, though my voice faltered at the end at the mention of OPTI. I couldn't help the joy I felt hearing that my mother was back on her feet.

"It requires more of my time." She went on. "But I'm sure you and Scarlett can babysit Renée for me, right? Also I'm dating a nice man named Florian. I hope you two might meet sometime."

"Yes, of course," I said to both requests, though when I glanced at Scarlett, I noticed a deep frown on her face.

"I'd better go," Scarlett said to me and began to climb the stairs to her room.

CHAPTER 14

Tartuffe

I carried a bouquet of flowers in one hand as I made my way down the hall to the dressing room after Scarlett's play. My mother dropped me off half an hour before the show and went on a dinner date with Florian. Renée had a sleepover since Scarlett planned to throw a party. Before the performance, Scarlett invited me to go backstage after the performance. I reached the door and put on my brightest smile as I walked inside. My eyes scanned the room for Scarlett and I inched forward, trying not to be noticed.

"Are you looking for someone?" A voice called my attention. I turned my head and met a tall lean boy dressed in a blue button-down shirt tucked into a pair of beige pants. His dark-brown hair was combed over, and he had a handsome face.

"Yes, my sister, Scarlett."

"You're Scarlett's sister? What's your name?" he asked. "I'm Jake Chambers." He extended his hand. His kindness and cordiality refreshed my mind after living for months as a prisoner. I hoped it would last.

"I'm Abigail." I seized it and shook it firmly. "Abigail Richardson. You were wonderful in the play this evening."

"Thank you," he said. He held my gaze for a second with his murky-brown eyes. I felt a sense of release. "That's...a...uh...pretty name," he murmured seeming to jump back to the present. "Let me help you find Scarlett."

He put a hand on my back and guided me to the back of the dressing room where Scarlett removed a pin from her flowing wavy dark hair.

"Scarlett," Jake said, "your sister Abigail has come to see you."

"Who's that?" she asked, barely glancing up from the mirror.

"Jake Chambers," I replied. I stretched the bouquet of flowers toward her as she spun around. "You were amazing, Scar."

"Oh. Hi, Jake," she muttered, and then she grinned proudly at me, her eyes twinkling. "I performed brilliantly, didn't I?" she said, reaching for the bouquet.

"Ow!" I cried as my finger brushed against a thorn. Scarlett caught the bouquet as it nearly slipped from my grasp. I held my hand and watched as blood pooled.

"Let me get you a tissue," Jake said. He hurried away and came back with a white Kleenex outstretched. I took it and pressed it against my bloodied pricked finger.

"Thank you," I said while Scarlett sniffed the pink roses.

"Mmm...Roses are my favorite flower—blooming beauties. Thank you, Abby."

"I'll see you later," Jake said and waved at me with a grin as he strode away. I turned back to Scarlett.

"You're welcome. While I watched, I almost forgot that you were acting," I said.

"Well, enough about me," Scarlett said though she beamed. She looped an arm around my shoulders. "Let me introduce you to the rest of the cast."

Scarlett led me over to a couple of beautiful tall girls. One had dark hair and a slender nose with a deep curve and the other had auburn hair. I remembered the dark-haired girl because she played Elmire. The other one, I think, had played Dorine.

"Hey, girls, this is my sister Abigail. Meet my friends, Betty and Rosalie," she said, "Betty and I did cheerleading together in middle school, and she used to be a flyer. Rosalie is on the field hockey team in the spring."

"Nice to meet you," I greeted them and found myself starved for words. Next to them, I felt shorter and I began to wonder if I had bad breath. "I...loved your performances."

"Aw, you're so sweet," Rosalie said. "Do you do any acting?"

"No," I said. "I used to...I just...I became too busy with other things in my life." I couldn't explain how I left home for the Edwins' several months ago and had to say goodbye to the life I had previously known.

"All right, girls, I've got one more person to introduce Abigail to," Scarlett said. "See you at our house."

Scarlett grabbed my arm and steered me away from Betty and Rosalie. Scarlett led me over to where a tall and broad robust boy removed a long, dark brown wig to reveal a mop of hair as black as the darkest night. The rest of his costume remained on and I realized he had played Tartuffe.

Scarlett coughed to get the boy's attention. He must have been used to Scarlett's impatient attitude because he chuckled.

"What do you want now, Scarlett?" he asked in amusement as he faced a mirror.

"I want you to turn around and say hello to my sister," Scarlett said.

"Renée?" the boy replied. "I didn't know you had any guests this evening."

"Not Renée," she said. "My other sister, Abigail."

The boy sighed as if Scarlett were a nuisance and turned around. His gaze went from Scarlett to me. I noticed his gray eyes were piercing in contrast with his dark hair. His gaze locked on me while a million thoughts poured into my head, making me horribly dizzy, and at the same time, I struggled to find words.

"So you're Abigail," the boy said and, with a flourish, bowed slightly at the waist, never dropping his gaze. "Nice meeting you."

It took me a moment to find something to say. I didn't expect his formality.

"N-nice to m-meet you too," I stuttered. My thoughts cleared. "And you are?"

"Heath," he replied, and I reached my hand out with my pricked finger to shake his. With a swift motion, he gripped my hand and held it long after we had shaken. His hand was warm and tough.

"I recognize you," I said as I shifted my hand out of his grasp. "You played Tartuffe."

I played with my hair while I waited for a response.

The raven-haired boy grinned. "I did," he replied.

"Well, I thought you had a very captivating performance," I said, feeling a shred of confidence resurface. "And you said all the lines perfectly with such tricky language."

"I have been studying for quite some time," the boy said, and I could see that my compliment pleased him. "I consider myself to be among the best. Even OPTI thinks so."

At that, my eyes flashed over to one of OPTI's screens. The brain became brighter and bigger than usual in satisfaction.

Scarlett rolled her eyes. "Don't get too over your head," she muttered, "I knew my lines too." Then she glanced at me. "Actually Abby probably knows the play as well as we do and she wasn't even in it."

The boy looked at me, and underneath his dark hair, I could see his eyebrows were raised. I could feel my cheeks reddening.

"I love to read plays," I said. "I mostly read books about chemistry and biology but I also read any pieces of classic literature I can find. Molière was an incredible playwright."

"Next time there's a play, you should audition," Heath said, his eyes gleaming. "You'd be a great addition to our acting group."

"Oh, I couldn't," I said, glancing at Scarlett. "I don't think I would have time for it."

"Oh, come on," Scarlett said. "You used to act in middle school. You got to play Red Riding Hood in *Into the Woods* in seventh grade. Not to mention the plays we created when we were kids."

I exchanged a glance with Scarlett and giggled. I remembered our childhood memories of putting on fairy-tale plays with Renée and Faith. Scarlett always starred as the princess, Faith played the fairy godmother, Renée put on whiskers and a tail to play a mouse, and my siblings chose me to play the prince. However, Scarlett would become jealous when I got to fight the dragon and complained that pretending to sleep bored her.

"You're the best actress in the family, not me," I answered her. "I don't think I should do it."

"Sorry to cut this conversation short," Scarlett said, glancing at her watch. "We have to be home soon for the party and I need to change. I'll leave you two to get to know each other." Scarlett hurried to the back of the dressing room to change. I watched her go and realized I found myself alone with the boy with raven hair. I could feel him watching me and I turned to meet his gaze once more.

"Is Molière your favorite playwright?" the boy asked, changing the subject.

"One of them," I said. "What about Shakespeare? You probably like his plays, right?"

"Of course," the boy said. "I'm quite gifted at performing Shakespeare too. We're only allowed to perform old plays so his works are the most commonly adapted at this school." His eyes gleamed as he spoke and I averted my gaze so I wouldn't become trapped in them again.

"So why haven't I seen you around before?" he asked, grabbing back my attention. "Why don't you come to Scarlett's plays?"

"I went to a boarding school for the last several months," I lied. I couldn't explain that I was in prison or in a dreadful foster home. "And before that, my mom was usually away on the weekends. So I was left to babysit Renée most of the time and couldn't go to any shows—" I interrupted myself when I noticed the boy gazed at me as if he were more intrigued by my appearance than my story. "I'm boring you, aren't I? You probably don't find my life interesting at all."

"Actually," he said, "I listened to every word. Scarlett never mentions Renée except that she doesn't like her."

"Um…yeah," I said, "I guess I shouldn't be surprised. Just know that Scarlett doesn't mean it. I know she cares about Renée as much as I do."

He nodded. "Are you going to be at the cast party tonight?"

"Well, I do live there," I replied. "So perhaps the question is whether you'll be there?"

Heath smiled so I could see his white teeth.

"Of course he'll be there," Scarlett said, causing us both to jump in surprise. "He's spending the night at our place. Speaking of which, I think you should get changed too, Heath. You're not coming to my party dressed like that. Come on, Abby, we'll wait in the car."

I gave the boy a small smile before following Scarlett out of the dressing room and then through the doors leading to the front entrance of the theater. We reached the black Jeep that belonged to Scarlett and got in. She started the engine, and together, we managed to back the car out without hitting the ones beside us. Scarlett seemed unconcerned about whether she scratched the car despite our mother giving it to her as a gift.

Scarlett pulled the car up to the front of the theater on the school's vast campus and honked the horn.

"Can't he change faster?" Scarlett asked as she pressed once more on the wheel. Then she gave her attention to me. "So how was talking to Heath?"

I shrugged. "He seems okay," I said, which was an understatement. I didn't want her to know I had a crush on him yet.

"Thank goodness," Scarlett muttered. "He doesn't like too many people but I guess he doesn't mind you. If he says anything mean, ignore it."

"Okay," I said, my eyebrows furrowing.

I glanced toward the doors to the theater as they opened and a shadowy figure walked down the path. As the figure drew closer, I could make out the black hair of Heath. He found the car, and although the windows were closed and tinted, he aimed a stare at me as if he had the eyes of a cat. On one shoulder slung a small bag and Scarlett asked me to open the trunk.

I climbed out of the car and opened the trunk as Heath reached it. He moved to put the bag in the trunk, and as he did, his hand brushed against mine, giving me goose bumps. I pulled my hand away as if it pricked me.

Heath grinned, his eyes as luminous as the full moon hanging in the sky above. "Oops," he said.

I tried to say something; it came out all slurred and my cheeks burned up.

"Hurry up." Scarlett honked the horn. "It doesn't take that long to put one bag in the trunk."

I sighed and moved to go sit in the passenger's seat. Heath climbed into the back seat and Scarlett drove off. On the way home, Scarlett led the conversation about the performance. She complained about how some of the other performers were being unprofessional and unconvincing as actors. Personally I thought all of the actors in the play were great. Arguing with Scarlett over such things wasn't wise though. I stayed silent most of the car ride, focusing on the road in front instead of the boy with inky black hair who leaned forward in his seat, not bothering to put on his seat belt. Every so often, I would feel his gaze on my back and turn my head to peek over my shoulder at him.

Finally Scarlett pulled the car into our long driveway, parking outside the garage. We got out and Scarlett hurried on ahead into the house, muttering something about getting ready for the party.

"She really likes planning parties," Heath muttered from beside me.

I uttered a small laugh. "That's Scarlett," I said. "Everything's always about parties, makeup, acting, and fashion."

We entered the house to find Scarlett flitting about to finish last-minute decorations for the party.

"Do you need any help, Scarlett?" I asked as I took off my shoes.

"Yes, please," she answered from somewhere in the dining room. "Can you and Heath get the food out? It's all in the fridge and there are chips in the pantry. Abigail, you know what kind I'm talking about and make sure any of the silverware or bowls you use are the right ones."

So I hurried over to the kitchen and got out the food which consisted of platters of shrimp and cheese. Scarlett went all out for her party, from appetizers to music; I could already hear a smooth beat of R & B blasting from the stereo in the living room, and streamers hung along the walls. I wondered how crazy it would be when Scarlett's wedding day came. She would have to plan the entire occasion herself with every detail met with precision. I worried for whoever Scarlett decided would be her maid of honor. I hoped it wouldn't be me.

"Keep setting up," Scarlett called to us as she raced upstairs in her eleven-inch ice-blue heels. "I'll be down in a minute."

I picked up the tray of shrimp and carried it over to the kitchen table. Heath had grabbed the bowl of chips and aimed to put it down beside the shrimp.

"Actually," I said, "the chips aren't supposed to go there. Scarlett says that 'shrimp and chips don't mix' and should be separate. The cheese can go beside the shrimp though."

"You sound like you've done this before," Heath said, handing me the bowl so I could place it apart from the shrimp. He fetched the tray of cheese and placed it where I directed.

"Many times," I muttered. "I may not attend many of Scarlett's parties. That doesn't mean I don't take part in the set up. Scarlett is picky about every little detail and not just about parties."

"Yes, I know," Heath said, looking bitter as if Scarlett had bothered him earlier about something.

"Well, don't take it too personally," I said as I moved to the fridge to grab the veggie platter and placed it in the exact spot on the table, "Scarlett likes things to go her way. If you think she's picky now, then you probably have never seen her when my mother's around. She's always picking at what our mother does or wears as if it's her decision."

The doorbell rang. Scarlett yelled for me to get the door.

"Do you think you can manage from here?" I asked Heath, looking up at his clean-shaven face.

His eyes were lucid, locking me to them again, freezing me. "I'll be all right," he said.

"O-oh," I muttered, unable to formulate words. The doorbell rang again and Heath turned away, breaking our gaze so I could finally think. I hurried for the door, opening it to reveal three guests, all of whom I recognized from the play.

Jake Chambers' tall lean figure stood in front of the other cast members, a bright smile on his face.

"Hello, Jake," I said, lighting up in his presence. "It's nice to see you. Uh, Scarlett will be down in a moment."

"That's quite all right," Jake said, "as long as I get to chat with you. You look absolutely lovely tonight." He took my hand and brought it to his lips, kissing my palm gently.

"Thank you," I said, taken aback. I'd never received a proper kiss from a boy, and even a kiss on the hand sent a thrill through me. "You're too sweet. Come in and I'll show you where the party is."

I shifted to allow Jake to step inside. Behind him, a younger boy with lighter hair and similar eyes clutched his pocket where I could see a notebook sticking out. A girl with glasses and chestnut-colored hair stood beside him and gazed at me with bright eyes.

Jake moved to put a hand on my arm. "This is Abigail, Scarlett's sister," he explained to the others. "We met this evening after the show."

"It's good to meet you," said the boy with light-brown hair. He held out his hand. "I'm Kyle. Jake's brother." I shook it. "This is my sister, Katie." He gestured to the girl who shook my hand as well. She looked artsy, dressed in a flannel shirt and a pair of dark jeans.

"You too. Thanks," I replied, "you were all so incredible in the play tonight. I'm glad I went."

Kyle's brown eyes darkened, his gaze lifted and I followed it.

Heath's bulky figure leaned against the doorway of the hallway leading to the kitchen. His eyes lit in amusement. Then his gaze flickered to me and a slow smile crept up on his lips.

"Oh, and there's our Tartuffe," Jake said, noticing the direction I looked. "I didn't expect to see you here and so early."

"Hello, Jake," Heath said in a low voice and it appeared as though he was sizing Jake up. "I would have taken longer but my ride was Scarlett and Abigail tonight. Fortunately they are both pleasant people to be acquainted with."

"Yes, of course," Jake replied, not appearing to notice Heath observing him. He kept glancing over at me. The awkward silence that followed made me hope that the rest of the party wouldn't play out this way.

"Ugh." I heard Scarlett groan as she bounded down the stairs and saw Jake in the foyer. She wore a tight low-cut black dress that hugged her figure. "I got ready quickly for *you*?" She rolled her eyes. "Well, Abby can take you in the living room for the party and I'll greet the rest of the guests."

"Sorry about Scarlett," I said to Jake and his siblings. "Come on." I led them down the hall past Heath. "Are you coming?" I asked Heath.

"In a moment," he said.

CHAPTER 15

Reckless

I sat on the couch in the living room, taking a break from awkward conversation with Betty and Rosalie for the moment. I observed people dancing and drinking until they were stumbling around the room amid chuckles. I realized I had no interest in any of this. Ever since my near-death experiences, I looked for something to fill my void. It seemed something that could only be filled and nourished by my faith. My mind lingered on this idea for a moment as I tried to figure out how I could incorporate my faith more into my lifestyle. As a young girl, Faith told me about the Christian practice of going to church on Sundays. However, most of the churches in this town and outside were abandoned. I had no way to express my faith at all. As I thought about it, I noticed Heath coming toward me, carrying two cups of some kind of alcoholic beverage in his hands. He raised one as he approached.

"I got you a drink," he said, sitting down on the couch beside me. "I hope you like alcohol."

"Oh, I can't," I said, waving the drink away.

"Oh, come on," he said. He took a swig from his own cup. "It has rum in it."

"Oh no," I said. "Did Scarlett open my mother's liquor cabinet?"

I should have known that Scarlett would do anything she could to get on my mother's nerves. For instance, serving her alcohol at her party without asking our mother, leaving her to find out when she arrived home to empty bottles.

Heath shrugged. "There's nothing wrong with it," he said, "so long as we get to enjoy it."

I laughed and shook my head. "Try telling that to my mother," I said. "She's strict about drinking and big parties. Scarlett told her it would be a small gathering and now…"

I gazed at the crowd that had quickly formed in our living room and could barely make out anyone's face in the dark.

"There's nothing wrong with drinking," he said. "It's pretty normal."

I pursed my lips. "I don't know. I don't normally drink."

"Don't be such a prude. It's just a rum and coke," Heath said. "Who doesn't drink at a party? It's about time you tried it. I know your type. You never let yourself have any fun."

I frowned. He might have been right. I couldn't remember the last time I enjoyed myself. I didn't experience much enjoyment in prison and, before that, living with the Edwins for half a year was nightmarish. Within the last year, I spent all my time trying to escape some kind of punishment or suffering and the consequences were catching up to me. My brain felt fogged, my mind numb, my soul empty. I needed a release, a distraction. I wished I could have been going to school here instead of in prison all these months. I longed to be a part of the school plays like Scarlett was and pursuing my passion for science in a real laboratory. Then I remembered OPTI's words to me before I left prison. My life belonged to OPTI. I hated that—I wanted to serve God. And tonight, I thought, I wanted to have fun. I *deserved* to have fun.

"I am not a prude," I retorted at last, snatching the cup from his outstretched hand. I brought it to my lips and took a small sip. I felt Heath's pressing stare though and I drank more of it, hoping for the shame to fade away from him calling me a prude; but it suffocated me, haunting every move I made.

"Drink it all," Heath said. He looked pleased. "If you're going to drink, you have to do it all in one go. Watch." He took his cup and brought it to his lips. He drained it in seconds, grimaced, and then placed it on the table.

I brought my cup to my lips again and squeezed my eyes shut as I downed the rest of the drink. I felt it go straight to my head. The drink's strength made my face scrunch like I'd taken a bite of a lemon. I set the drink down on the end table and almost knocked it over. The room started spinning.

"There," I said, giggling, "are you happy?"

"More?" he asked with a wink.

I shook my head. "No more rum," I said. "How much did you put in there? If I have any more, I might puke. How about something with less alcohol?"

"How about a light beer?"

I nodded and Heath left. I didn't have much knowledge about alcohol, after all, this was my first real high school party.

In a few moments, he came back with two cups of beer.

I grasped mine in excitement, hoping to ease away all of my burdensome guilt and drown out the cloud of darkness that seemed to lurk wherever I went.

"So now that that's settled," I said, brushing my hair behind my shoulder. I eased my back against the sofa. "How did you come to be such a great actor?"

"I would say I'm more than that," he replied. "I started young and worked my way up to lead roles."

"I did theater as a kid too," I said, pausing to take another sip, feeling more relaxed. "I played Wendy in *Peter Pan* a few years ago."

"No way," Heath said. "That's a great role and Red Riding Hood too. You must be talented."

"I haven't acted since *Into the Woods*," I said. "And my director didn't like my performance."

"Why did you stop?" he asked. "Not even at your boarding school?"

"Life got complicated," I said. His eyes darkened as he gulped down some beer.

"I know about that," he said. "Did you have a good childhood then?"

I shrugged. "It was decent," I lied. "I don't like to linger on bad memories too much." I averted my eyes and took a deep sip of beer.

"I can't say I disagree," Heath muttered.

"What plays were you in when you were a kid?" I asked.

Heath grinned. "I played Oliver in *Oliver*," he said.

"I can't picture you as Oliver," I said and worried I offended him. "Not in a bad way."

"A truly gifted actor can play any role even if it's wildly different from him or herself," Heath said. "Actually the director originally cast me as Fagin. The boy who the director cast as Oliver got sick."

A fleeting pause.

"Do you want to take a walk outside with me?" he asked.

"It's a bit chilly," I said. "Maybe not."

"I'll let you wear my jacket," he said. I looked into his captivating gray eyes and it made me want to wear his jacket all the time.

"All right," I said.

"Don't go anywhere," Heath said. I waited, longing for him to return.

Heath came back with his jacket and walked over to the back sliding door. I got up and followed him. All of my movements seemed out of my control. I felt my heartbeat speed up as he helped me put on his jacket. When I had it on, he opened the doors and stepped outside ahead of me. I headed out after him and lingered behind to close the doors.

When I turned around, I found Heath fixated on me. His eyes always seemed to shimmer, even in the dark. I felt as if he could see right through me. I didn't know what to say now that we were alone. I glanced back at the sliding doors. I could see the bright colors coming from everyone's outfits and the colorful lights that danced along the walls.

"What are you looking at?" Heath asked, and I could feel him standing behind me now, following my gaze.

I turned my attention away from the party and looked at the blue shirt he wore rather than look him in the eyes again.

"Just…thinking," I said.

"About what?" he asked.

"Nothing," I said while I shook my head. I hurried past him before his eyes could ensnare mine again. However, his height had its advantages, and in no time, Heath had caught up to me.

"Nothing?" he said. "Let me in on your thoughts. I want to know everything about you."

"It's not important," I said and then flashed a grin of my own. "Let's keep it a secret." I gave him a playful nudge.

I walked down the steps of the deck and followed the path past the gate to our pool and to the garden where a white bench perched. I sat down, my eyes cast downward at the dying plants.

Heath had walked over to the bench as well; he didn't sit down. I could feel his eyes on me while I gazed out into the woods. My back began to hunch as if danger lurked nearby. When I looked back over at Heath, my fears vanished.

"Walk with me," he said as he held out his hand.

I stared at it, wondering if I should take it or not. I snuck a glance up at his face and his eyes settled on mine. At last, I stuck my hand out to take his cool one, his touch sending a shock through me. I rose from the bench to let him escort me back up the path in the direction of the pool.

"So tell me," he said. "What was it like at your boarding school?"

"Not that interesting," I said, shaking off my unease. "I took similar classes, and I spent a lot of time doing sports."

"I can tell," he said. "You're looking fit. What sports?"

"Swimming and kickboxing," I answered and watched him carefully for his reaction.

Heath chuckled. "I can't picture you kickboxing," he said as we reached the gate that surrounded the pool.

"Well, a lot of things I've done may surprise you," I said and gave him a playful punch.

Heath opened the gate and began to step inside.

"We're going in here?" I asked. I allowed my hand to slip from his grasp and paused. "Why?"

Heath only smirked and then moved over to the pool. He opened the cover and began to pull it off.

"What are you doing?" I asked.

When Heath removed the cover and tossed it aside, his grin widened. He put down his phone on the edge of the pool, walked over to the diving board, hopped on, and, in a flash, did a cannonball into the freezing-cold water. I watched in bewilderment.

Heath surfaced. His mop of black hair was saturated with chlorine water and his clothes clung to his skin. He wore a toothy smile and then raised a hand to beckon me.

"Come on in, Abigail," he said.

"In there?" I said. "Are you insane? It's freezing!"

"Come on." He swam over to the side of the pool. "You can do kickboxing but you don't have the guts to do this?"

"I don't care. I don't want to dive into freezing-cold water."

Heath climbed out of the pool. His clothes dripped with water as he walked over to me. I put my hands up in defense.

"Don't try and get me wet," I said, "it might be interesting and fun for you but I'd like to stay dry and warm."

His grin returned as he moved closer and I found myself moving back.

"Go jump in or I'll throw you in myself," he said with a laugh.

"You wouldn't," I said. "There's no way I'm going in there."

"I would." Heath took a step closer. "Now jump in."

"All right, fine," I groaned. I put my phone down next to his, took off his jacket, and walked over to the diving board. Heath jumped back into the water. He floated on his back and pointed to the diving board.

"Get on," he said.

I rolled my eyes and climbed on top of it. A chilly autumn breeze blew. I clutched my arms as I shivered and surveyed the water that I knew would be nearly-zero degrees.

"I'm not so sure I want to get my clothes wet," I said.

"You can take them off," he said, grinning in amusement. "I don't mind."

"Ugh," I grumbled, "I change my mind."

"What are you waiting for, Abigail?" He threw up his hands. "Jump in!"

"I will. Just be patient."

"I don't like waiting," Heath muttered. "Hurry up!"

I scowled and then moved my feet along the rough surface of the diving board, inching closer to the edge where the board began to bounce. I thought about how Heath called me a prude. Again I felt that irritation and bitterness about how he saw me. Everything that had happened to me before now was wrought with misery and I never got much of a break from it. I wanted to stop living a miserable life. I wanted to have fun, to find meaning in my life again, and maybe, just maybe, I've found that meaning through my faith and now Heath as well. I wanted to jump into this pool even though I would probably freeze my butt off. I was exhausted from having so much pressure on my shoulders. I had a small secret desire to do something totally crazy. I didn't want my life to be bound by OPTI's endless demands of me—I wanted to be free.

"Just run and jump in," Heath urged. "It's like taking off a Band-Aid. It hurts less if you rip it off in one swift motion."

I nodded and backed up. I took a deep shaky breath and, remembering my desire, I began to run across the diving board; and when I reached the end, I sprung off. I tucked my knees to my chest and wrapped my arms around myself in a cannonball. I hit the icy surface with a splash, cursing in my mind from the cold, and sunk deep enough that my ears hurt. The frigid water sent a thrill through me as if I was a live wire. I swam to the surface, gasping and shivering. As I treaded the water, I burst into laughter. It felt so good to laugh. I couldn't remember the last time I had done so. I laughed even harder.

"I'm definitely going to have to find a way to get you back for that," I said in between giggles. "I think you gave me way too much to drink."

I swam over to the shallow end to reach Heath and then leaned back in the water so I floated on the surface. I gazed up at the full moon and the bright stars that surrounded it. I wanted the freedom to look at the skies for as long as I lived, but I knew that in three years, I would lose everything I'd gained so far.

Heath waded over to me and his head blocked out the moon's glow.

"Thank you," I said. "Finally I've done something thrilling and fun. It's been too long since I have. I had a lousy time at boarding school."

I stopped floating and let my feet touch the bottom. We were in the shallow end, near the side of the pool.

"You must not be happy that your parents sent you there," Heath said. "I wouldn't have been."

"What are your parents like?" I asked.

"Well, my father is a brilliant man," he said. "Perhaps one of the most brilliant men I've ever known. My mother is the same—a brilliant woman with a striking personality."

There was a moment of silence.

"I lost my father," I said. "It was awful."

"Were you close with him?" he asked, his volume dropping as well.

"No," I said, "not as much as I wish I'd been."

"Scarlett never likes to talk about it," he said. "She never did say exactly what happened."

"I don't like to talk about it either," I said, averting my eyes.

"Good," Heath said, and I looked back at him. Looking proved a mistake as his luminous eyes froze me. Heath brought his hand out of the water and cupped my cheek in his hand. "Because I'm tired of talking."

I froze as he leaned toward me and his warmer lips met mine. The kiss sent a thrill through me that encompassed any other feeling, the last of my somberness subsiding into bliss. Time seemed to melt as heat surged within me. Our kiss began as a small ember and then transformed into a combination of fiery passion with a chilled breeze of ice, Heath holding me close to him as his hands intertwined with my wet hair. A kind of hunger unearthed in me that made me realize I would never be the same like the succulent bite into a sweet yet poisonous apple. I let him deepen the kiss, stupefied.

I didn't realize he had been moving me backward until my back touched the side of the pool. One of his hands found my waist and then slithered underneath my wet shirt, up my back. He moved even closer to me, so now, we were pressed together; and he placed his other hand on my waist, pulling me closer.

The hand that he had laid on my waist moved to pull my wet top up. Then suddenly, my mind cleared and I pulled away, prying his hands off of me.

"Look," I said, "I'm not interested in that sort of thing. So if that's what you've been thinking, then you're wasting your time."

"Oh, come on," he said, moving toward me again.

"No," I said. I shoved him back. "I barely even know you."

Heath narrowed his eyes. "Don't you want it?" He closed the distance, grabbing my waist and yanking me toward him. I put a hand over his mouth before he could begin to kiss me again.

"No." I spat and wrestled my way out of his grasp.

He scowled but stopped his advances. "Looks like our fun is over." He climbed out of the pool and stormed back up the path into the house, leaving me alone in this freezing-cold pool.

I sighed, feeling like he had slapped me. Could that be all he wanted from me?

I left the pool deck and walked back up the path and into the house. I took the route through the kitchen to avoid soaking the living room carpet and angering my mother. Partygoers turned to stare at me as I entered and whispered to each other. Heath wasn't inside and I suspected he left. Jake stood in the kitchen with Kyle and glanced at me as I passed by them.

"Abigail," Jake said in concern, "are you all right? Did someone push you in the pool?"

"No, I'm fine," I said, wishing I could hide from view. "I'm going to head upstairs. I don't want to talk about it."

I began to move past him and he placed a soothing hand on my wrist. If any other boy had touched me this evening, I would have pulled away. But Jake's hand made me feel safe. I turned to meet his kind eyes.

"Take care, Abigail," he said, giving me a small smile. "I'll see you in school."

"Thanks for your concern," I replied.

"Well, good night," Jake said. "I hope you're all right."

"Good night," I said to him and Kyle.

I bounded up the stairs without running into any more trouble and went inside my room, closing the door behind me.

I took a shower first, not allowing myself to even think for a second about what had just happened. The hot water helped me relax and wash off the chlorine. I used soap nearly everywhere, making sure to scrub extra hard to fully erase the filthy feeling I had. I still refused to let myself think about it and got out of the shower to clear my thoughts again.

I decided to let my hair dry naturally tonight and slid on my most comfortable pajamas. When I finished brushing my teeth, I had nothing to else to do to keep my mind off of the ordeal. I lay in bed, praying in desperation to not have those thoughts slip in my brain. I curled around myself and clutched my knees to my chest while I sobbed. I should have known, should have predicted that he would want to sleep with me and pressure me into doing it. Was that his main goal the whole time? And the worst part was that I'd carried deep feelings for him that weighed on my heart and now they were shattered. If only I hadn't jumped in the pool with him or even kissed him, and now, this event would mark my entrance into my new school. I couldn't bear to think about what people might say if they heard about it.

In the next moment, Scarlett knocked on my door and came into my room.

"Is the party almost over?" I asked, wiping my tear-stained cheeks as I sat up.

Scarlett nodded. "Jake told me you were in the pool," she said. "What happened?"

I averted my gaze. "Nothing," I said.

Scarlett frowned. "Did someone push you in or did you jump?" she asked.

"I was with Heath," I said finally. "He dared me to jump in so I did. That's all."

"Of course he did. That's how he is," she said. "Where is he now?"

"He left, I think. It didn't end well…"

"What did he do?" she asked.

I wanted to tell her but all I could hear were Heath's words, *Don't you want it?* And I wondered if it were true. Should I have taken things further with him? Had I wanted it? My mind screamed *no*. My mind felt like a whirlwind, and I didn't know what to believe.

"He was mean to me. I don't want to talk about it."

"I'll talk to him on Monday," Scarlett said, "and straighten him out."

"I guess it's a little my fault. I shouldn't have bothered with him."

"No, don't say that," Scarlett said. "It was all his fault. I'd rather you hang out with Jake than him. And you know how much I can't stand him and his brother. I should have known Heath would spoil your night. I know he only targeted you because you're my sister."

"Do you think so?" I asked and felt my heart drop even more.

Scarlett averted her gaze to a painting displaying a field of wild flowers on the wall. My father gave it to me a year before he left. I never took it down.

"Yes," she replied so quietly I almost didn't hear her. My attention shifted back to her. Then she turned back to me. "Actually we kissed at the first party I ever invited him to this past summer. He wanted to take things further but I rejected him. It made him pretty angry. He must have been trying to get back at me in some way through preying on you. I thought he might behave better tonight. Clearly I was wrong. I'm sorry."

"Don't blame yourself," I said. "You're not at fault. I'm sorry for spoiling your evening. And please don't do anything to him on Monday. I don't want more attention drawn to myself."

"If he tries to tease you about that or anything," Scarlett said, "let me know and I'll make sure he'll never be able to utter a single word ever again."

"All right," I said, though I probably wouldn't tell her at all. I didn't want anyone to know what happened.

CHAPTER 16

The Absentee

School on Monday daunted me. I slid into Scarlett's car after Renée boarded the bus and her morning pep talk consumed me while I prayed in silence that I would survive the day and perhaps make a friend.

"Relax and breathe. It's not going to be that bad," she said as she pulled out of the driveway.

"Yeah," I muttered, averting my gaze to stare out the window at the neighboring homes surrounded by trees.

"Aren't you excited to show off your outfit? That's what first days are for anyways. When people lay their eyes on you, they'll see how lovely you are inside and out."

Since most of my clothes were old by now, Scarlett let me borrow an outfit from her closet. She promised to take me shopping at some point for a brand-new wardrobe. I wore a pink V-neck sweater with a pair of denim jeans. Scarlett even fixed my blond hair, pulling it out of my face in a half-up half-down hairstyle. I hoped I would blend in with the rest of the school.

Scarlett pulled crisp and smooth into the parking lot. We parted ways as soon as we entered school, and I ducked my head to avoid all the stares and whispering. I tried to find my locker. My heartbeat quickened as I checked for any signs of Heath as though he stood right behind me. I made it all the way to my locker without running into him. I sighed in relief.

"Hey, Abigail!" A voice called to me and I tried to turn my head away. The person's deep welcoming voice sounded familiar. I glanced up to see Jake hurrying to catch up to me as I placed my books inside my locker.

"How are you doing after the party?" Jake asked as he approached.

"Fine," I said. "I don't want to discuss it."

"Right," he said with a nod. "As you say. How is your first day of school so far?"

"Too soon to tell. Thanks for asking though." I closed my locker and started in the direction of my class along the same hallway.

"I'd be happy to help you catch up on classes," Jake added as he walked alongside me. "What's your first class?"

"Intermediate chemistry," I said.

"That's my first class as well," Jake said. "Down the hall."

I kept walking amid the curious glances from other students and felt more courageous with someone I trusted beside me.

"Do you want to meet sometime this week to go over the material?" Jake asked.

"Sure," I said with a smile, though I didn't need the help. I wanted to spend time with him. I welcomed his kindness like the drizzle of rain over a flowerbed.

"I'll meet you in the library, perhaps tomorrow afternoon?"

"Sounds like a plan," I said and a bubble of excitement rose in me, knowing that I would get to spend more time with Jake. It made getting over Heath feel lighter and easier. It seemed like an answer to my prayer and perhaps Jake could be that relationship that gave me joy. Though I couldn't help but feel nervous that something would go wrong as it had with Luke and then Heath.

I found the chemistry classroom, thanks to Jake's help, and he waited for me to enter the classroom first. When I settled along the side of the classroom and the rest of the class entered, one seat remained unoccupied a row behind me. Jake sat further in the back because the teacher gave us assigned seating. I wondered who hadn't shown up to class.

When the bell finally rang on Monday afternoon, I breathed a heavy sigh that I'd reached the end of my first day as the new student.

I hoped as time passed, I would make friends rather than people giving me pointed stares and asking me if I was the new girl from the party who jumped in the pool. One aspect that relieved me is that I hadn't run into Heath all day, though I spent most of it looking over my shoulder as if he was about to appear. At lunch, I ended up sneaking a bag of chips into the library because I couldn't find a table with anyone I knew.

As the sound of the bell subsided, I hurried out of the classroom and to my locker. I had half an hour before track practice started. OPTI required me to join the track-and-field team so I could stay in shape for OPTI's plan and I found out about it this morning before I left the house. To wait, I decided I would probably head to the library to get a head start on my homework. When I reached my locker, I stuffed some books I would need into my bag and slammed the locker shut, only to nearly have a heart attack upon encountering a tall robust boy leaning against the locker next to mine.

Not just anyone. The one person I least wanted to see today.

"What are you doing?" I cried. "You nearly gave me a heart attack."

Heath looked amused by that and straightened up. "I came to see you," he said. "We got cut short at the party this past weekend. Let's continue from where we left off."

I scowled. "Look, you can save your breath because I'm not interested," I said, slinging my backpack over my shoulder before brushing past him.

Doing so proved a poor attempt to lose him. He caught up to me in seconds.

"I know we got off on the wrong foot that evening," Heath said. "I think it would be great if we could see each other again some time." He leaned his head down so his lips were right at my ear. "Alone."

I shoved him away with my elbow. "I don't want to see you again," I said. "In fact, you'd better get out of here. I told Scarlett not to bother with you. If she sees you troubling me again, there's no stopping her. Plus this weekend, she bought a new pair of shoes with extra-pointy heels. You don't want to cross her."

"I can take Scarlett," he said. "I'm not afraid of a flimsy pair of shoes. Scarlett doesn't need to worry. I'm going to treat her younger sister with absolute respect." He placed a hand on my shoulder and I pushed it away with my hand.

"You're unbelievable," I growled and tried to quicken my pace which proved futile and I even heard him chuckle.

"Don't think I'm oblivious," he said. "I know you liked that as much as I did."

I frowned. "I don't think I enjoyed having you force yourself on me," I said. "Pushing someone away is not a sign of enjoyment."

"Maybe you got nervous," Heath said. "You did enjoy all that transpired before. After all, you kissed me back."

At last, I found the ability to divert my gaze, choosing to look out one of the large windows where students stretched out on the grass, reading or talking among themselves. A group of people who had attended Scarlett's party gawked at us as they passed.

I avoided the question. "I know the only reason you're into me is because I'm Scarlett's younger sister. Well, in case you didn't notice, Scarlett and I are not that similar when it comes to boys."

"I know," Heath said. He stepped closer to me and grabbed my hand. "Scarlett may be attractive but you're definitely the more appealing one."

"You kissed her first," I pointed out. "You didn't even mean it."

"You're the girl for me, Abigail. If you want, you can meet me at the edge of the forest and we can get to know each other all you want. Come on."

He grabbed my arm and started to pull me outside. I braced myself on the door. "I have practice now," I said. "I can't go anywhere with you."

"Ah yes," Heath said, "I almost forgot you're on the track team."

"How did you know that?" I cried.

"It says so on your jacket," he said with a smirk.

I looked down at my jacket that read "Greenfield Track Team" in green letters and scowled.

"Well, then I'd better go," I said. "I don't want to be late."

"Practice doesn't start for half an hour, I'm sure you have plenty of time," Heath said. "Don't worry, I know how important it is to be on time."

"And how would you know?" I challenged. "How do you know it doesn't start in ten minutes?"

"Because..." Heath said with a grin and reached into his old-looking bag to pull out a small black spiral notebook. He handed it to me, and I realized I held my agenda. "You have the time written down in here."

"How did you get this?" I demanded, moving out of the way of some students coming through the doorway.

"You dropped it on the floor in the hallway," Heath said which I knew was a lie because I rarely took it out of my backpack, except to write my homework down and usually I did that in class. "You should keep better track of your belongings. They might fall into the wrong hands."

"Clearly it already has," I said. "You didn't have to read it."

"How else could I have planned to meet with you after school?" he asked. "There was no way you were going to explain all those things in person. You shouldn't put so much information into one flimsy notebook."

"Well, I didn't expect you to read it," I grumbled and then looked at my watch. I had twenty-five minutes. Why couldn't time move quicker? "Now that I think about it, I have to go change for practice so I have enough time to warm up. Please leave me alone." I started back inside the school toward the girls' locker room. I glanced behind me and relief came over me to know he stopped following me.

The next day, in midafternoon, I entered my intermediate chemistry class filled with excitement at the prospect of seeing Jake. To my dismay, I found out Heath was also in this class. He had been the absent student. What could he have possibly preoccupied himself with aside from showing up to class yesterday?

Jake flashed a smile my way and my heart soared. I smiled back at Jake and sat down. My hands searched my backpack to find my notebook safely tucked away. Class began and I did my best to focus.

It took everything I could to ignore the temptation to turn around and look at Heath. When I looked around to check, he met my eyes. His eyes turned cold and I scowled at his frustrating attitude and behavior as if I had wronged him in some way. I wanted Heath to leave me alone so I could move on from the incident. I hoped—I prayed—for some relief. I wished my life would go back to how it was before Heath had pressured me to sleep with him. Admitting this wish to myself presented difficulties because at some point up until the incident, I had genuine feelings for him. I missed the person he had been before. Why did he have to destroy the relationship we had? I found it disappointing that my love interests so far always came with a burden attached to them.

When my second day ended, I was excited to spend time with Jake and study the class material. I met up with him in front of the library.

"How much do you know about chemistry?" Jake asked.

I began to feel sweaty. "Um…a lot, actually… It's my favorite subject," I said. There seemed no point to our meeting except to spend time together. "But…I'm sure there's something I've missed."

"Well…great." He opened the door and gestured for me to walk inside.

My eyes flickered immediately in the direction of the front desk where, of course, Heath lounged on a wheelie chair next to the librarian. I heaved a sigh of disappointment. Heath noticed me and glowered over my head at Jake.

"Let's go find a table," Jake said. I glanced behind me at him. He busied himself with scanning the room for an open table and didn't notice Heath's glare.

"Can I help you, dear?" Heath projected at me.

Now Jake's head turned.

"Heath," he said in a cheery tone. "Great running into our Tartuffe. We're doing fine, thank you."

"Just trying to be of assistance," Heath said with a shrug as if he were oblivious to the reason I glared at him. "You looked lost."

"When did you start working here?" I asked, hoping Jake didn't notice my irritation.

The librarian's eyes glowed. "Since the beginning of this year. He's a wonderful man, a true gentleman." She patted his shoulder. "Quite the expert when it comes to theater, public speaking, and history."

Heath brandished a triumphant smile at me and then winked. He adjusted the blazer he wore over his shirt.

"We're just trying to find a table," I muttered. "Come on, Jake."

I headed away from the entrance to the back of the library where I found a couple of empty tables. Only a muted hum filled the library at this point, and I sat down at a table. Jake slid in across from me, and soon, we focused on our chemistry work. It consisted of Jake quizzing me on the atom's properties and me lecturing Jake on the atom model, electrons, and protons while I visualized the components in my head like a map. I finally stopped myself once I opened a discussion on electronegativity.

"Can I walk you to the change rooms?" Jake asked and I found myself beaming as I replied with a yes. As we departed the library, I glanced at the front desk, expecting to see Heath but he had departed from his seat for which I was glad.

I continued to walk with Jake, reflecting on the unexpected joy that consumed me around him, and I realized with relief that there remained a promise of romance in my life that made me feel safe. In some ways, I'd found a doorway to freedom; and with every subtle brush of the hand, I clung to hope in Jake and I wanted to cherish this feeling while I had it. I felt this sense of safety came from Jesus. I knew my prayers of freedom had received an answer. I couldn't believe my luck.

"I have something for you," Jake said, and I stopped in the hallway as he pulled out a small bunch of light-blue flowers. He held them out in the palm of his hand.

"For you," he continued as he placed the bunch into my palm. I felt a tug in my chest. One activity I missed over the last year involved spending the spring and summer gardening, watching the beauty of seeds spring to life in elaborate assorted colors. "I thought they matched your eyes." Jake went on. "It's from a Cape plumbago bush. These flowers grow in bunches. They're evergreen, and they need very little water so they're very strong…like you." Now he looked nervous.

I didn't expect the compliment and now I stumbled over my words. "I…well…thank you," I said. "You're…um…very generous."

Jake smiled. "There's something else I'd like to say to you," he said and his nerves appeared to return. "Would you like to go to dinner sometime?"

I hesitated. That was a pretty big step for me. How could I refuse?

"I would," I replied. "Just name the time and place."

His smile brightened and he looked relieved. "I'll surprise you. Well, then I'll see you on Saturday. How about at eight?"

A small cough from behind Jake caught my attention. A little ways down the hall, Heath stood in front of the doors to the library, looking like he scrawled something in his notebook. I knew he hung on every word Jake and I spoke.

I scowled in his direction.

"What's wrong?" Jake asked, looking behind him, and then he saw Heath standing there. He looked back at me. "Is he bothering you?"

"Yeah," I said, loud enough that I hoped Heath heard it. He buried his face deeper into his notebook and his pen moved at a faster pace than usual. "He won't leave me alone."

"Well, I could talk to him," Jake said.

"No, it's okay," I said. "He'll go away eventually. I want to focus on us. You don't have to surprise me. I don't like surprises. Where should we go to dinner?"

"All right. Wherever you want to go," he said.

"How about a French restaurant?" I asked. "*Claude's* is a good place."

"Then it's settled. Can I have your number?"

Keeping my voice low, I gave him my phone number and address, and when I looked behind him again, Heath was gone. Good. I hoped I wouldn't have to deal with him anymore.

Jake walked me the rest of the way to the locker rooms for track practice. Unfortunately when I entered the locker room, despair crippled my mind once more and the fluttery happiness I had gained from spending time with Jake faded away into solace. Here I stood, left with the darkness of my thoughts, the utter exhaustion of my brain, and the feeling that I wanted to die just to escape the wall of darkness I'd stepped behind ever since I left the prison.

CHAPTER 17

Intrusion

On Saturday evening, Jake and I arrived at the restaurant in the center of town. The room was crowded with diners in fancy attire, sipping martinis, and indulging in fresh soft baked bread. I realized I must have picked the wrong restaurant because I felt underdressed and I worried that the bill might be too expensive for Jake.

Jake announced our reservation to the host and the host escorted us to a booth at the side of the restaurant. We both took our seats.

"Thanks for treating me," I said. "The food is excellent here."

"It is," Jake replied. "Actually I used to be a food critic for the school newspaper. Gave this restaurant a lovely review. Don't order the escargot if you can't handle it though."

I laughed. "Thanks for the tip."

I looked around the room and examined the decor on the walls, ranging from French quotes of *Je t'aime* to illustrations of the Eiffel Tower. Right in the center of the restaurant stood a pillar surrounded on all sides by the familiar OPTI screens. I turned my attention away from OPTI to survey a painting and hoped to retrieve a subject to get the conversation started.

"Ever been to Paris?" I asked.

"No," Jake said. "My family doesn't travel very often. It doesn't look good to OPTI."

"I've never been abroad," I said. "It seems like such a different world."

The waiter came over to ask about drinks.

"Speaking of traveling," Jake said when she left, "where were you before...um...before you moved here?"

"I, uh, stayed at a boarding school," I said. "I wanted a change in atmosphere from this small town."

"What was your school like?"

"I mostly studied similar subjects and trained physically," I said.

His eyes widened. "Really? How did you train?"

"We kickboxed and had swim trials."

"Were they your extracurricular?"

"No. I was required to train every day. OPTI wants me to go into law enforcement. I suppose it was preparation."

"Really? I have a passion for journalism on crime. We could work together." He smiled, though I tried to hide my frown.

"Are you the editor of the school newspaper?" I asked. I hoped to change the subject.

"No. That's my goal. I focus on reporting crime and natural disasters."

"That sounds like a hard job," I said. "Does it upset you to be around so much tragedy?"

His face fell before he answered. "Well, my father was murdered when I was a child. It drew me to the career path and made me determined to help in some way. I guess my job is more about making sense of tragedy for those who don't know how to cope with it."

"I'm sorry you lost your father that way," I said. "Did you ever get his...murder...solved?"

"No," he said. "I hoped I would someday investigate it myself. All the evidence is in the police department's hands, and well, too much time has passed."

"You can still make a difference now," I said. "Getting information of a homicide to the public could help you catch the criminal."

Jake nodded. "Do you want to go into forensics?"

"Forensics?" I asked.

"Only because you're very gifted at chemistry. You could become a forensic specialist."

"I don't know," I said, shaking my head. "I don't know if I'm qualified."

"You know more about the subject than I do and we're not even in the same year."

I smiled and cast my eyes downward. "Thanks. I guess I'll think about that career."

"I wondered," he said after a pause. "Why did you transfer from your boarding school? If you don't mind me asking."

"I had a terrible time there and I wanted to be with my family," I said. I felt guilty for pretending I went to boarding school. I couldn't tell him OPTI put me in prison for murder. "I thought I would like my boarding school. Instead it was way too demanding."

"That's understandable," he said. The conversation subsided and I began to grow nervous that this date wouldn't go well. The waiter spared us an uncomfortable silence when he asked to take our orders. We both ordered the steak frites.

I glanced to my right and stiffened. A burly man sat at a table nearby, across from a slender dark-haired woman. The man held my attention the most. He had a strong build with familiar striking black hair. His luminous gray eyes were engaged with the woman in front of him. *Heath.*

"Abigail, is everything all right?" Jake asked as he noticed I wasn't focused on him anymore.

"Um…yes…" I said. My eyes flitted back to Heath as I tried to recover from bewilderment. Our eyes met and a wide grin spread across his smug face. He adjusted his tie and looked back over at the girl he dined with.

"Abby?" Jake said.

I'd zoned out quite a bit. I dragged my attention away from Heath and faced Jake. My eyes settled on his kind face and I tried to pretend I hadn't seen anything. He looked concerned. "Are you okay?"

"Um…yeah, yeah…I'm fine," I said. "I'm sorry. I got distracted."

"Do you want another drink?" Jake asked, and I also noticed my glass had emptied.

"No, thank you," I said. "So what were you saying?"

He started to talk about his involvement with the school paper. I tried to listen and nod at the right times. I couldn't keep my focus from Heath's large figure. His eyes gleamed like he'd won something. Our dinner arrived, though I felt too nauseous to take a single bite.

"Are you going to audition for the play?" Jake asked, his dark eyes were soft, and for a moment, I thought it might be enough to get Heath off my mind.

"Yes, I think I will," I said. I forced myself to take a bite of the steak I ordered. My stomach churned. "I don't know if I will even have time to do it though. I have mandatory practice for the track team every day after school. Not to mention there's always Renée to take care of. My mother isn't always there to do it, and well, I worry if Scarlett and I don't take the time to take care of her, she'll be neglected. So I don't know how I would have time for play rehearsals too."

"It won't hurt to try at least," Jake said, "and if you ever need anyone to maybe babysit or do any favors, let me know."

"Oh, you're too kind," I said with a grateful smile. "Thanks for the offer, I'll think about it."

I stopped when I felt the hair on the back of my neck rise. I stiffened. I had the strangest sentiment that someone watched me. I craned my neck to take a glance around me and I found myself locking eyes with *his* gray ones again. He held my gaze the way he always does, looking triumphant.

Finally I broke our gaze. Now my mind freshened with thoughts of him. Of Heath and his eyes that allured me.

"Will you excuse me for a minute?" I said to Jake, trying to stay calm. "I have to use the ladies' room."

"Of course," he said.

I got up, grabbed my purse, and headed for the bathroom in the back of the restaurant. I had to climb down a small staircase to reach it. Luckily no one was in the bathroom when I entered and I leaned back against the door, squeezing my eyes shut, wondering if what I saw could be happening or not.

Why did he follow me here? Was he obsessed? Why couldn't he leave me alone? It was bad enough that I couldn't keep him off my mind, and now, I had to see him practically everywhere.

I sighed and moved to the sink. I tossed my bag to the side and turned on the cold water to splash it on my face. I hoped it would help me make sense of things. I remained lost and now my makeup ran in streaks down my cheeks.

"Darn," I muttered and grabbed a bunch of paper towels. I tried my best to clean it up so I didn't look like a complete mess.

As I did, I thought about what I should do. I knew I probably should confront him and tell him to leave me alone. Hadn't I already asked him to leave me alone?

That thought came from the sane part of my mind. The other part wished that Heath hadn't tried to force himself on me. Maybe then, I would have wanted to come to this restaurant with him and fall for him.

Ugh, why couldn't I get those thoughts out of my head? I rubbed my forehead, feeling a headache about to come on. Something about Heath captivated me and I couldn't let go of that feeling—the fact that whenever we met each other's eyes, it left me speechless. I wanted the Heath that I'd known at the party before he took things too far. My mind lingered on that night when he kissed me while enveloping me in a warm embrace. Heat filled my cheeks, and when I looked in the mirror, they were red. When I'd kissed Heath that night, I had lost all control. He had such a hypnotizing effect on me and it frightened yet thrilled me all at the same time.

I shook my head, again and again, breathing deeply, in through my nose and out of my mouth. A bowl of mints perched on the counter. I took one, tossed it into my mouth, and hoped I could freshen more than my breath.

When I felt ready to leave and came to my nervous decision to confront Heath, I exited the bathroom. As I entered the tiny room outside the bathroom, I walked right into someone.

I stumbled back; a strong hand caught my wrist before I could fall. I looked up into the eyes of the one person I tried so hard not to think about.

"Sorry about that," he said, "I didn't see you there."

I gaped, unable to formulate a sentence. "What…"

"Did I startle you?" he continued. "Sorry about that."

My mind finally cleared and I lowered my voice. "Heath. What on earth are you doing here?"

"I'm here to eat and I'm on a date," he replied. "Like you and that stupid boy you agreed to come here with."

"He's not stupid and at least he doesn't follow me around," I said. "I don't care if you say you're on a date. It's no coincidence that you're here."

"Of course it's a coincidence," he said. "I'm not here to see you. I have a wonderful girl with me. She's on the field hockey team."

"That's hard to believe," I said. "You followed me here on my date for—for what purpose? Is this all some joke to get on my nerves? Well, no one is laughing except for you."

"Actually," Heath took a step closer, causing me to step back. "There's a reason why I followed you here." He took another step toward me, and I knew if I took another step back, he would have me trapped against the wall. So I stayed in the same spot.

"What reason could you possibly have for stalking me and—and—"

Before I could utter another word, he leaned forward, about to kiss me, but I turned my head sharply so his lips met my cheek instead. Before he could try to kiss me again, I pushed him back.

"Stop it," I said, "you can't do that. We're not together. I'm seeing someone now."

"So?" Heath said, taking a step forward. I moved to the side so I no longer stood in between him and the wall. "So what if we're not together?"

"I don't want to be with you," I said, "I—"

"Don't want to be with me?" He clenched his jaw. "Is that why you finally agreed to go out with that Jake Chambers? Was it really because you don't want to date me? Or were you trying to make me jealous?"

"I wasn't—"

"Don't lie to me," Heath said. "You're very bad at it."

"I didn't lie," I said. "You can't kiss me. Jake and I are dating."

"Which makes this even more exciting, don't you think?" Heath said, grinning devilishly. "I watched you all night at dinner. I could tell you don't really like him. And then when you looked at me, I knew you wanted me."

"Well, you were wrong," I said, shaking my head furiously. "I like Jake. He's sweet, funny, charming, smart, and—"

"Completely boring," Heath muttered. "Why would you even waste your time with him? Well, I guess it was worth it since it's fun knowing he's completely oblivious to the fact that you're cheating on him with me."

"No, I'm—"

As I spoke, Heath strode forward and his lips came crashing down on mine again. I refused to kiss him back. I could tell it irritated him because at one point, he bit my lower lip. I slid down and tried to go under his arm. He moved quicker than me and easily pulled me back to him, pressing his body close to mine. My back pressed against the wall again.

"Stop trying to get away," he muttered. "It's tiring having to pull you back."

"I mean it," I said stiffly. "Let me go. I don't want this."

"Yes, you do," Heath said. "You just won't admit it to yourself." He moved his lips to my ear and murmured, "Now kiss me, Abby, you know you want to."

I shook my head.

"The truth is," Heath continued and reached a hand up to cup my chin, "I want you back too." He leaned his forehead against mine. "So let's get back together, that way we won't have to pretend not to like each other. Now kiss me, Abby."

He tilted my chin up and tried to kiss me again. I had enough of these games and I swung my fist up and forward, meeting his cheek. He staggered backward, clutching his sore cheek, his luminous eyes clouding in anger.

"Stay away from me," I growled and strode past him back up the stairs to where Jake waited for me.

The date ended well, though it left me in a haze and Jake had to repeat some of his questions while he adjusted his collar, appearing nervous as if he thought I lost interest. I didn't see Heath for the rest of the evening and I relaxed a bit. He left the restaurant as soon as he returned from the bathroom and I hoped it meant he would leave me alone for good. I didn't tell Jake about him following me there. Although I knew it wasn't my fault, I still felt guilty for Heath kissing me like that. If I told Jake about Heath trying to kiss me, it would have ruined the evening and would he believe me that it wasn't mutual?

After dinner, Jake drove me home and then walked me to my door. He gave me a gentle kiss that felt warm and refreshing. Despite Jake's presence, I couldn't stop thinking about how Heath had actually followed me to my date and tried to force himself on me again. I wanted it to stop. I didn't know what to do.

When I walked inside the house, I braced myself to find even more of a disaster. Scarlett, the babysitter for the evening, slept on the living room couch and Renée fixed her gaze on the television displaying one of Scarlett's favorite reality TV shows.

"How was it?" I asked Renée as she came to give me a hug.

"Dreadful," Renée said. "I'm so glad you're home."

"Did you eat at least?" I asked.

"Yes," Renée said, "Though I had to order the pizza."

I sighed in exasperation. I looked back over at the sofa where Scarlett lay, rubbing her drooping eyes.

"You couldn't even order a pizza, Scarlett?" I cried.

"Renée knows how to use the phone by now," Scarlett said as she sat up. "I was teaching her how to be independent."

"You're the worst babysitter ever!" I shouted a little louder than I intended.

"Whoa, Abby," Scarlett said, getting off the couch to come up to me. Renée did the same. "What happened to you?"

"Nothing," I said, "I had a good date."

"It doesn't sound like it," Scarlett said. "How could you have a good date with Jake? He's not nearly that attractive."

"Well, I like him," I said. "He's a nice boy."

"Tell us about it then," Scarlett said. "Why do you look so upset?"

"I don't feel like it," I said and started past her toward the stairs.

"Oh, come on," Scarlett said. "You have to explain why you're in such a bad mood."

"Heath was there!" I blurted. "He showed up at the restaurant with a date of his own."

"Heath?" Scarlett said, her eyes wide. "Why on earth would he show up there?"

"He's been bothering me ever since the party," I said, "and he was there when Jake asked me out. That's how he knew where I would be."

"You should do something about it," Renée said, looking concerned. "He shouldn't be following you around like that."

"What can I do?" I asked. "He won't leave me alone."

"Call the police then," Scarlett said. "Or better yet, I'll take him on."

"Don't do that," I said, "I don't want him to hurt you."

"Then call the police," Renée urged.

"What would I say?" I said.

"Tell them he's stalking you," Scarlett said.

"I-I...I don't know," I said. "I don't want him to get in trouble or anything."

"Why not?" Scarlett said. "If they investigate, you'll know the truth of what happened and he'll know to leave you alone."

I hesitated.

"Do it, Abigail," Renée said, taking my hand. "It's not okay for him to do that."

Scarlett gazed at me with a pressing stare.

"All right, all right," I said and pulled my phone out of my purse while my sisters returned to the living room couch. I dialed the number for the police and waited for someone to pick up.

"Hello?" came the voice of a male officer. "Can I help you?"

I swallowed back my nerves. "I want to report a crime," I said.

"What crime?" the officer asked.

"I'm being stalked and...um...I don't know the word for it... well, he sort of...forced me to kiss him," I said and kept my voice low as if Heath were in the room.

"By who? What is their name?"

"H-heath, Heath Harrison."

"And what is your name?"

128

"Abigail Richardson," I answered.

"Explain what happened."

"I went out to dinner tonight…on a date at *Claude's*. And he was there."

"What was he doing?"

"He was on a date too," I replied.

"That doesn't sound like stalking. Maybe he was actually on a date. It's a small town, after all."

"I know he stalked me," I insisted. "He followed me to the bathroom and—"

"Are you sure you're remembering it correctly? How much did you have to drink? He was probably trying to use a restroom."

"I didn't have anything to drink," I lowered my voice again out of embarrassment. "And he kept trying to kiss me."

"Have you dated this man?" he asked.

"Well, no, we didn't date because—"

"If you weren't dating then there's not much I can do. That stuff doesn't happen unless you're dating, honey. Your mind must be playing tricks on you. Perhaps you need to move on. He's clearly moved on if he's dating someone else. There's nothing I can do."

The officer's words confused me. It only mattered if we dated? What mind tricks? Had I wanted Heath to kiss me tonight? My lingering feelings for Heath made me uneasy. Did that mean I encouraged him to make advances on me? Then my mind recovered my memory of turning my head away from him and punching him in self-defense.

"Please help me," I said. "He is stalking me and I highly doubt he's moved on."

"I'm sorry but I don't have the time to investigate a case with no real leads and with no factual evidence. He was most likely on his own date. Try not to provoke him to kiss you next time."

"What?" I cried. "I didn't—"

The officer didn't say any more and I realized he hung up. I lowered the phone from my ear. Despite the officer's reassurance that Heath didn't stalk me, I held onto my belief that Heath came to the restaurant to see me, not for a date. Now I had to deal with Heath on my own.

"I'm tired," I said to Scarlett and Renée who looked dismayed by the phone call. "I'm going straight to bed."

"I'll clean up then," Scarlett said and I mustered a smile.

"Thank you. Renée, you should go to bed too. Mother will be home soon."

Renée nodded and the two of us ascended the front staircase to our rooms. I gave Renée a kiss on her forehead before I went inside my room. I couldn't settle my buzzing mind. What would Heath do if he found out I called the police on him? I wanted him to leave me alone so I could move on. I lay awake all night, worrying that Heath would keep showing up in places where I happened to be. Every time I pictured his face, I even questioned whether I should have reported him and the officer's insinuation that I provoked him left me wondering if that statement rang true. It seemed as if Heath acted like two different people: one that I'd fallen for and the other that wanted more from me than what I could give. Had I provoked him? Perhaps I shouldn't have agreed to date Jake while he had stood in the same hallway. But nothing could change what he did. He still forced me to kiss him tonight. I was certain of it.

CHAPTER 18

Stalker

The next week and a half in school brought additional stress to my already-burdensome problems. The classes I enrolled in to prepare me for OPTI's program for a career in law enforcement or the military demanded a good amount of my time and my workload climbed in piles until I felt like my hair would fall out. I found time to audition for the next school winter play of *Richard III* and excitement filled me at the chance to explore Shakespeare, an opportunity lost in my English class which mostly focused on grammar and stories about OPTI's greatness. Track-and-field practice was grueling. I developed shin splints over time and had days where I could barely move without pain. The worst part was we had a meet this weekend, and no matter how hard I tried, I still struggled to compete against the other runners. Meanwhile the lack of help from the police left me on edge. My mind was preoccupied so much with searching for signs of Heath that sometimes I lost focus whenever I spoke with Jake. It was a shame because I wanted to keep dating him. I knew Heath would most likely be on the lookout.

"I'd like to go out with you again," Jake said when we were both standing at my locker. He tucked a strand of hair behind my ear. His eyes were softened, warm and brown. "Do you feel the same?"

"Yes," I answered and looked over Jake's shoulder in case Heath happened to be standing in the vicinity, taking notes. He had even been absent in intermediate chemistry for which made me glad.

Jake smiled. "Good."

I returned it. "I'm busy this weekend though," I went on. "I have a track meet...Do you want to come?"

"I'd love to," Jake said, "I'd go anywhere with you."

"That's sweet," I said. "It'll make the meet a lot less miserable. I'll text you the details."

"I could give you a ride there," he offered. "That way, you can focus on your meet."

"Thanks. I'll be too nervous anyways."

"You'll be fine," Jake said, and the gentleness of his gaze almost gave me hope.

He leaned forward to brush his lips against mine. As he did, thoughts about Heath kissing me at the restaurant on our date swirled around in my brain. Guilt overwhelmed me and I tried to push it away. I wanted to enjoy Jake's warmth and the security he made me feel. When we broke away, I immediately glanced behind Jake again and thought I saw a head of black hair among the crowded hallway. A couple of students moved to leave the hall and I could see that it wasn't Heath at all, just a boy I didn't know. I sighed, aggravated that I had to be on the lookout.

"Are you okay, Abby?" Jake asked.

"Um...yes," I said, "I'm just...I'm not looking forward to this meet."

"You'll do great," Jake replied. "Nerves are normal. Take some deep breaths."

"Okay," I said, wishing all of my problems could vanish with a few breaths.

"Don't forget," Jake added. "Callbacks are this Friday. Congrats on getting one! I can't wait to hear which part you're going to get."

"Oh, well, thanks," I said. "Same to you."

He gave me a pat on the shoulder. "We can discuss the results on Saturday."

The rest of the week flew by and I occupied myself with homework, staying in shape for the meet, the final audition for the play; unfortunately Heath was present—and taking over Scarlett's job of looking after Renée despite not being able to drive. Scarlett started teaching me because with all of the household duties falling to her, she needed all the help she could get. Fortunately I learned to drive quickly and did my best not to crash the car. Mother wasn't around as usual, either out at work or out on dates with her boyfriend, Florian.

On Saturday, I waited in the living room with my track uniform on, hoping Jake would be on time. I absorbed myself in reading a book about the components of the atmosphere compared to the elements in the sea when my OPTI-Phone buzzed. I picked it up from the side table beside the sofa.

"Hello?"

"Abigail," a voice replied and I instantly knew who it was.

"Heath," I growled. "I'm hanging up so—"

"Wait," he said, "let's talk. We never seem to have time for that."

"That's because I don't want to talk to you," I said. "How did you get this number anyways?"

"I stole your notebook," he said. "You shouldn't put your number down unless you want people to call you."

"Well, normally decent people don't steal others' notebooks," I muttered.

"Don't be so bitter," he said. "I only wanted to talk to you."

"All right," I said, "let's talk. What do you want to talk about?"

Before I could hear a reply, the doorbell rang.

"Someone's at the door," I said. "Bye."

I hung up the phone and went to answer the door, expecting to see Jake. When it opened, I saw Heath's large figure leaning against the doorway with a triumphant grin stretched across his face. I scowled and went to slam it closed. He caught the door with his foot.

"Not so fast there," he said and pushed it open so he could step further inside. "I thought you said we could talk."

"I thought we were going to talk on the phone," I said a little nervous now that he had entered my house and no one else was home. "How did you get here so fast?" I asked peering around him, expecting to see some kind of plane or helicopter. "Did you fly here or something?"

Heath looked amused by my confusion. "Not this time," he replied. "I haven't been able to get a plane of my own yet. I'll let you know when I do. You can have the first ride if you want."

"No, thank you," I said, and then it occurred to me that he must have called me from outside my house. "Why did you have to call me to talk to me when you're already here?"

"I was desperate to hear your beautiful voice," he said

"I don't want to hear yours," I said. "So don't call me again."

"And what's going to happen if I do?" he said.

I didn't answer, my mind on my conversation with that officer. I guess I couldn't report him unless we were dating. All I depended on were my desperate pleas in the middle of the night that this would stop and I could enjoy my relationship with Jake. I tried to give my trust to God as I had done other times before, however, I still struggled to believe that my life would turn out okay.

"Why did you come here?" I asked Heath finally. "Are you here to force me to kiss you again? It's getting old."

"And yet I know you love it," he replied.

I looked at his phone again. He had a very expensive kind.

"Isn't that phone expensive?" I asked. "My mother refused to buy Scarlett one. It was also probably because my mother is old-fashioned."

"Do you want it?" he asked, holding it out.

I raised my eyebrows. "You're just going to give it to me?" I asked in shock. "I don't think your parents would like it if you gave that phone away."

"They can always order another one," Heath said. "One phone lost wouldn't hurt."

"No thanks," I said.

"If you'd like, I'm sure I could trade it for something else," he said. "How about some jewelry? Perhaps a diamond necklace."

I scowled, catching on to his game. "You're trying to buy me with gifts, aren't you?" I said. "Well, I don't want anything from you. I can't be bought."

"Suit yourself," Heath said and then moved past me to sit down on the living room sofa. He patted the spot next to him as a gesture for me to sit.

I kept my distance though and chose to sit on the arm of the sofa instead.

"You shouldn't be here," I said. "My…um…boyfriend, Jake, is coming over soon. I'm not sure if he'd like it very much if you were here."

"All the more reason to be here," he said, putting his feet up on the coffee table.

"Please don't do that," I said, "you're going to get dirt all over the table. You haven't even taken your shoes off. My mother will freak if she finds even the tiniest speck of dirt."

"Sounds like your mother needs to relax," Heath said.

"Don't say that about my mother," I snapped. "Are you going to take off your shoes or what?"

"I will," he said. "Come sit here first." He gestured to the spot beside him.

"No way," I said, "I'm not falling for that."

"Then the shoes will stay on," he said.

"Fine," I said, standing up and moving over to the coffee table. I grabbed it and pulled it far enough away so he couldn't put his feet on it. "Two can play at that game."

Heath smirked and then put his shoe-covered feet down on the cream-colored carpet.

"All right, fine," I grumbled and plopped down on the sofa beside him. I kept my distance though. Finally he took off his shoes and tossed them toward the front door. They landed in the front hallway.

"Do you like my socks?" he asked, noticing me staring at his feet.

I rolled my eyes. "Yes, I love them," I said sarcastically. "You're not doing a very good job at trying to make me want to be with you."

"I'm not?" he said.

I gave him a look and then glanced out the front window with hope that Jake would arrive soon.

"I had a nice time seeing you at callbacks for the play," he said. "I knew all you needed was a little persuasion."

I glanced at him. "I didn't need any sort of persuasion," I said. "I decided to do it on my own."

"Well, something must have changed," he said, "and I'm curious as to who inspired that change. You are aware that I always participate in every theatrical event in the school and I always get the best roles. What's going to happen when the director notices how perfect we are for each other and decides to pair us up?"

"I don't think they're going to give a newcomer a big role," I said. "Besides *Richard III* doesn't have many big roles for women. You should do your research before you start making assumptions. If anyone is going to get a big role for a woman, it will most likely be Scarlett. So I don't think I have anything to worry about."

"You know what I think?" he said. "I think you joined the play because of me."

"That's ridiculous," I said. "In case you didn't notice, I don't particularly like you."

"Are you sure about that?" he asked.

"I'm quite sure," I replied. "I don't get why you're wasting your time trying get me to like you. Don't you have any other girls you can chase after?"

"I do," Heath said, looping an arm around the back of the sofa where I sat. "But none of them are nearly as lovely as you."

"Nice line," I muttered, "but I have a boyfriend now. For quite some time, actually."

"I don't care," Heath said and slid his hand up my arm, moving his face closer to mine. I kept telling myself to pull away and stop anything from happening. As soon as I met those bright silver eyes, they paralyzed me. Our faces were inches apart and any moment he would—

The sound of an engine broke me from my daze and I jumped back. I looked out the window and saw Jake's car in the driveway.

"Damn." I heard Heath mutter under his breath.

"Jake is here," I said, jumping up from the couch. "You'd better go. Make sure you leave through the back sliding doors so he doesn't see you. He can't know about this."

The doorbell rang and I went to answer it. Suddenly Heath caught my wrist, spun me around, and crushed his lips against mine. It took me a moment to push him off of me.

"What the heck did you do that for?" I spat. He chuckled and left for the backdoors. I shook my head to clear my thoughts as the doorbell rang again. I took a deep breath, put on a smile, and opened the door.

"Abby," Jake said, a smile breaking across his face. He stepped forward to kiss my cheek. "How are you?"

"I'm great. Just need to gather my stuff," I lied. I still felt a little dizzy. Heath sent me in a panic over trying to cover up him showing up to my home, and I felt like my world spun out of my control. "How about you?"

"Better now that I'm here," he said. "May I come in?"

"Of course," I said, stepping aside. I hoped Heath saw. Maybe he could learn a thing or two about not barging into people's homes without asking.

As if on cue, Heath appeared in the front yard and headed toward his sleek black car that sat in the driveway, looking over his shoulder to watch me as if he waited for something.

"Abby, is everything okay?" Jake said, his smile fading. "You look a little distracted."

Heath winked as I closed the front door. I shook my head again, mostly to focus my attention back on Jake rather than Heath.

"I-I'm fine," I said. "Actually I got distracted because of the book I've been reading. It's quite good. And...I missed you." Before he could reply, I wrapped my arms around his shoulders and kissed him. I felt good knowing that at least this time, I actually wanted to be kissed. Jake wrapped his arms around my waist and I deepened the kiss. I pulled back after a moment and hoped that Heath saw us to make my rejection of him more clear.

"I missed you too," Jake said, kissing my forehead. "Let's get you to your meet."

He opened the front door and waited for me to grab my bag, my water bottle, and my jacket from the living room.

"Whose car was that in the driveway?" Jake asked as I noticed Heath and his car were gone.

"My mother's," I lied. We both settled in Jake's car and he began to drive down our long driveway to the bottom of the hill.

"Have you seen or read the news lately?" he asked.

"No," I said, "Anything new?"

"Several people were found in an abandoned church," he said. "They were singing hymns and one of them preached. OPTI sent forces to stop them."

I frowned. "What happened to them?" I asked.

"They were killed," he said in a firm tone.

I felt a sick feeling in the pit of my stomach. My mind screamed, *How could OPTI do such an awful thing?*

"That's awful…" I swallowed a lump in my throat. If those people were killed, what hope did I have of surviving with my faith?

Jake nodded and remained silent as he drove. I struggled in my mind to keep myself gripped on my faith. It felt like my life depended on it.

"I didn't mean to bring you down just before your meet," he said finally as he noticed my distraught. "I thought you should know."

I couldn't find my words.

"I'm supposed to write a story about it." Jake went on. "For the school paper. I don't know quite yet what to say."

"I'm sure it will come," I managed. "I believe in you."

"Thanks," he said.

We exchanged a fleeting smile, and then he refocused his gaze on the road in front of him.

CHAPTER 19

To Be Wed or Not to Be?

The meet went poorly for me. I came out fifth in the mile. My times still did not impress my coach. Jake was impressed though and his encouragement made me feel better about it. My love for him grew even more and I felt grateful to have him around.

Monday came quickly and I barely finished all my homework. At the end of the day, the bell rang and everyone crowded to exit the classroom. Today the director of the play put up the cast list in the theater building. I walked among a group of students making their way to the theater building to see their part. I spent the whole day fidgeting in class as I worried about what part I would get. I headed for the exit of the main building at a sluggish pace so I wouldn't run into Heath.

When I walked out of the main building I ran straight into Betty.

"What are you walking so slowly for?" she asked me. "Don't you know the cast list is up?"

"I know," I said, "but there's going to be a big crowd."

"Exactly why you should get there right away," she said. "Come on."

I adjusted my walking pace and hurried with Betty to the building where most of the acting, dancing, and singing classes were held as well as the stage. Some people were already gathered around the list. Some were cheering while others looked a little glum with their roles. I honestly didn't care which role I was cast as. I'd probably have a small role anyways.

I lingered on the edge of the crowd, trying to squeeze in. I accidentally knocked into someone and stepped back, muttering an apology. I took another step back and bumped into someone else.

I glanced behind me as I gave another apology and jumped when I met a pair of gray eyes.

"Hello," Heath said. "Have you seen the list yet?"

"No," I replied, turning to look ahead again as I tried to squeeze through.

"Out of the way, idiot," Heath said to a boy. He turned and I recognized him as Kyle Chambers, Jake's brother. "Let the lady through." Heath nodded to me and I scowled. I gave Kyle an apologetic look.

"That won't be necessary," I said, "I don't mind waiting." I gave him a kind smile, hoping to make up for Heath's rudeness.

"Actually I was just leaving," he said, frowning at Heath as he did. "I hope to see you at rehearsal," he said to me.

Heath started pushing his way toward the cast list, nudging a few people aside. I didn't want him to find my name first so I hurried to squeeze in beside him, trying not to push anyone. He beat me to the front.

"Did you find me yet?" I asked.

"I did," Heath said. He sounded thrilled like he had won the lottery. "And I think you're going to love your role."

"We'll see about that," I snapped. "Where is it?"

"Right there," he said, pointing at the list.

I followed his gaze and saw my name beside the character Lady Anne Neville. My eyes widened and I knew if I looked up, Heath would be wearing one of his wicked grins. Lady Anne Neville is a widow of Edward, prince of Wales, and then marries Richard III. Of course, when I looked at the top of the list, I found Heath's name printed in neat font beside Richard III of Gloucester. Richard III and Lady Anne have an important scene where he pleas for Anne's love. Heath had been right—with my luck, I did happen to be chosen to play his wife.

Heath looped an arm around my shoulders. "I just knew it," he said, "even the rest of the world thinks we'd be great together."

I scowled and pushed his arm away. "Don't get too excited," I said. "I've read this play and Richard III doesn't care much for Anne. He tells the audience that he wants to discard her later."

"You're right," he said. "There are some differences between Richard III and myself. For one, I don't have a hunchback, I'm much more handsome and a true gentleman. And I certainly wouldn't discard you."

"I'm not sure if I believe that," I said with a chuckle. "You have no problem forcing me to kiss you. If you're willing to force yourself on me, you'd definitely be willing to discard me."

"You'd be surprised," Heath replied. "I haven't given up on you for this long and you can bet my pursuit of you will last the rest of the year if I have to."

I scowled. "You're unbelievable." I turned away from the list as a gasp came from behind me.

"I'm *not* Lady Anne Neville?" Scarlett cried suddenly to her friends.

Uh-oh. I guess there were two reasons why this role would be the death of me. Beside me, Heath snickered as Scarlett approached the list. Her eyes lit in surprise when she read my name.

"Well, I'll be…leaving now," I said to Heath and turned to move past him. He stuck out his arm.

"Oh no," he said. "You're not going anywhere."

"Abigail?"

I turned and saw Scarlett glaring at Heath. "I thought I told you to stay away from her or I will smother you in your sleep."

Heath didn't seem at all bothered by that. "Oh, Scarlett, you make me soar with your sweet words of endearment," he said as if he were reciting a sonnet. "Anyways I think you two have a lot to talk about. I wouldn't want to get in the way."

He left and I turned to Scarlett, praying I wouldn't meet a spiteful angry glare.

"So I saw that you're Lady Anne Neville?" Scarlett said, looking like she didn't know whether to be angry with me or not.

"Yes," I said and wrung my hands together. Scarlett didn't say anything for a moment. I reached out and touched her arm. "I'm sorry, Scarlett. I really am. You know I wasn't looking for a big role when I auditioned. I never meant to upset you."

Scarlett sighed. "Well, congratulations," she said, sounding forced.

"Why are you upset?" I said. "It's not a big role."

"It's the toughest scene in Shakespeare," she said and her eyes hardened for a moment. Then her intensity dwindled. "But if I could lose the role to anyone, I'd rather it be you."

"What part did you get?" I asked.

"I'm Queen Elizabeth," Scarlett answered.

"That's the female lead!" I cried and wrapped her in a hug. She returned it after a moment.

"Abigail." I heard from behind me. I stepped out of Scarlett's arms and whirled around to see Jake standing there with a big smile on his face. "Congrats on your role."

I walked up to him to give him a hug as Scarlett scowled at him and then went to meet up with her friends. "Thank you," I said. "Who are you?"

"I'm King Edward IV," he said. "It's not the lead, although it should certainly be a good role to play."

"That's great," I said. "We can probably practice together then. How's your article coming?"

Jake's face fell. "I tried to tell the story right, you know?" he said. "I wish more could be done."

I sighed and my hope flickered as I struggled to understand how I could serve God in a world where Christians' voices were silenced in horrific ways. Could death be the only release or freedom for me and other people of faith?

CHAPTER 20

Stranded

A couple of weeks later, I found myself driving one of my mom's cars to the grocery store from after-school play rehearsal. Scarlett went with some friends to a group study session on a Thursday night and it was my turn to go to the grocery store to pick up dinner for Renée and me and food for the following week. I could drive well enough to get my license by now but nerves filled me. I tried to reassure myself that I drove better than Scarlett who often got distracted by how she looked while doing it.

I took the back roads to be safe. I maneuvered along a windy road and slipped the car around each bend when I heard a sudden thud and the car jerked as though it had hit a bump and the wheel lagged on one side. To my dismay, I had to let the car slow and wobble onto the side of the road, putting on my blinkers as I did. I put the car in park and lowered my face into my hands, terrified that I would now be caught driving without a license.

I decided it would probably be foolish to get out of the car. I didn't know how to fix a flat tire and I didn't have a spare in the trunk. I debated whether I should call a tow truck.

Suddenly there were a pair of headlights behind me and I squinted at them. I rolled the windows down, hoping to ask for help. A small black car pulled up beside mine. The window rolled down and out poked a face I recognized as Heath's.

"Need a hand?" he said, looking amused.

"What are you doing here?" I asked. "Did you follow me?"

"No, of course not," he said. His eyes made it impossible to believe him. "I was headed the same way. We just had play rehearsal, remember? What happened to the car?"

"Flat tire," I said. "I hit a pothole."

"Let me take a look," he said.

"Sure, I guess," I said, giving him an odd stare. I didn't expect him to help me in any way. I opened my door to step out onto the pavement. A gush of chilly air met my cheeks and I wrapped my arms over my coat to warm up. Heath had pulled his car to the side of the road and slipped out, trudging over to the front of my car.

He paused at the wheel on the side I pointed to and bent to inspect it.

"My mother is going to freak," I said. "Renée is home by herself for far too long and now we'll have to pay for a new tire..."

"It's definitely flat and there are even punctures. I know how to replace a tire. I'd do it for free...for you."

"Yeah right," I muttered. "And what do you want in return? Another kiss?" I turned away from him to face the empty road, wishing someone else had stopped to help. "I'll call a tow truck."

"I don't want anything in return," Heath said. "You've won, Abigail. I'm not going to chase you anymore."

"Then why are you here?" I spat, though I hoped his words were true.

"To help you," he said, "that's all."

I stared at him and his face set; not a trace of a smirk on his lips.

"All right," I said. "You can replace it but I don't have a tire. I'll still need to call a tow truck."

"And a ride home," Heath said. "I can take you."

"I'll wait for the tow truck," I said.

"And let them find out you're underage?" Heath asked.

"What else can I do?" I cried and sent up a prayer for help, though I also felt guilty for not obeying the law. I had to take care of the house or we would have no food or clean dishes or clean clothes.

"I'll tell them it's my car," Heath said.

"No, Heath," I said. "You don't have to do that. I'll face the consequences."

"You can't afford to," he said. "I'll keep your secret. You can trust me."

"Trust you? How can I after everything?"

"Everything I did came out of love," he said, "I suppose I didn't express it in the right way."

I studied him and blinked. I wondered if I heard or even saw him in the right light. "This sounds like one of your games to take advantage of me," I said, stepping away from him. "I wouldn't be surprised if you did follow me here."

"You might think so," he said. "But I know the truth. I did nothing of the sort. Now come in my car. It's warm. I have seat heaters."

"I'll wait," I argued.

"I'm not leaving until you're safe," he argued back.

"I doubt I'm safe with you here," I muttered and crossed my arms. In silence, we both waited. A couple of cars passed by and I sighed in relief that none of them were police cars.

"They must be busy," I said.

"Get in," he said and walked over to the passenger side door of his small black car. He opened it and waited for me to come around. "Warm up." His hands moved to my back and he guided me toward the car. "It will be faster."

I sighed. "Fine," I said, "I'm not kissing you though."

I climbed in on the passenger side and he slid into the drivers' seat, pressing the button for the seat heater. I kept my arms crossed as I warmed up.

"Where to?" he asked, flashing me a grin.

"My house, of course. It's about ten minutes away," I said. I gave him the address. "In case you don't remember, it's up on a hill and surrounded by a forest. It's secluded. I like having some privacy."

"Yes, yes," he said as he drove. "Must be nice to be able to keep secrets."

I didn't speak as he drove, embracing the warmth of the car.

"Do you live around here too?" I asked after a moment. "Is that where you were going when you ran into me?"

"No," he said, "I have friends that do though."

"Really?" I said, my voice wry. "I'm sure you must have followed me, of course."

"It's true actually," he said. "I do have friends that live in this area. There's a party tonight. It won't end well though."

"How would you know?" I asked.

"Because I'm not there," he said with an even wider grin.

I scowled. "You're so…" I trailed off.

"What?"

"Arrogant," I said.

"I'm not arrogant," he said. "I'm confident. Are you?"

I didn't answer and turned to watch the forest on the side of the road.

"You don't go out very much, do you?" he asked me.

"No," I said. "I don't have time."

He smirked. "Well, maybe you should make time," he said. "Life is short. You might as well have fun."

I scoffed. "Just because I don't go to huge house parties doesn't mean I don't know how to have fun," I said. "Before you tried to sleep with me, I certainly had a great time at Scarlett's cast party and all it took was a freezing-cold pool."

He gave me a knowing look.

"It took much more than that," he said with a one-sided smirk and his eyes gleamed in the darkness.

I remained silent and stared at the road ahead, feeling relieved to see we had reached a neighborhood lined with beautiful homes, the windows lit like lanterns, permitting release from darkness.

"I do wish I had more time to have fun sometimes," I said. "I'm always focused on my schoolwork and being a good daughter, sister, mother, and caretaker. I forget to let myself have fun."

"Mother?" he asked, his face scrunching up in a mix of confusion.

"Not actually," I said. "I mean that I care for my younger sister, Renée, like a mother would."

"What happened to her actual mother?" he asked.

"At her spa retreat this week," I said. "She'll be back though. She always comes back. That's the one thing we can count on from her."

"Then why did you come home?" he asked. "You could have easily stayed at your boarding school."

"To be with my sisters," I said. "But it's not the same...I guess...a part of me wishes that one day, that house could become my home again..."

"I'd say not to hold onto too many wishes," he said as he turned a corner. "They never come true. And they only keep you waiting. You have to make it your home on your own...or leave until you find a new one."

My face fell at his words. My mind prompted me with a memory of my dream where Jesus baptized me after I nearly died. My wish had been fulfilled at that time, and when OPTI allowed me to leave, I felt God had intervened to give me a chance at freedom and to be with my family. On this lonely road of my life, I reminded myself that I could hope in Jesus to bring me joy and comfort. Like the lit homes on either side of us, I felt that God guided me through the darkness, step-by-step, to a better brighter future, although I couldn't always see a clear path ahead.

"I disagree," I said. "I think if you believe deeply enough, any wish you have can come true. Like a miracle."

"I've lost my belief in miracles," he grumbled. "The world is too dark for them."

"Believe me," I said. "I nearly died twice and God saved my life. God's beaming light can break through even the darkest night. My faith gives me the strength I need to keep going when life is hard."

I realized I spoke the words I needed to hear most as my mind reminded me of those Christians who were killed in church. I clung to hope for a miracle that would put an end to that violence.

Heath glanced over at me and our eyes met. I felt something deep within me that I couldn't explain and the feeling was so unwanted that I buried it down. I feared this inexplicable sentiment in my heart. What was happening to me?

I broke our exchange and averted my gaze, wishing I could conceal my face. I also realized I'd revealed my faith to him. At this point,

I didn't care about the consequences. My faith had become one of the only aspects of my life that truly made me happy.

"There's something I've been meaning to say," he said, and when I looked over at him, his eyes softened. "I'm sorry I've been following you around and forcing myself on you. I've realized I made a mistake out of weakness. Do you think we could start over? Be...friends?"

He stopped at a stop sign and our eyes met again. I kept my gaze on his eyes and couldn't break it as hard as I tried. His eyes glistened with what I could gather as tears and a guilty wounded expression. My heart ached for him.

"Okay," I said in response, though I felt trapped in a fog and my voice grew distant, its volume diminished as if I wasn't here. I wanted to forgive him, to take away his pain. "Let's be friends."

After a short stretch of time in silence, while Heath called for the tow truck, Heath pulled the car up the hill into the driveway. He hung up, and I had to admit, it relieved me that I didn't have to fear a punishment from the police. I would have to tell Scarlett I can't help out with groceries anymore. It's way too risky.

"Thanks for doing that," I said and seized the handle to open the door. "I can't face any more trouble." I stepped down to the ground and stopped when I noticed him getting out.

"I'll walk you to your door," he said, sliding his hands in his pockets as he reached me.

"Sure," I said and started up the steps of the path that led to my front door. I reached into my pocket to pull out my key ring. As I pulled them out, I fumbled with them; they slipped from my grasp onto the paved driveway. Heath and I both bent at the same time to pick them up and our heads bumped into each other.

"Oops," I said.

"I'll get them." Heath's hand reached the keys, and when he rose, we stood in close proximity to each other.

"I have to go," I blurted before anything transpired and turned to climb up the stairs to the front door. Heath trailed behind me. I stopped and craned my neck around when I reached the porch.

"Looks like you won't have a car for some time," Heath said from the bottom of the stairs. "Do you need a ride again at all?"

"Jake can give me a ride," I said.

"Right," he said and turned around.

"Why did you give me a ride anyways?" I asked.

"Because that's what friends do," he said with a glint in his eyes. "Good night, Abigail."

"Good night, Heath," I said and turned to unlock the front door. I glanced back at him with my last words already on my lips. "I hope we can remain friends."

He turned and strode toward his car. I opened the front door to my house and stepped inside, closing it on the shrouded night while I tried to piece together what I experienced tonight with Heath. I leaned back against the door with my hands over my face and sunk to the floor.

CHAPTER 21

Truce and Tragedy

Heath kept his distance from me over the next month. I mostly saw him in rehearsals, and we busied ourselves with rehearsing the scene where Richard III persuades Lady Anne Neville to marry him. To my surprise though, Heath had stopped making advances on me and even stopped his grins whenever we ran the scene. Outside of rehearsals, he had stopped forcing himself on me and he didn't follow me around. I could turn my focus to my relationship with Jake and I enjoyed being his girlfriend. He gave me more flowers on one of our dates. I persuaded him to pick the movie we watched on another date. Finally some part of my life felt more in my control despite OPTI looming in the background, a reminder of the life OPTI sentenced me to have.

Meanwhile I struggled to keep up with assignments from each of my classes along with track and caring for Renée. Perhaps I shouldn't have committed to the play on top of all my responsibilities but I did want the chance to perform. I didn't even want to do track. OPTI had become the reason why I had to run laps every day until my entire body trembled. I lost sleep, having to pull several all-nighters to complete my homework or study for exams. I barely had any time to take a break.

Relief came with the coming winter break, a time of rest and the Christmas holiday. I knew it celebrated the birth of Jesus and I wanted to make the most of it, though OPTI didn't consider it a holiday. I had grown tired of keeping my faith concealed and not having the freedom to express it under OPTI's watchful gaze. I wanted to celebrate it anyways, to do something—anything—to share my spiritual experiences with other people so it might create change to have more religious freedom. I dreamed of the day when I could look up at the starry night sky and feel *happy*. It seemed so simple; an ocean of sorrow seemed to separate me and other people from that possibility.

After school ended the week before break, I met Jake at my locker.

"Ready for the break?" he asked and gave me a kiss.

"Yeah," I muttered with a sigh. "It's exhausting having to keep up with all this work."

"I know. I've noticed how busy you are. Have you ever thought of dropping one of your responsibilities?"

"Yes," I said, "but I don't want to lose my role in the play. It makes me happy to perform."

He nodded in understanding. "What are your plans for break?"

"Well, we're having a family dinner at my house," I said. "Which reminds me, you should come if you can."

"Who's going to be there?" he asked.

"My mother's boyfriend, Florian, is coming," I replied. "It makes me nervous. If you came, it might help ease the tension."

"Of course," he said. "I'd be happy to come for you."

We exchanged another gentle kiss.

"Now I have something to invite you to. I'm going to the lake to write a report on an incident that happened there recently. Do you want to come?"

"Oh, yes," I said. "Let me know the date and address and I'll be there."

Jake gave me a light kiss on the lips and then sauntered off for the newspaper club. I busied myself at my locker, dreading having to go to track today.

"Abigail!" an assertive voice called that belonged, without question, to Scarlett. I turned to see Scarlett rushing toward us with Heath clutching her arm. His eyes rested on me and I returned his stare with my mouth agape.

"What's up, Scarlett?" I asked, looking from her to Heath

"I wanted to um…let you know," she said, looking at Heath. "That we're dating now. I hope it won't be uncomfortable, you know because…"

"Yeah, I know," I said while Heath's eyes pleaded with me like a child who had been caught stealing a toy.

"Heath told me he saved you when you were stranded on the side of the road and that he apologized for his behavior," she said. "And well, I forgive him. He's sorry for how he treated you." Her eyes glistened with genuine forgiveness. "You don't mind if we date, do you?"

Heath pressed me with his stare as if he had asked the question. I didn't want to let Scarlett down so I decided I would permit it.

"No, of course I don't mind," I said while my heart jumped in my chest and my mouth fell open. "Go ahead."

"Good," she said. "I hope you can get to know each other better. Well, see you, sis."

She turned and walked away with her arm linked with Heath's. He turned back as she did and flashed a beaming smile. I stood, watching them leave in the middle of a whirlwind of emotions.

Practice pushed me extra hard today. We ran three miles at a fast pace around the gym with little break. By the time it ended, I felt ready to collapse.

"Abby," the coach said, "you're not in the shape you need to be. What's going on? Have you not been practicing?"

To be truthful, rehearsals for the play took some time out of my regular practicing. That and the exams I had coming up this week.

"I have, Coach." I tried as I headed for the locker room.

"Well, keep running harder," he said. "It's disappointing, honestly."

I sighed in frustration and entered the locker room to change. When I emerged, I gasped when I found Heath standing there.

"What do you want?" I growled.

"Nothing," Heath replied. "I came to give you a message from Scarlett."

"I don't want to hear it," I said and started past him.

"Why are you mad?" he asked. "I did what you wanted and moved on. I've held up my end of the truce, haven't I?"

I stopped and turned to scowl at him. "I know the only reason you're dating Scarlett is to get to me. You shouldn't waste your time because it's not working."

"I'm not doing it for you," Heath said. "I'm actually quite fond of your sister. What's not to like about Scarlett?"

"Would you stop playing these games?" I spat. "You're only doing this to make me jealous. You don't realize that it will hurt Scarlett if she realizes."

"I don't intend to hurt Scarlett at all," Heath said. "I had plenty of fun while I chased after you but you didn't want me to do so. Why can't you accept that I've moved on? Are you jealous?"

"No." I fumed. "You know that I have a boyfriend whom I care about very much. In fact, I care about him so much that I've invited him to dinner to meet with my family this break."

"If you aren't jealous, then why do you have to prove it to me?"

"Once again, I am not jealous," I said, my voice rising. "You have no clue about how I feel because if you did, you would not be traipsing around with Scarlett on your arm to eventually hurt her. We had a truce and you are not sticking to your words. So let me make myself clear. Stay the hell away from me and my family, you complete and utter asshole!"

His face fell. "You know," he said above a whisper, "you're not living up to the truce either. I seriously am pursuing Scarlett because I want to be with her. Why can't you accept that and be civil with me?"

My anger fell away as I watched his sad eyes, and instead, I carried on his sadness as if it were my own. Maybe I had falsely accused him of trying to make me jealous with Scarlett. And he did help me that night when my car's tire flattened. Perhaps his apology was genuine and maybe I was the one who hadn't let what he did go.

"Okay," I said, "I'm sorry that I accused you of using Scarlett and for calling you an asshole. I'll try to be more accepting of you two together. You did help me that night. Like I mentioned, we're having a family dinner this winter break. Why don't you come...as Scarlett's date?"

I didn't quite know why I invited him. How else could I make up for my behavior?

"What's the message?" I asked.

"Florian is planning to propose to your mother at the family dinner."

I wanted to scream.

Scarlett drove me to the lake the following Tuesday morning where Jake told me to meet him. At first, I couldn't see the lake because a forest surrounded it. However, I noticed an opening with a trail leading up to the oasis in our desert town. The sky was overcast, not even a trace of the sun. It saddened me that once I left the car, I would be learning about some sort of tragedy that had taken place here. Two police vehicles were pulled over on the side of the road. Another bluish-gray car pulled up and parked along the side of the road in front of Scarlett's. My sister waved as I stepped out of the car and walked over to Jake's. Scarlett drove away while Jake's door opened and he stepped out, his dark-brown hair looking especially tidy and combed over. I took his hand and together we walked toward the deputy who stood at the entrance to the forest's trail.

"Reports are saying that several people were using this lake to perform secret baptisms." Went on the deputy whom Jake interviewed. He wore a white uniform and it reminded me that someday, I would be wearing that same uniform, forever in OPTI's control. "OPTI's screens were not able to detect this activity until recently. It's uncertain who participated. A couple of the leaders have been arrested."

I exchanged a distraught look with Jake.

"How many people do you think were involved?" Jake asked.

"We don't know due to the lack of surveillance," he replied. "This has led to the construction of screens in the forest surrounding the lake. Unfortunately it will still be difficult to detect illegal behavior."

"Who discovered the problem?" Jake asked.

"Lynn conducted surveillance of the area once OPTI detected suspicious activity. Thanks to Lynn, we were able to capture two of the leaders."

An officer wearing a white uniform strode toward us from the forest.

"And there she is," the deputy said, gesturing to the officer. The woman who the officer called Lynn had fiery hair, slick and long, accenting her lean yet fit body. In spite of her leanness, Lynn bore the muscles of a woman who probably trained much harder than me to keep her look. Her eyes were fierce and green.

"Lynn," the deputy said. "This is Jake Chambers, a high school reporter, and his uh...date."

"Abigail," Jake reminded him. "She's my girlfriend."

"Pleased to meet you, Jake," Lynn said and stretched out a slender pale crisp white well-manicured hand for Jake to take. He shook her hand. "And, Abigail."

She turned to me to take my hand. Her hands were cold, probably due to the temperature; it seemed to suit her.

"How did you manage to capture two of the leaders?" the deputy asked Lynn.

"While I patrolled the forest," Lynn said, "I saw a few people enter. I monitored the trail close to the edge of the lake when I heard people reciting what sounded like prayers. When I arrived at the edge of the lake, the men and women there started to run away through the forest. I managed to restrain two of the leaders who were performing the baptisms."

"What's going to happen to them?" I asked. Like when those people were killed at that church, this story left a sick feeling in the pit of my stomach. It disturbed me that these Christians were hunted for practicing their faith. I worried over what their consequences would be.

"They will all receive the death penalty."

My stomach churned again and my hands balled into fists.

"Is there something wrong?" Lynn asked me.

"They were *innocent*," I cried; all my fear gave way to anger. Jake yanked my arm back as a fist hit my cheek and I fell to the leaf-covered ground. Then a memory hit me—of my sister Faith falling onto the sidewalk after a police officer struck her as well and me clutching her hand. If I had known that I would lose her then, I would have gripped her hand tighter.

"Praise OPTI," Lynn hissed at me from above me. "Without OPTI, we would never get justice against those criminals. How dare they worship anything else besides OPTI?"

"Yes, yes," the deputy said, his face beet red as Jake gave me a hand. "It's very unwise to defy OPTI. You both better leave now and don't speak another word against OPTI. I'll let him know what you did so you can be appropriately punished. Remember if you're caught practicing, little girl, you'll receive the death penalty as well."

Jake and I hurried away toward his car. Jake drove us away from the scene without a word. I kept my gaze averted from his face. He pulled over to the side of the road and then burst into labored sobs.

"That was beyond terrible," Jake said between gasps. "I had no idea they were after Christians. There's something I didn't tell you…" I couldn't look at him, couldn't stand to hear him in pain. Did Faith cry such tears after that blow to her face? I couldn't remember. I wished I could have held her, told her I loved her, and maybe then, I wouldn't have lost her. I took a deep breath and looked over at Jake. A tear slid down his cheek and he shook with anguish. "My father lived as a rabbi in secret. My family is Jewish. I couldn't quite piece it together, but somehow I knew, I felt that his murder was an attack on his faith."

"I'm sorry," I said and placed a hand on his shoulder. I couldn't conjure any other words. "I lost my sister Faith as a young girl. A police officer struck her, like me, for not bowing to OPTI. I'm beginning to wonder whether hate became the motive for her death." And as I spoke it aloud, I knew in my heart, like Jake did, that it was the truth. "No one should die because of what they believe. It has to stop. I don't know what on earth to do about it."

"Thank you for trying," Jake said as he straightened up. "I'm glad someone stood up for them. If only more people tried. The world would be a better place. No one is good or bad simply for their faith. We all deserve to belong in this world. We're all children of God."

I nodded at his words, and I cherished his message, recognizing that I was a child of God like him; we both belonged in God's kingdom. My heart warmed with God's love at a time when I needed it most. Faith had lived as a child of God too and it pained me that someone killed her because of it.

CHAPTER 22

Christmas

"Scarlett. Could you answer the door, please?" my mother asked as she glared down at her from the kitchen. I stood at the stove, steaming the broccoli, wafts of vapor heating my face. "It's probably my future fiancé and soon to be your stepfather. Scarlett, get up off that couch and answer the door."

Scarlett didn't look up from her spot on the sofa, admiring her freshly painted nails.

"First of all, that man is *not* our stepfather. And second, I don't think so," she answered, "I'll sit right here, Mother."

"Scarlett," Mother retorted. "When are you going to learn to accept Florian? We may marry at this point and I would like for you to treat him with respect."

"That man does not deserve my respect or time," Scarlett said. "When are you going to exchange him for someone new?"

The doorbell rang again.

"Someone please answer the door," our mother demanded.

"I'll get it," I offered, though she didn't look at me. "I'm finished anyways." I removed the broccoli I cooked from the pan, into a strainer, and then in a large bowl. I sighed as I headed over to the door, trying to drown out my mother and Scarlett's bickering. Just as my mother said, Florian stood at the door.

"Abigail," he said. "Don't you look nice?" He gave me a creepy smile, peering down at me from the rims of his glasses. He sported a fancy suit as if he dined at *Claude's*, and once again, I felt underdressed.

"Thanks," I muttered. "Come inside. Renée is setting the table."

I led Florian into the kitchen and looked away with a slight grimace as he went to give my mother a kiss.

"Is Heath here yet?" Scarlett asked me, looking up from a magazine.

"No," I answered. "It's Florian. Don't you remember?"

She didn't even look at Florian.

"Ugh," she grumbled for my ears. "At least we could have some-one more interesting present."

Florian listened though because he chuckled. "Looks like your sister's in a bit of a mood, don't you think?" he asked me as if hoping to bond with me.

"That's her usual," my mother said. "Most difficult child I've ever had."

"Most difficult mother in the world," Scarlett shot back. I exchanged a glance with Renée who looked about ready to plug her ears and leave the room.

"Isn't Heath coming soon? Why didn't you invite him?" I asked, hoping to change the subject as I sat down on the arm of the couch.

"I planned on it," she said, "but you got there first...why did you ask him to come again?"

"Because I knew you would forget," I joked. The doorbell rang again. "That could be him or Jake. Want to answer it?"

Scarlett waved me forward, going back to sniffing a perfume sample in her magazine.

I answered the door to find Jake there and beamed at him. I leaned up to give him a soft kiss.

"I'm glad you made it," I said. "How are you doing?"

"Not good," Jake said in a low voice. "I'm glad to see you though." The twinkle in his eyes muted.

"Come in," I said, placing a hand on his back to guide him inside. I wished I could cheer him up. "Help yourself to some refreshments."

He took his shoes off and then followed me into the kitchen.

"Oh, Abigail, is that Heath?" Mother asked, squinting at him brightly as she looked up from the cranberry sauce.

"No, it's Jake, my boyfriend," I answered, giving Jake an apologetic look. "I've been dating him for a few months. Don't you remember?"

"Oh, well, you know me," she said, "always busy. Nice to meet you."

Jake crossed the kitchen to where my mother stood and shook her hand like a true gentleman.

"It's a pleasure to finally meet you, Ms. Richardson," he said. "Your home is beautiful."

"A polite young man, you are," Florian said in praise and clapped him on the shoulder. "Welcome to the family."

I swear I heard Scarlett hiss like a grumpy cat.

I glanced over at the sofa in time to see Scarlett wearing the biggest scowl I'd ever seen on her face. She jumped up from the sofa, tossed her magazine on the coffee table, and stormed away up the stairs.

The doorbell rang again. I retraced my steps to answer it.

I came face to face with a familiar tall strongly built boy with dark hair wearing a white button-down shirt and nice black pants. His inky black hair looked especially clean and trimmed so it no longer hung around his ears. He had a clean-shaven face as well. Even his eyebrows looked like they'd been trimmed. In his hands, he held a small box with a bow tied tight around it.

"Hello, Abigail," he said, flashing me a wide grin.

"H-hi," I stuttered like a fool as I tried to recompose myself. "You look...um...well...nice."

"As do you," he said, his eyes meeting mine.

"Come in," I said, bringing him into the kitchen as Scarlett clamored back downstairs.

Mother's gaze fell on him and she wrinkled her nose as if something smelled. She didn't bother to greet him.

"Heath, darling!" Scarlett cried as she hurried into the kitchen to hug him close. I walked past them to Jake who stood at the island counter, talking to Florian. My eyes flickered away from Heath and

Scarlett as they kissed and I wasn't sure whether to feel uncomfortable or confused. I still had that image in my mind of Heath when he drove me home after my tire went flat.

"Abigail, can you bring the turkey over to the table?" my mother asked.

I picked up the sliced turkey dish. "Do you need anything?" Jake asked my mother.

"Yes," she said, smiling. "Could you grab the broccoli? It's on the counter."

We both helped carry the dishes to the table.

"I've almost finished dinner," Mother said. "Why don't we all sit at the table?"

We all sat down except for my mother, me beside Jake, Scarlett beside Heath, Florian at the head, and Renée beside me. Mother guided the mashed sweet potatoes into a large dish. I chatted with Jake about his latest report.

"I still want to write it," he said. "People should know the truth about what happened no matter if the truth is controversial to those who worship OPTI."

"That's an honorable way to lead," I said. "Someone needs to tell the truth."

I noticed Heath glance at me. Having Heath here was awkward. I didn't know what to do with myself. I tried not to look at him because every time I did, my eyes locked with his without meaning to do so. Scarlett hardly noticed. She was discussing her new favorite pair of boots with Heath.

"I need to send them back right away," she said. "It's a nightmare trying to get around when they kill my feet. I planned to buy a pair for Abigail as a gift, however, she's stubborn about it and now I see why."

"I can hear you, Scar," I muttered while Heath chuckled.

"Everyone can," Florian said with a chuckle of his own. "Let's focus on one conversation."

Mother agreed and placed the mashed sweet potatoes on the table. Then she sat down next to Florian.

"Thanks, OPTI, for this wonderful meal," Florian said.

Jake and I exchanged an uncomfortable glance. I had nothing to thank OPTI for, though I already received a warning from OPTI that if I spoke like that again, especially to an officer, I would be sent back to prison. I couldn't promise that I wouldn't do it again. Exhaustion hit me from having to stay quiet and meet OPTI's never-ending demands.

Next up was trying to survive this dinner. I picked at my plate of food and glanced at the OPTI screen attached to the wall in the dining room as though he could hear every thought. Nothing happened and I turned back to my meal.

"I heard you say you're writing something, young man," Florian said to Jake. "Would you like to share with the rest of us?"

"Uh, yes," he said. "I'm writing a report on the secret baptisms that occurred at the lake."

"I heard about that," Florian said. "Two of the leaders were arrested. Betraying OPTI like that is a serious crime."

"You should have seen Erica last night—" Scarlett told Heath.

"There's no crime in practicing your faith—" Jake said, his jaw set.

"She threw shade at me all because of the boots that she desperately wants."

"The loss of lives to preserve order for OPTI is worth it," Florian said. "Don't you know your history? If you're going to write an article, you need to understand the situation from OPTI's perspective."

"I was over at her house and she told me I was ridiculous for wearing boots with high heels because they would scuff up her floors as if she has the right to tell me what to do—"

"Isn't that a cruel punishment for such an innocent act?" I asked. "And can OPTI be allowed to interfere with something so precious as belief?"

Florian's face dimmed as if I'd slapped him.

"But I heard that she's been fooling around with one of the football players while she has a boyfriend, and if she dares utter another word against my fashion sense, I'm going to expose that bitch's secret—"

"Scarlett, no cursing at the dinner table," Mother scolded her. Scarlett scowled when she realized she'd become the center of the conversation.

"Oh, well, it's not as if you're so innocent." She sneered. "You did it last night."

"I did not," Mother replied, although it wasn't true. "Don't give me that attitude either or you can skip dinner tonight." She glanced at Florian who had stopped eating.

"Ignore it, Florian." She went on. "These girls have been going on about belief for years and nothing will change it."

"Yeah," Scarlett soured. "You'd probably like it better if you didn't have to deal with us and any of our beliefs at all. You usually do. How long has it been since you've been home? Five days?"

"I was out of town for a meeting with a client," Mother said, "and I don't like it better without you. Why else would we be having a family dinner tonight?"

"Maybe for Florian. Maybe we're having a family dinner tonight because you're pretending to play the part of our mother. The part that you should have done since our father left."

"That's enough," I said before my mother could open her mouth to argue.

Renée had her face down against the table as if she couldn't bear to hear another word.

"Renée, please don't sit like that." Mother turned to her now. "Sit up straight. This is a family dinner."

She grimaced but did as our mother instructed her.

"Yeah," Scarlett said, "what were you doing, licking your plate like a dog?"

"Oh, leave her alone, Scarlett," I said.

"Don't take her side," she growled at me. "Like you always do."

"How did you find out that Erica's been cheating?" Heath asked her, seeming to try to redirect the conversation for which I was glad. It worked because Scarlett launched into a new discussion about this Erica and the rumor about her.

"What classes do you take, Jake?" Mother asked, calmer now and attempting to redirect the conversation further.

"I take a journalism course," he said. "I'm taking English, chemistry with Abigail, geometry, computer science, and a history course called OPTI's New America about the history of our country."

"Very impressive," she said. "What is your preferred subject?"

"I prefer English and journalism," Jake said. "I find writing about and solving crime so important to spread awareness about societal issues."

"Quite different from Abigail. She's into sciences. I've never understood it. I suppose she gets it from her father. It's not so much a girl thing, is it?"

I grimaced. "I just find it fascinating," I said.

"I don't think it's not a girl thing," Jake said. "My sister, Katie, is very adept at sciences and well, it has nothing to do with gender."

Mother nodded, looking pleased. Florian remained frowning as if he'd tasted something bitter.

"Belief and science?" he said. "How can you possibly reconcile the two?"

It took me aback as the conversation suddenly focused on me.

"There's a way," I said, though I knew where this conversation headed. I glanced at the OPTI screen with unease. "Science is our way of understanding and appreciating the wonder of God's creation such as the complexity of an atom beyond our vision, our smallness in comparison to a vast universe, a reminder of our limitations, learning about concepts and theories that are beyond human comprehension, such as the big bang, and is a gift for improving our health and overall life expectancy."

"And that's how you and your father differ," Mother said.

"Well, I hope that perhaps you might agree with your father," Florian said. "After all, faith is illogical and superfluous in such a technical world as ours."

"But how can you ignore our basic humanity, the depths of our emotions, our diverse personalities, the intangible power of art, the expansiveness of human imagination, the existence of good and evil, the power of love, miracles, free will, and the concept and depth of our souls? We're more than walking automatons. Those are aspects of ourselves that are hard to measure yet they exist so how can belief be illogical?"

When I finished, everyone at the table quieted. Both Jake and Heath were gazing at me with distinct yet equally curious expressions.

"That's enough talk about belief, Abigail," my mother said. "I don't know how many times I've told you not to discuss it. Especially with your duty to OPTI."

She turned her gaze on Heath and frowned.

"And you? What courses do you take?" she asked.

Scarlett stopped talking to wait for Heath to speak. "I'm mostly into history," he answered. "Theater and public speaking. Those are my specialties."

"He's the lead in our school play," Scarlett said. "*My* boyfriend." She grabbed his face and kissed him. I averted my gaze.

"Which play is that?" Mother asked, sounding uninterested.

"*Richard III*," I answered. "I'm Lady Anne Neville."

"That's a great role!" Florian said. "I could definitely give you both some tips. I was quite the expert in Shakespeare back in my day. I played Petruchio in *Taming of the Shrew*."

"I want to hear from Heath," Mother said. "How is rehearsal going?"

"Excellent," he answered and gave me a grin. Scarlett stared at her nails, uninterested in the conversation. I knew she was jealous of the part I received. This time, I could understand more now since I acted in a scene where I agreed to marry her boyfriend. "We've blocked most of the play. I have most, if not all, my lines down. And Abigail and I were given a huge compliment from our director for our scene together."

"Did my nail polish chip?" Scarlett said, her voice rising an octave. "I'd better go fix it." She hurried off upstairs, not looking at anyone, even though her nail polish sat on the coffee table in the living room.

"That's great to hear, Abigail," Mother said. "Let's toast to it."

"To Abigail," Florian muttered, raising his glass without much enthusiasm.

"To Abigail." I heard Heath say and his eyes gleamed for a moment.

I raised my own. Our glasses clinked together.

Scarlett came back then. "Close call—a trick of the light," she said as she sat back down.

Mother scowled. "Don't leave the table again until we've all finished eating," she said.

"I had an emergency," Scarlett retorted. "In any case, while it's very nice that Abigail is playing Lady Anne Neville and Heath is Richard III, I'm playing as Queen Elizabeth. It's quite a big role. I think we should do a toast."

She raised her glass.

"To Scarlett," I said, raising my glass. I waited a moment before everyone else joined in and our glasses clinked together to celebrate Scarlett.

"What about Renée?" I said then. "She got an A in math this semester."

"To Renée," Jake cheered with a raise of his glass and everyone else, including me, followed.

These toasts turned into every one of us getting a toast—Jake for his part in the play, and Florian and my mother for their upcoming anniversary. I'd waited all evening for the moment of the proposal but it never happened, and Florian seemed in a bad mood for the rest of the meal. We engaged in a conversation about the corporate law firm where they were employed.

After dinner, we all settled into the living room, reclining back against the cushions. My head leaned on Jake's shoulder while he watched the hockey game on television. Scarlett and Heath were watching it with an intensity that made me wonder whether they should have been there in person. Florian sat in one of the reclining chairs, nursing a glass of scotch. My mother sat with Renée and asked her about school. I was the only one who didn't engage in some activity.

My mind drifted far away, thinking about Christmas and wanting to do something to commemorate it tonight. I excused myself from the living room to head up to my bedroom and closed the door. I lit a candle and placed it on my windowsill. On my knees, I prayed for my country and for the Christians involved in the baptisms. I prayed for Jake and his father, that Jake and other Jewish people would be free to express their faith as much as me. I wished for freedom from harsh treatment from having faith. I wished my family could be more peaceful. I wished for love that seemed hard to find in this world—for a miracle that would save us all from OPTI. I prayed to know what I could do to help, that God would lead me in the right direction. I prayed I wouldn't be under OPTI's control anymore. I couldn't imagine how devastated I would be when the time came to say goodbye. Was this OPTI's intention—to allow me to revel in everything that I would inevitably lose? The punishments at the detention center seemed benevolent in comparison to how I would feel if I lost all that I'd gained these past few months.

I looked up from my window to see a wondrous star-sprinkled sky, a million glistening lights beaming down on earth, seeming brighter than usual with a full moon singing to the human eye. The nighttime scene filled me with a sudden joy beyond words. My eyes found the North Star and found it gleamed brighter than I'd ever seen it on this holy night.

At ten o'clock, Jake decided he would leave and head home. I walked with him to the door and wished he could stay.

"Thanks for coming," I said.

"Thanks for inviting me," Jake said, though he looked glum. His usual cheery disposition had disappeared and I didn't know how to mend it. "The meal was delicious. Tell your mother that she's an excellent cook. She seems nice."

I grimaced. "Sorry for all of the fighting. I hope I can make up for it." I leaned up to plant a gentle kiss on his lips. I held the kiss and thought of how much I would miss Jake when I had to say goodbye in less than three years, if either of us lived to see the day.

A sound of a door opening caught my attention and I broke away from the kiss. Heath stood in front of the hall closet and he pulled out his black coat.

"Did I interrupt something?" he said as he turned to face us.

"Don't worry about it," Jake said. "Go ahead." He pulled open the front door and stepped aside so Heath could walk out to his car. I expected Heath to make some sort of flirty comment to me.

Then I remembered our truce. "Good night, Abigail, Jake."

Heath headed out the door and down the front steps and toward his black car. Jake stepped outside then, and I followed to walk him to his car.

Heath started the ignition. Jake came to a halt.

"Wait a minute," he said. "Isn't that your mother's car?"

I realized what he meant in that moment and my eyes widened. He looked at me and I struggled for words.

"I saw that car here about a couple months ago and you said it belonged to your mother," he said, narrowing his eyes.

"I...um...you don't know the whole story," I said, placing a hand on his arm.

"Heath came over, didn't he?" He stepped back away from me.

"Well, sort of...yes, but not for what you think," I said quickly and my arm fell back to my side. I felt tears brim my eyes. I didn't want to lose Jake of all people.

"What am I supposed to think?" Jake said. "Is something going on between you?"

"No, Jake," I said. "I'm sorry I didn't tell you."

"Tell me what?"

I tried to find the words that could explain what had happened that day and all those other times when Heath pursued me; I didn't even know where to begin.

Jake scowled. "Never mind, forget it. I'm leaving."

He spun around and strode over to his bluish-gray car. It unlocked and he climbed in without another glance in my direction. When he pulled away, I headed back inside the house with tears running down my cheeks. I swelled with fury at Heath. He was to blame for Jake thinking I lied to him. Though I couldn't help the guilt that came to me for the times Heath had kissed me as if I had wanted him to do so. Not only that but I recalled that fleeting feeling I'd experienced when Heath drove me home that night. I still didn't know what to do with that ambiguous feeling, and I hurried up the stairs to my room.

I lay back on my bed and stared at the ceiling. A moment later, I heard four knocks on the door and I knew Renée stood behind it. We came up with that signal a long time ago whenever one of us felt sad and we needed to talk to each other.

I got up off the bed to open the door.

"Thanks," I said, "I think I'll be okay. Go back downstairs."

"Would you do that to me if I were sad?" Renée said with a smile.

I smiled at her through my tears. "Come in."

Renée stepped forward and launched herself at me in a hug. I squeezed her tight and then sat down on my bed.

"What happened?" Renée asked. "Why are you crying?"

"Jake found out that Heath came to our house," I said. "It happened last October after he came to the restaurant, and Jake thinks I'm cheating with him."

"Didn't you explain that he stalked you?" Renée asked.

"I didn't get a chance to," I said. "He wouldn't listen."

"Don't feel bad," Renée said. "You've done nothing wrong."

"I know, I know," I said, "but ever since Heath drove me home that night…there's been something different between us. He stopped pursuing me and I…well…I see him in a different light and I don't know what it means. I can't explain that to Jake. He'll never understand."

"Are you saying you like him?" Renée asked.

"No, of course not," I said. "I don't…know what I felt. All I know is that I want to be with Jake. I don't want to break up."

"You'll need to tell him the truth," Renée said. "He won't be angry with you if he knows why Heath came. Call him tomorrow."

I nodded. Her words comforted me. If I had a chance to explain, he would understand. I put my arm around Renée. "Thanks for listening," I said.

"Of course," she said.

I wiped away the last of my tears. I would call Jake tomorrow and explain—most of it, at least. Then maybe this pressing guilt I had would release and I could move forward.

CHAPTER 23

The Winter Festival

The next day I called Jake but he didn't answer. I lost my motivation to do anything except lie on the sofa and watch television. That afternoon Scarlett came home from running some errands in town and announced that Florian ended up proposing to our mother at a lunch at a local restaurant without any of us around and she said yes. She even knew what kind of ring—a large Tiffany Soleste oval diamond ring. While she spent time with her fiancé, I had the responsibility to make lunch, and later dinner, for Renée while loading and unloading the dishwasher.

I grew tired of sitting around, crying over the weekend; so instead, I distracted myself with getting ahead on my homework for school as much as I could. This meant hours spent in my room at my desk, working on geometry problems in the textbook, making flash cards for the next chapter for intermediate chemistry, reading for history, and rehearsing lines for the play. I also needed to stay in shape and knew I couldn't afford to take any more breaks under OPTI's close watch. Both days, I ran around my neighborhood until everything hurt—and everything did, inside and out. I tried Jake again the next day. He didn't answer. On Monday afternoon, I returned home from a workout to find Scarlett lounging on the living room sofa with shopping bags scattered around her.

"Abby," she said when she noticed me. "I barely saw you this weekend. What have you been up to?"

"Mostly homework," I said, taking my earphones out of my ears.

"Oh, how boring," she said. "You should have told me. You could have come shopping with me."

"I don't have time to go shopping," I said as I entered the living room. I took a large gulp from my water bottle. "I have way too much on my plate."

"Why do you have to do track again?" she asked, sitting up.

"Like I told you, I have to train now so I can go into law enforcement or the military on OPTI's orders."

"I've never seen you as that type. No offense."

"Well, OPTI does. It's more like a punishment. I'm just lucky to be home with you, Mom, Renée, and...hopefully Jake."

Scarlett smiled. "I'm glad you're home too."

I sat down beside her on the sofa, my eyes turning to the television screen. Her favorite reality television show was on.

"What happened to Jake? Did you break up?"

"No," I said, "I don't want to talk about it." I hadn't told Scarlett either about the time Heath came over and barged his way into our home.

"Well, you wouldn't believe all the gorgeous clothes I found," Scarlett said. "Look at this."

She grabbed one of the shopping bags and pulled out a pretty light-blue sweater.

"Lovely," I said. "You did well."

"Do you want me to get you one? There were only a few left. I'm one of their best customers so I'm sure I can pull some strings."

"Sure, if you can get one."

"You could wear it to the winter festival tomorrow night. I'll let you borrow mine until we can get you one of your own."

"Are you sure?" I asked. "Wouldn't you want to wear it?"

"I already have my outfit picked out," she said.

"You can wear it if you want," I said. "I'm not going."

"You're not going? Why on earth are you going to miss it?"

"I don't have time to go," I said. "I'm way too busy. I have to make flash cards of the next chapter in chemistry, read for history, and practice lines."

"That's hardly a good excuse," Scarlett said. "School hasn't even started yet and you're already getting ahead of yourself."

"It's a must," I said. "I need to be prepared."

"What about Jake?" she replied. "Isn't he going?"

"I don't know," I said. "I can't reach him."

"Well, then call and leave him a message to invite him," Scarlett said. "Come on. I'm going with Heath. If you went, we could go together and have a double date."

"No, thank you," I said. I didn't want to see Heath, especially with my anger at him over interfering with my relationship with Jake. Although he'd been surprisingly accepting of a truce, I remained uncomfortable around him, especially with Scarlett there too.

"Please come," Scarlett said. "It will be so much fun."

"You really want me there?" I asked, raising my eyebrows.

"Yes, come on," she said. "We haven't had a chance to hang out for a while."

She stared at me, her eyes hopeful. They convinced me. It would be nice to spend time with Scarlett and do something to relax. I could use a break.

"Okay," I said, making her smile. "I'll tell Jake and we can go on a double date."

"Yes," Scarlett said and she gave me a hug. "I can help you with your hair and your makeup. You're going to look stunning."

"Thanks," I said. "Now I have to get back to work."

I turned around and headed upstairs. Now that I knew I would be going to this festival with Heath there, it made my mind unable to focus on anything but the thought of ending up as the third wheel on their date.

Lights dazzled and surrounded me as I walked through the crowded streets in the center of town. Even though we weren't at liberty to celebrate Christmas anymore, the tradition of hanging lights in this period of winter remained and we were told to thank OPTI for them. I didn't, of course. Passersby wore mostly white hats, gloves, and sweaters. I stood out in my light-blue sweater and gathered some stares. The shops carried on the winter theme with decorations in the form of garlands and figurines of deer, elk, bears, and wolves. An antique shop even contained ceramic statues of Santa Claus, though we all knew he doesn't exist. Despite the decorations and the icicle-shaped lights, the snow on the ground remained fake as it had for years during the winter. For years, we've lacked proper natural snowfall. Snowstorms occurred in the winter though were rare.

Earlier in the afternoon, before we left for the festival, I finally reached Jake and he agreed to let me explain myself. He suggested it would be best to talk in person and that he had plans tonight. I knew he was most likely celebrating Hanukkah with his family and had to keep it hidden from OPTI. I sent a prayer that OPTI wouldn't find out to ease my worries. I didn't want to lose Jake like those people at the church and two of the leaders of the secret baptisms.

Scarlett invited me to come to the winter festival anyways and I didn't want to disappoint her so I went as her third wheel. As we made our way through the busy streets, Heath draped his arm over Scarlett's shoulders. They had already exchanged two prolonged kisses that I had to hide my eyes from and pretend like I wasn't here. They even took a selfie of the three of us with me standing behind them. I tried to focus on the positive and enjoy myself. But the busy crowds and Scarlett and Heath's presence made me feel terribly lonely. A month and a half ago, he fought for my affection. Could he really have moved on from all that and so fast?

As we reached the park, we came across an ice sculpture contest. OPTI was the judge of the winner, of course, and we walked by each sculpture to observe the artistic shapes. A figurine in the shape of two swans with their heads together stood out. Another sculpture looked like an intricate flower, and one of them appeared OPTI-shaped. Even as a sculpture, it radiated with OPTI's oppressive power and I couldn't stop staring at it out of fear. Although I knew the sculpture wasn't OPTI, I felt like its gaze hovered over me and I kept myself immobile as if even the slightest movement in the wrong direction would infuriate OPTI.

"It's no contest," Scarlett said. "I think it's obvious who's going to win."

"That's because you're so smart," Heath said and poked her on the nose.

"I know," Scarlett said. "What else is new?"

She turned back her bright eyes to rest on the other sculptures.

"Don't you like the other two, Abigail?" Scarlett asked me.

I didn't answer and hoped OPTI wouldn't detect my fear.

"Will you take our picture?" Scarlett asked me and passed me her OPTI-Phone which already had the camera app open.

"Sure," I said and held the phone up. Heath put his arms back over Scarlett's shoulders and they stood in front of the swan ice sculpture. I began to grit my teeth. Heath was at fault for ruining what I had with Jake and now I ended up stuck on a date between him and my sister. Why couldn't he stay out of my life? I took the photo and then passed the phone to Scarlett who studied it. Scarlett had blinked and asked me to take another one. Before I knew it, I had taken several pictures of them.

"That's enough," I said after the last picture. I grew increasingly irritated with both of them. It only made me feel guiltier because I knew my irritation at Scarlett, at least, wasn't justified. Scarlett invited me to be kind to me, not to make me a miserable third wheel.

We finished looking at the ice sculptures and continued on inside the park. An ice rink sat at the center of this park with more twinkling lights attached to trees surrounding it that gleamed brilliantly against the smooth icy surface. Scarlett and Heath wanted to ice-skate so I stopped with them to sit on a bench and watch.

"Are you sure you don't want to ice-skate?" Scarlett asked. "You know you can rent skates, right?" She gestured to a stand near the rink with a man standing behind it, distributing the rental ice skates.

"I'm sure," I said, "I don't feel like ice-skating."

"Let us know if you want to join," Scarlett said and hustled over to the stand while grasping Heath's arm. He must have said something funny because she giggled.

I watched them skate together, Heath, at first, holding Scarlett's arm like a gentleman, and then, eventually parting from her to attempt to skate backward—I guess to impress her because she laughed. Watching it made me want to cry. I didn't know why it bothered me so much. Maybe I was bothered because I cared so much about Jake. I didn't mean to hurt him by not telling him the truth.

I waited and continued to watch them skate for twenty minutes. After that time passed, I saw Heath leave the rink. He removed his hat, ran his hand through his hair, and then walked over to where I sat.

"Isn't it freezing out?" Heath asked and looked down at me. "And you're not even wearing a hat."

"I forgot to bring one," I said, adjusting my coat so that I covered my torso.

"Want to wear mine?" he asked.

"I'm fine," I said without hesitation. "Where's Scarlett?"

"She ran into her friends at the rink and needed some girl time," Heath said. Then he sat down on the bench beside me and started undoing the laces of his skates.

I kept my gaze turned away from him, on the brink of an outburst.

"What's wrong?" he asked.

"I don't want to talk about it," I said and looked down at the ground to avoid his searching eyes.

"Is it about Jake?" he asked.

"I said I don't want to talk about it," I grumbled.

"Fine," he retorted. "But I'll tell you one thing. That boy is an idiot for not wanting to talk to you."

"How do you know what happened?" I asked. "I never told you anything. And he does want to talk to me. I spoke to him today. Don't call him an idiot."

"Scarlett told me," Heath said. "And I don't think he deserves you."

"How do you know?" I argued and stood up. "How do you know what I deserve? You know nothing about me."

I looked him in the eyes by mistake and they hooked me. I managed to turn my head away and hid my face in my hands.

"I lied to him," I said, my arms falling back to my side. I kept my gaze ahead of us toward the rink. "I thought it would be better for him if he didn't know…" Tears formed in my eyes as I trailed off and turned away from him. Then I became heated and turned my gaze back to Heath. "You're right…I did nothing wrong. It was you. You're at fault. You stalked and forced yourself on me and you didn't care what happened in the process."

"Go ahead and blame me." Heath fired back and he stood up from the bench with his boots back on his feet. "However, I was not the one who lied about it. You did that."

"Oh, so now I *did* do something wrong?" I retorted. "None of this would have happened if you had stayed out of my life."

"Maybe I will stay out then," Heath growled, his eyes lit with anger. "Don't worry, Abigail, you don't have anything to worry about. I'll stay far away from you, if that's what you want."

He began to stride away from me.

"Tell Scarlett that I left," he said over his shoulder.

I scowled. I thought saying those words to him would somehow make me feel better. It didn't. My heart carried more guilt to the point where it ached and I burst into tears.

Scarlett came off the rink and frowned when she noticed I stood in front of the bench alone and crying.

"Where's Heath?" she asked.

"He left," I answered.

"Why?" she asked. "Why are you crying? What happened?"

"We fought," I admitted, looking away from her.

"What was it about?"

"You told him that Jake isn't speaking to me and I told Heath he was to blame for Jake thinking I cheated on him," I said.

Scarlett's frown deepened. "Why would you say that?" she asked. "I'm sorry that I told him. I tell him everything. I didn't mean to upset you. But you shouldn't have said that to him. He didn't do anything," she said. "He cares a lot about you, Abigail, and didn't he help you that time when your tire went flat?"

"There's a reason…" I said. Although I knew it was Heath's fault, now that I faced communicating it to someone, I feared that she wouldn't believe me. Had I provoked Heath to stalk me with my attitude toward him? Perhaps I led him on; I couldn't explain how.

Heath confused me. Could he really have changed since we made a truce?

"Never mind," I said. I hung my head in shame and wondered if she could be right. I probably made a mistake in accusing Heath of ruining my relationship with Jake. I had to forgive him. Hadn't he proved he was worthy of forgiveness?

Scarlett and I found Renée with her friends nearby in town and left the winter festival together. Scarlett barely said a word to me the whole way back. I knew she remained mad at me and it only made me feel worse. It felt like I was a disappointment to everyone. I could never do anything right. No matter what I did, I always found a way to anger or upset someone.

I wondered, could I be a disappointment to God too?

CHAPTER 24

On Edge

I spent the rest of winter break getting ahead on my work and trying to reach Jake again. We made an agreement to talk in person after and give us both time to concentrate on our studies and, in Jake's case, his article on the secret baptisms. Scarlett didn't stay mad at me for long. It made me feel better, however, she remained frustrated that Heath wouldn't come over anymore. I didn't understand why it upset me too. I thought I would be glad when he stopped invading my life. More pain consumed me.

When the break ended, nerves filled me over having to return to a place that put so much stress on my shoulders. I knew I would be seeing Jake at school and I worried about what he would think of my explanation. Would he believe me? I didn't even tell Scarlett so how could I tell Jake?

When I took my seat in intermediate chemistry, Jake wasn't at his desk. I wouldn't have an opportunity to talk to him and tell him the truth. He came in late, and as he made his way to his desk, he looked at me with uncertainty. I hung my head and tried to keep myself from looking over at Jake. I couldn't stand that he still had the impression that I might have cheated.

I waited, my anxiety climbing throughout the period and then peaking when the bell finally rang. Jake left the classroom, and I hurried after him out into the hall and to my locker where he stopped.

"All right," he said, "let me hear you out."

"Heath didn't come to my house that day because we were together," I said. "Ever since Scarlett's cast party, Heath has been... pursuing me. He showed up in places where I happened to be and he tried to force himself on me. I didn't feel anything for him and I tried to stop him. Nothing worked...not until...well, the night he drove me home from rehearsal."

Jake's eyes softened. The silence that came between us made me uneasy. Finally Jake broke the silence. "Why didn't you tell me about any of this? Why wait until now?"

"I couldn't reach you, and I didn't know how to tell you," I said. "He showed up at the restaurant on our first date and I felt...guilty even though I knew it wasn't my fault."

"He came to the restaurant where we were on our date?" Jake said and now his brown eyes were hard. "Why did he do that?"

"To win my love or something," I said. "I know I don't love him though. I don't feel that I wanted his advances. I love you, Jake. You're the one I want to be with."

His face fell. "I'm sorry I accused you of cheating," he said. "And...I love you too, Abigail."

Our eyes met and his reflected genuine love.

"It's okay. I'm sorry I lied," I said. "I forgive you."

"Don't apologize," Jake said. "I understand why you didn't tell me. But...why did you let him drive you home?"

I groaned inwardly.

"He found me on the side of the road after our late-night rehearsal...I...I had to go to the grocery store. Scarlett needed my help to care for Renée. I didn't have anyone else..."

"Why didn't you call me?" Jake asked. "I could've come to help you. If he pursued you like that and forced himself on you, why would you trust him to give you a ride home?"

"I don't know," I said. "I...he said he would say it was his car so I wouldn't get caught for driving illegally."

"Where is he?" Jake said, and his face reddened as he looked around the hallway as though expecting Heath to appear.

"Don't be mad," I said, reaching out to grab his arm to get his attention. "We have a truce. I don't want to break my end of the truce...again."

"He stalked you, Abigail," Jake said. "And he forced himself on you. What good is a truce after that?"

"Well, he stopped," I said, "and now he doesn't even want to see me. Things have turned out for the better."

"Stalking is a crime, Abby." Jake went on as if he hadn't heard. "You should go to the police."

"I already tried," I said. "They said it didn't count because I wasn't in a relationship with him. But, Jake...please don't worry about it. He's dating my sister now and he treats her well. She told me he's sorry for what he did. Maybe we should let it go."

"Let it go?" Jake repeated and threw up his hands in exasperation. "You actually believe his apology? And why would Scarlett date him?"

"She doesn't know he forced himself on me, only that he stalked me on our date. She forgave him. I want to keep a truce with him so he'll leave me alone," I said. At the same time, my head spun; I believed in Heath's sincerity, especially because he stopped chasing me. And the distance he kept from me right now gave me more proof, right?

"But you let someone like him give you a ride home," he said. "You weren't worried he would do it again?"

"I needed the help," I said. "He promised he wouldn't ask for anything in return...he was already there...I...and he didn't do anything to me."

"I can't believe it," Jake cried. "I think I need some time to think about all of this, Abby. I don't understand why you accepted a ride from him after what he did."

I felt like a stick prodded at my heart. I had already spent so much time apart from Jake—I couldn't stand anymore. I tried my best to keep my tears at bay.

"I don't want to split up because of this," I said, taking his hand. "That's one of the reasons I didn't tell you."

"Look, we're not splitting up," he said. "It's overwhelming news." His eyes glistened. "Just...give me time."

His hand left mine and I watched him turn to walk back down the hall. When he disappeared down the next corridor, I put my head in my hands as the tears that I had tried to push down flooded my eyes and slipped down my cheeks. What I feared most happened. Heath's pursuit of me had divided Jake and me which—now that I think about it—must have been his plan.

But he apologized. The thought intruded my mind and muddled my brain. I remembered Heath's apology, the sincerity in his eyes; he said everything he did came out of love, and perhaps, I'd led him on that night at the cast party. Also I witnessed Heath's treatment of my sister and it seemed like he had changed into a different person. Or he had become two people—one that played games and chased after me out of love and the other that was heartfelt and deep—as deep as a well. Like something unexpected, the depth remained there all the same. After this, I didn't know how to feel about Heath. Scarlett had forgiven him, I'd made a truce with him; but Jake held onto the incident as if it had happened at this moment in time. I had no clue where I stood on Heath now. I couldn't say; I found myself torn between anger at him and compassion for him. I recalled Faith's lessons as a child. She often mentioned that love and forgiveness was at the heart of Christianity. Did that mean I should have forgiven Heath instead of having mounting anger toward him?

Like slime, guilt clung and weighed down my bruised heart.

Rehearsals for the play brought me closer to Heath despite his attempts to avoid me. The director loved our chemistry so much that we had to run the scene multiple times which left Scarlett in a bad mood and made me worried that Jake might think I had an attraction to Heath. When the end of our big scene concluded, Heath and I stood so close that I felt the warmth of a fireplace; yet at the close, he would turn away and give me the cold shoulder. By the end of the evening, he would storm out of rehearsals without speaking to Scarlett or me. Scarlett seemed conflicted as if she didn't know who to be angry with.

The rehearsals became more time-consuming, lasting all evening. Performing became my sole enjoyment aside from chemistry because it had become one of the only tasks that felt good at the time. In spite of this pleasure from performing, as opening night came closer, I busied myself so heavily with juggling track, my schoolwork, and the play that during one of the rehearsals, I froze in the middle of my scene with a blank memory of what my lines were. I had two weeks left until the first performance and the director gave me a solid lecture about knowing my lines or else my understudy would have to take over.

Heath wouldn't speak to me anymore and Scarlett threw me irritated looks or sighs in disapproval whenever Heath left if I approached them in the hallways or at rehearsals. The only person who would talk to me in my life was Renée, however, I barely had a moment to spend time with her. I would feel so much relief once this play ended. I didn't plan on auditioning again which left me torn. I couldn't have any extracurricular aside from track-and-field, according to OPTI.

All of these pressing thoughts consumed my mind all day and every day until I felt like I suffered from information overload. Not to mention, I couldn't stop thinking about the two Christians who had been captured and the horrors they must be facing while captive. Their bravery and sacrifice for Jesus inspired me. I wondered how I could make one of my own. In spite of the inspiration, my mind and heart were tormented with guilt and loneliness, keeping me up way into the night. During the day, I busied myself with work and exercise without feeling the full impact of those emotions and states. At night, the pain caught up to me and I sunk underwater in a sea of impenetrable night. I said many prayers in my head for relief from it; I cried that I wouldn't sink deeper. I was on the verge of a breakdown. Ever since the secret baptisms, my hope for relief from my anguish dwindled.

The image of that starry night sky on Christmas and its ever-present awe inspired me to keep moving and rise from my bed each day. Even though I'd studied stars and space in Earth science lessons taught in middle school, I couldn't describe the awe it inspired in me. Despite my despair, it seemed that God listened and I prayed he would lead me on a path toward correcting all the wrongs in my world.

On the morning at the end of January and of the first performance of the play, I woke from a long restless night. I slept for a few hours and immediately felt my chest tightening as my mind flooded with endless thoughts about everything I needed to do on this day. Friday had arrived so I had to pull myself together to focus on concentrating in school for one more day and then concentrate on the piles of homework the next day. Today I had an exam or quiz in every class, starting with computer science, and I only had a few hours each night of this week to study for all of them. I climbed out of bed and dragged myself across my room to my bathroom. As I brushed my teeth, I examined myself in the mirror, my blond hair knotted and tangled and feeling like a zombie. I hurriedly washed my face and splattered concealer on my face where pimples had sprouted, making sure to get the darkness under my eyes as well.

I pulled on a pair of jeans, the same top as yesterday, and a sweater. Then I grabbed my backpack, and as I made my way down the stairs, my body ached all over from my workout yesterday. I tried to hurry, but with each lift of a leg, my limbs burned and the stiffness led me to place my legs down on each stair as carefully as if I were on a balance beam. I found Scarlett already in the kitchen by the time I reached it and she rummaged through the fridge.

"Looks like Mother forgot to go grocery shopping again," Scarlett said and turned around as I entered. She appeared in much better condition than I was and sported neat fitting colorful gym clothes.

"Going for a run?" I asked in confusion.

"Later," she said. "Oh look, there's some yogurt left." She pulled a carton of yogurt out of the fridge. "I bought this cute outfit yesterday and I figured…why not show it off?"

"You've been going shopping a lot lately…" I said.

"Don't tell Mother," Scarlett said and opened the yogurt carton. She opened a drawer built into the counter and pulled out a silver spoon.

"Please don't make her angry," Renée's voice met my ears, and I glanced over my shoulder to see her standing beneath the arched doorway, her auburn hair in pigtails. "I don't like when Mother yells."

"Don't worry," Scarlett said after a spoonful of yogurt. "I'll let Mother borrow my outfits."

"That's not the point," I said in irritation which had grown from my exhaustion. "Neither of us want to hear you two yelling at each other constantly."

Scarlett glowered at me. "Huh, well, if you're so worried about *arguing*, why don't you make peace with Heath already so he can finally come over to see me?"

"I can't make peace with someone who won't even talk to me," I countered. I wished I could tell Scarlett the truth; her anger at me made me nervous. "Anyways, let's go. Renée might miss the bus. And neither of us can afford to be late."

Scarlett gave both of us a haughty look. She closed the lid of the yogurt carton and put it back in the fridge. I didn't bother to eat breakfast; I had too much to think about. Scarlett strode ahead of Renée and me, and we followed her out to her black Jeep, and soon, we all settled inside. We dropped Renée off at the bottom of the driveway and waited with her for the bus to come. When it arrived she climbed on the bus to leave for school.

Scarlett and I remained silent throughout the drive. Since my argument with Heath, most mornings, like this, began in silence until Scarlett turned the radio up to the most popular station. She stopped asking me if I wanted to listen to my favorite station. Our tastes in music were wildly different; Scarlett favored electronic music and hip-hop while I enjoyed classical and pop music. I didn't speak up about Scarlett's treatment of me because I didn't want another argument. Besides the radio put an end to the awkward silence that we always seemed to share nowadays. My mind sifted through thought after thought without even a slight pause. I attended to each of them as if I might say something bad or out of anger at Heath. I had to forgive him as Scarlett urged me to do. If I did forgive him, what would my relationship to Heath be? All those times he went after me, I never imagined feeling friendly toward him; or perhaps it was best to regard him as an acquaintance. However, we'd already reached a stage of close proximity that would make picturing him as an acquaintance next to impossible. Before he tried to take things further with me at the party, I admit I had liked him beforehand and I wondered how I could ever simply be his friend either. I fought with him more than any other person in my life. Would we ever be able to have a civil conversation? How could our truce truly hold up?

I must have fallen asleep on the way to school because I suddenly felt Scarlett nudging me awake.

"Didn't sleep last night?" she asked.

"Not at all," I managed to murmur in spite of my grogginess.

"You realize the opening of the play is tonight," Scarlett reminded me.

"I know," I said.

"Maybe you should go back home and sleep," she suggested. "You have to be awake for the performance and be able to remember your lines."

"I can't," I said, "I have exams or quizzes in every class and track practice that I can't miss."

"There's no way you can do any of that without any sleep," she insisted.

"There's no way around it," I said. "If OPTI hears that I've missed these exams, I may be punished. My chemistry exam is a midterm."

"Have you even studied?" Scarlett asked.

I sighed and looked away to avoid the question. "Barely," I muttered under my breath.

"Doesn't sound like it," she said. "Sounds like a nightmare—"

My eyes shifted to the screen of the radio in which OPTI's unforgettable image appeared as if in response to what I said. Scarlett looked from the screen to me with her forehead wrinkled with worry. I was no longer tired; my brain seemed to switch on to alert mode at the sight of OPTI. We both fell silent and waited as if OPTI was about to say something. Then finally, he spoke.

"Don't miss the exams. There will be consequences."

"But she's barely awake," Scarlett said, and I grabbed her arm to capture her attention and to warn her not to say anything. Scarlett shrugged my arm off her and looked back directly at OPTI. "Can't you give her the day off? Well, except for the performance tonight."

"No," OPTI responded. "These are important exams for your future. If you skip today or fail them you will be punished. And another word from you, Scarlett, and you will be too. You may not have a mother who gives you discipline but I will. Get to class before you are late. Both of you."

My stomach dropped and my brain began to whir with rapid firing thoughts. My brain seemed about to shut down from all the built-up tension. Scarlett frowned and left the car. I followed suit, hoping I wouldn't be late.

I had my first exam of the day in computer science and discovered that most of the questions weren't related to the study guide. With a heavy heart, I had to guess at every question. The rest of the exams were just as brutal, and by the time the afternoon came, I found myself rushing to my afternoon intermediate chemistry class. I needed extra time to go over the flash cards. I had a lot of them with a messy scrawl of the terms.

When the exam met my hands, I stared at the first page and I didn't recognize any of the terms or equations. I started guessing, trying to remember books I'd read on molar mass uses, trying to circle the right answers. But when I arrived at the section on calculating molar mass, my brain froze. My palms sweat profusely, my heart jumped in my chest, and my brain ran on overdrive as I searched it for answers. I thought about track practice coming up today and the play tonight. How could I do all of it when I hadn't slept and on the verge of burnout? How could I make it through the rest of the day? Everything in my life had fallen apart and I held on for dear life. My hands trembled and it made it difficult to even write out each problem. OPTI's threat of a punishment—if I failed the exam—occupied my mind the most; would OPTI send me back to the detention center to live out my endless sentence without my family? I felt at the end of all hope, doomed to fail everything today. My heart lurched in distress.

My tired panicked gaze zoomed in on an O_2 symbol for oxygen. Why did it look like it was etched in bold ink?

I slumped over sideways and darkness overcame me.

CHAPTER 25

Accused

A cool breeze met my skin and woke me from what I thought could have been a nap. My mind tried to calculate molar mass equations and it took a while to realize I no longer wrote a test. When my eyes settled on the IV attached to my right arm, I gasped in horror that I had somehow ended up in a hospital, my test unfinished and riddled with exhaustive mistakes. I looked around the rest of the room and noticed the cool breeze came from a fan attached to the ceiling. I lay limp on a hospital bed, by myself, in a sickeningly white room. When I remembered my last moments of consciousness before I passed out, a surge of terror infiltrated my mind. It felt as if someone sat on my chest and I struggled to breathe. I couldn't sit still. I sat up and hugged my chest. Nausea made me gag; nothing came out. I had one more exam to complete and I felt my heart lurch again. I put my head in my hands in despair. I also missed track practice, and when I looked outside the dark windows—the *Richard III* performance. I thought I might burst into tears; I looked forward to that day more than any other since the beginning of the New Year. My heart was crushed and I didn't know how I would keep going with all the pressure on my shoulders.

At that moment, the door to my room swung open and in marched Scarlett, her hair all done up in a complicated elaborate hairdo fit for a queen. She wore her workout clothes, making her appear more like a sports fashion model.

"Abigail—" she started when she saw me clutching at my chest.

"I missed it?" I asked, though I already knew the answer.

Her eyes glistened with fresh tears. She hurried over to smother me in a hug so tight it hurt. My breath came out quick, sharp, and painful.

"You made me so worried," she said. "I'm so sorry I took my anger out on you."

"It's okay," I reassured her. "It's my fault that Heath doesn't want to be around me."

"You just had a fight. That's all. You can make up, right? It's been long enough," she said.

"Where is he?" I asked.

"Here, in the lobby," she said. "He's worried about you too, as much as you might have thought he didn't care."

"Heath came?" I asked and my stomach flipped. I felt confused then. Why did it matter that Heath showed up?

"Yes," Scarlett said. "He wants to see you…if that's okay."

"So the play is finished?" I asked.

"Yes" Scarlett replied. "The play ended twenty minutes ago. It was excellent but it would have been way better if you had performed in it. Perhaps you'll make tomorrow night's performance."

I put a hand to my forehead. "I really wanted to be there," I said as tears gushed from my eyes, and then I collapsed into sobs. "I've lost grip on everything in my life. Playing Lady Anne Neville was the one thing I looked forward to the most since the New Year."

"I know, I know," Scarlett replied. "Your understudy, Rosalie, had to take over. I came to visit you earlier to try and wake you up. The nurses wouldn't let me."

As she said it, a nurse entered the room.

"Lie back and try to rest," she told me. "You need to relax your body."

"What happened?" I asked her as I shifted back into a lying position.

"No worries, nothing serious. You had a panic attack," the nurse answered as she pulled out what I realized was a large needle and four small vials. "Now that you're awake, we'll need to draw your blood for testing. You'll receive a physical and meet with a psychiatrist."

Reluctantly I held out my arm for the nurse to tie something rubbery around it, and then she stuck the needle in my vein on my left arm. Scarlett turned away and cringed, however, I didn't feel very squeamish. My mind pondered the various facts of the components of blood from red blood cells to oxygen and carbon dioxide transportation and exchange. Scarlett gazed out the window; she cringed.

"You can see a psychiatrist tonight before you leave," the nurse said. "You're free to go home tonight if you choose."

"Thank you," I said as she left.

Scarlett drew her gaze away from the window and toward me again in time for her to see me panic-stricken despite the nurse's advice to relax. How could I relax when I most likely faced the danger of returning to prison and losing everything I gained, losing the freedom I'd only just tasted?

"I have a problem," I said. "I didn't finish my chemistry exam and I probably failed the other ones."

"Don't worry," Scarlett said in a hushed voice, her olive-green eyes firm despite the pressing situation. "You'll be okay. We'll explain it to OPTI. You won't be punished. Maybe you can retake them. And there's always tomorrow night's performance if you're up to it."

"I'm not so sure that I won't be punished," I replied. "He warned both of us this morning."

"But you've been doing so well otherwise, haven't you?"

"No," I said. "The rehearsals took up so much of my time that I'm not getting the grades I should or the results I need to in track."

"Just relax," Scarlett said. "Recover, and if OPTI allows you to retake them, you'll have more time to study for them this time."

"Thanks," I said, "I hope I hear the same from OPTI." I swallowed and my heart thumped. I strongly doubted it. I wished I could have remained unconscious.

Scarlett emitted a heavy sigh and sat on the edge of my bed.

"I wish I could help you," she said. "I've never been in your situation. You have so much to do in such a small amount of time. No wonder you panicked."

I nodded. "Well, you've done all you can, Scar."

"If only it had been me." Scarlett carried on. "If only I had been punished. I should have been the one to put those petals in Mr. Edwin's tea."

"OPTI still believes I did it," I said. "If OPTI knew the truth, would I be free from imprisonment?"

"There's no way to prove it, unfortunately," Scarlett said, her eyes cast downward.

I agreed with Scarlett. Maybe from the beginning, if OPTI knew the whole story about Mr. Edwin and how he died, maybe then I wouldn't have been convicted of murder. If only Mr. Bourdin had listened and helped us, if only our mother hadn't broken down, if only our father had stayed, if only Faith hadn't died because of her beliefs, if only OPTI wasn't our ruler, if only we were all free—how different would my life be? How different would all our lives be?

I didn't know what we could do to achieve freedom. What kind of rule would grant us freedom? I prayed that God would grant us a better ruler. I prayed God would give me the opportunity to create change in my world.

"Anyways," Scarlett said, dragging me back to my dismal reality. "Heath wants to see you. Should I tell him to come or are you avoiding each other?"

"Send him in," I said with my own heavy sigh.

"Will do," Scarlett said and then left the room for the waiting room.

I waited in my bed and nearly regretted my acceptance to see Heath. How could I even talk to him? Could we make peace again and keep it? I didn't know what to say to him.

He entered the room and his gray eyes burrowed into mine as if he hadn't seen me for a long time. However, something was different about the look in his eye that I couldn't figure out.

"Hey," he said and came over to my bedside.

"Is that all you have to say?" I asked, sitting up and crossing my arms in defense. "Why did you even come?"

"You should already know why I came."

"Because you have a habit of showing up wherever I am," I replied. "So it shouldn't surprise me that you're here yet it still does."

"I came because I saw you faint in class and I needed to—"

"To what?" I said in a soured tone.

"To see you. You had a panic attack and a fainting spell. Isn't that the right thing to do?"

I stared at him for a moment and then shifted my gaze to the window before he could begin to conclude that I had any sort of attraction to him. I didn't.

"I thought you didn't want to see me after what I said." I turned my head back to him, avoiding his eyes. "I'm sorry for blaming Jake's reaction on you. I didn't hold up on my end of our truce again."

Heath grinned. "Well, I admit I may have had some part in it," he said. "But who can blame me? Like I told you before, my motive is and has always been love."

I shared another look with him by mistake and the glint in his eyes mesmerized me. I blinked. Again I saw it; I realized I saw him as the person he had been before we kissed at the cast party, before I had rejected his advances—before we became enemies, mysterious and captivating.

"And now you realized your part in it?" I asked in annoyance. Then another thought occurred to me. "Why couldn't you have come to that conclusion earlier? And aren't you dating my sister?"

Heath's eyes flickered from the window to my face, however, I couldn't read his expression. Finally he said, "I am. And now my motive is to love your sister. I came with her, didn't I?"

The sound of the door opening interrupted our conversation.

"Abigail." I heard and recognized Jake's strained voice. Then he came into view followed by the same nurse who took my blood. The nurse left as soon as he entered. "I saw you faint in class," he continued, his eyes focused on me, "and I had to come see you."

Then his gaze settled on Heath and he frowned.

"Why is *he* here?" Jake asked.

Oh no.

"He…he came to see…if I'm okay," I explained.

"What about me?" Heath said. "Can't I be here when Abigail is ill?"

"You're not her boyfriend," Jake argued. "I am."

"I haven't seen you two together in weeks," Heath said. "Abigail and I were closer to each other in rehearsals than you two have been since winter break."

"That's enough, Heath." I snapped. "We're taking a break."

"I don't think you should be here, Heath," Jake said with finality. "She's had enough of you."

"I don't think she has," Heath said. "She isn't bothered that I'm here. Are you, Abby?"

I exchanged a look with Jake for a moment, unsure of what to say. He stared at me, waiting for my answer. I couldn't give him an honest answer without him becoming angry.

I averted my gaze. No answer came from my lips.

"Oh, I see," Jake said. He started back out the door.

"Wait," I said before he could close the door behind him.

He halted and turned his irritable stare back on me.

"I need you to know that there's nothing going on between Heath and me and nothing ever did," I explained. "But we've come to a better understanding and a truce. So I'm not bothered that he's here because I know he won't hurt me anymore."

"Will you?" Jake said, turning a fuming glare on him.

Heath's face contorted into a scowl. He aimed it at me before he stormed out of the room, shouldering Jake in the process. It stung my heart. I sighed out of exhaustion with keeping up with Heath's moodiness. I thought Heath and I made progress; now he hated me again. When would this emotional roller coaster end? And how? With us as friends or enemies? I couldn't figure out what to do to repair our relationship. How could he be mad when he claimed he had moved on with Scarlett?

I suppose something had occurred between us before Heath tried to sleep with me in the pool. However, he's the one who broke our connection to begin with, unless perhaps I had broken our connection by making him believe I wanted to sleep with him. Before Heath stormed out, I only spoke what I thought was the truth from my end. I realized then that I didn't think Heath had gotten over me. I sighed a great sigh, wishing for an ounce of peace.

"Sorry," I said to Jake. "I thought we were on good terms."

Jake crossed his arms and shook his head. "He still likes you," he said. He walked away from the door to stand at the foot of my bed.

"I guess he does," I said and hoped to change the subject before Jake became angry. "Believe me when I say that there is nothing between us."

After Heath left so suddenly, sadness overcame me. I didn't know why. I started to question my words. Something strange had developed between Heath and me ever since the truce and I began to figure out what it could be. I reflected back on the night we went to the winter festival. Would Heath act as gentle, humorous, and affectionate with me if I had been in Scarlett's place?

Jake stared at me as if deciding whether he should march out of the room or come to my side and mend our relationship. Then without another word, he came over to my side, leaned down, and kissed me, gentle and long. As my mouth moved with his, I had a brief image in my mind of Heath in Jake's place. As soon as the image entered my mind, I broke the kiss fast to shake it from my mind. Jake looked confused.

"What happened?"

"Oh, nothing," I said. "I...I'm happy that we can be together again."

"Me too," Jake said. "I'm sorry I became angry. I just didn't understand...why you would speak with him alone and that you weren't bothered by him visiting you."

"I get it," I said. "I've tried my best to forgive him. He's a different person now and he's stuck to his word over no longer pursuing me."

"I hope it stays that way. He has feelings for you while dating your sister," Jake mused.

"This is the only time he's ever appeared interested in me since he started dating her," I said as I reflected on my past memory of Heath at our family dinner having a blast watching the game with

Scarlett. Heath's interactions with Scarlett differed from how he acted with me. "Maybe his feelings...came back?"

"I doubt it," Jake said, growing tense like he would leave again. "Perhaps he didn't move on."

"Look," I said to calm him down, "whatever it is. They're his feelings, not mine. I have feelings for you, not him. So can we please go back to how things were...before? Heath probably won't speak to me after this. Today was the first time he spoke to me in a month. Now I most likely won't speak to him until he moves on again."

Jake sighed. "Okay, Abigail. I trust you. Let's go back. It wasn't your fault that he pursued you so I'm sorry I got upset with you."

"It's okay," I said, "I trust you too. Just give us another chance."

"Okay." Jake nodded. "Let's start over."

He sat down on the chair beside my bed and took my hand. He looked deep into my eyes and I stared back. As I did, instead of seeing Jake's comfortable brown eyes, I saw Heath's silver ones alit like the moon against the dark night. I squeezed my eyes shut in a cringe, trying to push it from my mind.

"What's wrong?" Jake asked.

The image vanished from my mind like a wisp of smoke.

"Um...nothing I...I'm just thinking about..." I trailed off as I tried to come up with an answer. "OPTI. I'm worried OPTI won't be happy with me." I grew tense after I said it and looked around the room at the OPTI screen. Fortunately it was blank. Though somehow, the screen appeared just as irksome.

"Why?" Jake asked. "You just had a panic attack."

"I know," I said, "but I didn't finish my exam, failed the others, and I missed practice."

"You can just retake them, Abigail," he said. "And honestly, I think you have too much on your plate. You're trying to be on the track-and-field team and in the school play on top of school. Why don't you just let go of one of your commitments?"

"I suppose now I'll have to drop the play," I said. "Though I love to perform."

"Why not drop track instead?" Jake asked.

"OPTI...wants me to do track. I have to do it."

"Are you sure?" Jake said. "Why would OPTI need you to do track?"

"It's what OPTI ordered me to do."

Jake sighed and nodded.

"By the way, did you ever submit your newspaper article on the baptisms?" I asked.

"I did," Jake said and frowned. "The chief editor of the school newspaper refused to publish the article I wrote and I'm no longer allowed to write about crime. If I write anything like it again, I'll be kicked out of the club. How will any change or progress occur? That was one of the most important subjects to write about for our time."

"That's disappointing," I said, wishing I could have helped. Attempts to make change were more difficult than I thought. Still a fire of determination was lit in me as I searched for an opportunity to do the same. "We'll figure it out." Would my attempts to speak out make any difference? Was OPTI's control of us too powerful?

Scarlett and Jake both stayed in the hospital until I met with a psychiatrist who prescribed me some antianxiety medication. I felt a sense of relief, however, I knew that the true relief would be freedom from OPTI. Other than a lack of sleep and anxiety, the nurse announced that I was healthy. As I left the hospital with Scarlett, after a goodbye kiss with Jake, I thought about what awaited me and the drive home felt slow like we were in a funeral procession. I dreaded returning home to what I knew would be a rage-filled OPTI. I began to wish I had perished instead of waking up to this nightmare. I wondered if I might have another panic attack once I got home.

Scarlett didn't speak until she pulled the car up our long curved driveway.

"What happened when you and Heath spoke, Abigail? Why did he become so mad? He broke up with me and then left without telling me why," I noticed her inaudible crying, a tear making its way down her cheek.

I stared at her tear-stained face and my heart plummeted in my chest. I couldn't bear telling her that Heath stormed out and probably broke up with her because of me—because he still has feelings for me.

"It's my fault," I lied. "I got mad at him again and we had a fight."

Scarlett crossed her arms and looked down. "I haven't told him this…" she said. "But I think I'm in love with him. And now, well…I don't know what to do." She put her head in her hands and started to cry.

"I'm sorry. I'm sorry we fought…"

"You should be!" Scarlett cried, her anger rising. "Why do you always have to drive him away?"

"I'm sorry," I said, and it was all I could keep saying without giving away the truth. She would be even more miserable if she knew.

She exited the car and hastened to the front door. I followed after her. The temperature was cool and the driveway wet from precipitation. I hugged myself to warm up.

"Please, Scarlett," I said, "I understand why you're mad. Maybe Heath wasn't the best guy for you. It's better—"

"*Better?*" Scarlett whirled around at the door. "How could anything be *better* right now?"

Droplets of rain fell in delicate splatters from the night sky; a full moon shone down upon us. "I know it's hard," I said. "But you can get through it." The rain came down harder, beginning to seep into my clothes and dampen my hair. Scarlett remained dry and untouched under the awning of the front porch.

"He was my first…my first love…" She spat back. It was hard to take but I didn't know what else to do. "What did you say to him?"

"I…I don't know…he got mad…"

"Are you seeing him behind my back?"

"What? No, of course not."

"You know, your chemistry during rehearsals was far from invisible."

"I was acting. Nothing more."

"Why else would he break up with me? He probably has a crush on you while you're with Jake, doesn't he?"

"Scarlett…please…" I shivered from the cold and ran a hand through my wet hair that dripped as if I was having an icy shower.

"Does he like you, yes or no?" Scarlett demanded.

"I think so…"

"And do you like him?"

"No…I-I don't think so."

"You *think*? So you do."

"No, Scar. Please…"

"Don't ever speak to me again."

I hung my head and tears fell from my eyes as Scarlett spun, opened the door, and stomped inside. The lights were on so I knew my mother was home.

When I got to the door and opened it, Renée waited behind it and gave me a tight hug when I entered.

"I'm so glad you're okay," Renée said. "Mom is in the family room, waiting for you before we go to bed."

"Oh okay, thanks," I said.

"Why are you crying? Why was Scarlett so upset?" she asked.

"Heath still likes me and he broke up with Scarlett," I said. "Scarlett figured it out."

"Oh, no," Renée said, putting her hands to her face. "But how is that your fault?"

"Because she thinks I like him back," I said, "but I don't."

"She'll get over it," Renée said. "You didn't even do anything."

"Yeah," I agreed. Even though what Renée said was true, a sliver of guilt remained in my heart as I recalled Heath's face when I kissed Jake. I didn't know what it meant and I shook it from my mind, hoping it would stay out.

"Abigail, you're home." I heard my mother say as she entered the foyer. She came over to wrap me in a hug and it confused me so much that it took me a moment to hug her back.

"You're home too, I see," I said.

"Well, I have more time now with my new job…" She trailed off. "Did I tell you I'm opening a private law practice?"

"Congrats," I said. "I'm very happy for you."

"This way, I'll be able to schedule my own work time and try to be around you all more," she said. "And in no time, Florian will move in and join our family."

"That's great," I said, trying to sound sincere. Mother spending more time at home rather than commuting a distance sounded wonderful, but I didn't want Florian around as my stepfather. We'd already had a previous stepfather named Gunther who used to force us to eat spinach soup and perogies. Aside from that, it seemed like I'd waited for this moment ever since Faith died and Father left.

"Why don't you go to bed? You look exhausted." She patted me on the shoulder.

Before I could respond, the screen on the wall of the family room turned on and OPTI appeared.

"I need to speak with Abigail before she goes to bed." Came OPTI's digitized voice without a trace of hesitation. "Clear the room immediately."

My mother looked at OPTI's icon in what I read as concern.

"You'll be fine." I heard my mother whisper and then she started up the stairs, urging Renée to leave too. Renée gazed back at me in worry and fear and I tried to put on a brave face for her. I doubted it worked.

I started into the family room and realized I trembled from head to toe. My chest hurt again, despite the medication, and I wondered if I would have another panic attack. When I dared look at the screen, it started to pulse at the speed of my pounding heart, and then he spoke.

"Abigail, didn't I warn you against failing your exams and track practice? I've gathered the results of your first exams and you failed all of them. I thought we had an agreement to prepare you for your life serving me. It was never in our agreement for you to be in the school play and you were chosen, even though I don't think you have the qualities fit for being an actress. Your understudy did much better. And don't think I haven't taken notice of your newfound faith. You've done so many things deserving of death. However, I can offer you a life fit for you. Serving me will give you a beautiful life of riches and power, if you have what it takes. But after what I've seen today and over the past months, it's clear that you have no appreciation for the life I've given you so far. If you don't pull your act together, things will get much worse for you. I guarantee it. In fact, I think it's time for Jake to learn the truth about you. You are in a relationship, right?"

OPTI's pulsing came to a halt and remained on the screen, making me freeze along with it.

"Abigail." He spoke again.

"Um, yes," I answered as fast as I could, feeling like OPTI was smothering me. I wanted to cry, though I knew it would only make things worse.

"Well, let's put it like this—I think Jake deserves to know exactly what you did and where you came from. Don't you think so?"

"But I didn't do anything. I didn't kill Mr. Edwin."

OPTI's colorful orb stopped pulsing. The swirls of colors left me dizzy.

"*You didn't kill Mr. Edwin?*"

"No...it was an accident." My voice choked in almost a whisper. My mind went blank, and suddenly, the memory of Mr. Edwin's death was blank and blurry and nothing I could do would resurface it.

"Explain to me what happened that night." OPTI began to vibrate once more.

"Well..." I feared explaining to OPTI exactly what happened because if I did, he would know that Scarlett and I put those flower petals in Mr. Edwin's tea to make him sleepy. "I don't know..."

"Well, I remember and I saw you put those petals in the mugs for Mr. Edwin to drink."

"They weren't poisonous. They were...for...sleeping..."

"Sleeping? You wanted to put a generous man to sleep?"

I didn't answer.

"Those flowers weren't valerian. They were poisonous."

"N-no...no they weren't," I said. Fear choked my throat as I thought back to that nightmarish evening. I believed they were valerian—I picked it out myself. What if I had been wrong? I felt my stomach drop and I became dizzier until I thought I might hurl. I may have actually killed someone.

"You were the one who put them in, and therefore, *you* are the reason that man died," OPTI said and stopped pulsing again.

"N-no...no...I didn't...I..."

My memory fogged again, and as I tried to remember that night, all that appeared in my mind was the image of Mr. Edwin's lifeless face—dead, eyes wide, and empty before Scarlett and me.

"No...I didn't kill him...I..." The dam broke, and like a rushing river, tearful sobs burst from the very core of my being so much so that it seemed like the walls should be shaking. My words came out in wails like the roar of tidal waves. "I didn't mean to. He hurt us so bad. They hurt us...We needed to escape. Please...Oh...Please... We were so *alone!*"

I clutched my chest in agony. My sobs continued for several minutes before they subsided, leaving a hollow and empty silence.

"Tell Jake about who you are." OPTI spoke as if I hadn't broken down in sobs. "Or I will tell him for you. You have one week. And if I don't see improvement in your performance in school and on the track team, I will find more ways to punish you. You're a murderer. You should be grateful that I've given you freedom."

OPTI vanished from the screen. The all-consuming guilt of having killed Mr. Edwin penetrated my heart and mind and all I could think about was Mr. Edwin slumped over in his chair, not breathing. After what felt like a very long time, I rose to my feet and ascended the staircase, one stair at a time.

Blinded by my tears, I stumbled through the hall to my room and into my bathroom. I started brushing my teeth and tried not to look at myself in the mirror. My hands shook, making it difficult to brush, and I ended up slipping and marking my cheek with toothpaste instead. My thoughts raced yet my mind was numb and I could barely concentrate. I kept thinking about Mr. Edwin's eyes, how empty and dark they were and how ghostly white his face was under the sharp bright lights in his kitchen.

Claustrophobia seized me, as if the walls of the room were closing in, and I couldn't breathe. It felt like I'd been shot. I noticed my eyes in the mirror and they were wide as if I'd seen someone die. And in a way, I had.

I couldn't breathe. My head pounded and seared as if I had a massive headache.

"N-no...no...no..." I said to myself. I put my head in my hands. "It's my fault...my fault...my fault..."

I fell to my knees again. My hands clutched my heart. Then I clasped my hands in prayer.

"I'm so sorry...I'm so sorry. Oh, please...I didn't know...I didn't know!"

I remembered what Faith taught me long ago about repentance.

"I repent. I repent. I repent. I'm so sorry...I..." Images of Mr. Edwin slumped over on the chair flashed in my mind. Then another memory surfaced from the Edwins' house—something I never wanted to remember. I was lying on my back; no—I couldn't remember. I could hear screaming, I didn't know where it came from. The ceiling was dark, everything was dark—hot breath met my cheek.

"No...no...no...I can't." I shuddered. The memory fled away as suddenly as it came and my heart wrung with agonizing guilt. I couldn't live with it. I couldn't live with myself. "I couldn't take it," I wailed. "I couldn't breathe. We were trapped. My body wasn't my own. There was nothing I could do. I couldn't breathe...I couldn't breathe..."

My eyes flitted around the room and then settled on a razor. I imagined it—all this pain would end. I got to my feet, staggered to the bathtub, and turned it on. Then I reached for it—the razor. I removed the blade. I gasped as it nipped my finger and a tiny drop of blood oozed from the cut. I tossed the plastic of the razor in the wastebasket. I pictured it in my head—lying in the bathtub, bleeding out until the water was deep red. A *murderer*—I couldn't live with it.

My focus channeled on the blade. My hands still shook and it was hard to grip it. I put the blade against my skin. A bead of sweat slipped down my arm and my heart jumped. It felt like my heart split open, raw and bleeding. I breathed in heavy gasps. I stared at the blade and then—

"Ahh," I groaned as I made the first light cut. Blood pooled in the crevice and dripped onto the white linoleum floor. I was drenched in a cold sweat and the room spun. My heart wrung with each beat. My vision blurred and my ears rang. I slumped back onto the floor, clutching my bleeding wrist, feeling weakened.

"Abigail!"

It sounded like Renée's voice. I couldn't answer. I couldn't warn her. Then it was dark.

All I could see were pearly white clouds beneath me, above me, surrounding me. Then I noticed a hand on my forehead and I looked up to see a wonderful face—the kind face of Jesus. He wore a glorious smile. His face left me speechless.

"It wasn't you." I heard echoing in my ears like a gentle hush of wind.

The guilt weighing my heart was swept away; my soul's anguish subsided into peace. I wanted to remain in this moment forever.

CHAPTER 26

Rescued

I woke. Disoriented, my surroundings a blur. I knew I had left heaven behind, returning to earth, broken yet breathing. My heart radiated with a joyful glow. I didn't know, couldn't explain what it was. Then a memory came to me—it was a hot summer day and I remembered sitting in the flower garden, listening to Faith telling Scarlett, Renée, and me all about the Holy Spirit. It felt as though it rested in my heart.

When I examined my surroundings, I was left dismayed. I realized I had returned to the hospital surrounded by the same queasy white walls. The only light coming into the room was from the window and the sky was dark aside from a pinkish-orange light of the rising sun behind the trees. An IV was attached to my left arm and my other was bandaged. I grimaced from the dull pain in my wrist and was careful not to move it.

The door to my room swung open and a nurse walked in.

"I'm glad to see you're awake. I'll need to replace your bandage," she informed me. "Then you can go back to sleep."

As she carried on with her task, I cringed when I saw the black stitches that sealed my cut. The sight brought back a wave of sheer terror from what happened last night—the pounding of my heartbeat echoing in my ears. The guilt that had weighed down my heart had disappeared, now a faint sensation. I thought I had died and made it to heaven. As much as I wished I hadn't woken up, I remained mystified by the great release from my burden. I didn't kill Mr. Edwin after all. Jesus's whisper proved it; my chains were broken.

I burst into sobs. All this time, OPTI tried to coerce me into believing that I'd murdered someone. Jesus's appearance and soothing words gave me a sense of liberty that couldn't compare to any I'd felt in a long time. Finally I could return back to the person I once was—a young girl with a broken bleeding soul and a flickering faith. Except OPTI still believed it.

"Your family is here," the nurse said. "They've been here all night."

"My whole family?" I asked.

"Your mother and sisters. Your father must be on his way."

"My mom is here?" I blurted. "I don't really have a father."

"Oh," she said and the nurse gave me a polite smile. "Yes, your mom is here. Should I tell her to come?"

"Tell them all to come," I said.

The nurse nodded and left.

"Abigail!" I heard Renée cry as she entered the room ahead of my mother. Renée rushed over to my bedside and wrapped me in a hug so tight as if we hadn't seen each other in weeks. Tears streamed down her cheeks and seeing her kind and innocent face in distraught made my heart ache. I couldn't bear to have to explain what happened to Renée. I wished I could protect her from knowing what I almost did to myself. It was too late. "Please never ever, *ever* do that again. You scared me."

I stared at Renée's broken expression and her words echoed in my mind. I thought about what might have happened to Renée if I had been successful. I couldn't bear that thought—of putting her through that kind of pain. As much as I wanted to leave this world behind, I couldn't do it to Renée or Scarlett or my mom or Jake or all the people I cared about.

"What happened, Abigail?" my mother asked. "I'm disappointed that you would do such a thing."

I couldn't speak and I was on the precipice of weeping over all that I had endured since OPTI's scolding.

"I thought I killed Mr. Edwin," I said and the pent-up sobs burst forth. I looked at them both in desperation. "OPTI made me believe it."

"Abigail, you didn't do it," Renée said at once. "Scarlett said there were more petals in the mug that he drank from, remember?"

"Why would OPTI send you to prison if you didn't do it?" my mother asked. "I expected you girls to be on your best behavior."

"We were," Renée said. "The Edwins were the problem."

"What did you give him, Abigail?" my mother demanded.

"I…I…we. Mom, we just wanted to get out of that house."

"What did you give him?"

"V-valerian. To make him sleepy."

"Why on earth would you try to make him sleepy?" my mother cried.

I exchanged a wary glance with Renée. I shuddered on the inside from the memory of that night spent with a dog collar around my neck.

"It wasn't safe there," Renée answered for me and another tear fell from her eye. "We already explained everything."

"How did you know it was valerian?"

"I remembered what it looked like from when we used to garden," I said. "And I read a book about botany from Father's study."

"When did you go in there?"

I grimaced. "A long time ago," I said. There were two rooms in our house that none of us were to enter: Faith's room and our father's study. My mother never cleared them out; there they sat, the last remains of Faith and my father.

"Never mind that. Did you give him poison by mistake?"

"N-no. I didn't."

"How do you know?"

"Jesus told me."

My mother appeared confused. "What do you mean?"

"I had a dream—"

"Enough about religion, Abigail," she said. "You need to focus on OPTI. He gave you a fair punishment for what you did and he even allowed you to come home. You should be grateful that you're free from that prison. I hope you've learned your lesson. I'll wait in the waiting room."

I lowered my gaze to my bed, wishing I wouldn't cry. The wind was knocked out of me and the ache in my heart resurfaced as if I had done it.

It wasn't you, I heard in my thoughts again, in the same distant tone, and I clung to Jesus's words with all my strength. I prayed that I wouldn't forget. As I thought about my dream of Jesus, I found solace in his comforting words and the tender hand placed on my forehead. I knew Jesus watched over me and even loved me. Tears came to my eyes at the thought of Jesus granting me such mercy. The dark tunnel that I'd traveled through up until now was beaming with a bright light like a burning beacon, my fear cast out, my weakness turned into strength. I wasn't alone.

Renée placed a hand over mine as a lone tear fell from my cheek. "What happened in your dream about Jesus?"

"He told me I didn't do it. I didn't kill Mr. Edwin."

"Of course he did," she said with a smile. "He saved your life too. Don't we all need to ask for help from God? I couldn't make it through life without him."

Neither could I. Jesus saved my life. If I hadn't fainted and gone to the hospital, I might have bled out. Renée was right. I wouldn't have made it this far in my life without help from God.

"Where's Scarlett?" I asked as I remembered our fight the night before.

"In the waiting room," Renée responded. "She wouldn't come. She thinks it was her fault."

"Tell her to come in," I said. "It wasn't."

Renée left the room, and after a moment, Scarlett entered. Like Renée, it looked like she'd been crying; and when she saw me, she broke down, her face in her hands.

"Oh, I'm so sorry!" she cried and came to my bedside. "I didn't know you would—"

"It wasn't you," I said before she could cause herself any more grief. "I thought I killed Mr. Edwin because OPTI convinced me that I did. OPTI claimed that those petals were poisonous, not valerian."

"They were valerian," Scarlett said. "I recognized them too from gardening. But I guess to OPTI, it must have looked like you did it… That's why you did…this?" Her eyes shifted to my bandage.

"Yes," I said. "I thought it was me."

"You're not a murderer, Abigail. You have one of the kindest hearts I know." She went on quickly. "Trust me, we only grew up together. Also I'm sorry I got mad at you. It's not your fault if Heath still likes you. I should be mad at him and not you."

"It's okay," I said. "I understand. I didn't hurt myself because you were mad. It wasn't your fault."

"Never do that again," Scarlett demanded with as much emphasis as Renée. "Promise me you won't do it again."

I stared up at her. Her request made me uneasy. However, I didn't want her to worry about me. I swallowed. "I promise."

"I'm sorry I let you take the fall for that," Scarlett said. "It should have been me. I should've been the one who went to that detention center. Not you."

"You didn't do anything," I said. I was glad it hadn't been Scarlett. I wouldn't want her to suffer like I did in that prison. There was one thing that lingered in my mind—OPTI's punishment. I would have to tell Jake.

"You have one week," OPTI reminded me when I was alone with him. There was a screen in my hospital room with OPTI's brain on it and it watched me until it was time for the lights to go out for bed. I felt nervous under OPTI's close surveillance, but what could I do? I doubted I would get much sleep.

I spent the rest of the weekend in the hospital while my cut healed and as a precaution so I couldn't make another attempt. I wasn't planning on it now. I kept having memories of me clutching the razor blade and blood dripping crimson onto the pale floor. I spent more time praying for the intrusive images to go away and asking Jesus for guidance. Just as my first dream had inspired me, this one made me yearn to follow Jesus even more as I became more and more free with myself, free from OPTI's accusation.

CHAPTER 27

Defamation

On Sunday, the hospital discharged me and my mother drove me home. I was nervous to return, and when I entered the front room, my eyes narrowed on the OPTI screen where I had been pressured into believing I murdered Mr. Edwin. My sobs and screams from that night echoed in my ears. Renée offered to let me use her bathroom since I was afraid to go in mine. My mother took all the razors and put them in her bathroom temporarily with the door locked, except when she was in it. Now I couldn't make another attempt. It felt good to be at home again and not to feel all that guilt crushing my heart. However, as I thought about the week lying ahead of me, my heartbeat increased and I found it difficult to relax. I had one week to tell Jake the truth about my past. I also needed to restudy all the material for all my school exams until I felt more confident about retaking them.

I didn't sleep the night before Monday arrived and instead lay awake while I tried to imagine what I would tell Jake. He may never speak to me again if he knew. Perhaps if I explained all the details, he would understand, especially my dream. Over the next week, I spent hours in class picturing what I would say to him while OPTI established a countdown clock that remained on the screen at home as additional pressure to tell him before OPTI did. Each day, in fear, I prayed for God's help—that maybe I wouldn't have to tell him. Or if I did tell him, I could have time to explain. Aside from this worry, I couldn't stop thinking about Heath. I saw him in class all week but he didn't look in my direction. I grew tired of his anger with me and I wanted to resolve things. When I was with Jake this week, I tried not to mention my irritation with Heath. In spite of this, it didn't stop gnawing at me, no matter how hard I tried to dispel it.

I retook all of my exams this week and felt more satisfied with my performance. However, my cut made it difficult to write and it ached throughout all the exams. OPTI was pleased with my performance and it seemed to be the only thing I did successfully this week. Friday arrived and I had to tell Jake before OPTI did so hopefully he might believe me. We sat across each other in the cafeteria, Jake munching on a sandwich while I picked at my tray of pasta. With so much stress lately, carbs were all I craved.

I played nervously with my water bottle while Jake bit into his salami sandwich. I looked around the room and noticed Heath having a laugh with some of his friends, patting one of them on the back. He caught my gaze and turned away. I sighed.

"You're quiet today," Jake said in concern. "Are you worried about something? Is it anxiety again?"

"No...nothing...well, sort of." I tripped over my words. A ball of stress squeezed my heart and I breathed heavier. Before I could say any more, Jake spoke, "Did I tell you I'm a candidate to become student body president?"

"No, you didn't. That's great news," I said, trying to sound happy. I doubted Jake was convinced. "I hope you get it."

"Have you ever thought about running? I mean, not many women run. I think it would be great if that changed."

"No," I said with unease. "I'm not sure."

"You could do well," he said. "You're very smart. You outsmart me in science, that's for sure."

"Thank you," I said. I cherished his compliment because so far, I didn't feel all that great about myself. Even though I knew I wasn't a murderer, OPTI's punishment was like another slap in the face and I continued to pray that I wouldn't suffer from amnesia.

"You're welcome," he said in a sweet voice. "Could you help me out with it? We're supposed to have presentations next week in the gym with our positions to persuade students to vote for us."

"Doesn't OPTI choose who gets the position?" I asked.

"Well, yes," he said, "but they're letting people vote before OPTI makes the choice. I suppose to increase participation and student engagement."

"I can help," I said. "What do you need?"

"I need you to come by my table and help pass out badges," he said. "Also I have to prepare a speech for speech night in about a month. That's when the president is decided. You could help me proofread it and practice. Unless, of course, you'd like to run yourself."

"No," I said. I couldn't have another priority on my plate after my anxiety attack. Though Jake's encouragement did make me dream a little. Wouldn't that be a position of leadership that could be used to influence and help others? I longed for an opportunity to create change. However, Jake was right—not many women ran and I knew there had been no woman president as far as I could remember. Faith even ran but was unsuccessful. If Faith couldn't make it, what were the odds that I would?

"I would vote for you."

"Me?" I said, staring at him and nearly dropping my water bottle. "You're just saying that."

He smiled. "Like I said, you're smart," he said. "You could make a great student body president. I tried to make a difference with the newspaper and that didn't work out. This race may be a better chance at creating change, don't you think?"

I nodded and my eyes shifted to a poster on one wall announcing the start of the student government election race. What better way to take a stand than to lead the school? I longed for that type of position. Perhaps this was the opportunity God was presenting me with to speak out about injustice.

"Yeah," I said, "I want to run. Thanks for the encouragement."

Jake looked as though he was about to speak when his OPTI-Phone beeped. He gazed down at it with a frown and then unlocked it. To my sudden horror, I could see a video of myself from seven months ago, placing flower petals into all three mugs. Mr. Edwin presented us with the mugs and then drank his. Once again, I had to watch him struggle and die. I closed my eyes and lowered my head as if I were guilty. My heart felt like it had been torn open once more. OPTI had beaten me to the punch. I held onto my memory of my dream so my brain wouldn't slip out of my fragile grip on reality.

"What's this?" Jake asked. "That girl…it looks like you."

"I didn't do it." I opened my eyes though I knew it was too late. "I didn't do it. Jake, I—"

"Then what is this?" he cried, rising from the table. "Did you… did you poison a man?"

"Please, Jake. It's not what you think."

"Tell him the truth," OPTI's voice whispered from Jake's phone, the video replaced by OPTI's orb.

Jake looked from his phone to me.

I couldn't find the words to explain myself.

"Abigail did not go to boarding school, Jake," OPTI said while I trembled in silence. "She was in prison. For murder. And I graciously allowed her to go free on the condition that she serve me."

Jake stared at his phone.

"Prison?" he looked up at me. "You were in *prison*? For *murder*?"

"Please, Jake," I cried though I knew my efforts were futile.

"I can't deal with this right now," Jake choked. Students at other tables were turning to watch. Heath had paused in his laughter to stare at both of us as if he were listening to every word. "It sounds to me that OPTI is right. I can't believe you would do that. And you've been keeping that a secret this whole time? *Really*, Abigail. You actually *killed* someone?"

He snatched his tray and strode away before I could say any more. I stared miserably down at the table on the verge of tears. I didn't even get a chance to explain it myself. I felt like an entire river of tears might flow from my eyes, if that was even possible.

I rose from the table and stumbled my way out of the cafeteria, my mind numb, my soul bleeding. I wandered blindly through the corridors until I came across my locker, though I'd forgotten why I was even there. I stared blankly inside it while tears blurred my vision. The life I'd thought I'd regained a grip on crumbled.

In my miserable desperate state, I accidentally bumped into someone as I attempted to leave my locker. I looked up, feeling ready to apologize, when I met Heath's unmistakable handsome face. His black hair still hung down to his ears; it looked neater as if he'd just had it groomed and trimmed.

"What happened?" he asked with no trace of humor in his expression.

I met his eyes as though I might drown in them and forgot where I was, back in the fog. Then a locker slammed shut nearby, jolting me back to the dismal present. I couldn't allow these feelings in and I couldn't explain what they meant.

"I thought you were mad at me," I said when I found my voice.

"What's that bandage on your wrist?" he asked, his eyes resting on my wrist.

I scowled when I realized some of the white bandage remained visible underneath the sleeve of my shirt.

"I can't tell you," I said.

"Did you and Jake break up?"

"It's none of your business." I snapped bitterly and sought to move past him. He caught my arm.

"I can keep a secret," he said, and his eyes were like stones in his sincerity.

"I can't tell you here," I said, glancing around nervously at the other students in the hallway.

Heath stepped closer to me and a sense of warmth encased me. "I know a place," he said under his breath.

I followed him outside of school and we walked across the back parking lot to the beginning of a trail in the surrounding forest. I practiced sometimes on this trail after school, and the nature around me put me at greater ease. I kept my distance as I walked beside him along the trail. Twigs and leaves crunched and crinkled under my feet. It felt weird to be alone with him. Not just alone but completely away from the world—a small sanctuary in OPTI's world. Something called me to close the distance between us; I fought against the urge.

"It's been a while," Heath said and nodded at me with a slight smile.

"You mean it's been a week," I said. "And you've been angry with me for most of it."

"I've had my reasons," he said.

"What are they?" I asked. "Tell me why you've been angry."

"You said there was never anything between us," Heath said. "But if I remember correctly, you enjoyed that night, our first kiss."

I was about to protest. He raised his eyebrows and I stopped because I knew he would know if I lied. "Maybe I did. But you crossed the line with me, remember? Whatever was between us vanished that night."

"Vanished?" Heath argued. "I highly doubt that."

"I thought we had a truce," I said. "You accused me of not abiding by it and now you're not. I was about ready to let go of it all."

His face darkened. "When I made that truce, I apologized for all of what I did. It didn't mean I would never have feelings for you again. How could your feelings have vanished when you weren't bothered that I was at the hospital to see you?"

I didn't answer and looked away. My mind reminded me of kissing Jake that night and picturing Heath's face in his place and the change that had occurred in Heath, in me—could it be that I felt love?

"In any case, we're here to discuss your bandage," Heath said, bringing me back to the present moment. "How did you injure yourself?"

"How do I know you're not going to be mad?"

He stopped suddenly and stuck his arm out so I walked into it and stumbled, our proximity was comforting and eased my wounded heart. Then he leaned close to my ear.

"Because nothing you say could change how I feel about you," he said. My heart thumped. Should I get it over with and tell him the truth? I barely understood all the feelings that came to me in his presence. It seemed like we were linked by an invisible thread that compelled me to get closer, to lean my head on his shoulder, to stretch up and—

I realized the distance between us had shrunk so my arm nearly brushed against his. I didn't try to step away. I knew I was in trouble, but despite the screams in my mind, my heart's call was stronger.

Then I was reminded of something.

"But…you and Scarlett," I said. "You said you weren't using her."

"I wasn't," he said, and he started to stride at a steady pace again. "I cared a lot about her…but…she wasn't you."

I didn't answer again. I kept walking alongside him and, once again, felt my heart trying to draw me closer to him as if the pull was against my will.

"I tried to…kill myself," I said and kept my eyes turned away from him.

"Why would you do that?" Heath asked. "What's the matter?"

"I didn't come here from a boarding school," I said. "I came from a detention center and used to be a prisoner there…"

"For doing what?" he asked, looking surprised.

"For…murder…OPTI thinks I killed a man. I know I didn't. I gave him valerian to make him sleep, not poison. Out of desperation—to end our suffering at the Edwins' hands."

I explained the rest of the situation—how we had to stay at the Edwins' while our mother recovered. Then I elaborated on how the Edwins mistreated us and, finally, how Mr. Edwin drank poisoned tea and died right in front of us. I watched his expression carefully the whole time. I thought he would be disgusted and would walk away from me, declaring I was a murderer. However, instead of anger, I saw understanding. Instead of accusations, I heard, "I believe you, I don't think you killed anyone."

I felt like a weight had been lifted off my shoulders. Heath believed every word, and this time, it didn't come from OPTI. Gratitude swirled in my heart so much so that I didn't notice how close I stood next to him.

"So it's true then," I said in a hushed voice. "Your feelings haven't changed."

"It's like I've known you for years," Heath said. "A connection that can't be explained simply."

I stopped trying to fight all the urges to get away, to force myself to remember the past with Heath. Yet none of those urges could overpower my greater desire to unite myself with him.

Before I could stop myself, I stepped forward and leaned up close to his face so my lips brushed against his. He caught my lips and deepened the kiss. Despite my misery earlier today, this kiss cast all of it away as if I'd entered a new world of bliss, privacy, and freedom. I put a hand on his arm and leaned closer to him so I was encased in his embrace. I wanted to melt into it, to forget all of our history and succumb to my heart's longing to be with him, to be near to him, to touch him, to be held by him.

However, I knew I couldn't love him. Not after he broke up with Scarlett and not when my relationship with Jake had been torn apart. There was more to it—I couldn't trust him after that whole phase of him chasing me around.

I mostly felt confused. So I broke the kiss suddenly and stepped away from him.

"I-I have to go," I said.

I turned around and stumbled along the trail to find the exit, fighting against branches and tripping over the roots of trees, hoping I could leave as soon as possible. I couldn't comprehend what I just did. Kissing Heath? For so long, I tried to get him out of my life, and now, I couldn't stop myself from dreaming about him. I still loved Jake, but after today, it seemed that our relationship was irreparable. Every fiber in my being was falling in love with Heath, the only person outside my family I'd ever felt deeply connected to in some strange way.

CHAPTER 28

Courage

I spent all of track-and-field with my mind like a live wire, buzzing with thoughts of Heath. Fortunately we ran a continuous mile and a half around the track for conditioning purposes. I performed better, I thought, yet my coach had corrections to give me on my form and time. Scarlett picked me up and drove me home afterward. I barely spoke to her, trying to hide what I'd done while my heart weighed down with guilt once again. I tried desperately to shut down my thoughts of Heath. They remained fixated on every memory I had of him after he stopped chasing me: sitting beside him in his car, greeting him on my doorstep, dressed up in a button-down shirt, his hair trimmed, him appearing at the hospital to see me. I found I preferred him with his wilder hair. After we arrived home, Scarlett stepped out of the car first and I trailed behind her into the house.

"I only told him the truth," OPTI said as I entered. Scarlett had already disappeared, most likely upstairs.

"I'm running for president," I responded through my anger. Somehow that kiss had refilled me with courage and strength.

"Fair enough," OPTI said, not seeming the least bit bothered. "Good luck. You might get it if I think you're the right candidate. Watch what you do or there are more punishments for you to face."

His image disappeared in a blinking blur, and despite my courage, I tasted a sliver of dread rising in the back of my throat. My heart ached over Jake's reaction to the video and OPTI's announcement about my time spent in prison. It almost made me think, maybe I had done it—*No*, my mind reminded me. They were valerian petals. Jesus told me himself that it wasn't me that killed him.

I hurried upstairs and to my bedroom. I threw my backpack to the ground and knelt at my bedside with my hands folded.

"Please help me, Jesus. Oh, please. Jake thinks I'm a murderer. I don't want to lose him. And I'm so confused...I don't know why I suddenly have feelings for Heath. I want to go back to how things were before...before I developed a crush on him. Should I be with Heath? But what would Scarlett think? She thinks I don't like him but if she finds out...Please, help me. I don't know what to do...I need comfort, an escape from all my grief. Please help me run for president so I can make the greatest change possible in your name. I don't want to be under OPTI's thumb anymore. Please, I can't stand it. *Please*."

"Abigail?" I heard Renée ask from the other side of my door. "Are you okay?"

At the sound of her voice, I rose to my feet and opened the door. I thought about Renée's reaction to my suicide attempt. I didn't want to upset her like that again.

"Yeah, I'm fine," I said. "I...I needed to...pray."

Renée gave the hall a furtive glance as if someone might be watching.

"I pray too sometimes," she said. "It gives me hope."

Hearing her say it brought tears to my eyes because for me, the faith I had discovered reignited the flame of hope I had lost as a child when Faith died and Father left. After Jesus rescued me again from suicide and OPTI's blame, the flame grew brighter.

"I'm glad," I said, my voice choked. "It does for me too."

I put a hand to my mouth and burst into sobs. I cried as I remembered a long time ago when I'd given up on my faith that my father would return and that Faith would come back. My dream of having a family was destroyed. The sorrow remained today, however, my faith had become like an anchor that grounded me in my despair, like the powerful glow of a lighthouse amid a darkened sky and a raging storm.

Renée stepped forward to give me a hug and I held on tight as if I might lose her.

"I love you so much," I told her.

"I love you too, Abby."

I sent a silent prayer in my mind that I would never lose my siblings. We'd already lost Faith a long time ago. I couldn't bear to lose Renée or Scarlett too.

My thought about Scarlett made me step apart from Renée and tense up. As I did, I heard Scarlett's bedroom door open.

"I'm going to be in my room," I told Renée. I hurried to close the door behind me, hoping not to see Scarlett at this point in time.

I sat down on my bed, mentally exhausted and sleepy.

"Why do you look so sad?" I heard Scarlett say to Renée.

I opened my door again. "We were having a moment."

Scarlett looked close to tears too.

"Why are you sad?" I asked.

"Isn't it obvious? Heath broke up with me, remember? And I had to put on a sweater today because apparently, it's unladylike to have exposed shoulders. This is just like the time I got detention for wearing a skirt above my knees without nylons. Things have got to change."

"Actually Jake broke up with me today," I said. "Sorry about the sweater and the skirt."

"So that's why you look like you've been crying?"

"Yes," I said with a nod.

Renée sighed. "I'm going to do homework," she said.

"But it's Friday," Scarlett said, looking incredulous. "Nothing better to do, I guess?"

"Leave her alone," I said to Scarlett who frowned again as Renée retreated back to her room.

Her frown faded once Renée was gone. She turned to me with expectance.

"So it looks like we're in the same boat," she said. "Let's go share a tub of dairy-free frozen yogurt, watch a movie, and talk about it."

"I'm not in the mood, sorry," I said and began to step back into my room.

"Don't make me do it alone," she said. "Come on, Abby, I need to talk about it, and from the look on your face, I can tell you need to talk too."

"I want to take a nap," I said. "Also since when do you not eat dairy?"

"Please," she said. "Well, I wouldn't say it's a trend…but it kind of is now. If you don't like it, there's always regular ice cream. We haven't had a chance to hang out since the winter festival and you deserve a nice post-breakup remedy."

"I don't think anything could make me feel better about this," I said. She looked at me with gleaming eyes that pressed me to finally say, "Okay. If you really want to hang out, then…all right, fine."

"You're still in track clothes," she said. "You can't have a proper post-breakup party without being comfortable."

We both changed into T-shirts and sweatpants, and I reluctantly met up with her downstairs.

She was waiting for me, reclining on the sofa with her eyes fixed on the television as she flipped through channels. Junk food covered the coffee table, and as exciting as the thought of this party was, all I could think about was kissing Heath, the warmth of his breath, the flush of my cheeks. I didn't want to tell her, and I knew I would have to be on guard not to let it slip. Also although it was off, the OPTI screen remained in the living room and I felt more afraid of having any sort of conversation about what I did today.

I sat down on the small space on the sofa at her feet.

"What movie do you want to watch? Oh, wait, there's that cool thriller television show…I've seen most of it though. What do you suggest we do?"

"I don't know," I said, "I don't know what's good. I haven't paid attention to movies lately."

"I'll pick then." Scarlett scrolled through the menu of movies and put on a romantic comedy.

"Can you grab the frozen yogurt? It's in the freezer."

I retrieved the frozen yogurt and two spoons. I rejoined her, feeling more cheerful not to be alone right now. It made me glad it was healthier because I needed to eat like this to improve my fitness in track. I worried about eating the junk food and whether it would hinder my performance.

"I can't eat it alone," Scarlett said, and I sighed as I ate a spoonful. It tasted so good but I knew later I would regret it.

We were watching the beginning of the movie and I had already eaten a good portion of frozen yogurt and chips. Then Scarlett started to cry after the couple's first kiss in the movie.

"What's wrong?" I asked.

Scarlett sat up. "Remember what I told you?" she asked. "Well, like I said, Heath was my first...love...ever."

"I'm sorry, Scar," I said and felt guilt settling in my throat as I thought about what I did today. I put a hand on her shoulder. "I didn't know how much you cared about him."

She looked up at me with tears dripping down her cheeks. "I never got a chance to tell him," she said. "And I don't know if he... felt the same."

"I don't know," I said. "I wish I could tell you..."

"How could anyone love me?" she asked. "He probably didn't."

"I love you, Scar," I said. "And perhaps...he did love you."

"He broke up with me because he likes you," she said. "I know it's not your fault yet it feels terrible to know that he probably didn't love me back."

My face fell and I was so overcome with guilt that I thought I might explode into tears in front of her. Instead I tried to keep it together out of fear of her knowing. I mentally repented, wishing I could go back and hold myself back from kissing Heath. I leaned forward and gave Scarlett a hug. She returned it in the midst of weeping.

"I'm sorry he hurt you," I said. "You're better off without him."

She continued to cry and I tightened my hug, wishing it could take her pain away. I felt the urge to tell her, to admit to my mistake. No words came out.

"How did Jake break up with you?" she asked as she pulled back. "I thought you made up at the hospital."

"Well, part of my punishment from OPTI was to tell him that I murdered Mr. Edwin," I said and swallowed. "OPTI showed him a video of it before I could and then told him that I went to prison." I looked at the blank screen where OPTI might appear.

Scarlett deepened in her sadness. "I-I'm sorry that happened," she said. "Don't worry, I can tell him the truth. I'll back you up."

"I don't think he'll speak to either of us," I said. "He seemed pretty upset. I don't want you to take the fall for me."

"I don't care," she said. "I'm going to tell him."

I mustered a small smile. "If you think it will help, then go ahead. But I don't think he'll believe you either...OPTI showed him a video of it. It's hard to disprove. Perhaps during my candidacy for president, I can show him who I truly am."

Scarlett snorted as she drank her soda and it came out her nose. "Did you just say you're running for president?" Scarlett said through a gasp. "Why didn't you tell me?"

"I just decided it," I said. "I hope I can make some changes."

"Lucky for you, you already have a campaign manager," she said, standing up and pacing. "I know how to help you win. We have to go shopping immediately, and what about social media accounts? You'll need one of those and have you scheduled a hair appointment? I'd say long but neat with layers. How much time do we have—"

"Scar, calm down. I just decided this," I said.

"Okay, okay," she said and sat back down. "Tell me when your first event is."

"Next Friday," I said.

"That's not a lot of time," she said, her forehead pinching. "Do you know your position yet?"

"No," I said, "I haven't even registered yet. Jake is running too but he already knew about it in advance. I have a lot of homework piling up and I have to stay in shape."

She shot up from the sofa, looking ready to burst into action. "Then what are you waiting for? Register now, if you can. I can help you get it done in time."

"I thought this was a post-breakup party?" I said.

"And now it's a presidential-preparation party so there," she said. "I'll go grab my laptop and yours." She practically bounced upstairs in excitement, and I decided it wouldn't be a bad idea to have help with this. I had no clue what specific stances I would take. I'd been so busy juggling my studies, track, and the play that I didn't have time to think about addressing problems with the school. I sent up a prayer for guidance. I knew based on what I learned about Christianity that it should be about love. I remembered Faith told us Jesus healed the sick and taught to care for vulnerable people. So I did my best to identify problems at school in which people were in need. I asked God to show me how I could help.

Scarlett returned with her silver laptop with a mint-green protective cover. She brought my bulky black one with her. Unexpectedly Renée rushed down after.

"You're running for president?" she asked, her hazel eyes bright and inquisitive. "I want to help."

"You know it's not of your school," Scarlett said as she plopped down on the sofa beside me. Renée sat on top of the coffee table, facing us. "Don't sit there."

"Oh relax, Scar," Renée said. "I can sit wherever I want. I can even sit on you if I'd like to." She rose and moved toward Scarlett, squatting on top of her.

"Ugh, you're going to get lint on my pants, no way," she said, nudging her away. "Go back to the coffee table."

Renée crossed her arms in triumph and then sat back down on the coffee table.

"Now, Abby." Scarlett poised herself to type on a blank document. "Running for president is a huge deal. You'll have complete control over some of the policies of school, though unfortunately, the principal can still override your leadership. That's why you have to be smart. If you get the school on your side, you have way more influence."

"What about OPTI?" Renée said. "Doesn't he have power over what you do?"

"OPTI chooses the president usually based on how many votes you receive, though I recall some past exceptions," Scarlett said, "which means your policies must align with the ones he wants for the school. Try to think of all the things that could be improved about school."

I grimaced as I realized she was right. How could I reach people if my policies were against OPTI's wishes? OPTI wouldn't allow me to convince people to allow religious people to live freely and without threats of violence. I suppose my changes would have to be radically different if I wanted to stand out and attract people. If the majority of the votes went to me, how could OPTI refuse?

"Let Abigail decide," Renée said. "She's the one running. What policies do you want to happen?"

"What's one thing about school that you would change?" Scarlett asked.

I thought deeply about what she asked, but as I did, I was reminded of the piles of homework I had to do this weekend and the exercise I needed to stay in shape. Then it came to me.

"Well, I struggle sometimes with my work," I said, "and I'm sure I'm not alone. I could…start a tutoring program where upper-classmen volunteer to tutor younger students."

"I think we need a better dress code," Scarlett said. "I think everyone should be able to express their fashionable tastes without ridicule and especially without detention. We should be able to choose how we present our bodies without judgment."

"That's your idea," Renée said. "What do you think, Abby?"

"I agree with that," I said. "Detention sounds harsh. All right, write those ideas down."

Scarlett nodded and started typing away, her face set with determination.

"There's one important thing we haven't mentioned…" Renée said and looked sad suddenly. "Faith…"

"Oh," I said and then fell into my own grief over my sister. "Maybe I could advocate for better security to prevent…and not allow students or any individual to bring guns in or around the school campus."

"Yes," Scarlett said. "That should be one of your central positions. If only someone had done something before Faith's death. She would be alive."

We sat in a glum mournful silence. Imagine how different my life would have turned out if my sister was alive and free from violence as a result of her faith. Thinking about Faith reminded me of my own experience with death. That gave me another idea.

"What about suicide prevention?" I suggested. "I could set up counseling services for students and a number to call in case they're at that point. I could also implement a plan for punishing bullies, particularly ones who hurt based on someone's race, ethnicity, religion, gender, or sexual orientation. Everyone deserves to be free from threats of violence. How can you have freedom without it?"

"That's a great idea," Renée said. "That could help a lot of people."

Scarlett typed away, nodding her head as she did so.

"One more thing…" I said. "I could propose a conference for women of all races, ethnicities, genders, religions, and sexual orientations to share their experiences to encourage students to be more accepting and aware of the issues."

"All right," Scarlett said. "That's enough."

"I'll have to put together graphics to present these ideas. I'll need to pass out fliers and hang posters too."

"I can post your ideas on OPTI-Social and share it with my friends. We'll need a headshot of you as soon as possible to go on OPTI-Photogram."

"I'll tell my friends to ask their siblings to support you," Renée said.

"If the first event is next Friday, then we must go shopping this weekend," Scarlett said. "Do you have any business attire?"

"No, I don't think so."

"I'll help pick it out," Renée said. "I know what would look good on you."

"She won't like your taste in fashion," Scarlett said, raising her chin. "Mine, on the other hand, would suit you perfectly. I'd say you go with business casual at the first event and formal for the headshot and speech. Jumpsuits are a great way to make a fashion statement. They would look great on you."

"No way," Renée said in a huff. "You should buy a dress or wear a suit, whichever you prefer. Not a jumpsuit."

"Maybe I'll go by myself," I muttered, sensing a fight about to rise between them.

"No, no," they both said at once and then exchanged a glare.

"I really want to help," Renée said when she looked away.

"We'll try to get along," Scarlett said and crossed her arms.

"We should probably go to the store and try different outfits on first," I said. "That might help."

"We'll go tomorrow then," Scarlett said. "We'll do headshots on Sunday after I do your hair and makeup. I have a friend whose gifted in photography. Don't worry, Abby, with my help, you'll win for sure."

"With me too," Renée said.

"Yeah, yeah," Scarlett said.

"I don't have much time to put everything together."

"That's where I come in," Scarlett said.

"*We*," Renée insisted.

"I guess I'll go get started on my poster board," I said and jumped up from the sofa. "Can you share those notes with me?" I asked Scarlett who nodded.

I headed upstairs and began my work on this presentation for president. As soon as I found myself alone, I recalled my exchange with Heath today and imagining the kiss we shared today gave me goose bumps. Once again, my heart plunged into guilt and I prayed for forgiveness. I didn't know how to bring it up to Scarlett. As I set up the information for my poster board on my bulky laptop, provided by OPTI, all of my feelings for Heath came rushing in and I couldn't escape the desire to kiss him again. I knew we had a complicated history and I wondered if I could trust that he had put his past behavior behind him. I didn't know what to expect on Monday when I saw him. Also as I put this presentation together, I worried that I might have another panic attack. The medication I consumed earlier helped ease some tensions; however, I knew there would be another storm coming. Change wouldn't be easy. I was determined to fight for it.

CHAPTER 29

Assertive

"Mmm…now this looks wonderful! It's a must-have." Scarlett gazed at me while I spun around so she could see the black sleeveless dress I had on at every angle. "Chic and professional."

"This is the fifth outfit we tried, and so far, they are all a must-have," I said. "I think we need to narrow it down to three."

"Well, lucky for you, I have excellent taste," she said. "Which three are your favorites?"

"I like the navy suit the best," I said.

Scarlett sighed. "What about the scarlet jumpsuit? Didn't you think it looked gorgeous on you? It's also my name and favorite color. What could make a bolder statement?"

"It's too bold for me," I said. "I'd rather do something more classic. What do you think, Renée?"

"I agree," Renée said. "The gray suit is a safer choice and you also looked lovely in it."

"I guess all my efforts will go to waste then," Scarlett complained with a dramatic sigh, crossing her arms. Then her arms uncrossed and her voice returned to a louder pitch. "I am your campaign manager and I insist you follow my advice if you want to win. You can't play it safe. The bolder you are, the more people will take notice."

"All right, fine," I said and began to understand her perspective. "Relax. One of the outfits can be the scarlet jumpsuit."

"That's what you'll wear when you make your speech," Scarlett said in triumph. "It's decided."

"Won't it be distracting?" Renée said.

"Exactly," Scarlett said. "If you're lucky, people might forget the other candidates."

"I think the focus should be on my policies." I pointed out.

"It will be," Scarlett assured me. "Trust me. The outfits will make you look and feel like a real president."

"I trust your judgment," I agreed. "So I'll get the jumpsuit, this navy suit, and…the beige dress."

"Sounds good to me," Renée said and I could see her begin to accept it.

"Oh, what about the black one?" Scarlett said. "Black is bolder."

"All right, fine, Scarlett," I said before she could become annoyed with me. "Let's go with that one."

"Wait but the beige dress makes you look more innocent. Now you have four outfits total. And what about the gray suit?"

"Look, I have enough outfits," I said. "If I become president, maybe then we could come back here and buy more outfits."

"Oh, then, we'll definitely have to get you a brand-new wardrobe. I can't wait!"

The next day began with Scarlett storming into my room at 7:00 a.m. and opening the curtains so light streamed into my room, directly on my face, alerting me and blinding my tired eyes.

"Time to get in the shower," she said. "I'll be doing your hair, makeup, and nails. You'll be wearing the beige dress with the white blazer."

I rubbed my tired eyes, trying to fight the urge to fall back asleep.

"Come on," she said. "Your sleep must be disrupted if you want to get everything you need done. I know you have a lot on your plate and that's why I'm helping you."

I sighed and rolled out of bed, knowing she was right. Scarlett did make a good manager.

"You can get ready in my room. I have everything set up," Scarlett said and led me down the hall to her room.

I'd been using Renée's bathroom since the incident, and I almost never entered Scarlett's room, so it came as a surprise when I found every inch of the white carpet immaculate and pristine as if we had just moved in. The headboard of her bed captivated my eyes. It looked as though someone had splattered it with paint in varying shades of magenta that settled into a deep-purple hue, all against a white background. The duvet's calm-gray hue soothed my eyes like a bed of soft clouds before a storm. A couple pillows with a touch of light pink gave a pretty compliment to the rest of the bed. Beside the bed rested a white side table accented with pink tulips in a vase perched on top. A magenta rug stretched out underneath the bed, completing the bold serenity of the room.

"How is your bed already made...and so neat?" I asked as I followed her inside.

"It took plenty of practice," she said. "It wouldn't feel right to start the day without my bed made. I can make it pretty quickly now."

She urged me into her bathroom.

My grogginess made me underestimate Scarlett's claim that everything was set up. When I entered the bathroom, I felt like I'd walked into a professional beauty salon. A collection of makeup was positioned on the counter arranged with precision, a stool placed before it. On the other side of the sink sat an assortment of hair products in addition to a blow-dryer and a hair curler, both set up and plugged in.

"When did you do all this?" I asked.

"I organized it last night before I went to bed," she said. "Well, except for the blow-dryer and hair straightener. I've been waiting for the opportunity to use it on someone. I bought the organizer and some of the makeup and hair products once I was cast in *Tartuffe*. I did my own makeup for that show and for *Richard III*."

I gaped. "You did that all by yourself?"

"Of course," she said, "I wouldn't have dared let anyone else do it."

"What time did you go to bed last night?"

Scarlett didn't answer. Instead she stepped out of the bathroom and closed the door behind her.

"Shower quick and let me know when you're done."

I did as she said and showered as fast as I could. Once the hot water met my face, it awakened me to all the problems I had to face. I'd had a restless night with my mind preoccupied, wondering what Heath could be up to and if, perhaps, he was thinking of me. I'd spent so much of my time trying to get away from him and now my breath caught each time I imagined holding his hand or even standing close to him.

As I stepped out of the shower and wrapped a towel around myself, Scarlett swung open the bathroom door and nagged at me to sit down at the bathroom counter. She began putting a bunch of different hair creams in my hair to add volume, to make it soft, to protect it from heat—I never put this much effort into my hair. I hoped I could trust Scarlett's judgment. She blow-dried my hair with care, to make it even straighter than usual.

"Why didn't you tell me you started?" Renée's voice carried into the bathroom as she hurried inside. Her auburn hair was disheveled as if she'd just rolled out of bed.

"Why are you in my room?" Scarlett asked. "Get out."

"Renée is a part of this too," I argued.

Scarlett stopped blow-drying my hair, put it down on the counter, and crossed her arms. "What are you going to help with? You're only eleven years old. What do you know about hair and makeup? You don't even wear it."

"I'm good at art and I know what colors look good together," she answered, her arms crossing as well.

"Why don't you show Renée how to do it?" I asked. "Isn't it great that you both share similar interests?"

They both remained throwing bitter glares at each other as though they were having a staring contest.

"All right, well, I guess I'll finish on my own then," I said.

"No way," Scarlett said, uncrossing her arms and facing me. "I'm your campaign manager."

"And I want to be her assistant," Renée said, looking at me, her eyes gleamed with hope.

"If we're going to do this, then you two have to get along," I said.

Scarlett huffed and then shrugged. She raised the blow-dryer again to finish. Renée sat down on the edge of the bathtub. They both helped me throughout the process—Scarlett finished styling my hair with the curling iron so that my hair fell in soft waves down my back.

"It looks great," I said. "Thanks, Scar."

"I know, you look gorgeous," Scarlett said. "Wait until I put some makeup on you. What color eye shadow do you think I should put on?"

"Pink would look nice," I said.

"Uh-uh. I think we should go with a more natural color like a soft brown."

"I like pink too," Renée said.

"Oh, come on," Scarlett said. "Pink is fine but you need something that's natural that also makes you stand out."

"A soft pink could make her stand out," Renée argued.

"I'm doing soft brown," Scarlett decided. "I know what I'm doing."

"All right," I said finally, though I grew annoyed and I could tell Renée felt the same.

We went with a soft brown, and Renée ended up helping Scarlett put the eye shadow on my face. To finish, Scarlett added a neutral-pink lipstick.

"You look so beautiful," Renée said when my makeup was done. "Your beauty enhanced."

"You look absolutely marvelous," Scarlett said and her eyes sparked with excitement. "Wait until after we're done."

"For what?" I asked.

"Well, I figured we have to announce that you're running as soon as possible. You'll have to prepare a social media post on OPTI-Social and OPTI-Photogram alongside your headshots."

"I don't have many friends on there or even at school in general," I said. "Who will support me?"

"Don't worry," Scarlett said. "I'll share it on mine and I know tons of people."

Thinking about social media gave me a sinking feeling despite Scarlett's help. I was far from popular at school. I had some acquaintances in track-and-field as well as from *Richard III*. Other than that, most people didn't notice me. How would I become the popular vote? The play might have directed attention to me, however, I didn't even get to perform and that still upset me.

Once we were done, Scarlett urged me to put on the beige dress and the white blazer. Scarlett's photographer friend arrived fifteen minutes later. His name was Julian and he had a very pretty face with curly brown hair. His high-definition camera hung from his neck. I noticed Scarlett blush as soon as she answered the door.

"Hello, Julian. How are you this morning?"

"Pretty good, Scarlett," he said with a white smile. "Are you ready to get started?"

Scarlett's eyes widened as though she just woke from a nap.

"Oh…yes. This is my sister Abigail," she said, making a half-hearted gesture in my direction. "As you know, I'm her campaign manager and I think the best shots we can capture are outside on the front porch. What do you think?"

"I think the lighting outside is excellent," Julian said. Then he extended his hand out to me. "Nice to meet you, Abigail."

"You too," I said. I took his hand and shook it a couple times. "And this is Renée, our younger sister." I gestured to my sister who held out a tentative hand to shake his.

"All right, we're losing time," Scarlett said as he and Renée shook hands and quickly walked past Julian to the front porch. "Come on, Abigail."

Julian smiled at me and then turned to follow Scarlett outside. I looked over at Renée. We shared a long sigh.

"This is going to be a long day," Renée said as we both walked outside and closed the front door behind us. The air was dry and cold. Goose bumps rose on my legs as a shiver ran down my spine.

However, the sun shone down on my face, the heat warming it with gentle rays.

"You picked a good day to do this." Julian noted to Scarlett.

"Oh, thank you," she said with her eyes fluttering. "I'm Abigail's campaign manager. She's definitely going to win with my help."

"I'm sure she will," Julian said and gave me another warm smile. "Why don't you sit down on the porch swing over there? I'll start taking shots once you're settled."

I crossed the porch to the chair swing to sit down. Julian held up his high-definition camera and began taking shots of me sitting on the chair.

"Try putting your hand on the armrest," Scarlett said and I followed her direction. Julian took several pictures and held out his camera for Scarlett to look them over.

"No, this isn't working," Scarlett muttered. "You need to look more...more..."

"Confident?" Renée finished.

"Exactly," she agreed for once. "Could you take it at an angle to make her look more assertive?"

Assertive? I asked myself. I didn't feel assertive at the moment. It seemed like a quality that only men could possess with OPTI as our ruler. I wanted to be strong though. I didn't like feeling weak and helpless. So I followed Scarlett's direction and tried my best to present myself as strong and assertive to the camera. I tried to think of a time when I felt strong and remembered the feeling in my heart during my dream of Jesus after I nearly committed suicide. I felt so much peace and freedom from all that chained me. I found freedom to praise and love Jesus with my gifts and talents; I found freedom in his perfect love that swept away all my fear like a mighty breeze. As I posed, I recalled that strength I obtained in that special moment and hoped it would emanate through the photos. I could sense a glow in my heart, especially when I thought of Jesus. It motivated me to use this opportunity to honor Jesus and make a difference at school.

"Don't smile, Abigail," Scarlett said while I posed.

"She looked fine." Renée spoke up. "Do you want to smile, Abigail?"

"No, she doesn't," Scarlett said. "Should she smile, Julian?"

"Maybe you should ask Abigail," Renée said.

"Maybe you shouldn't be involved in this," Scarlett retorted.

Julian looked between both my sisters and then at me.

"Well, I think you have a pretty smile," he said.

"Thank you," I said, averting my gaze.

"*Doesn't she?*" Scarlett said. Her voice fell flat in her anger. "Go ahead then, Abby. Why don't you smile?"

"I don't really feel like doing this anymore." I rose from the chair swing.

"What?" Scarlett cried. "No, sit back down right now. We're not finished."

"We're finished with you," Renée said as she crossed the porch to the front door.

"Go ahead and leave, Renée," Scarlett said in a voice that emanated false kindness. "You probably have homework to get done, don't you?"

"It's better than spending time with you." Renée shot back and departed through the front doors.

"I have other things to do as well," I said as my irritation grew. "On my own."

"But I'm your campaign manager," she called after me as I headed for the door.

"I don't want you to be my campaign manager anymore," I said. "It's too frustrating."

Scarlett's face reddened. "Fine. I won't be. Good luck on your own."

"I can do it with or without your help." I snapped. Then I looked at Julian who watched everything in bewilderment. "Thanks, Julian. Send the photos to me when they're touched up. Scarlett can give you my contact information."

As I went inside, my anger surged. I knew she had tried to help me, however, she controlled every aspect of the campaign without listening or acknowledging Renée's or my opinions. Her last comment frustrated me even more and motivated me to prove that I could do it on my own.

"Can I still help you?" Renée asked me as we climbed up the stairs to our rooms.

"Of course," I said. "I need some time alone though."

We parted at the top of the stairs for our rooms. As soon as I got there, I changed into some more casual clothing and started working on my presentation board again, advertising my goals as president. I had to make posters to put up around school. Not to mention I had schoolwork to get done and I hadn't exercised yet today. I grew anxious that I wouldn't be able to keep up with my work again. Having so many tasks to do at once tired me and I had little time to take a break from it. However, I couldn't think of a better opportunity to act on my faith.

After a couple of hours, my stomach began to growl so I went downstairs to make something to eat for all of us and ran into Scarlett lounging on the sofa, flipping through the channels on the television.

"Any progress?" she asked as I crossed the room to the kitchen.

"Yes," I said, "I'm halfway done with the poster board."

"That's good," she said, and it seemed she had calmed down.

I walked inside the kitchen and began cooking some rice and vegetables for Renée and me. Scarlett rose to her feet and came over to sit at the island.

"I'm sorry, Abigail," she said. "I didn't mean to make you upset."

I glanced over at her and knew from her sad eyes that she meant her apology.

"I guess I got carried away with the position," she said. "I've been feeling pretty awful lately. Being your campaign manager was a way to get my mind off of Heath and stay busy. I'm sorry I took my anger out on you."

"I get that breakups are hard," I said, and I felt my guilt return with full force. "I can't work with you if you won't let me have a say in how I go about it."

"I'll try to listen more," Scarlett said. "Can I be your campaign manager again?"

"Only on two conditions," I said. "One, that you let me make more decisions, and number two, that you're nice to Renée and that you apologize for mistreating her."

Scarlett scowled at the last part. I gave her a hard look.

She sighed. "Fine. I'll be…nice…to Renée. And…I'll apologize."

I finished in the kitchen and ate while Scarlett examined the headshots from this morning on her phone. Renée came down to eat and, at first, seemed reluctant to join us.

I looked at Scarlett.

"I'm sorry, Renée," Scarlett said, though she also appeared hesitant. "I'll try to be…nicer to you."

"Thank you," Renée said.

We spent the rest of the afternoon planning a social media post. Scarlett found the right headshot, and with her and Renée's help, I put together an announcement that I was running for president and a summary of my goals to help those in need at school, from tutoring to banning weapons on school grounds to holding a women's diversity conference. Scarlett shared it on both her accounts with some success. They both received some likes, though as Scarlett scanned through her news feed, the other candidates received more attention and approval. One of them promised scholarships and grants for research, internships, and college to affluent white men of OPTI's choice. Another candidate promised more punishments for men and women for wearing clothing unsuited to their gender and tightening restrictions on which bathroom both men and women were allowed to use.

Finally I looked over Jake's post which advocated for more diversity in the school newspaper club and other student-run clubs—a pretty daring position to take. Racial minorities were often excluded from important positions and involvement in certain clubs. Unfortunately Jake didn't have much popularity with people either. It upset me to see the post and remember that Jake thought I murdered Mr. Edwin because of OPTI's lies. I didn't know what to do or say to get him back and now I competed with him for president. How could I start over with Jake after I kissed Heath? My feelings for Heath grew so much stronger after one weekend. It left me in confusion.

"You're the only woman running," Scarlett said as she scanned through her news feed on her phone. "That can either be a good or a bad thing. Actually I don't remember the last time there's been a woman that became a student government president."

"You'll stand out," Renée said. "And offer a unique perspective."

I nodded, though I doubted that I could win. "If a woman has never won, how am I supposed to suddenly get the position?"

I exchanged glances with Scarlett and Renée as if they might be able to answer my question. None of them said a word.

CHAPTER 30

A Storm Draws Near

I opened my eyes the next morning and wished I didn't have to climb out of bed. I didn't know what I might face after I announced my run for president. First, students knew me as a candidate for school president and the only woman running. I knew it would come with a certain amount of attention. I was apprehensive to know what kind. Second, I would have to face Heath and I had no idea how to act. My feelings for him still confused me. A part of me told me to end my relationship with him fast. Another voice in my head told me to pursue my feelings for him. Third, I would have to face Jake now that OPTI had turned him against me.

Scarlett drove us all to school today as an effort to be kinder to Renée and, throughout the drive, gave me a long pep talk about how to handle the attention. However, the discussion made me even more nervous.

"Just be you," she added at the end of her lecture. "Let people get to know the real you and they'll vote for you for sure."

I didn't know how to do that. I was so adjusted to others not noticing me and not fitting in that I feared that if I acted as myself, I would be teased or ridiculed.

Scarlett and I parted once we were inside the building and I stood in the front entrance for a moment, watching students crowding the hall, laughing, chatting, patting each other's shoulders, snick-

PAIGE TREVISANI

ering, and whispering. I took a deep shaky breath and dared to enter the halls with students that may have only just noticed me.

As I expected, people turned away from their respective conversations to stare at me as I walked by. A couple of girls turned to giggle with each other and a boy I didn't recognize put up his hand to give me a high five. I met his hand, unsure of what else to do. The girls giggled again and I lowered my head when I realized I was the butt of a joke. Then I noticed the flash of a camera, and before I could stop the nameless photographer, they hurried away. My confidence in my campaign dwindled with every step.

"You look scared," a girl with a nose piercing informed me.

I rushed past her with my head down in further embarrassment. I didn't want to look scared, however, I didn't know how to fix my expression. As I took each step, I walked past a wall of windows and the clouds parted to reveal a beaming sun shining down on my head. I lifted my chin and kept walking through the storm, my bravery revived.

As soon as I entered intermediate chemistry, I noticed people eyeing me. Jake wasn't here yet, his desk empty, and my heart sank that he might not come at all. I swallowed the lump in my throat and tried to ignore both my classmates and my sadness as I sat down. I withdrew my notebook from my backpack. I examined the board to assess the homework due for tomorrow's class. As I did, Heath entered the class with his usual grin though it brightened. He walked past my desk, close enough so that his arm nearly brushed against mine, making my heart thud in my chest. I concealed a shy smile. He sat down in his usual spot in the back of the class, in the row next to mine. I could feel Heath's yearning gaze on my back and tried to pretend to be focused on my notes in my notebook. His stare made the hair stand up on the back of my neck.

When the teacher entered the class, all the chatting and whispers died down. She smiled, and as she looked around the classroom, her eyes settled on me.

"I'm thrilled to announce that Abigail Richardson received a 98 percent on the recent exam, the highest grade in the class. Congrats to one of our presidential nominees."

I shrunk in my seat as the class turned to stare at me. Some people appeared curious; some stung me with sharp glares. I stiffened and flashed a shy smile. Once more, I could sense Heath's stare on my back and the part of me that had feelings for him welcomed the attention. The teacher gathered our focus to the lecture and the stares shifted off of me for the moment. Receiving a high grade felt amazing after all the stress and misery I'd been under since my anxiety attack. It felt like a huge blessing and I sent up a prayer in thanks. It made me realize that with God on my side, I could overcome any difficulties. With my faith, I could gain support in my election process.

At the end of the lecture, I tried to pack my backpack as fast as I could, hoping to avoid more attention.

"Congrats on the exam grade," a girl to my right said as I threw my bag over my shoulder. She had a sleek bob and wore a black leather jacket over a black V-neck top. A pair of black jeans with rips hugged her thin legs. I'd sat next to her since I started at school but we never spoke a word to each other. I knew she was a popular girl though. I saw her spend time with Scarlett's friends, Rosalie and Betty. A rush of joy filled me, knowing I'd received praise from her. "And on entering the race for president. You have a lot going for you."

"Thanks," I said. I admired her haircut and thought she seemed nice.

"I'm Chelsea," she said as she zipped up her black glossy backpack. "I'm running for vice president. I would change to president but the deadline was this weekend. Anyways do you want to sit with me and my friends at lunch today?"

"Sure," I replied and felt hopeful.

"See you then, Abigail," she said with a sweet smile and turned to walk away.

I hurried out of the room shortly after replying quick thank yous to the other students who congratulated me. When I reached my locker and opened it, once again, I found I wasn't alone. As soon as I turned to close it, Heath stood there, his eyes luminous.

"Good morning, Abigail," he said, brandishing his enticing smile.

"Good morning," I replied as I dropped off my chemistry textbook.

"Congratulations," he said. "You must feel good."

"Yeah, I do," I said. "And thank you."

Then he reached his arm over to put it around my shoulders. I stepped away, though I wished I didn't have to do it.

"What's wrong?" he asked, looking confused.

"Well…I…uh," I stammered.

He stared at me.

"I can't be with you," I said finally.

His eyes narrowed. "Can't? What about that kiss we shared? Why shouldn't we be together?"

"Look," I said, putting a hand on his arm. "I can't deal with it right now. You broke up with Scarlett and if she ever found out… she'd never speak to me again."

"Who cares?" Heath said. "She'd have to deal with it eventually, why not break the news sooner?"

"I can't do that to her," I said.

"Don't you want to kiss again?" he asked, his luminous eyes becoming gentler. We stood close to each other and I felt an urge to close the distance.

"No," I blurted both for my ears and his. "I have to go to class."

"I'm not going to wait around for you to change your mind," he said with a scowl. "I've chased you enough and all for you to walk away from what we have."

"I'm sorry if you're hurt," I said and felt close to tears. I felt like I hurt myself as well. "I can't have a relationship right now. I'm sorry."

I closed my locker and started down the corridor, tears obscuring my vision. Jake hadn't appeared either, and the rest of the day stretched out while I prayed for it to end. I had ended my momentary relationship with Heath and I had lost Jake. The pain felt unbearable. For a moment, I started to doubt myself, wondering if I truly could be the murderous girl he believed me to be.

At lunch, I set out in the crowded cafeteria, carrying my tray with a dismal-looking ham sandwich, searching for the girl from my intermediate chemistry class. I felt on the spot, and if I didn't find a place to sit soon, then people would know that I didn't have any friends.

"Abigail?" I heard a voice from behind me and I spun around to see that I'd walked past her table.

Chelsea sat there with a couple of other girls who were all dressed in similar edgy fashion; their hair shone as if it had been done.

I sat down in an empty chair. Chelsea introduced me to her friends, Lucy and Allison. A beat of silence followed and I ate my sandwich to have something to do.

"Are you excited for the election?" Chelsea asked. "You must be excited that you might be president of the school."

"Yes," I said, "I'm hopeful."

"So...how do you know Heath?" she asked while running her hand through her hair. "He's pretty...popular, you know? Wasn't he the lead in both school plays?"

"It's a long story," I said. "And yes. Actually I was a female lead in *Richard III*."

"Oh," Lucy said. "We didn't see you."

"You went?" I asked.

"Yeah, we go to every performance that Heath is in and we've never seen you," Chelsea said.

"It's a long story," I said again and wished I could hide my face. "I couldn't perform."

"You seem to have a lot of long stories," Allison said with a giggle.

"Wait a second," Chelsea said and then looked at me meaningfully. "I think I recognize you. Aren't you that girl from the cast party? Scarlett's sister?"

"What do you mean?" I asked.

"A rumor spread last October about Scarlett's sister making out with Heath in the pool," Chelsea said and shared a giggle with her friends. "Someone said you left with Heath and came back soaking wet from the pool. Are you together or something?"

"Um...no," I said and felt sick, knowing someone had taken notice of that private personal moment. "That ended because he wanted to take things to a level I wasn't ready for."

"You mean sex?" Lucy asked.

"You almost had sex?" Allison probed.

"Um…no…I…" I said.

"Why wouldn't you want to have sex with Heath?" Chelsea said. "He's hot."

"I wasn't ready," I said.

"Are you a *virgin?*"

Before I could stop it, a dark image fluttered into my mind. Something heavy crushed me against the floor. A single tear fell from my eye—my screams futile, unheard, and useless.

"I-I need to go," I managed. I left my tray behind and hurried away to the nearest bathroom. I entered a stall and puked until nothing came out. I'd tried so hard to keep those memories quiet, to stuff them down, to do everything I could to forget the moment when a man neglected to treat me with dignity. It wrung my weary heart to think about it. I was not a virgin. That had been taken from me long ago.

CHAPTER 31

Presidential Presentations

Over the next few days, the initial attention I received subsided. I knew it wouldn't last long because the presentations were fast approaching on Friday after school. I would have to miss track practice and that meant I would have to do a makeup practice Saturday with the coach there to push me until I collapsed. Regular homework took up so much of my time all week that I ended up having less time to design my posters. Fortunately Scarlett and Renée helped me and I printed them Thursday night, around midnight. After getting through another exhausting day of school, I was about ready to go home and take a long nap. I had no time. I had to face this moment. I couldn't run away from it. I had to do it for God. I found the bathroom and changed into my suit as fast as I could. Scarlett straightened my long hair and put on my makeup this morning. I spent a few moments examining myself quickly in the mirror to make sure I looked good. I noticed a pimple on my nose and worried that the concealer might not have covered it up enough. Then I worried that my skin looked too pale and it felt like I wasn't in my body, a ghost-like reflection. Scarlett said this morning that I looked good so I tried to believe her, even though I didn't feel it. At that moment, I sent a prayer to God that I could feel more confident and make a good impression today.

"Where have you been?" Scarlett cried with her hands on her hips as I entered the gym with my poster board. "The presentations start soon. We need time to prepare."

"I was changing," I informed her. "I haven't had much time to get here."

"All right, well, you look great. Really sleek and cutting edge. Now let's set up," Scarlett said and grabbed my arm to pull me along.

Numerous tables with white tablecloth were set up in neat rows in the gym with poster boards perched upon them. Each of them had a paper nameplate. This event was also hosted for the other student government positions and a number of people stood by their decorated poster boards. Scarlett led me to the table reserved for me and I placed my poster board on top. It displayed my headshot in addition to my slogan, "Love thy neighbor," and objectives as president. Scarlett reached into her bag to pull out the stack of fliers.

"I gave some to Renée to pass out at her school," Scarlett said.

"Why would you do that?" I asked. I was also surprised to hear Scarlett and Renée working together.

"If we pass them out to as many people as possible, your message will spread faster," Scarlett said.

Two of the presidential candidates, William Reynolds and Dylan Matthews, were using holograms to display their presentations. I wasn't sure how they were able to afford something so ostentatious. I suppose OPTI had already stepped in to help them win. Jake and I were the only presidential candidates using poster boards. I looked over at Jake's board and noticed his advocacy for supporting minority students in clubs like the newspaper. It endeared me to see how much he cared about other people. It made me feel tired of being under OPTI's rule where loving people like Jake weren't accepted and couldn't become leaders. I had to be strong if I wanted a shot at winning. If I publicly expressed my faith and disapproval of OPTI's treatment of religious people, what might happen to me? I felt myself trembling and tried to calm myself down for the presentation. I prayed in my mind for help to calm down. I tried to fill my mind with the peace and serenity that I'd felt in my dream of Jesus. I prayed that I might find that same feeling on earth, if that was possible, even if I had to fight for it.

Students began crowding the gym and walking around the tables. Most of the people went to William or Dylan, amazed by the holograms that reflected their intended policies. Jake gathered some attention but I also saw someone laughing after he spoke. At first, no one approached my table and I grew anxious as I hoped to gain some attention.

"This is ridiculous," Scarlett said. "We had everything set up perfectly for today. You're the one with the best policies."

"Scarlett?" A student came up to us to ask. A couple of other girls followed her.

Scarlett whirled around to address her.

"Are you running for president?"

"No," she said, "I'm an actress. But my sister Abigail is." She gestured over to me and I gave the girl a small smile. "Isn't she great?"

"Yeah, totally," she said and then smirked. "Aren't you sleeping with Heath?"

"What?" Scarlett and I said at the same time.

"Someone told me that you made out with Heath at a party and nearly did it in a pool," she said with a giggle.

"I didn't nearly sleep with him," I said, afraid to look at Scarlett. "We just kissed. It happened a long time ago. At your cast party, Scarlett."

Scarlett gave me a funny look. "You kissed Heath? I thought that was just a rumor. Why did you never tell me?"

"It's not a rumor anymore." The girl sneered. "Everyone knows you're secretly together. You don't have to hide it anymore."

"They're not together," Scarlett said. "Maybe you should keep your nose out of our business."

"If you don't believe me, then look at this," the girl said and held up her OPTI-Phone. The screen displayed a video of Heath and me in the pool, making out. "And this." She began to swipe through her phone.

"Enough," Scarlett said and waved her hand. I finally peeked at her. She didn't look mad and I sighed in relief. Though I also wanted to cry, knowing that such a personal moment in my life was used to discredit me. "I don't care what you have on her. Don't you try to discredit my sister!"

"Don't worry, it's already viral. Good luck becoming president, *slut*." The girl snickered with her friends joining in, and they all turned to head straight over to Dylan and William's tables.

Scarlett glared after the girl as she slipped away. "Remind me not to invite *her* or her friends to my next party."

I tried to shut out and ignore what they said about me. I shortly realized I couldn't because when Scarlett checked her social media accounts, all of them displayed the video and a photo of Heath and I close together by my locker a week ago with the caption, "SLUT."

"Why didn't you tell me about making out with Heath?" Scarlett asked me. "And why were you together at your locker?"

"He just...he wanted to know why I had my bandage," I said. "He was concerned. And I didn't mention kissing Heath because nothing really became of it. I didn't want to take things further that night. Heath became angry and left. That's all. Then he started showing up wherever I was and tried to continue a relationship with me. But I had already moved on with Jake. I suppose I led Heath on that night. He told me everything he did came out of love and even made a truce with me that he would stop. And he did. He moved on with you."

Scarlett looked crushed. "He never said a word about having kissed you or any sort of relationship," she said.

"Maybe he didn't want to hurt your feelings and it didn't matter. We barely had a relationship at all."

She pursed her lips. "And then his feelings came back," she said her eyes cast downward. "For you."

I nodded and began to feel nauseous with my guilt at having kissed Heath just a week ago. I thought that ending my relationship with Heath might help me move on, might take away these feelings. On the other hand, at times I couldn't breathe without him around. Something about him chased away my despair and fear. A platelet that sealed my bleeding heart.

It nerve-wracked me to know that other people knew something so intimate about me. My chances of becoming president were abysmal now. Scarlett did her best to hand out fliers to passersby. More people were responding with jeers and laughter. People steered clear of my table, as if I had a plague, and now I knew why. I gritted my teeth as I realized that my reputation had been ruined before I even had a chance to promote myself.

"Don't let it get to you," Scarlett said. "I'll find whoever spread the rumor, sent the video, and the photo. They won't dare do it again."

"How will you find out?" I asked. "It could have been anyone."

"Oh I will," she said. "Don't worry."

As she spoke, I was surprised to see three girls walking toward us—Chelsea, Allison, and Lucy—looking amused.

"Hey, Abigail," Chelsea said. "Wow, your presentation looks great. Not surprising since you're so smart."

"Thank you," I said.

"I'll spread the message to vote for you," she continued. "Since you seem to be struggling."

"Who are you?" Scarlett asked, her eyes looking at Chelsea from head to toe as though she was conducting surveillance.

Chelsea glanced over to Scarlett with a similar look.

"I'm Chelsea," she said and stuck out her hand. "I'm a friend of Abigail's."

"And when did you become friends?"

"On Monday," she responded. "Why do you want to know?"

"Did you take this photo?" Scarlett asked. Her voice came out tight and her eyes narrowed as she practically shoved her OPTI-Phone in Chelsea's face. It displayed the picture of Heath and me standing at my locker.

Chelsea and her friends snickered.

"What do you mean?" she said.

"I think you're responsible for this video and photo going around," Scarlett said. "And I think you're the one who spread the rumor about Abigail sleeping with Heath in a pool at *my* party."

They burst into scornful laughter again.

"Just so you know," Scarlett continued. "Heath was my boyfriend. Abigail never dated him."

"Oh, so both of you are sluts then." Chelsea rounded back. "I guess it runs in the family."

They laughed again.

"Don't you dare—!" I cut myself off as Scarlett's fist swung back. "Wait, Scar, don't—"

Scarlett's fist flew forward anyways and smacked Chelsea's face. Chelsea stumbled backward and her hands moved to cover her face.

"Ugh, my nose...I'm bleeding," she whimpered. Then she straightened up and gave us a furious glare. "Watch your backs, both of you. You've messed with the wrong person." At that, she turned on her heel and hurried out of the gym with her friends behind her.

"This is quickly becoming a disaster," I said, unable to shake my fury with Chelsea. Students in the gym had abandoned their interests in the other candidates to gawk at Scarlett and me. "I think we should leave."

"What about our goals for you to run for president?" Scarlett said. "We can turn things around."

"No one is coming to my table," I said. "And my reputation has already been ruined."

Out of nowhere, I felt someone's hand lay on my butt and a pinch. I turned around and saw Dylan, a devious smile on his face.

"Perky," he mused. "Let me know when it's my turn." Several of his supporters watched and laughed.

I jumped away from Dylan's hand. "Don't touch me!" I exclaimed.

Dylan's eyes were piercing. "I thought you would want it. You're too pretty to be president but you'd be a great lady to me."

"No, thank you," I said. My stomach churned. "Find someone else."

"Well, you're so arrogant you wouldn't know how to even be a president with integrity," Scarlett thundered back while the crowd of students watched in amusement as though it was a reality television show. Some students gasped while others continued to laugh and jeer at Scarlett now.

"Silence, all of you." A voice boomed from behind Scarlett, and I whirled around to see a large tall man that I recognized as the school principal. Right next to him, Chelsea clutched a tissue to her bloody nose and had tears lining her cheeks. Her friend Allison stood by her. Dylan and the crowd surrounding him quieted.

"Who punched you, Chelsea?"

"Scarlett did," she replied, tears ran down her face as she pointed her carved fingernails at my sister.

"I only did it because this little brat posted a private video of my sister to humiliate her and ruin her reputation," Scarlett said. She looked at Chelsea. "I'd do it again," she added, crossing her arms with a triumphant look.

"Don't look so smug," the principal said. "We don't tolerate aggression or rudeness in this school. Please come with me, Scarlett, so OPTI can assign you a punishment."

Scarlett scowled at Chelsea and followed the principal out of the room, turning to shoot another glare her way. Chelsea left with a triumphant grin on her face, clutching her bloody nose. I took Scarlett's departure as a sign that I'd better pack up my things and leave. Now I was alone. I turned around and began to pack the fliers in my bag.

"Are you Abigail?" someone behind me asked. It came as a surprise and I jumped, halting in storing the fliers. I faced a girl around my height with innocent doe eyes. She gazed at me in curiosity with a polite smile.

"Yes," I answered.

"I'm Maddie. I saw your post online," she said. "I liked how you want to set up a tutoring center. My friends and I struggle in our classes sometimes and we could use some help. Someone told me you're very good at chemistry—could you tutor me in that subject?"

"Yes," I said. Her kindness took me aback. "I would be happy to. I'm pretty busy right now but I could help you when I have more time after the election."

"Could I have a few fliers?" she asked. "I can pass them out to my friends."

"Yes, you can," I said and pulled out some of the fliers. I handed them to her.

"God bless," she said in a low melodic voice and hurried away before I could say another word.

I remained in that position for a long moment, stunned. Calm swept over me like the hush of the wind. Her courage to speak so openly to me amazed me and her kindness, in spite of all the hate thrown in my direction, bewildered me.

I put my face in my hands. A lump rose in my throat. I was not alone in my faith.

My hands shook as I grasped my poster board and my backpack before I left the gym. I began to wish I'd never kissed Heath, never even met him. Perhaps I was a slut for kissing Heath right after he broke up with Scarlett. My heart tore.

I rushed to the nearest bathroom, breaking down in tears before I could even push open the door. I couldn't comprehend how much love I felt from just that one girl. Maddie had shown me much kindness, a kindness foreign to me; and through her, God had breathed love into my soul, casting out my humiliation and hurt. I didn't know—barely understood—the love God had for me in that moment. I sank to my knees in my pain and sobbed for a long time. Then as though an invisible hand had been placed on my chin, it lifted toward the ceiling of the bathroom. In that same moment, one of the automatic sink faucets turned on, the water gushing out in a heavy stream like a waterfall. I stared at the stream of water in amazement and the sense of love I felt in my heart surpassed the pain, raising me from my sorrow and insecurity and into joy at the sight of what I knew was another sign from God. He loved me and he was with me when it seemed like no one cared about me. An indescribable sense of joy emitted from my heart, my burden lifted. I could trust God's love for me above all else.

"You've been suspended?" I asked in surprise when I met up with Scarlett outside the school. She stomped toward the parking lot. I trailed close behind her, anger rippling through me as well.

"Ugh, I'm going to get that little brat *Chelsea*," she declared as we reached her car. "How dare she call us sluts just for having a relationship with Heath! She's just jealous that she could never get a man like him. And to post a video of you and Heath together from months ago when you're totally not!"

THE LIGHT IN AN IMPENETRABLE NIGHT

I remained silent as Scarlett drove us home, continuing to rant about Chelsea. I knew she had a right to be mad. Even so, I wished I could escape from having to be reminded of it over and over again.

When we reached the house, Scarlett stormed inside. I entered in time to see her toss her purse onto the couch and fall back against the cushions. I nervously checked the OPTI screen, expecting to be punished for my poor performance. I heard nothing. The silence was eerie. I hoped Maddie and her friends might help spread awareness of my campaign—a small shred of hope.

"How did it go?" Renée asked as she came downstairs.

"Don't ask." Scarlett cut in.

Renée grimaced. "No supporters?"

"Worse than that," I said and sat down on the arm of the couch. "There's a rumor about me and a viral video of the night of Scarlett's cast party where I kissed Heath in our pool."

"You kissed Heath?" Renée cried.

"Yes," I said. "Nothing came of it though. That's why I never mentioned it."

"Now Chelsea and her other friends are calling us both sluts for our relationships with Heath."

"Abigail and Heath together?"

My heart leapt from hearing our names said together. I wondered what Heath could be up to right now. I imagined he must be angry again. Rejecting him made me distraught but I had to refrain from hurting Scarlett.

"That's rude to call someone a slut," Renée added. "No one is."

"Don't worry," Scarlett muttered. "She'll be sorry I received a suspension."

"Don't go after her," I said. "You don't want something worse to happen."

"What could be worse than suspension in my junior year? I have colleges to apply to in the next year—"

"You could get expelled!"

"Well, I could use this time to go shopping a lot but—"

"Mom will take away your credit card again—"

"Then I'll spend my time plotting ways to get back at Chelsea—"

"You could get expelled!" I cried again. "Revenge is not the answer."

"There's a difference between revenge and justice." Renée pointed out.

"Ugh, I hate Chelsea!" she cried, throwing her arms up and shooting up from the couch. Then she looked over at me. "Why did you even become friends with her?"

"Well, she seemed nice at first," I said. "I didn't know she did that."

"Sorry, Abigail, it doesn't look like we're going to win." Scarlett spoke what we all knew. Perhaps I should drop out of the race. Except Maddie's request made me feel good about my policies and my desire to make a difference at school for God had developed.

"One good thing happened," I said. "A girl came up to me after you left and she said she would tell her friends about me and my campaign."

"That probably won't help much though," Scarlett said. "Unless she has many friends."

"I passed out posters to my friends," Renée said. "But no one else would take any from us. The other students thought we were weird. If only I was popular like you are, Scarlett."

"It didn't help me that much either," she said. "I could lose some of my popularity from today. I won't let Chelsea destroy my reputation any further or yours. Never."

"Just be careful," I said. "It could backfire on you."

"Yes, yes, yes," Scarlett said as she grabbed her purse and headed for the stairs. "I'll just act in secret."

CHAPTER 32

Slander

I had a more peaceful weekend than the last two. Aside from track practice, I didn't have anything to prepare for the presidential race. Speech night would occur in about a month. I was unmotivated to write it though. Would anyone even listen to what I had to say? Scarlett spent the weekend either sulking on the living room sofa or out of the house at her yoga class at our local gym. I joined her, after much persuasion, and found the experience cathartic. Engaging in such a serene activity cleansed me from the pressure I dealt with for the moment.

However, when I awoke Monday morning, my chest and throat were constricted in a panic about having to go to school. I almost considered staying home and lying in bed all day, sleeping, escaping into my unconscious mind. I secretly wished I had been suspended with Scarlett, though if I had, OPTI would be furious with me and grant me another punishment. I couldn't win. I always faced some kind of danger in my life that left me paralyzed. I also wished that things could go back to the way they were before I had become a candidate—invisible, known from a faint rumor that never reached my ears. I sent a desperate plea to God that I would survive the day.

I opened the doors of the school. Déjà vu struck me and I visualized last Monday. This time, I knew, would be far worse. I closed my eyes as though I might escape. I took a deep breath.

Before I could even reopen my eyes, I felt someone knock into my shoulder, making me stumble forward, drop my phone, and a couple of books I carried.

"Watch where you're going, klutz." A girl's voice chimed as she walked away, a smug grin on her face as she joined the flood of migrating students. I picked up my books and phone and continued to trudge forward, hoping that push would be the worst of it. When I entered the crowd, students paused to stare at me. They seemed to part again as if there were something wrong with me.

"How long have you been sleeping with Heath?" A girl with a pinched nose sneered. "Is he your first?"

"Try to keep your legs closed from now on, honey." Another curly-haired girl hollered.

"Your bra strap is showing." Came another punch from a girl beside her. "And I can see your boobs. Cover up."

I heard a whistle. "Nice legs." This one came from a boy whose eyes surveyed me from head to toe and then stared straight at my chest. I moved my books to cover it. "Want to show me some love, babe? Don't be shy."

"You have a fine ass!" Another guy called at me. The other boys surrounding him hooted and hollered.

"No one wants a whore to be president!" A girl shouted. I noticed it came from Allison. The girls surrounding her chortled.

I kept my head down, as if by doing so, I could become invisible. All I heard was a torrent of insults and taunts. I struggled to breathe and my face scrunched as I tried—prayed with all my might that I wouldn't cry. Tears leaked from my eyes.

"Toughen up, girl," another boy said from beside me. "It's just a joke. Don't be so sensitive."

I looked up, eager to find a bathroom so I could be alone and skip my first class or perhaps the entire day. I stepped toward the door for the ladies' room but a group of burly boys blocked my way, wearing varsity lacrosse team hoodies.

"Want to try the boys' bathroom?" one of them mocked.

"Give us a treat, won't you, babe?" said another.

"Don't you have a sister? We could have a threesome, you know," another said with a wink.

"Don't speak about my sister like that!" I blurted in fury and tried to move back along the corridor, pining for an escape.

"You should speak more kindly to us," one of them said. "We'll put you in your place!"

Suddenly I felt a hand on my arm push me and my entire body slammed against the door to the boys' bathroom, my head hitting it first while the rest of my body sunk to the floor like a rag doll. I held my breath out of terror as I tried to scramble to my feet.

"Leave her alone!" a fierce yet sweet voice cut through the jeers and laughter.

My vision blurred. The room spun. A coarse hand gripped my arm and tried to pull me into the boys' bathroom. I even prayed I might faint so I wouldn't know what was about to happen—again.

Then I felt another softer small hand on my other arm. More hands were added and they tried to pull me in the other direction. More coarser hands grasped my other arm in a vice grip, much stronger than the girls'.

My head spun from hitting the door. I did my best to fight against the coarser hands and got to my feet. When I did, the coarser hands pushed me inside the bathroom. I fell onto the hard floor and hit my head again. I prepared to try to throw a punch as soon as they closed in, if only I could get the right angle. One of them, the tallest one, stood over me with his eyes illuminated like a jack-o'-lantern. The two boys beside him were leaning down to grab ahold of my arms. Drips of sweat pooled under my armpits, my forehead, and my feet. A chill ran through me and I lingered on the edge of unconsciousness. I felt ready to give up, urging my brain to shut down before I had to watch it happen. As if this moment could be lost in space, my life forgotten. A flood of images flashed before my eyes, of myself in the pitch-black, hearing grunting noises, lying underneath a heavy unidentifiable force, my cries bouncing off the ceiling.

The sound of rushing water awakened my mind. My eyes searched the room and landed on the sinks' faucets from which water streamed while the basins overflowed and water splashed in waterfalls onto the floor.

"What the—" one of the boys said. Now their attention drew to the sinks too. I took that moment to rise from the floor, my entire body quivering.

"Looks like you're some kind of witch freak too," one of the boys said. "Let's get out of here."

All at once, they left the bathroom. The door opened again, and at first, I despaired that they changed their minds. Instead a group of young girls slipped inside. The sound of water flowing ceased, and when I looked behind me, I saw that all the sinks were off. A large pool of water remained on the floor and I could hear the water in the basins draining.

My mind ran at high speed as though it might shut down as I wished. The bright lights above me stung my eyes, and I realized I might have a concussion. It took me a moment to gather my surroundings and to process what almost happened to me. I was alone—with four girls I didn't know, staring at me in concern.

"Are you okay?" said the girl with the kind voice. It took me a moment to recognize her as Maddie and the friends she mentioned. I gazed back at them, unsure of what to say or do. I did not even have any sense of the time.

"I can get you some ice from the nurse's office," another girl said. "Does your head hurt?"

As soon as she asked, I felt a pain on the back and side of my head. It broke me out of my shock and I could finally focus.

"Are you okay?" one of Maddie's friends asked. "I mean, of course you're not okay. What's your name?"

"Um…yes…I mean, no," I said. I shifted my feet. I didn't know them well but something about their presence gave me a sense of security. I savored that feeling, wishing I could fully know it.

"It's Abigail," Maddie said to the others. "Her name is Abigail."

"Thanks…for…helping me," I said. I burst into tears in front of them, feeling embarrassed. The girls stepped forward at once to wrap their arms around me, one of the girls with black hair rubbing my back gently. I barely knew them yet I clung to them like the anchor of a rocking ship.

"I'm so sorry about what almost happened to you. I'm Jaylyn by the way," Jaylyn said as she and the other girls stepped back. She had dark-brown hair and looked similar to another one of the girls. "This is my twin sister, Isabelle, and our friend, Rachel."

"No one deserves to be treated like that." Isabelle said. "Why did they stop though? And why is the floor wet?"

"I-I...I don't know," I said, looking down at the puddles of water around the bathroom. "The sinks just turned on."

I feared they might accuse me of being a witch too or question whether it happened.

"Perhaps God saved you," Isabelle said. "Just like he saved us."

I couldn't comprehend it. They were most likely right. I didn't know why, couldn't fathom God's unfailing protection and the depth of his love for me. I felt like wailing out of relief and joy amid my shock. Then it occurred to me that I should be in class. My heart leapt in my chest and my throat tightened as I hurried past the girls to open the door to the bathroom. I feared an impending punishment from OPTI for it.

"I have to go to class." I managed to gasp over my shoulder before I left.

I found my backpack on the ground outside the bathroom and put it back on my shoulders. I raced down the hall, though my effort seemed futile, and it felt like I ran toward more danger. I had no desire to be at school right now. I wanted to leave. *Now.* I had no escape—nowhere to run or hide. I was on the brink of tears. I tried to contain myself. I couldn't handle any more grief over this campaign. Although I didn't like the feeling, I felt incredibly angry with all the people responsible for my pain. I almost hoped Scarlett might find a way to get back at Chelsea for spreading this rumor about me. However, it would be useless and probably wrong to seek revenge. I entered my chemistry class and apologized for being late amid stares and dirty looks cast on my fractured heart. Heath sat at his desk. I tried not to look at him and settled in my seat. I spent the period trembling and crying silently, wondering with hope that maybe Heath might care.

The bell rang for the end of class. I found myself staring in dismay at the blank page of my notebook. I noticed Heath walk by my desk quickly and picked up a black designer backpack that belonged to none other than Chelsea.

"Thanks, babe," she said to him. Her short hair wasn't sleek and straight today. Instead it swayed as she moved and the ends of her hair were blond in an ombré. She threw a smug look in my direction before they both walked away.

I hurried after them as my anger resurged.

"Heath," I cried to his back as he walked alongside Chelsea.

He looked behind himself at me and stopped. Chelsea turned too with a cutting glare.

"What do you want, Abigail?" Heath asked. Then he looked concerned. "Why are you crying?"

When I first went after him, I felt like I would know what to say. Instead I was speechless. What could I say to make things better? What could I say so he would end things with Chelsea?

"I don't know," I finally admitted. "It's nothing."

"Come on, Heath," Chelsea said with a smirk at me and then pulled on his arm. "I need to get to class."

I sighed and watched them walk away, my heart in pieces—a cut deeper than he might ever know.

CHAPTER 33

Light in Impenetrable Night

I spent the rest of the morning feeling depressed as I meandered from class to class and trying not to look anyone in the eye as they hurled insults at me. I couldn't understand why they would keep going when I already carried so much pain. How could they not care? Why couldn't any of them ever give me a break? I was bleeding and broken before everyone and no one cared. That was the worst part. I considered ending my life so all this pain and torment could end. Perhaps that might be easier.

I looked outside the windows on my way to the cafeteria and noticed it rained, streaks of raindrops splattering the glass. It reminded me of the sinks turning on in the bathroom and I almost had to shut it out so I wouldn't burst into tears in front of the crowd of students filling the halls. Like Maddie and her friends said, God saved my life as he had all those times before. Crying proved unavoidable and tears rushed like a stream down my cheeks. I couldn't comprehend it, the kind of love that never gave up on me.

I considered heading for the nearest bathroom rather than the cafeteria. The crowd cleared somewhat, and then I saw Maddie and Jaylyn hurrying toward me.

"Do you want to sit with us, Abigail?" Maddie asked.

"Here's a tissue," Jaylyn added, handing me one while I thanked her and wiped my wet eyes. "We came looking for you because we thought you must need some company so no one hurts you again like before."

"Yes," I said, "thank you for your concern." I was hesitant to give them my full trust after what happened with Chelsea. However, I remembered how Maddie, Jaylyn, Isabelle, and Rachel had all comforted me and made me feel loved when no one else did. That reassured me.

I followed Maddie and Jaylyn to their table where Isabelle and Rachel sat. "Why were you crying just now?" Jaylyn asked, putting a hand on my shoulder and rubbing it.

"I just…well…all the teasing," I said. "It seems like no one cares here, except you all, my sisters, God, and Jesus."

"I know," Jaylyn said, her eyes soft in understanding. "I've been there before. It gets better. Trust me."

Hearing that touched me with a depth I couldn't express. It illuminated my hope. Tears weren't far away again.

"By the way," Maddie said as we all sat down. "You would make a great president. You're such a strong person."

"Thank you," I said and gave her a small smile.

"Let me go grab the both of us some lunch," Isabelle said. "It's on me, Abby. Do you mind if I call you that?"

"Thank you," I said again, unable to believe their concern for me. "That's fine with me."

Isabelle left to get me some food.

"How was the rest of your day after this morning?" Rachel asked.

"Not good," I admitted, and my eyes flickered to each of their faces to survey their reaction. "I was late and then Heath…well…"

"You mean the Heath from the video?" Rachel said. "Are you in a relationship?"

"No," I answered. "All we did was kiss that night and that's all. But he's dating Chelsea and she's the one who released the video and the photo."

"Maybe he doesn't know it was her," Maddie suggested. "I can see that would hurt though."

"I'm sorry," Rachel said as Isabelle returned with a burger for me and for herself. I thanked her as she sat back down. "Is there anything we can do to help?"

"You already are helping," I said. "I don't know what to do about the teasing though. It seems like everyone hates me."

"Well, it's their loss," Maddie said. "You're a wonderful person, and I think you're very brave to be running for president."

My spirits lifted, the bleeding in my heart quenched.

"Thank you," I replied.

"I can think of one thing we could do," Isabelle said. "Maybe it would help if we walked you to class. You know, so no one can try to hurt you again."

"Thanks for the offer, however, I wouldn't want to put you in danger."

"I would do it," Rachel said. "I don't mind."

I looked from Rachel to the other girls, and they all nodded.

"Don't you have classes though?" I asked. "I wouldn't want to make you late."

"We can alternate based on our schedules," Jaylyn said. "People might still tease you, though they won't be able to become physical like those boys. You won't be alone."

"Can you show us your schedule?" Rachel asked. "If you don't mind sharing."

"Are you sure?" I said. "It wasn't as bad as this morning on my way to the cafeteria."

"Maybe it died down for now," Maddie said, "but speech night is approaching, right? That's when the final votes are cast and OPTI makes the decision."

I put my head in my hands. Then I felt embarrassed. I looked up at them again.

"I know how you feel," Isabelle said. "With us, you'll be okay. We'll make sure of it."

"I might as well drop out of the campaign," I said. "I'm not going to win."

"Don't worry about it," Jaylyn said. "And don't blame yourself. People are mean in this school. It's not a reflection of you."

I nodded and realized it must be true. It wasn't my fault that the other students bullied me. The blame rested on their shoulders.

"Don't give up," Maddie said. "You have such great ideas. Don't let mean people try to intimidate you. The best way to beat them is to keep going and show them that they can't defeat you."

Maddie's words struck a chord with me. She was right. If I backed out now how could I make an impact and spread the word about freedom for people of faith. I couldn't make a difference if I backed out of the campaign. Maybe I wouldn't win but maybe I could change people's minds and bring God's grace to people who need it most. Perhaps my speech could alter how those mean people saw me. Perhaps their hearts might be moved.

I exchanged my schedule with my new friends. For the rest of the day, they took turns walking with me to class. Their presence and kindness were like shields on the fearsome walks through the halls—God's enduring protection of me. My strength was restored and I found it easier to breathe. I wanted to do what Maddie said and continue with the election to prove that all the hate I received couldn't hinder my mission.

Maddie gave me a ride home after a miserable track practice. She had choir rehearsal and it ended around the same time. When we parted, I entered my home to a scene I hadn't encountered in a while—Scarlett leaned back on the sofa, making out with a boy I didn't know at all.

She broke away from their kiss and looked up at me while I shifted my gaze away from her, wishing I could avoid this awkward situation.

"Oh, hi, Abigail. Looks like the mood's been broken, Tim. See you later."

They both sat up and the golden-haired boy ran a hand through his messy locks that reminded me of Heath. I had to stop myself from picturing him with Chelsea or I might explode.

"Call me soon, Scar," Tim said as he exited through the front door. Scarlett blew him a kiss as he departed.

"How was school today?" Scarlett asked, straightening up and stretching her arms.

"Are you okay?" Renée asked and came downstairs. "Finally he's gone." She added, "I can come downstairs."

Scarlett looked like she was about to shoot a sour look at Renée.

"Can you please just get along for today?" I asked. The horrific day I had irritated me and I couldn't stand to hear them start a fight.

"How was school today?" Renée asked then.

"Not good," I answered, my despair returning. "As worse as it could get."

"What happened to you?" Scarlett asked in alarm.

"People teased me and shouted insults at me," I said. I neglected to tell them about the worst part. The terror I'd experienced was too hard to express aloud.

Renée grimaced. "People were mean to me today too," she said. "Word has spread about you and this rumor, unfortunately. I felt so bad all day because I thought you might be getting the worst of the treatment."

It upset me to hear that Renée had faced bullying too, especially because it was related to me.

"I can take you to speak to the principal and report those bullies," I said. "You don't need to get hurt because of me."

"It wouldn't work," Renée said. "The principal probably wouldn't believe me. It's not because of you. It's Chelsea's fault that this rumor was spread in the first place."

"I would help," Scarlett said. "But all I can do is sit at home or run errands. I never thought I would actually miss school."

"You won't be happy to hear this then," I said, "Chelsea and Heath are dating."

Scarlett sank down onto the sofa, her head in her hands in exasperation. "Chelsea and Heath?" She nearly shrieked. "Why on earth are they together? How do you even know?"

"I saw them together in class this morning. He walked her to her next class."

"That little brat," Scarlett growled. "She accuses us of being sluts for dating him and then she does without any of the same judgment or ridicule. I wouldn't call *her* a slut. It's a degrading word.

Anyways it's probably not serious. He'll dump her as soon as he finds out about her."

"He probably already knows," I said. "It's clear that she was jealous that she heard a rumor about me kissing and talking to Heath and that you dated him."

"I can't believe he would date her after the rumor she spread about you," Scarlett said. "When we were dating, whenever you came up, he went on and on about how much he cares about you and I believe him. He wouldn't knowingly do this to either of us."

"You're right," I said, remembering how Heath had believed that I didn't kill Mr. Edwin. He told me that afternoon that nothing could change his feelings for me and he seemed genuine. I felt like kicking myself for telling him we couldn't be together. "He cares about both of us."

"Maybe I could tell my friends to spread a rumor about Chelsea," Scarlett said. "Then the attention will be on her."

Although I resented Chelsea after today, I knew I wouldn't wish to spread rumors about anyone. All I wanted was for the bullying to end.

"No," I said to Scarlett. "It's miserable to have a rumor spread. I wouldn't want to put her through what I went through today."

"How bad was it?" she asked.

"Very bad," I said and glanced at Renée. I couldn't elaborate in front of her. "But I met these girls who tried to help me escape and they said they would walk me to class from now on until it stops I guess."

"Be careful who you trust, Abigail," Scarlett said. "Chelsea claimed to be your friend too."

"I know," I said. "They seem like nice people though. I spent my lunch period with them. They took care of me and made sure I was okay."

"That was nice of them to do that," Renée said. "They seem like good people."

"What are you going to do about the campaign though?" Scarlett said. "Your chances of winning are next to none. No offense."

"I want to keep running," I said, though my voice quivered. "I don't want their treatment of me to prevent me from taking a stand with my faith to serve God."

"What if it gets worse?" Renée asked.

"I don't know how it could get any worse," I said. And then, in a shaky voice, added, "I was almost..." Then I remembered Renée stood here too, far too young to know.

"What?" Renée asked.

"I need to be alone," I said. "I have homework to do. Life doesn't stop even if you wish it would."

"Are you sure you're okay?" Scarlett said. "Maybe you should take time off school until it dies down."

I glanced over at the blank screen, always poised on the living room wall, and back at Scarlett and Renée.

"I don't think I could," I said, "I can't get behind in school. Are you okay?"

"Of course I'm not okay," Scarlett said. "I'm going to use this suspension to get important things done. Did you know I'm going to miss the audition for the next school play? That Chelsea is going to seriously pay."

Even though I still thought it wouldn't do any good to get back at Chelsea, when Scarlett set her mind on something, it was difficult to stop her. I just hoped nothing worse would happen to her.

"I'll make dinner for us soon," I said to Renée. "Mom won't be home until eight o'clock tonight, as usual."

Scarlett huffed and rolled her eyes at the last part.

I walked past Renée and up the stairs to the second floor. I continued down the hall to my room and quickly entered, closing the door behind me. I wasn't ready to be alone. I lay back against my bed, covered my mouth with my hands, and began to sob without restraint. I couldn't be certain if I would endure another day of the bullying. As I cried, suddenly the room filled with a pool of sunlight. I dared to think about what those boys almost did to me and remembered how the sinks had turned on instantly without any explanation. I knew it was the Holy Spirit. God saved me from a terrible fate, another miracle. Just like when the sink had turned on for me after the presidential presentations. I knew then, like I know now, that God had saved my life today. So despite my pain, I clung to the growing faith that so long as I had God with me, I could survive. I knew God gave me those friends who came to my side and lifted me out of darkness.

I lifted my chin up at the dazzling sun that cast its glorious glow inside my room. For the first time in a long time, I knew I was safe.

CHAPTER 34

My Friend

According to Scarlett, who remained active on her social media platforms, word went around the school about those boys nearly violating me. It didn't make anything better because most people claimed I provoked them or that I had consented to it based on what I wore and because they thought I was a slut. I admitted to Scarlett that it had happened and she immediately suggested that I should report them and see a doctor. My irritation with bright lights and loud noises confirmed that I must have a concussion. I reluctantly told the doctor how it happened and he seemed sympathetic. He advised me to report those boys to a guidance counselor. I nodded. I was too afraid they would retaliate if I even mentioned their names. Scarlett understood why I didn't report them. She looked especially somber lately, and I knew she wished, as I did, that something could be done about it, some kind of justice.

Scarlett couldn't go to school with me either so she lost that battle. It devastated me to learn that I would have to miss track practice and our upcoming meet until I healed. Under OPTI's orders, my chemistry teacher gave me detention for my tardiness though she seemed apologetic about having to do so. My track coach told me I had to make up all the practices that I missed every weekend, except for spring break, once I recuperated. Maybe I shouldn't have stood up to those boys. Maybe it would have been better if I had stayed quiet and kept walking with my head bowed.

Anger flowed through me toward OPTI for his harshness with me when I already faced a miserable situation. I received no mercy as though I was to blame for arriving to class late or missing track practice. Trying to please OPTI felt like a never-ending battle and I always came out on the losing side. The taunting didn't subside when I returned to school, and I even saw the posters I had hung in the hallways defiled with profanities or torn down. I didn't take them down completely because I was determined to stay in this race. The chances were that I would lose but I hoped I could make a difference somehow. Having new friends helped restore some confidence in my life's direction and, more importantly, knowing that I had God on my side no matter what I faced. I felt a yearning to learn more about God and for my relationship with him to flourish. It made me want to talk to Maddie, Jaylyn, Isabelle, and Rachel more and try to understand their own relationships with God. What had they experienced? What did they mean when they said God saved their lives too? How did they live under OPTI's rule knowing they would die if they practiced their faith?

I didn't want to have to hide my faith anymore. I wanted to tell my new friends about my experience with faith and how God rescued me. However, it saddened me that as much as my faith has made my world a better place, my destiny, according to OPTI, was to serve him once I finished high school. My choices in deciding my life were limited and I wondered if I should hold onto hope for a different path. I wanted to serve God instead. However, I knew God was on my side, and if he saved me from all my past turmoil, perhaps I would be saved from this. I couldn't imagine a world without OPTI's presence in every nook and cranny. But my heart longed for something more to this life, something greater, and I knew the only way I could feel complete would be through walking by faith in God, trusting in his love for me, like my sister Faith had.

Thinking of Faith deepened my sadness. She had suffered a cruel death for defying OPTI and staying true to her faith. How could I face OPTI with my faith and survive it? I longed to be able to talk to Faith, to see her bright smiling face and the glint in her green eyes when she laughed. I had so many questions for her about my faith.

I had no idea how I could get answers to all my questions about it. The thought of entering Faith's room made me hesitant. Sometimes I couldn't even look at her closed door without welling up with tears and longing to hear her voice again. I needed her guidance far more than ever.

Throughout the week, I spent time getting to know my new friends on my walks to class. When I met up with Isabelle on Tuesday morning, I barely said a word to her apart from a greeting. I racked my brain for something to say to break the awkward silence as we walked the hallway. Nothing came. She didn't look fazed and wore a bright smile whenever I snuck a shy glance at her. I wanted to discuss my growing faith without OPTI overhearing and putting our lives in jeopardy.

"Is English your favorite subject?" Isabelle asked finally as we walked down the hallway toward my class.

"No," I said. "We only read memoirs of people who OPTI favored or intellectual essays about the government. I wish we could read more fictional literature."

"Me too," Isabelle said, "I've written a few fictional stories myself. I don't think people would care to read them."

"Why would you think that?" I asked.

"Well, I wrote one story last year about a fantasy world and OPTI called it childish. My classmates made fun of it too so I lost my confidence in writing them. I have some experience with bullying myself so I know how you must feel. Eventually people forgot about it or lost interest."

"I'm sorry that happened to you," I said. "I hope you keep writing. I would read one of your stories."

Isabelle thanked me. "They remind me of home. I've been away from it for so long, my memory has become fuzzy. But Jaylyn remembers more clearly. We're twins, you know? Fraternal."

"Where's home for you?" I asked.

"Mexico," she said. "Quite far away from here."

I looked at her in surprise. "Wow. I've never been there. That is far. What's it like there?"

"Not good, unfortunately," she said. "My family suffered from famine, drought, and threats of violence so we made a long journey to New America, hoping to find a better living situation. We lived outside the border for some time but the conditions were far too dangerous. Leaving was the hardest part. My parents feared my sister and I wouldn't survive. Then the security officers at the border gave us a court hearing where OPTI decided our true parents were not fit to raise us. Jaylyn and I were taken from our parents, leaving our country, everything we knew behind." A tear fell from her hazel eyes. "We could only take the clothes we wore on our backs. OPTI placed us in the foster care system and we moved from home to home whenever our guardians grew sick of providing for us. Then our adopted parents discovered us and took us in as their own when no one else did. Jaylyn and I don't know, to this day, what became of our real parents. I know God led us to our new home and saved us from abuse, to provide a sanctuary for us in the midst of our dangerous world. However, as much as I love my guardians, I pray every night that God will reunite us with our true parents again. I miss them so much that my heart aches every day."

"I'm so sorry. I can relate," I said. Her story touched me to the core. How could anyone separate children from their loving parents? "My father left when I was young and my mother...well...she doesn't seem to notice my siblings and me. We might as well be living on our own, except we don't have the money to provide for ourselves. I had an experience in foster care and my siblings and I received such harsh treatment that we did everything it took to escape."

"I'm sorry as well," she said, her eyes glimmering with tears. "Well, if you're feeling down, you can come over to our house. We'd love to treat you for dinner sometime. I'm sorry for your difficulties with your parents. It's said in the Bible that if your parents forsake you, God will take you up and care for you as his own. You're in good hands. You don't have to fear with God on your side."

I nodded, speechless and grateful to hear that all the love I could possibly need came from God. He was my one true parent when my own parents neglected my siblings and me.

Over the next two weeks, I spent several walks to class with Isabelle, Rachel, and Jaylyn and started to get to know them all. I discovered that Rachel had great skills in computer science and geometry. I struggled in computer science and not many girls had made it into the intermediate level class, though Rachel had. Jaylyn's favorite subject was global history, however, she explained that the class didn't touch on topics concerning Latin America; and she wanted to research it as much as possible to spread awareness of the history, culture, religions, and politics occurring in those places in recent history, as well as current events, with the hope for more inclusiveness of Latin Americans in our country.

Although I spent much of my time walking to classes with Isabelle, Rachel, and Jaylyn, I didn't have as many opportunities to talk to Maddie. I wanted to know all of my new friends' stories about how God saved their lives, and I figured Maddie might know much more than I did about the Christian faith. She confided in me, on one of our walks, that her mother was a privately ordained priest. If I could have another private moment with her, hopefully away from OPTI's prying eyes, perhaps I could discuss my faith with her and she could help me know more about how I could make a difference and act more on my faith. However, her schedule didn't line up with mine as often, and at lunch, the OPTI screen always featured his luminous brain, surveying us all no matter where we went like the *Mona Lisa*. After two weeks, the teasing died down and students lost interest. I still received dirty looks and the whispering didn't stop; however, I found it easier to ignore while I had a friend by my side.

By the time the upcoming Monday arrived, I didn't need to have anyone walk me to class. Even so, Maddie met me at the front entrance of the school that morning and we began our trek.

"How are your siblings?" Maddie asked.

"Good," I said. To Scarlett's delight, she returned to school only after two weeks and went on a dogged mission to persuade the drama teacher to let her audition for the next school play, especially when she found out it will be *Hamlet*.

"No one can play Ophelia but me!" she declared to me last week while she paced around the living room, trying to call the drama teacher. "I've been dying to play her for years." Her persistence and, most likely, her talent paid off and the drama teacher gave in to her incessant demands.

"Scarlett's happy to be back from her suspension," I informed Maddie, "and she's busy preparing for her audition for the next school play. Renée received an A+ on a painting for her art class. She painted our backyard's flower garden the way she remembered it from when she was a six-year-old. I told her I would frame it in her room. Our garden's never looked the same."

"Excellent," Maddie said with a bright smile. "Renée must have a good memory. Why did Scarlett get suspended, if you don't mind me asking?"

"She punched Chelsea, the girl who posted the video and photo, in the face during the student government presentations for calling us sluts," I said.

"Oh, wow! Now I remember. I didn't know she was your sister."

"Yes, we're related, even though we're not that much alike," I said.

"What do you mean by that?" Maddie asked.

"Well, she's pretty popular at school and I've usually been unpopular," I said, giving her a shy smile, embarrassed to admit my unpopular status. That didn't waver Maddie's disposition and it felt refreshing to surround myself with the kind of people who wouldn't judge me. "And she's very much into fashion," I continued. "So is my younger sister, Renée. She's in middle school."

"Aw, that's sweet to have a younger sister," Maddie said. "They must get along well then."

"Um...not really," I said. "It used to be Scarlett and me who couldn't get along and now it's turned into her and Renée fighting."

"Hopefully they'll work things out," she said. "Would you like to meet up outside of school for lunch today?" she asked as we reached the hallway where my intermediate chemistry class was located. "Isabelle, Rachel, and Jaylyn all have to study for a Spanish test and it would be nice to eat outside now that it's not raining as much."

I agreed and parted from Maddie, my heart sinking at the thought of having to see Chelsea and Heath together. My heart broke all over again whenever they exchanged a significant glance or laugh. I wished that somehow Scarlett and Heath had never been together at all and then I would be freer to pursue something with Heath. I thought about that kiss more often than I bargained for, despite how confusing my feelings were. I knew imagining a better future with Heath wouldn't be possible. He'd moved on from how he felt about me, and now, it was too late to change my mind. Had I lost him forever? My heart couldn't bear it. Despite my efforts to try to move on, my breath caught whenever he walked by my desk to get to his, and when he dropped a pencil in class with a clatter, my eyes immediately flickered behind me to his. I usually had to shake myself to stop from staring into their mysterious depths that possessed the glinting allure of jewelry after it has been polished.

Lunch arrived and I met Maddie outside the cafeteria's entrance, a little ways away on the vibrant green grass that surrounded a concrete walkway leading to the senior parking lot. She withdrew a small blanket from her backpack that she spread on the ground, turning our meeting into a picnic. At first, I stayed quiet as usual while we both munched on our sandwiches. The sun shone above our heads and provided us with a gentle warmth. Maddie spoke and grabbed my attention.

"I'm sorry again about how poorly you've been treated at this school," Maddie said. "You're very strong to put up with it. Not many women run and this is the reason."

"Really?" I asked. "Has this bullying happened here before?"

"Yes," Maddie said. "Last year, a girl ran for the election but students cyberbullied her because of her race and her registered legal sex so much that she stepped down right after the presentations." She leaned forward. "People even told her to go back where she came from, even though she was born here, and to commit suicide. By the end of the year, her body was found in a river in the woods underneath a willow tree. She drowned."

"That's—" I lowered my voice. "That's terrible," I replied.

"The media reported it as suicide," she said. "I sometimes wonder if…never mind. The point is, it's very dangerous to be a woman and run for president at this school or any school for that matter. That's why it's so important for you to continue because if you overcome the misfortune of it all, then that could give other women hope and, man, we need it."

"Other women?" I asked. "Hope? For what?"

She leaned closer again. "For a freer, peaceful, love-filled life. That's what the Gospels are all about—Jesus commanding us to love unconditionally and giving us freedom through his sacrifice. He loved people for who they were and what was in their hearts, not based on any sort of characteristic. We're saved through faith alone..." She trailed off and glanced around as if she were nervous that someone watched her. "It's something that can't be earned through good works because we all fall short, we all sin, we all make mistakes. God's grace and love are free gifts. As Jesus said when he came, 'The Spirit of the Lord is on me, because he has anointed me to proclaim good news to the poor. He has sent me to proclaim freedom for the prisoners and recovery of sight for the blind, to set the oppressed free, to proclaim the year of the Lord's favor.'"[1]

"What are the Gospels?" I asked. I couldn't help but revel at the thought of freedom from oppression. That's what I had yearned to have for what seemed like forever.

"The Gospels are four books in the Bible that contain evidence of Jesus's life and teachings," she explained.

My eyes widened. "What kind of freedom do you mean?" I asked.

"Jesus came to earth, in biblical times, as God incarnate, born from the Virgin Mary," she said. "He spent his life teaching and preaching God's law, healing the sick, and performing miracles through the Holy Spirit. He had twelve male disciples and many women followed him as well. He befriended and spent time with sinners and the marginalized, especially women and ethnic minorities. He was persecuted, crucified, and then resurrected after three days. He revealed himself to Mary Magdalene, one of his beloved female disciples, and she, with a few other women, delivered the news to the other male disciples like Peter. Jesus made the sacrifice on the cross to open the gates of heaven so that anyone who believes in him

---

[1.] The Holy Bible, New International Version, Luke 4:18–19 (International Bible Society, 1984).

will not perish but have eternal life. All your sins are forgiven if you have faith, especially if you repent, and we are instructed to forgive each other in that way, though sometimes it can be hard and take time. Forgiving does not mean you have to forget though. When we repent, our sins are cast in the sea of forgetfulness for all our lives on earth and in heaven. All you have to do to be saved is to have faith. We are saved through grace alone and not through good works."

While I listened to Maddie, her words absorbed my attention and I lost all sense of my surroundings. It seemed as if I'd been transported to another world. I never knew that we were saved through faith and tears came to my eyes at the thought. For so long, I thought I'd fallen short as a good person. To know that I didn't have to be perfect to enter heaven was refreshing and lifted my burdens. I had finally received another taste of freedom.

"Why would Jesus make that sacrifice for us?" I asked.

"Because he loved the world," Maddie answered with a beaming smile. "He loves everyone, even his enemies. The two greatest commandments are to love God with all your heart, mind, and soul and to love our neighbors as ourselves. Jesus lived by these commandments especially."

"That's wonderful," I said, in complete awe of Jesus's incomprehensible love for humankind—the greatest blessing of all. "What is heaven like?"

"No one knows for sure," she said. "It's the kingdom of God, the Promised Land, a place where sin and suffering don't exist—a place of eternal peace and rest. It will be true freedom. The truest you'll ever experience. Jesus is the King of kings and the Lord of lords. Hallelujah."

I remembered my dream after I attempted suicide. I could imagine what that kind of freedom felt like—like my eyes and my heart had been opened to a new understanding of life, the world, and all existence. The freedom I'd been in search of all this time, I'd already received without even knowing it; Jesus' sacrifice gave me and thousands of others a miracle beyond anything I could imagine. His sacrifice granted me the promise of freedom in heaven, and after what I'd endured, I would give all that I had for unlimited peace; no more cries of agony, no more hate, or injustice—just peace, laughter, love, and joy.

"What was that word you said? I've never heard it before. It sounds wonderful."

"It's *hallelujah*. A simple way to explain it is that it means 'praise God.' I try to say it, even when I'm sad, and it makes me feel better."

I fully understood why she said it after what I'd heard about Jesus. "I'm a believer in Christ," I told Maddie. "I've believed for a while now. I wanted to share it with people I know but I was afraid."

"I understand. I was afraid once too," she said. "There's a way you can share it. Easter Sunday, which celebrates the day Jesus rose from the dead, is coming up soon, following this season of Lent. We've planned to gather at the abandoned church in the old center of the town and have Eucharist. That refers to the Christian ceremony of receiving Communion. My mother will be the priest. She's already prepared the sermon and the prayers. I'll give you a copy of it and the directions to the church."

"I'd love to come," I said, beaming at her. For the first time in a long time, I felt joy about my future. Maddie told me the date and time of the service, and after a brief hug, we parted. We'd been so engrossed in our conversation that we both arrived late to our classes. All I could think about was our conversation and all I ever wanted to think about. I finally understood that Faith gained her strength to defy OPTI from the one and only God. Just as I had, Faith had discovered and experienced God's kingdom on earth—the Promised Land.

I seemed to float through the rest of my day in such high spirits that I nearly forgot about all my misery from the presidential campaign and OPTI. My fears and my sorrows were cast in the sea of forgetfulness for the moment, just like my sins, and I felt more liberated than I ever felt in my life. I could lay all my burdens down to God and Jesus and gain some relief from all my woes. I could finally breathe easier, and I wanted to do something to repay Jesus for all that he'd done. I couldn't think of anything that could compare to what he did for all of us. I settled for my repayment to be following Jesus and to do what I could to spread this feeling of freedom and love to all people and reach those in need.

When I made it home on the bus, this time, I prepared to share all that I learned with Scarlett and Renée. As I stepped inside, instead of seeing Scarlett with another boy, I found both my sisters sitting as stiff as soldiers on the sofa, their eyes glued to the television screen while the OPTI screen was alit with its eerie glowing brain.

"What's going on?" I asked. I noticed the familiar yet morbid hum of the news. I felt like the world had stopped and everything happened in slow motion. As I inched closer, I noticed the headline—"*Breaking News.* OPTI's Latest Victory," appeared on the bottom of the screen. A picture of—my breath caught—Maddie was displayed as the news reporter said, "OPTI triumphs once again with the death of sixteen-year-old Maddie Stephens who was caught praying over the *Book of Common Prayer* on school grounds. She was also one of the defiant teens who were baptized in the lake last winter. The police killed her mother, Lauren Stephens, at her home around the same time. When faced with death, she proudly admitted that she was an ordained priest and had organized the baptisms movement. Both Ms. Stephens and her daughter died at the hands of the police. Her husband perished five years ago from terminal cancer and there is no evidence to demonstrate whether he was also engaged in unlawful activity. Maddie was an only child and is survived by no one, making OPTI's victory complete."

In the background, the people behind the reporter cheered. Was I seeing the world backward? How could anyone cheer over someone's gruesome death? An innocent girl and her mother vanished from the earth forever.

My backpack fell from my shoulders and onto the floor beneath me. I remained stuck in the same position as though I'd been turned to stone. My body was so numb, dead from all feeling. I wondered if I would ever experience joy or even breathe again. I fell to my knees as Scarlett and Renée focused their attention on me to rush to my side.

"She was my friend…" I managed to whisper in a choked voice. "She was my *friend!*" A torrent of sobs burst forth from my tired lips, my soul torn apart and releasing labored aching breaths. Scarlett and

Renée wrapped their arms around me. I looked up in time to see OPTI's glowing, pulsing orb vanish from the screen.

Rash fury occupied my mind. I pulled out of my sisters' arms, opened my backpack, and took out a hard-covered book. With all my built-up strength, I hurled it at the OPTI screen, causing it to erupt into an ear-splitting sound of glass shattering, an echo of my soul. Lightning flashed across the overcast sky, accompanied by thunder's deafening roar, and the house fell into utter darkness. Rain hammered against the roof.

My siblings and I all huddled on the sofa in fear and sorrow. When the storm ended silence fell all around us. We remained in the same position, immobile as the sun broke through the clouds and began to set—a fiery, blazing red.

CHAPTER 35

Be Still

Like an apparition, I roamed the grassy unkempt field, drifting among the dead in this decrepit graveyard behind the actual cemetery. Christians, Jewish people, Muslims, or anyone of another faith or anyone who didn't worship OPTI couldn't be buried in the same cemetery as OPTI worshippers. Racial or ethnic minorities, members of the LGBT community, and immigrants had to be buried here as well no matter their belief. Alone. Although I probably should have been at school, I couldn't pull myself away from the austere wind-broken tombstone roughly carved with the name "Maddie Stephens" beside the one for her mother. They didn't receive much of a crowd for their funeral, only a small gathering of brave souls. The funeral home director refused to even receive either of their bodies so all that could be done was have the holes filled up with empty coffins containing a photo of Maddie in one and of her mother in another. The only thought that gave me peace was my knowledge that they were both in heaven, a much happier, peaceful place. At last. *Free.*

I kept apart from the group at the funeral. I feared knowing the other mourners in case they were next to go. I couldn't stand to lose another soul the way I lost Maddie, the way I lost Jake, the way I once lost my father, and the way I lost Faith. Ever since the funeral, I kept returning back to this same spot as though drawn here by a silent call in my otherwise empty mind. I didn't want to be at home and I didn't want to be at school. I hadn't even spoken much to my other new friends. Isabelle, Jaylyn, and Rachel all came to the funeral and we spent it with our arms around one another's shoulders while we wept, a shared friend slandered as a traitor and killed because of it. My faith, at this time, wavered. I held onto it anyways, believing in Maddie's final words to me of Jesus's sacrifice and love for us all. On her gravestone was carved:

Psalm 46:10 "Be still, and know that I am God."[2]

A sense of ease embraced my somber heart when I saw it, and it reminded me that God remained in my heart no matter how dark and despairing life could be. I clung to my faith and belief as though my life depended on it despite the agony and weakness I felt. As I stood on this Friday morning, shivering from the breeze in my tear-stained black dress, I sent all the prayers I could to God that this nightmare would never happen again. Anger boiled underneath my sadness; fits of anger consumed me that left my room a mess from throwing pillows and kicking my garbage can while I screamed broken prayers at the ceiling.

Part of the reason I didn't go to school was to defy OPTI's strict rules. I expected to be punished. At this point, I didn't care. OPTI was the reason I had to be here anyways, in between life and death. In my room earlier, I spent my time crying out my window in fractured prayers to God that I wouldn't lose anyone else and all this pain would stop.

One of my only slivers of hope and potential joy became my opportunity to make a speech. I didn't feel the need to prepare. I already knew what I wanted to say. I only counted down the days. I already spent the morning of the funeral putting up the new posters and all of them had a picture of Maddie with the caption, "Hadn't she suffered enough?" I expected they would all be torn back down but I stood my ground. I couldn't go back to the fearful girl I had been. I feared death, however, Maddie's words inspired more confidence in me that I would be saved and go to heaven. Staring at the

---

2. Psalm 46:10.

grave only upset me. Leaving upset me even more. Maddie had been so kind, so loving, and so innocent. I couldn't imagine why anyone would want her dead. Especially not for her Christian faith—or any faith at all. Once again, my heart ached knowing that OPTI aimed to destroy such a person's precious and beautiful faith.

I thought I was alone until I heard shoes thudding against the grassy and muddy ground. I looked around me. Not in fear, for I already felt dead inside. I looked because I wanted to stare right in the face of whoever would insult or hurt me for grieving here. The figure surprised me, even though his raven hair was unmistakable—Heath.

"What are you doing here?" I said, a little irritable.

"I was about to ask you that same question," he said as he reached me. I noticed he wore a particularly nice all-black suit.

"Are you going to a party or something?" I asked.

"If that's what you call a funeral, then yes," he said, no trace of humor in his voice.

"The funeral was two days ago…I think," I muttered.

"Actually it was three."

"How would you know?" I rounded on him. "I didn't see you there."

"I didn't know her, Abigail," he said. "I thought I should pay my respects at some point."

"What do you want from me?" I nearly spat at him. "You know we can't be together and I've seen that you moved on. You don't need to suddenly reappear in my life as if you know…as if we were even friends to begin with."

"We could be friends, Abigail," he said. "You're right. I have moved on. Have you?"

"Yes, of course I have," I muttered before he could detect my disappointment. "Things can finally go back to how they were before Scarlett's cast party."

"They can't," he said, "because neither of us are the same people."

I studied him closely for a second, and despite my biting anger, I knew he had a point. I could never go back to the naive girl I was then, especially to think that my life would turn out all right if I followed OPTI's demands of me. I knew I probably should feel afraid. After all, I'd smashed an OPTI screen to pieces. That didn't deter me from doing the same thing to my phone before I even went to the funeral. I had no one to talk to, nothing I wanted to say. I just wanted to die. I stood here, waiting to be resurrected like Maddie had promised.

"You're not alone, you know," he said under his breath. "I lost a family member as a boy to a similar fate. My...my younger brother. He found God when he almost died on a playground. Bullies, you know how it is. His faith saved him, and when OPTI came for him, he wasn't afraid of death anymore. He died peacefully despite the agony of being shot in the chest. I saw it happen. With my own eyes. I'll never forget how happy he looked when I saw him at his wake. Miracles do exist, I suppose, even if you don't understand them."

"She was my friend..." I whispered. "She's gone...dead...and we only just met!" Grief swallowed me like a tidal wave, and I launched myself into Heath's waiting arms. He held me as I released one of the most debilitating wails I'd ever known. Memories swarmed into my mind of sitting in my math class while my sister Faith was killed, just like Maddie, my father's disappearance and my endless waiting for him to return, having to run for my life in the pitch-black to escape the coyotes at the Edwins', watching Mr. Edwin take his last breath, and nearly drowning to death because I couldn't meet OPTI's high demands; it felt like my whole life, I traveled on that same endless road, trying to escape the Edwins, trying to escape unceasing danger, loneliness, tragedy, and despair. A road that went on forever, that no one should have to travel on, a road with no lights and the haunting sound of sirens. More sobs burst forth from my chest from it all, from all that pain that I'd experienced on that long winding road. I let him hold me in a way I'd never been held. I realized I had one more person in this world and that was Heath.

"I'm sorry I told you we shouldn't be together, Heath." I tilted my head upward and caught his eyes, as smooth as a dart hitting a bull's-eye. "The truth is, I love you, Heath."

His eyes smoldered. "I love you too, Abigail," he said. I leaned upward, ready to embrace him with an unforgettable kiss, but then I remembered—

"You're dating Chelsea." I realized as I loosened myself from his grip to step back. "I can't date you if you're with her. It wouldn't be right."

"Always the moralist, aren't you?" he said and chuckled. "I wouldn't mind it either way."

"Wait a second," I said. "Didn't you say you moved on? How can you...say..."

"I didn't move on, Abigail," he said. "Chelsea is a...nice girl, I suppose. But my heart lies with you. I can't help that. Love is love. You know that as much as I do."

"How could you even date Chelsea?" I said. "She's the one who posted that video and photo. She's responsible for all my misery since. Did you know I was almost...well, I don't know what to call it..."

"What video? What photo?"

"How can you not know?" I cried. "Everyone knows. The video showed us kissing at the cast party and people think we slept together. Then Chelsea somehow took a photo of us together at my locker. Ever since, I've been called a slut, a whore, everything in between, and bullied all because of the claim that I slept with you. Then Chelsea started dating you and I didn't see anyone call her a slut. Not that they should."

Heath stared at me as if this was the first time he heard any of this.

"I never knew," he said under his breath. His eyes narrowed and his nostrils flared. "I wouldn't have dated her. What happened to you?"

"I don't want to get into it," I said. "It's how Maddie and I became friends. She...she and her...my new friends...they helped me when I was at my worst." I almost wept again, my body trembling. "I wouldn't be here if it weren't for Maddie, Jaylyn, Isabelle, and Rachel..." And then I did. "Oh, it's so painful...all of it..." I shouted in prayer. "Make it stop, God. Please, make all of it stop. I can't go through this any—" Heath's arms enveloped me as I leaned into him, releasing all my anguish in a spinning tornado of confusion.

Then another thought hit me. I looked up at Heath.

"Do you love Chelsea?" I asked.

"No, Abigail," he said. "I love you."

"But you dated her," I said. "That must mean you love her in some way. Don't you?"

"Abigail," he said and captured my face in his hands. "How many times, how many ways do I have to prove to you that I love you? You're the only girl for me."

Then I asked an even more pressing question.

"Will you break up with her?" I asked.

"Yes," he said. "I'll do it soon."

I felt like kissing him right now. I stopped myself. I couldn't do that to Chelsea despite what she did to me. I cried in Heath's arms for what felt like decades, my love for him stretched as deep and firm as the roots of an oak tree.

I returned home from the segregated cemetery, feeling lighter from Heath's comfort and promised love. Scarlett and Renée remained too hesitant to speak to me and I couldn't discuss Maddie's death over and over again without wailing and screaming. I could tell they were nervous because they kept staring at the shattered screen where OPTI should have been. I didn't know what would happen as a consequence for that. I knew I was in danger.

Fortunately Scarlett took over caring for Renée and had a meal ready for Renée and me. I didn't eat it though and instead headed for my bedroom. I entered the room and flopped onto my bed. I just wanted to sleep and sleep and sleep. Only then could I escape my torn heart. I couldn't sleep though. I was far too alert. I rolled onto my back. The candle I had lit for Maddie's memorial had blown out. Sadness enveloped me. I didn't have much to give to Maddie's memorial aside from a photo of her and some pink tulips from my spring flower garden. We hadn't been friends for very long.

I sighed, figuring it would be a waste to relight it. I decided to enter my bathroom to get ready for bed. I gazed at myself in the mirror. I felt a disconnection with myself as though I'd split into two people, as if I left my body. I looked pale and my hair was light enough to make me look like a ghost, surreal and ethereal. A tear stained my cheek.

Then a memory flashed into my mind of me in my bathroom holding the razor to my wrist and making the first cut. I felt called to that level again, that sinister voice that told me that maybe things would be better, better if I wasn't here. All my pain, all my sorrow—gone. It seemed so simple. I felt scared though because a part of me realized that when I thought I would take my life, I feared I would regret it when it was too late. Also I realized after that I couldn't put Scarlett or Renée or my mother in that situation of losing me to suicide. In another sense, I wouldn't be around when God finally freed us from OPTI's control. A part of me couldn't—wouldn't—give up the fight despite the unbearable pain.

When I woke up from my dream of Jesus in heaven, I'd been given a second chance at life. I didn't know what purpose I had. I wanted to know what it could be. I needed a reason, something—anything—for me to keep going. I sent a prayer to God that he would confide my life purpose to me and why I should keep going. I also sent up a desperate prayer that I wouldn't die by suicide and that someday, everyone in my country would be free—truly free—but that possibility seemed far off, as though I was on a treadmill in the dark with a small bright light hanging over my head. I couldn't picture a future for myself, couldn't imagine a life beyond the sorrows I endured right now. I barely knew myself. As another tear dripped onto the counter in front of me, I sent a prayer to God that I would have a future.

I left the bathroom and reentered my bedroom. My eyes narrowed on the candle and I gasped. It was lit. I blinked and studied it closer. The flame remained bright and beaming and cast a golden glow onto Maddie's photo. I fell to my knees and a well of tears streamed from my sunken bruise-like weary eyes; seeing the flickering flame was like a beacon of hope. God hadn't abandoned me. The candle burned with Maddie's memory, and like that, it seemed as though she'd come back to life. It reminded me of the gift of resurrection Christians are promised. At least I knew that in some way, Maddie lived on. In this time of darkness faith was my only light.

"Hallelujah." I exhaled.

I finally slept that night and was further surprised by my dream. I saw myself skipping around on a blanket of clouds, wearing a sparkling silver dress that swayed as I moved, gliding with little effort and filled with an insurmountable amount of joy. Above me, in the clouds, Jesus's face appeared, watching over me with a tender gaze that gave me a sense of security, using the Holy Spirit to guide me through my tumultuous life. I trusted that God has a plan for my life and that I would carry on despite my agony. When I woke, I held onto this discovery. It didn't feel like God's presence was just above me anymore; he was everywhere, near and far, all around me, with transcendence and immanence, holding my crumbled heart.

CHAPTER 36

Speech Night in Scarlet

I stopped visiting the cemetery. I felt glad Heath found me there because it ended my cycle of torment. Not going proved hard though. I feared what would happen if I forgot. It was similar to when Faith died and how sometimes I forgot what she looked like. Usually it left me in a panicked spiral, desperately racking my brain for a clearer memory of her. Unfortunately time worked against me, and although I didn't forget what she looked like, I just couldn't remember as much of our memories together. I could remember Faith preaching to us about the Bible, particularly about Jesus. I knew now that by preaching to me, Faith saved my life, just as Maddie, Jaylyn, Isabelle, and Rachel did. I wouldn't know what to do in this world without my faith. I held it close to my heart.

For some unknown reason, my mood lifted. Getting through each passing day became less difficult and allowed me to return to school. With Maddie's death and my heat-of-the-moment decision to break an OPTI screen, I was almost certain of my impending death. However, as the days passed, nothing happened. In the meantime, at lunchtime on Monday morning, I waited with anticipation in the woodsy trail, enclosed by nature. It was about ten minutes before I saw him.

"Did you do it?" I asked Heath when he appeared. He gazed back at me with a gleam in his eye that I could only gather as love.

"Yes," he said. "Chelsea and I are history, Abby. I want you."

I stepped forward with joy and wrapped my arms around his neck as he lifted me from the ground. Our lips met in our embrace, his strong arms gripping me tight. He put me back down and continued to hold me as we shared a deep kiss in a world that suddenly seemed full of wonder again.

We kept our relationship a secret from the rest of the school, especially from Scarlett. I didn't know yet how to tell her and I wanted to avoid having other students call me a slut once again. However, their words and judgment of me hurt more than I expected, and on our first meeting in the woodsy trail, I found it difficult to kiss Heath with the chorus of "slut" bobbing into my head with every movement of our lips. When our kissing escalated, I usually stepped back, feeling wary about taking our relationship to another level.

Fortunately Heath respected my wishes and keeping it a secret even heightened our passion for each other, something I both craved and feared. My love for him bloomed with each kiss and touch, and aside from my faith, it was the only part of my life that helped me heal from my grief and experience some happiness even. However, being apart during school and at home proved difficult. I didn't believe I was a slut—just a girl in love. The only thing that could make my life better would be the freedom to hold hands in the hallway or exchange a heated look in the middle of class. Heath was all I could think about and I feared losing control, of losing my attention in school and my grades slipping. At least in track, my mind could daydream while I jogged. Spending time with Heath dragged me out of my jaded outlook on life since Maddie's death and consumed every aspect of it.

Everything went well between Heath and me until Thursday came, right before speech night on Friday, followed by the final vote. As I closed my locker, a face appeared behind it—Chelsea. She stared straight at me with eyes like daggers.

"Chelsea?" I asked with slight nerves in my gut. "What are you doing here?"

"Heath broke up with me on Monday," she said. "Did you know that?"

I looked away and pretended to be busy putting a book away that I actually needed.

"No," I said. I don't think it was very convincing because she didn't waver.

"You little skank." She hissed. "You totally stole him from me."

"Do not call me a skank just because I'm dating Heath." I fired back, daring to stare back at her vengeful expression. I realized I admitted to our dating. I didn't care anymore.

"Watch your back, Abigail," Chelsea said, leaning closer to me. "You're going to regret that you stole him."

My anger ignited like sparks.

"I didn't *steal* him, Chelsea." I fumed. "He chose to be with me long before you were together. If you want to know the truth, we kissed one month ago, a week before you two became a couple. We're in love and he chose to come back to me when he found out what you did to me. And do not call me a slut or a skank. Just so you know, being in love with someone doesn't make you one. It just makes you human. Try spreading another rumor but you won't be able to because I have nothing left to lose."

"So you are together." She rounded back in a sneer. "What would your dear sister Scarlett think about that? Break up with Heath or I'll tell her the truth."

"Go ahead and try it," I said, though my chest tightened at the thought. "I don't care anymore."

She looked livid and with a huff, turned on her heels and stalked away.

The news spread like wildfire because the next day, as I waited to set foot on that stage for speech night, I overheard the other male contestants jeering at me and making dirty jokes when they knew I could hear them. One of them told me I looked pregnant. Fortunately Scarlett didn't seem to believe the rumor as she helped pump me up for my speech.

"Go out there and crush it, Abby," she said. "Who cares if you mess up, right? It's not like it could get any worse."

"Thanks," I said and gave her a hug that she returned. "Thank you for your support, Scar. I couldn't have done it without you as my campaign manager."

She nodded. "Oh, don't worry. People won't forget either of us. I'm hosting a party at our house after this with only my friends invited. Think about how fun the party will be and you'll do great."

At that, I stepped onto the stage. I wore the scarlet jumpsuit Scarlett encouraged me to put on to honor her part as my campaign manager. When I walked onto the stage, the lights were bright enough to cast the audience in darkness. I suppose it made it easier that I wouldn't have to see them glare at me while I spoke, and the color I wore attracted attention. I only had a short speech. What was the point?

"Many of you probably don't care what I have to say," I began. "You've all made it pretty clear that I'm an unpopular candidate." I cringed from the sound of *boos*. "But when I was at my worst because of the bullying, the only people who truly cared about me were Maddie Stephens, Jaylyn and Isabelle Guerra, Rachel Shapiro, and my sisters. It's thanks to them that I'm still breathing. I hope one day, we won't live in a world where people are killed for believing in God or discriminated against because of their race, ethnicity, gender, sexual orientation, religion, unbelief, or nationality. Maddie Stephens didn't deserve to die and neither did her mother, a beloved and wonderful priest. Isabelle and Jaylyn didn't deserve to be separated from their parents or unwelcomed in our country." I didn't mention Rachel so as not to put her life at risk for her Jewish faith. "I'd like to add, I do not serve OPTI. I serve the one and only God. Jesus is the Lord."

I waited in silence. Then out of nowhere, the OPTI screens surrounding the auditorium flickered and flashed on all sides like lightning while I heard a chorus of gasps from the audience, including my own. A video played on the screens of what looked like me hurling a book at the OPTI screen in my house. The audience gasped again, collectively, as the film replayed over and over again. I should have known, should have imagined the humiliation that awaited me from OPTI. I knew then that my credibility as a person in this school, town, and maybe even state, would collapse even more. I could only stand on the stage and watch OPTI throw another punishment at me. I thought about heading off the stage in my disheartened state when the video changed to reveal a video of me at the Edwins'. I saw myself putting the valerian flower petals into the three mugs of tea and then jumped to when Mr. Edwin drank the tea and subsequently died from poison. Once again, while the crowd gasped in horror, I had to watch that man die again as if experiencing it in real life wasn't scary enough. I studied his pale face as Scarlett and I rushed to escape the house with Renée, the rash decisions that seemed to determine my fate for the rest of my life.

The crowd inhaled again. As I listened, a flashback of me cutting myself in my bathroom—because OPTI made me believe I was a murderer—flitted through my mind. I couldn't go through this again.

The screens turned pitch-black then. Suddenly the OPTI brain appeared. Instead of being multicolored, it turned bloodred. The screen went blank again.

"She's a murderer!" a voice cried in the audience. "A cold-blooded killer!"

"She killed an innocent-looking man!" another voice shouted.

"She should be in a detention center!"

"She's a Christian too! A traitor to OPTI!"

"She should be in jail!"

"Lock her up! Lock her up!" the crowd chanted.

I left the stage, feeling beyond confused and in shock like I'd been punched in the stomach. I didn't know how to make sense of what happened. Scarlett waited for me in the same spot and threw an arm around my shoulder, escorting me to the nearest exit. She seemed as disappointed as I felt. Unfortunately despite what Scarlett said, my life did get worse.

CHAPTER 37

Uninvited Guest

Scarlett and I returned home later that night for Scarlett's speech night party. Dylan received the most votes, however, OPTI gave the position to Jake for some unknown reason. It made me happy that it went to someone like Jake. He didn't come to the party though. I waited in the empty front lobby with Scarlett until OPTI announced the results, wishing I could go home. OPTI even announced for emphasis that I only received six votes in total, making the crowd roar with laughter.

At the party, I stayed in the kitchen, hovering over the food and watching Scarlett dance with Tim. Renée had to stay upstairs in her room and I considered joining her. I left the kitchen, stumbling and squeezing through a crowd of students who gazed at me in disgust and moved away from me as though I were a pariah. The only reason they came to the party was because not all of them knew Scarlett and I were sisters. The glass from the OPTI screen had been cleaned up by now and replaced. The wires remained fried, most likely from the storm that came after I threw the book at it. The screen didn't work at all anymore.

"Hey," a voice said from the crowd, and my eyes found Heath, standing at the bottom of the stairs. He was dressed in a blue button-down shirt and black denim pants, his dark hair groomed and shiny rather than its usual wild nature.

His eyes called me to him and I found he remained the only person, aside from my immediate family and Rachel, Isabelle, and

Jaylyn, who didn't believe I murdered Mr. Edwin, even with that footage. My friends had found me in the lobby and gave me hugs though they were too disturbed by OPTI to come to the party. In this moment, Heath's undeniable acceptance of me despite everything deepened my love for him.

"Want to get away for a bit?" he asked and held out a hand to me.

I took it and our eyes locked again.

"Did you enjoy it, Abigail?" a triumphant voice asked behind me. "Did you enjoy poisoning an innocent man?"

I whirled around to see Chelsea, her bob now a dark shade of blond. Allison and Lucy stood by her side again, echoing her contempt for me.

"I didn't kill him," I said. Even so, with all the exposure publicly from OPTI during my speech and the cutting glares of my classmates, it felt like I had.

"She's right and I believe her," Heath said and glowered at Chelsea. "We're not dating anymore. Give it up."

"I don't care about you anymore, Heath," she said. "By the way, you weren't a great kisser."

"Then why were you so jealous?" I countered in Heath's defense.

"Not anymore. Fortunately, for me you won't be president. I made sure of it, *murderer*."

Before I could stop it, Chelsea raised her glass of what looked like some cranberry drink and dumped it on my head. I only had enough time to gasp. The ice from her drink gave me a brain freeze while the cranberry juice seeped into my hair and dripped all over my jumpsuit. Scarlett would be furious. Her friends started laughing. I felt ready to throw a punch but Heath grabbed my arms and held me back.

"You'll get in trouble," he warned me. "It's what she wants to happen."

"Get out of our house." I spat instead as I wiped some of the drink off my face while Chelsea and her friends snickered.

"Who invited *you*?" I heard Scarlett's voice from behind me.

Chelsea turned her attention to my sister. "No one," Chelsea said. "I didn't need an invitation. After all, I am vice president of the junior class next year."

"Too bad none of us care," Scarlett said. With her stilettos on, Scarlett looked taller than Chelsea and much more intimidating.

"Oh, I'm sure you'll care," Chelsea said. "Look around you. I sent everyone a video of you that I'm sure you'll enjoy."

I observed the room while Scarlett stared Chelsea down. All around me, partygoers gawked at their OPTI-Phones as they chimed and vibrated instantaneously. Mine remained shattered so I couldn't know what they watched. Scarlett's phone chimed and she took it out to examine the screen. I watched Scarlett's face, expecting her to look humiliated. Instead she looked up at Chelsea and gave her a smirk.

"What video of me?" Scarlett asked, and now, she was the one with a triumphant look on her face.

I finally caught a glimpse of her phone and saw a clip of Chelsea taking out a bunch of votes from my ballot and stuffing them into Dylan's ballot. Chelsea's face turned red. I brightened. Although I didn't come close to beating Dylan, I still received more votes than I imagined. Some people's minds had changed.

"Nice effort trying to take me down, Chelsea," Scarlett said. "I discovered that you probably hacked my phone while I was meeting with the principal to try to film me with Tim so I decided to flip the direction of the camera." She stared her down once more. "Should have checked it before you sent it, right? Now everyone knows you rigged the election and stole Abigail's votes so Dylan could win. I'm sorry to tell you this, Chelsea—justice is served."

Chelsea seemed so angry as she stared at her phone that it appeared as though it might break in her hands.

"Too bad Abigail lost no matter the measures I took," Chelsea retaliated despite her defeat. "Didn't you hear the rumors, Scarlett? Abigail made out with Heath behind your back probably the day I took that picture of them. She told me herself."

Chelsea tapped her phone, and suddenly, I could hear my voice.

"If you want to know the truth, we kissed one month ago, a week before you two became a couple. We're in love and he chose to come back to me when he found out what you did to me—"

"You recorded our conversation?" I cried. "Get out of our home! You and your friends don't belong here, ever."

"Good luck." Chelsea sneered at me, looking smug as she hurried for the door, pausing to slam her empty drink on a side table in the foyer. Her friends joined her.

I shifted my gaze to look with unease at Scarlett who fixated a glower where Chelsea had stood. Then she turned to me with a scowl.

"*Get out of my sight.*"

"Scar, please. I...I wasn't thinking."

"Don't, Abigail. Don't even try to talk to me."

"Hey, leave her alone, Scarlett." Heath's voice met my ears. "We got together when you and I weren't dating anymore."

"Don't *you* talk to *me* either and make up lame excuses." Scarlett fumed at him. "You fell in love with my sister while we were dating." Then she shifted her gaze back to me. "And *you* not only fell in love with him back, you kissed him a week after he broke up with me and lied about it to me for an *entire* month."

"I'm sorry, Scarlett," I said. "I...I didn't know how to—"

"Did it not matter to you how that would make me feel?" Scarlett said. "I was beginning to fall in love with him, Abigail. I never want to speak to either of you ever again! Especially not *you*," she said to me. "This party is over. I'm sorry I even threw one for you."

She was right when she said the party was over because everyone had tuned into our fight and the music cut from the stereo as soon as Scarlett said the word *off.* Then she stormed upstairs; I could hear her door slam from down here.

I gazed at the spot where Scarlett had been standing, frozen. I tried not to look at Heath. The guests began to leave the house until Heath and I stood alone.

"Come on, Abigail," Heath said and put an arm around my shoulder. "Don't worry about Scarlett. You did nothing wrong."

"I did do something wrong," I said. "I kissed you shortly after you two broke up. She's right to be mad."

"Don't let that separate us," Heath said and looked deep into my eyes.

"It has to," I said as tears fell from my eyes. "I couldn't be with you then and I can't now."

"We can hide it then," Heath said and his thumb brushed a tear from my cheek. "From Scarlett."

Finally I faced him. "I'm sorry, Heath," I said. "We can't be together. Not like this."

I leaned up to plant a kiss on his cheek and then began to climb up the stairs.

"I'm sorry," I muttered again as Heath left the house without another word. All the bliss I'd experienced this week with Heath vanished so suddenly. I had to do right by Scarlett. She was my sister and I didn't act the way I should have. It was too late to take it back. Now I had to spend all of spring break with Scarlett angry with me.

CHAPTER 38

Easter Sunday

On Easter morning, I woke early and climbed out of bed for the church service. Now that the OPTI screen didn't work, I didn't have to fear that he would know where I went. My guilt remained my only obstacle that weighed down on me like chains that dragged and slowed my attempts to move forward. I remembered what Maddie said about being saved through faith alone. I did repent for my mistake and felt a sense of release from my guilt. However, Scarlett wouldn't speak to me and I didn't know what to do to change it. I felt determined to make another move against OPTI, though doing so might result in my death. OPTI had already taken so much from me and my faith became my only shield, the fire that enriched my soul.

I stepped outside my house when I walked right into a bulky figure.

"Abigail." Heath exhaled, catching me by the wrist despite the fact that I'd already settled back on my feet. "Where are you going?" He noticed my white dress and the makeup touching up my face. "You look beautiful, by the way."

"It's a long story," I said. "I'd like to know what you're doing here. If Scarlett—"

"She won't know," he said. "I came to fight for you, Abigail." He raised his other hand and in it rested a crimson rose with the stem cut. "I know we're not supposed to be together. We were never supposed to when you consider our history. Being with you was the happiest I felt in a long time. Take me back, Abby, and we can be free to be together. Scarlett knows we're in love now. We don't need to hide it anymore."

"I have to go, Heath," I said, staring in apprehension at the rose as if I was about to be pricked. "I can't...I...I can't deal with this right now."

He grasped my hands as I started to move past him and held them gently in his own firmer hands. I stopped; his touch was electrifying. "You've said that before, Abigail. It's time we both fight for the love we know is unmistakable between us. I can't stop thinking of you."

"Me too," I said. "I really have somewhere to be though."

"Where could you possibly go on a Sunday?"

"To church," I said and held my breath.

"What?" he said.

I sighed and briefly explained what Maddie told me about having Eucharist at the abandoned church on Easter Sunday. Heath's expression turned to one of alarm.

"Abigail," he said, "if you go to that church, you could die. Did you not listen to my story about my brother?"

"My faith is all I have, Heath," I said. "I already tried staying quiet and obeying OPTI's commands. Look where that got me—the whole town thinks I'm a murderer, a slut, and a traitor. There's no going back, Heath. I can only go forward, and well, if I do die...At least I'll die happy like your brother did."

"Maddie probably didn't die happy, Abby. Didn't you see the clip of it? She was shot in broad daylight right after school." I cringed and he went on. "What do you hope will happen from doing this? That it will make things better?"

"It could," I said. "It could encourage more people to take a stand. My only option is to stand by Jesus on this holy day. When I couldn't breathe, when I was at my end all this time, this year and the last from OPTI, the one person who saved my life every time was Jesus because of his love for me. I need to go for Maddie and her mother too because neither of them deserved to die. Hopefully, one day, no one will have to hide their faith out of fear of death. One day, people could feel free to live by their beliefs and accept their differences. Don't we all want the same thing? To be free, to belong, to be loved, and to be valued for who we are."

"I believe in God too, Abby," he said, "because of my brother but going to church won't help, Abigail. OPTI is way too powerful."

"Don't you believe in miracles then? Don't you think God is more powerful?" He didn't say anything though didn't look happy about it. "I'm going, Heath," I said. "And there's nothing you can say or do that will change my mind." I started down the front steps and headed for one of my mother's cars.

"Let me go with you then," he called after me.

I halted because I found it difficult to think about putting Heath in a near-death situation so I understood his hesitancy to let me go. I didn't want to seem hypocritical so I opened the passenger side door of my car for him.

"Get in," I said, "I need to get there soon."

Heath sighed and hurried over to me.

"I'll drive. You're still underage, remember?" Then he held the rose out and a pin. "May I?" I nodded and pulled my hair back while he attached the rose to my dress over my heart. I couldn't suppress the thrill from the close proximity of his hand, and he gazed at me, his eyes intense as though he wanted to kiss me. I bit my tongue to wake myself from the trance his eyes put me under and turned away before he could.

As Heath drove, I rolled down the window, admiring the warm sunny day at the beginning of April. A touch of a breeze met my cheek. Only a few soft white clouds floated in the sky, blue like the sea. Heath and I didn't speak much aside from Heath giving me directions from the map. I didn't want to admit that I feared we would both die like those people who were shot at church last fall. I tried to focus my mind on the more important mission of taking a stand against OPTI's control of me and everyone in this town, especially people of faith. As my mind sifted through past memories of God's grace in my life, from my outside imprisonment at the Edwins' to the illumination of the candle for Maddie's memorial, I knew he remained by my side. The small flame continued to flicker and hadn't gone out since it had been relit. The candle wax didn't melt either. When we passed the cemetery, the rising sun's rays cast a radiant golden glow upon the graves of both the OPTI worshippers and the segregated cemetery as though they were all called to eternal life. Despite my fears that I may die today, Jesus's profound love for everyone revealed itself to me on this day, honoring his resurrection, and filled me with an unexplained joy that gave me peace in my coming death. Soon, I supposed, I would be home—my *true* home. *Free.*

We arrived at the old center of town where the local shops were boarded up and had missing bricks, piles of them strewn across the ground and cracked. The roads were riddled with potholes, gravel, and pebbles. The church stood at the far end of the street, and as my eyes focused on it, I understood why our town referred to it as an abandoned church. Stones were missing from the walls. The doors appeared as though the painter had adorned it with a pearly white paint, but had faded into an off-white color and chipped.

Thick vines stretched across the walls, a thriving green. The grass was overgrown, stretching out to conceal the cracked stone pathway. Behind the church rested a large forest, and when we stepped inside the building, it made sense. The church was empty with no roof. The floors were covered in patches of dirt and bushes with more vines stretching through the high, hollowed out windows and along the walls, making the building seem one with nature. The windows perched high up and were hollowed out. An altar perched in the back of the room in the center, still fully intact with a gold cross resting on top. The window behind the altar displayed a stained glass image of Jesus with his arms spread wide, wearing a long white robe, with women and children standing beside him. The women were covered from head to toe. The image left me awestruck as I rarely ever saw an image of Jesus, apart from my dreams, and felt deep love emanated from his eyes—a love greater than I could ever comprehend.

Under OPTI's control, we learned very little about history before OPTI came to power and most literature contained stories about OPTI so it was difficult to imagine a world where OPTI didn't exist. Seeing the image of Jesus gave me hope that one day, people would be free to worship him in harmony, knowing that God's love can conquer any form of evil standing in the way.

The sun shone through the open roof, beaming down to form a halo on the altar as though Jesus stood there. A couple of white clouds drifted in the sky, a marvelous, heavenly white like the robes Jesus wore.

"No one's here, Abigail," Heath said in a grave tone. "We'd better leave before OPTI discovers where we went. Nothing is going to happen without anyone here."

"Are you sure about that, Heath?" A voice came from behind us.

I jumped and spun around to see Isabelle and Jaylyn entering through the doors. They smiled at us.

"So I guess Maddie told you," Jaylyn said as she walked over to us. "Without her mom, we won't have a priest to deliver a sermon or give communion." She frowned. "Hopefully we can make do anyways."

"By the way," Isabelle said, "thanks again for what you said in your speech about Maddie, her mother, and us. It would have made her very happy to hear. We were happy you stood up for us and them."

"Thank you," I said as a tear came to my eye. "I wouldn't have found the strength to without you all. You saved my life."

They both smiled again. "You can always count on us," Jaylyn said. "That's what true friends are for."

We exchanged hugs. My eyes shifted to Heath who stood close to me, on guard, as though in preparation in case someone came to kill us.

"I still have my copy of the service," I said to Jaylyn and Isabelle and pulled out my leaflet from my purse. Maddie had stored it in my backpack before we parted that day outside the school, and I found it over spring break. It was already stained with my tears.

"What will we do without a priest?" Isabelle said with her eyes cast downward.

"One of us could lead us in prayers," Jaylyn said. "Do you want to lead, Abigail?"

"Me?" I asked. "Why should I lead?"

"Because of your story, Abigail," she said. "You have a great story of how your faith saved you from a tragic circumstance and your speech about faith as a candidate showed much bravery. People know you from the news ever since OPTI shared a video of your speech. If anyone knows you're the one leading, it could send a huge statement to OPTI."

"Don't set Abigail up to be killed," Heath said with a scowl at them. "Isn't it enough that she came?"

"Heath, it's okay," I said, "I agree with them. It would send a message. I'll lead the prayers then."

Heath didn't look happy with my friends or me. I gave him a pressing stare. "Please, Heath. It's what I want. I want to take a stand against OPTI and lead for Jesus. That's why I came, and if I die, it'll be worth it to glorify Jesus as the one who saves us all, who frees us all."

Heath didn't respond while he sulked.

"Who will lead us in the hymn?" I asked them.

"Jaylyn," Isabelle said. "She brought her guitar."

I nodded, noticing it slung over her shoulder, and moved to take my place at the podium near the altar.

Shortly after Isabelle and Jaylyn came, more people began to arrive of all ages and backgrounds, including Jaylyn and Isabelle's adoptive parents. Soon a large diverse group of Christians bravely stood together where the pews used to be. I knew our presence here would attract attention. I wanted to be free from fear and remained calm as I prepared to worship our Savior.

Isabelle and Jaylyn announced a moment of silence to honor the deaths of Lauren and Maddie Stephens, the two leaders of the secret baptisms, and the victims who died in the church shootings in the fall.

I took a deep breath and read the first prayer while everyone else followed along:

> You, God, are my God,
> earnestly I seek you;
> I thirst for you,
> my whole being longs for you,

in a dry and parched land
where there is no water.
I have seen you in the sanctuary
and beheld your power and your glory.
Because your love is better than life,
my lips will glorify you.
I will praise you as long as I live,
and in your name I will lift up my hands.
I will be fully satisfied as with the richest of foods;
with singing lips my mouth will praise you.[3]

As I read the words of this prayer specifically, I felt a lift in my spirits and my voice carried on as though magnified and coming from the depths of my soul. Like in the psalm prayer, we all lived in some form of a desert land under OPTI's control; and like the writer of this prayer, I longed to know God far more than I did now, to be given something—anything—like water to sustain me in my own trek through my perilous desert like the lake of the secret baptisms. Following the prayer, the leaflet contained a beautiful hymn called "Be Still" that Jaylyn led.

Child of God, oh, hear Him saying,
'In temptation look to me.
E'en when Satan's pow'r seems strongest,
Thy salvation I will be.
In the midst of fiery trials,
Thou canst walk without a fear,
For My presence shall be with thee,
Thou wilt ever find Me near.
When the journey's end is nearing,
When dark Jordan rolls before,
Falter not, I have redeem'd thee,
I will bear thee safely o'er.'

---

3. Psalm 63:1–5.

Be still, be still,
Be still and know that I am God,
Be still, be still,
Be still and know that I am God.[4]

The hymn eased my weary spirit and revitalized my strength in enduring the trials of my life, knowing that we all had Jesus as our Savior to bring us salvation from even the most oppressive evil. Then I came across a reading from the Gospel of John. I spoke:

> Now Mary stood outside the tomb crying. As she wept, she bent over to look into the tomb and saw two angels in white, seated where Jesus' body had been, one at the head and the other at the foot.
>
> They asked her, "Woman, why are you crying?"
>
> "They have taken my Lord away," she said, "and I don't know where they have put him." At this, she turned around and saw Jesus standing there, but she did not realize that it was Jesus.
>
> He asked her, "Woman, why are you crying? Who is it you are looking for?"
>
> Thinking he was the gardener, she said, "Sir, if you have carried him away, tell me where you have put him, and I will get him."
>
> Jesus said to her, "Mary."
>
> She turned toward him and cried out in Aramaic, "Rabboni!" (which means "Teacher").
>
> Jesus said, "Do not hold on to me, for I have not yet ascended to the Father. Go instead to my brothers and tell them, 'I am ascending to

---

4. Kate Ulmer, "Be Still" (HymnsUntoGod.org, 2014).

my Father and your Father, to my God and your God.'"

Mary Magdalene went to the disciples with the news: "I have seen the Lord!" And she told them that he had said these things to her.[5]

I listened carefully as I read each word of this passage from the Gospels and felt a sense of awe that Jesus rose from the dead and ascended into heaven. Not even death could defeat him. And all of it happened so that everyone could receive the grace of God, eternal life as long as they had faith. Jesus's disciple Mary Magdalene saw him first in his resurrected form, revealing the valued status of women as human beings in Jesus's ministry and with full and equal rights to preach, worship, use their talents, and live the truth as leaders and disciples. It inspired me to become a leader as well, to share my story of how Jesus helped me to survive in the darkest times, spreading his love to any soul I could.

I felt more alive than I'd ever felt in my life, my longing for God quenched with the spiritual power of these words, and my next words flew out as easily as a river flowing gently downstream.

"I know the saving power of God in my life. More than a year ago, OPTI placed my siblings and me in a foster home when my mother was too sick to care for us. The Edwins were cruel to us. Nights at the Edwins' proved intolerable. I had to...I had to...do things that no one should be forced to do. My body didn't belong to me. Mr. Edwin even put a collar around my neck like a dog, forcing me to spend the night in the backyard. Coyotes nearly killed me, and despite my dwindled hope in God, he still rescued me from them that night and proved that his love for me and everyone is boundless.

"When Mr. Edwin died from ingesting poison, OPTI accused me of murder and sent me to a detention center like a prisoner. I had to endure intense conditioning on OPTI's orders. I nearly died because I couldn't keep up, drowned in a glass cage." I took a deep

---

[5]. John 20:11–18.

breath to suppress the tears of endless grief in my eyes. "When I was in that cage, I screamed for God to save my life. And he did. I didn't drown, an enormous blessing. A man named Byte bargained with OPTI and a boy named Luke to save my life and allow me to train to a level that convinced OPTI to let me leave that place behind and go home to my family. Although I couldn't see it then, I feel as if God intervened to save me from prison and allow me to return home, a safer place, with my family. Unfortunately my family fell apart a long time ago—my sister Faith died in a school shooting that I'm certain was motivated as a punishment for standing up for her faith to OPTI, and my father abandoned the rest of us to pursue whatever other life captivated him more. I don't even know if he's even alive.

"Even so, I went home after my time at prison, the one place I wanted to be most. A place that always seemed distant from me, a place I had always been trying to reach. Where I lived wasn't nearly the same, however, because I lived under OPTI's control. I had to train physically and intellectually to enter the military or law enforcement on OPTI's orders. I couldn't decide an alternative path. At times, I felt like I didn't have a future. Whatever I faced, my siblings always brightened my life for me. My boyfriend named Jake made me feel welcome at a time when I didn't have any friends at school. He showed me kindness when I needed it most. He lost his father, a rabbi, in a hate-fueled murder like I lost my sister. Despite our differing faiths, God loves us just the same. Although our relationship didn't work out, I fell in love with a man who I believe could be my true love." I looked at Heath who gazed back at me with what I could only gather as deep love for me. My heart radiated with love for him and it felt magnified, knowing he was here and that he also loved Jesus as much as I did. I grimaced as I felt a sudden nip at my chest and realized the rose pinned to my dress had pricked me. I ignored it and went on with my story. "When OPTI punished me for having an anxiety attack, he tried to convince me that I murdered Mr. Edwin to the point where I believed it and nearly ended my life. Jesus appeared to me in a dream, saved me from suicide, and reassured me that I wasn't at fault.

"When students bullied me physically, emotionally, and ver-bally because of accusations that I was a slut, all because I kissed a boy I loved at a party, God rescued me from it all and gave me a group of friends who protected me from the insults and torment. They gave me the strength to keep going when I'd lost hope. They too had experienced God's saving grace. Isabelle and Jaylyn lost their parents because of OPTI, a horrendous injustice, and God rescued them to provide them with a better life. However, the loss of their parents, their true family, is a punishment that no child should ever have to endure, a pain that not even time can heal.

"When Maddie died, I felt hopeless and full of anger at OPTI for killing such an innocent girl or anyone for that matter. She taught me the true meaning of the Gospels, that Christianity is a religion of love through Jesus's courageous sacrifice, everlasting love for all people, and his teachings for us to love our neighbor as ourselves. I've come to begin to understand the love and the grace that God gives us. A life-saving soul-deep love that has allowed me to endure all of the suffering I faced all because of OPTI. Miracles do exist, thanks to Jesus. In Jesus, I found freedom, in Jesus I found a greater love than any man or woman could ever give me. He loves me for who I am. Above anyone, Jesus gave me strength, gave me hope, gave me courage, and empowered me when I felt weak. He saved my life more times than I can count. Now I know my true home lies in heaven with Jesus. Hallelujah."

The crowd echoed my hallelujah, and the sun seemed to shine brighter down upon all of our heads. Then as one, we recited:

> Our Father, Who art in heaven,
> Hallowed be Thy Name.
> Thy Kingdom come.
> Thy Will be done,
> on earth as it is in Heaven.
> Give us this day our daily bread.
> And forgive us our trespasses,
> as we forgive those who trespass against us.
> And lead us not into temptation,
> but deliver us from evil. Amen.

"Abigail, Abigail!" a voice shouted from the crowd of church-goers. I was awakened from my pleasant meditation on the prayer and the service. I looked up in time to see Heath approaching the podium. "I checked the news on my phone. OPTI's forces are coming for us. They're on their way to us as I speak, a block away. We have to leave now!"

Alarm swept over the room. The whole crowd of people tried to move for the doors to the church at once. I held onto the leaflet with the prayers and hymns and hurried with Heath to follow the crowd. However, as the doors opened, they slammed shut even faster with churchgoers turning around, bumping into each other.

"They can see us if we leave," a tall bearded man shouted. "They're too close. If we rush out of here, they'll see us and shoot. There has to be another way."

"Block the doors!" I heard Isabelle cry and saw her hasten through the crowd with Jaylyn behind her. "They're going to try to shoot us either outside or inside. If we block them from entering, we'll be safe."

I glanced up at the sky and noticed that a thicker layer of gray clouds had formed during the service, though the sun remained visible. Time seemed to slow down and I looked at Heath, knowing that we might die together on this day. I hadn't even left a note at home. I didn't tell my sisters because I knew they might have come too and I didn't want to lose them.

"We're doomed," Heath said to me. "I told you something like this might happen."

"We were doomed before," I said and took a long deep breath, "to OPTI's oppression and persecution. I don't regret coming here."

Heath grasped my hand and looked at me with care. "If we die, we might as well do it together."

I leaned forward. Heath closed the distance and kissed me back with a depth that made me forget about the danger for the moment. When we broke away from each other, we remained close and held hands as we rushed toward the doors. Jaylyn lifted a slab of wood.

"Help us block the doors," Isabelle urged, and while Isabelle helped Jaylyn place it through the handles of the doors to lock it,

Heath and I lifted several stone bricks to place them in front of the doors. I could hear the thuds of what sounded like people marching, the sound growing closer and closer.

"Hey," a man in the crowd shouted. "There's a back exit right under the archway."

I saw the man hurry to the exit, followed by the panic-stricken crowd.

"The door is blocked," the man cried, trembling, and I could hear him banging on the wooden door in despair. "We're trapped," he concluded as the crowd grew more and more frightened, knowing that our deaths were near. I couldn't breathe. No one could. I prayed in desperation for all the horrors to end; once again, I screamed for God's help, for God to save us. The clouds above our heads were becoming more and more dense.

Then I felt a sudden surge of heat against my skin. Smoke emitted from under the door and a crackling sound met my ears as I stared at it in horror.

"Fire!" Heath cried and began to push me back, away from the door. "The door is on fire."

More screams filled the air. Then I had an idea.

"If we're going to die here," I shouted, "we might as well die in prayer." Then I began to lead:

> Our Father, Who art in heaven,
> Hallowed be Thy Name.
> Thy Kingdom come.
> Thy Will be done,
> on earth as it is in Heaven.

The crowd settled down, and together, we finished the prayer.

> Give us this day our daily bread.
> And forgive us our trespasses,
> as we forgive those who trespass against us.
> And lead us not into temptation,
> but deliver us from evil. Amen.

We continued to repeat the prayer in hopes that God would hear it and rescue us. I found that even if I didn't live today, participating in this worship of God made me the happiest I'd ever been in my life.

The fire began to climb up the wooden doors and spread onto the bushes inside the church. We stayed back. Either we would die of fire or meet OPTI's forces on the other side. I felt ready to meet my fate.

A rumble resounded from the sky above us.

I raised my chin to gaze up at the sky. The sun had vanished completely behind the mass of gray clouds. A bolt of lightning flickered across the sky, followed by a thunderous roar like a mighty wave at sea. Rain poured in torrents upon us all. I watched it all, exhaling in relief.

"Hallelujah." I breathed in astoundment, transfixed upon the mightiness of the raging storm. "Hallelujah!" I cried, my voice breaking.

The rain drenched me from head to toe, quenching my thirst. The ground inside the church flooded so that the fire was put out as fearsome thunder reverberated from the sky. Lightning struck the wires attached to the poles outside one of the windows, making a deafening sizzling noise. The door to the church charred from the fire so I could sort of see outside the church. The police force tried to break down the doors and managed to split the wooden plank blocking the doors. Some of the stone bricks tumbled to the ground.

The rain ceased, with a suddenness I'd never seen in a storm, and the clouds parted, their color remaining dark gray, forming a sort of halo around the shining sun as it cast down its rich heavenly gold glow on the earth like a gentle stream, like a glimpse of heaven. My awe turned to incredulity and I fell to my knees. One by one, each of us fell before the heavenly power of Jesus. When I glanced over at the cracks in the door, I even saw members of the police force kneeling before God, before our glorious Savior. The clouds parted even more, revealing the sun in a background of an azure-blue sky. The sun illuminated the stained glass window so that it magnified Jesus in all his radiating glory, his robes glowing white and his face as marvelous as the sunshine, surrounded by a kaleidoscope of colors.

"Exit here!" a deep voice cried from the exit under the archway, one that I'd heard before, a very long time ago, but couldn't quite place. "It's not blocked anymore, run! To the forest!"

I gasped. I recognized his face, a calm peaceful expression emitted from his quiet brown eyes. Byte. He wore his police uniform with his helmet off. His face intrigued me because it looked distantly familiar, then it came to me—the parade. He had been the boy who people threw bottles at, the boy who wouldn't bow to OPTI. "I know the way to freedom," the deep voice reassured us and I felt a sense of calm wash over me. The crowd filed out of the room and Heath and I started to follow.

Then I heard the sound of wood splintering. I turned around in time to see a white slender figure emerge, holding a handgun.

"No!" I heard Heath and Byte shout at once as it fired, and Heath moved to knock me out of the way. He wasn't quick enough, however, and I felt the sharp bullet pierce my heart while I gasped in searing pain. My eyes rolled back in my head as I fell backward into a blanket of darkness.

CHAPTER 39

Rise Up

Time and space blurred. I began to see a sparkling light and moved toward it longingly. The sparkling light twinkled down upon me and then expanded into a blinding light. Suddenly I could see white clouds beneath me, covering every inch of my surroundings, and I knew then that I had somehow made it to heaven. I didn't feel afraid and I wasn't concerned that I even died. This time, I knew it wasn't a dream. Peace consumed my soul with happiness beyond what I had ever experienced.

Then I saw him.

He wore pure-white robes and stood before a golden gate. Like I had on earth, I quickly dropped back down onto my knees before my Savior.

"Hallelujah," I said, and it seemed like it came from the depths of my soul.

"It's not your time yet, Abigail," Jesus said. "There is much left for you to do on earth. You have a purpose." He paused. "The times ahead will be dark. Nevertheless, do not fear, for I will be with you always. Your faith has saved you. Remember, only Jesus saves."

Before I could open my mouth in reply, the image of heaven faded away. As it did, I heard what sounded like a verse from the Bible spoken in my head as though from God.

Do not fear, for I have redeemed you;
I have summoned you by name; you are mine.

When you pass through the waters,
I will be with you;
and when you pass through the rivers,
they will not sweep over you.
When you walk through the fire,
you will not be burned;
the flames will not set you ablaze.
For I am the Lord your God,
the Holy One of Israel, your Savior…
Since you are precious and honored in my sight,
and because I love you…[6]

I awoke with a gasp as air filled my lungs, my eyes settling on a blank white ceiling. My vision hazed and my ears rung. I felt nauseous. My entire body felt limp and heavy against the bed I lay in. I tilted my head downward, slowly, and noticed I wore a plain white hospital gown. My entire chest was wrapped in a thick white bandage like a mummy. Then my memory came back, and I had a vague recollection of the police officer that shot me straight in the chest. I'd caught a glimpse of her fiery hair—Lynn. Then I remembered, Heath, Isabelle, Jaylyn, Byte, and the crowd of Christians. What happened to them all? Did they make it out? Were they alive? I recalled Byte standing at the back exit. He said he would lead them to freedom. Were they successful in fleeing to safety? Would I see them again?

A doctor came into the room and his expression changed from serious to one of shock.

"You're—you're alive?"

I looked back at him in confusion. As my mind pieced together the sound of a gunshot, visiting heaven, and the heavy bandage around my chest, I realized how surprising it must have been for him to see me awake, alive at all. I gasped as I felt the same shock.

[6.] Isaiah 43:1–4.

He left the room without uttering another word, I supposed, to deliver the news.

Within moments, Scarlett burst into the room so fast and with such fierceness that the door banged against the wall. Her eyes were red and her face tear-stained. Renée was behind her, looking pale and like she'd just thrown up.

"You're alive!" Scarlett cried in a mixture of joy and grief. Then she broke down again, and I watched her painfully as she sobbed her heart out. Renée couldn't keep it together either and joined her sobs.

"Never...ever..." Scarlett choked through her heaves. "Do...that...again."

Renée opened her mouth as if to say something. A wave of sobs hindered her. Seeing them cry made tears escape down my cheeks.

My mother came into the room with the doctor, and he explained to her what happened. She was more composed than Scarlett or Renée and wore a stern expression.

"It's good to see you're alive and well, hun." She put a hand on my shoulder, patting it gently. "Your sisters are right though. You shouldn't have left the house without telling any of us where you were going."

Scarlett echoed my mother's words by giving me a stern look of her own. It surprised me to see Scarlett agree with something my mother said.

I didn't quite know what to say or how to explain myself. I didn't regret going despite dying and then coming back to life. Leading that service filled me with indescribable joy, more than I'd ever felt in my life on earth aside from my dreams of Jesus.

"I had to go," I said. "It was...important to me..."

"You should know better, Abigail," my mother said. "Going to church is dangerous. Don't make the same mistake your sister did."

"It wasn't a mistake," I argued.

Before anyone could reply, Heath strode quickly into the room, his eyes covered in dark circles and landing on me. His shoulder was wrapped in a similar bandage.

"There are too many visitors," the doctor said.

"I'm a patient," Heath said.

"Then you should go back to your room to get some rest."

He ignored the doctor and walked to the far side of my bed. I glanced with unease at Scarlett who grimaced. "You were there together?" she said. "I need to leave."

Without another word to either of us, she left the room. I could hear the thuds from her shoes as she stomped away. I guess she wouldn't be speaking to me anymore again and I sighed.

"How are you alive?" he asked me. "Did it hit your shoulder too?"

"No, I...I don't know," I said. "It's a miracle." I hesitated to inform him or any of them about going to heaven. My mind still processed it.

"Who's this?" my mother asked, looking at Heath.

"He's my..." I said, "um...boyfriend. Heath."

Heath smiled and placed an affirming hand on my shoulder. Then he looked up with a grin at my mother.

"All right, well, you could have told me you were dating someone, Abigail," she said. "And I hope you can help keep my daughter out of danger, Heath. Florian is here but he refused to come because you betrayed your allegiance to OPTI. Try to keep our family civil. Our wedding is in a few months." I noticed Renée frowned at our mother while my battered heart sank. "I'll give you and your boyfriend some privacy. Come on, Renée."

She put her hand on Renée's back and guided her out of the room.

Heath didn't seem to notice and only gazed at me with deep love emanating from his peculiar eyes. "To think, you've now come back from the dead," he said. "I thought I lost you. Jesus saved your life. OPTI won't be happy when he finds out. This is going to make the news for sure. You survived death, Abigail. No one has but you. OPTI will be furious."

"What happened to the others?" I asked, dreading the thought of OPTI's wrath.

"I don't know. The officer shot me shortly after you and I passed out. OPTI hasn't caught any of the people who escaped. They must have found a good place to hide. I'd like to know who dared try to kill us."

"I know who," I said. "Her name is Lynn. She captured two of the leaders of the secret baptisms. Don't go after her though. We don't need any more trouble from the police."

"We're safe for now," Heath said. "The storm made the power go out in the town so the OPTI screens and cellular data wouldn't work, not even with a generator. If the OPTI screens had been working, those Christians who escaped would have been found in no time. That's how they went undetected. The only question is where they went."

I burst into bittersweet tears knowing that Jaylyn, Isabelle, and Byte and the other Christians from the service were still alive, wherever they were. I missed all of them so much. Would I ever see Jaylyn and Isabelle again? Would I ever be able to thank Byte for saving all our lives? God saved my life and others' once again. The knowledge gave me a powerful sense of hope that the future would be brighter and OPTI's reign of terror against Christians and other people of faith would come to an end.

I leaned forward. Heath read my mind and joined his lips to mine with a depth of passion that I wouldn't forget.

CHAPTER 40

The One True God of the World

News spread at a rapid-fire pace that I survived. My heart suffered no damage with only a faint bullet-shaped scar, the remaining evidence that I'd suffered any injury. However, the doctors and nurses at the hospital asked to see me. Soon patients approached me in awe that I'd survived a gunshot, and it gave them hope that they would recover. Others denounced me as a witch who had used magic powers to heal myself.

The press featured the story, though they seemed to encourage the witch theory and that I had betrayed OPTI by attending church. OPTI even showcased footage of me hurling a book at my OPTI screen with the caption, "Angry Christian Woman Gone Mad."

On my first day back at school while standing at my locker with Heath, his phone chimed and when he checked it we saw a video posted on OPTI-Tube that was going viral.

"Poison her." OPTI's voice came from the television screen in the Edwins' living room. "She miraculously survived those coyotes the other night. Her belief is a threat to me just as her sister's was. We don't need another uprising. Take her out."

Mr. Edwin nodded, a gleam in his beady eyes. "We grow hemlock here for a reason. For misbehaved teens."

I shuddered, stunned, wondering who could have leaked this video. I'd come so close to death that night. Jesus had told me the truth when I needed to hear it. I didn't murder anyone. OPTI was the true murderer all along and I had endured endless punishments for something I didn't even do. I remembered the quote that Maddie spoke to me from the Gospels. Jesus came to free the prisoners, and this video released me from my own unjustified imprisonment. With the wires connected to the OPTI screen in my home fried and irreparable, I found additional freedom.

Unfortunately OPTI's rule in our town restored at a fast pace and he declared he would find out whoever had leaked the video. Following the release of the video, Jake resigned as the president of the junior class without much word as to why. I ran into him on the way home at the end of intermediate chemistry on the Friday following my release from the hospital.

"Abigail," he said in a choked voice. I turned around and stopped in my tracks. His eyes glistened with tears. "I'm so sorry about what happened to you. All of it. I didn't know you were bullied like that. I didn't know OPTI framed you. I hope you can forgive me. As I know you've heard, I stepped down as the junior class president, and instead, I want to give my title to you. You deserve it. I know you'll do a great job. You're going to do great things in your life."

I found my own eyes echoing his with tears of my own. "Thank you," I said. "You don't have to do that for me. I forgive you but don't blame yourself. OPTI is to blame. I hope we can be friends."

He nodded and pulled me into a hug while we both cried.

"Can I join?" a voice asked and Jake and I broke apart to see Rachel giving us a sad smile.

"Of course," I said and gave her a hug.

"Isabelle and Jaylyn are gone," Rachel said with a somber expression. "We'll have to stick together now until we can find our escape. I didn't get a chance to tell you, Jake and I are dating now." They took each other's hands.

"That's great," I said. "Congrats."

Rachel smiled brighter. "See you around, Abigail."

Together, Jake and Rachel walked away down the hall. My heart filled with joy that Jake and Rachel had found someone who made them happy. In this time, love and faith remained what we all needed to survive.

That weekend, Renée and I were watching television in the living room when Scarlett came downstairs. She noticed us on the sofa and scowled at me. I decided it came time to have a chance to explain myself to Scarlett if she would listen.

"Scarlett, can we talk?" I asked from the living room. I stood up from the sofa as she put on her shoes at the front door of our house, dressed for her yoga class.

She started to open the door.

"Please let me explain myself," I said. "I can't stand that you're mad at me."

"Fine," she said with a sigh and faced me. "What do you have to say about it?"

"I know I kissed Heath," I said. "I know I shouldn't have after you just broke up. I didn't plan for it to happen."

She scoffed. "Yeah right."

"Scar, you have to understand," I said, "I didn't act in my right mind. OPTI had just shown Jake the video of me looking like I poisoned Mr. Edwin. I had a breakdown. Heath and I met up to talk about it and he believed me when I said I didn't do it. I...it meant so much to me. I kissed him. And then I rejected him because I knew our relationship would hurt you so soon after you broke up. We didn't start a relationship until after Maddie died. I love him, Scar. I can't explain the reasons. Please forgive me."

Her face fell. "Oh, I'm sorry that happened to you," she said. "I approve if you want to continue to be together. I love you so much. I don't know what I would have done if I lost you."

We exchanged a tight hug.

"I couldn't have made it through any of this year or last without you and Renée," I said. "You're the best campaign manager ever. I hope you'll help me next school year as junior class president."

She looked confused.

"Jake stepped down when he saw the viral video and gave the position to me," I said.

"What?" The news stunned her so much that her mouth fell open and she dropped her car keys. "Are you kidding? Oh, congratulations." She launched forward in another hug. "I can't wait to take you back-to-school shopping." She stepped back. "Renée too. Love you both." She gave Renée a small smile, and she smiled back.

"Love you too," Renée and I said at once. We all came together in a group hug. My eyes settled on a picture of Faith that sat on a side table in the foyer, wishing she could have been here. The sun was cast on her image through the window and I knew she was happy.

On my return to school, some students stopped making snide remarks at me and resorted to ignoring me, I supposed, because they feared I did have some sort of supernatural power. A few would ask me how I survived.

"A miracle," I answered every time. "From Jesus. The Prince of peace. King of kings and the Lord of lords. Savior of the world."

Those who asked looked amazed by my answer. Some even asked me to explain more about Jesus. Each time, it gave me joy to share the good news—to spread word that God is and always has been the One and only true God of this world and not even OPTI possessed enough power to defeat him. With that knowledge, whatever came my way, I knew I would survive it as long as I had Jesus.

ABOUT THE AUTHOR

P aige Trevisani is an Episcopalian, a Christian fiction author, and graduated from Skidmore College in May 2019, with an English major and a business minor. Paige was raised and confirmed in the Catholic Church; however, after studying the Bible in college became a member of the Episcopal Church. In high school, Paige was a member of the National Honors Society and was accepted into Skidmore College's New York State Summer Young Writers Institute where she studied fiction taught by professional writers. Upon acceptance to Skidmore College, Paige took several courses in fiction writing and even had one of her short stories called "OPTI" published in her school's *Folio* literary magazine which became the inspiration for her first novel.

Paige was also a member of her college's Christian Fellowship Club and even coled a Bible study on women in the Bible. In 2016,

Paige was invited to be the vice president for finance by the founder and copresident of her school's Women in Business club and coproduced her school's first ever Women in Business conference called Liberal Arts Leads as well as a second annual conference called The Next Step as the vice president for operations.

Additionally Paige has a passion for theater and attended Stagedoor Manor for six summers, a performing arts camp where she was awarded with Best Featured Actress in a Drama for her role in the *Laramie Project* in the summer of 2014. In 2011, she performed in the opening act of the eighty-fifth annual Macy's Thanksgiving Day Parade.

CPSIA information can be obtained
at www.ICGtesting.com
Printed in the USA
BVHW031848231220
596371BV00011B/73

9 781098 053178